THEIR LOYALTY TO LEGEND

Book 2 of The Chimera's Requiem

M. A. Morales

FIRST EDITION: MARCH 2024

ISBNS:
979-8-9871958-9-5 (paperback)
979-8-9871958-8-8 (ebook)

FOR MORE CONTENT BY this author, go to:
    elleoaks.com

SEND INQUIRIES TO AUTHOR at:
   Gmail: mamoraleswrites@gmail.com
   Or contact via form on elleoaks.com

(CONTENT WARNINGS: VIOLENCE, blood, gore, mature language, mature themes, mentions of depression, suicidal ideation, PTSD, and allusion of child sexual assault.)

This is for those who never stopped believing in the magic of imagination.

Summary of HER CURSE AND LULLABY: BOOK ONE OF THE CHIMERA'S REQUIEM

Botalia Ulton lived in exile for 10 years, isolated on an island where her parents conducted countless experiments, one which led to her own hybrid creation. Within her lives the beast, tucked away and held there by Botalia's life force. But within her is also a curse, one which burdens her with the weight of the world. A curse that grants her unimaginable power at a torturous cost.

One day, a visitor arrives. Tanten Flynn, an ex-Council member of the very association to exile Botalia, invites her to join an alliance. There is talk of a schism within the Magistrate Association, and Tanten wishes for her to join his team.

She denies his request.

Days later, his son, Koepp, arrives on her doorstep. And days after, an assassination attempt occurs, an old friend among them. The friend is no more than a shell of the person from her past, Tenebrant, a necromancer who does not hide his bloodlust and rage well.

After a mishap of an atomic shift, and one of the assassins by the name of Nix begging to be her apprentice, the unlikely team takes form, and they uncover a secret they had hoped not to divulge. The schism is a red herring. Tanten and co. are after something much greater. With this knowledge comes the responsibility to try to stop them from achieving it.

Unfortunately, they arrive in Dominia too late. Tanten and his team have recovered the ancient altar piece from the Magistrate Association. They now make their way to Qoterra with hopes of restoring the piece to make the altar whole once more and open a portal to another dimension to claim the Staff of the Gods.

Botalia, Koepp, Tenebrant, and Nix are forced to team up with two Council members of the Magistrate Association, Cefni Medina and Merwyn Giacobbe. Together they will travel to Qoterra and attempt to take down Tanten and any other hoping to claim the staff for their own.

SO BEGINS OUR TALE.

Chapter One

And the books stack up with greater volume than that within the ancient vault of Tuqucuan. Botalia searches the rows, gathering what interests her, despite the assistance it may offer on their journey. A giddy school child comes to life within her as she beholds the collections of the most esteemed Professionals and Scholars, wandering through literature they deem critical to specific subjects of study, noteworthy to the history of certain branches, and evolutionary to the sciences or arts. Her heart excites despite her stomach reminding her of the nerves she should possess.

Orphacia Glatz, an Archaeological Scholar, and Lenora Kasper, a Literary Scholar, drop book after book on the stack Tenebrant holds. He follows them about, involuntarily, their chosen servant being one that none of the Association could have caught of their own accord. The necromancer had escaped the grasp of the magistrates for years, the juxtaposition of his current role as book collector for the Scholars enough to cause Botalia a chuckle from her vantage point.

"Ooh, and this one covers potential weather-related disasters and survival techniques for such situation," Lenora says, skimming the text before slamming the book closed and adding it to the pile.

"Boy, over here!" Orphacia beckons Tenebrant from a row they walked previously.

The necromancer releases an impatient sigh, his aura spinning faster about him. Botalia warns him with no more than a glare as he passes by. With a lick of his lips, peering at her through no more than the slits his eyes form, Tenebrant slows his aura and trudges over to the Archaeology Scholar.

"This is about druidic rituals. This one covers the Great Titan Wars of the First Era. Oh, and this concerns cryptids deemed otherworldly and able to teleport between marbled realms!"

Before placing the final book atop his stack, Orphacia opens to a seemingly random page and loses herself in its sporadically formatted text. Tenebrant bites his tongue and taps his foot on the ground.

Lenora approaches behind him and places a hand on his bicep, causing him to flinch. She scans him from head to toe.

"Your aura twists relentlessly, as if itching for a release." She grins, her hand moving to adjust the fabric at his shoulders. "Violence isn't the only way to-"

"Of course!" Orphacia screams in her epiphany. "The Book of Runes! It's the most important. How pathetic of me! Come, come little necromancer boy."

Lenora rolls her eyes and strolls to a nearby shelf, picking up a book and skimming its contents.

Meanwhile, Koepp and Nix flip through a comic book designed for scouts going on their first survival outing. The pages turn back and forth between watercolor images of young boys building shelter and a fire pit.

"Fire is most important. If you get too cold, you're as good as dead," Nix states, arms crossed.

"But what about food?" Koepp asks, peeking ahead to upcoming pages.

"Psshh," Nix swats the air. "During my training, I went twenty days without food."

Koepp's jaw drops, his friend never failing to astound him.

"Whoa! You must have been so hungry."

"Not really. I survived on cocoa crumbles and oat soup."

"Whoa! You must have been starving!"

Koepp's face contorts as he processes Nix's words.

"Wait a minute..."

Botalia, who feels no guilt eavesdropping on their conversation, giggles. She drops her stacks on a table, inhaling profoundly as she takes another look around the magnificent library. Shelves full of books most would never have access to, paintings from eras long lost to many history classes, busts of those Scholars who revolutionized the branch of their specialty, the energy gifted to one in such a space fills her more than any stimulant could have.

"I've finally made it," she whispers. Her fingers dig into the cherry wood headrest of the chair, overwhelming emotion enough to cause her body to tremble. She hurriedly takes a seat and organizes her texts before her.

Several encyclopedia-sized tomes open on the table in front of her, life force assisting where her arm length prevents her from doing so. To her left, a book opens to a detailed map of Qoterra. A diverse land of mountains, jungles, and active volcanoes on the upper shores of the island. An open space of obsidian plains and lava rock cover a great portion of the island to the north. No doubt that is where they would find the caldera.

To her right, Botalia flips through a translation guide, with languages and explanation of accents by those tribes which inhabit the island. Many of the terms derive from druidic origin, the druids who at one point cohabitated the island with these tribes. In this era, a new tribe formed, most had druidic blood in them, though very little remained of that culture. But where culture adapted to that of the other tribes, their life force did not. Based in a ritualistic format, their life force was a group effort, intention of several working together to form forces an individual could never conjure of their own will.

And yet, of all these fascinating texts, none interested Botalia more than the tattered book which lay before her. No doubt studied by many, an original text that Orphacia, other Scholars of her field, and informants hoped to learn from for their digs. Not as a guide to do so but used as a warning. Advice to never underestimate the power of an enchanted object, an artifact with residual life force attached. It was an adventurer's guide through Qoterra, and what occurred after the finding of the altar... the first documented account.

Mairo Phillips, a Pharmacology Scholar and council member, marches into the room with his informants. They carry small metal trays with tubes and syringes atop. Each is labeled with a member of the team.

Merwyn and Cefni greet the informants by name as each take a Pterosicaria vaccine to the arm, critically decreasing any possibility of a virus being transferred should a blood moth choose them as prey.

Nix rolls up his sleeve and turns his head away. Three pokes and the informant shares a grin before leaving.

Tenebrant offers a glare to the informant to step near him. The man pulls the tray near, as if to use it as a shield, and looks to Mairo.

"You have to take those if you're coming along," Cefni instructs. His patient tone fails to reflect in his distrustful eyes, creating no more than slits as he peers at the necromancer.

"What's the worst that can happen if I don't? Death? I don't fear death."

Cefni chuckles and shakes his head.

"There are illnesses with symptoms far worse than you could ever imagine. At that point, you'd be begging for death."

Tenebrant resigns from the conversation and snags the tray from the informant. An open hand gestures for the rest of the equipment. The informant reaches with a shaky hand into his coat pocket and drops the sealed needle tips into Tenebrant's palm. The necromancer shoos away the informant and sits himself on a couch nearby, performing his own vaccinations.

Two young women approach Koepp. Atop his tray are six syringes, two oral tablets, and a square patch. Koepp crosses his arms over his chest, hands grabbing near his shoulders. He gulps and looks to Botalia for help.

"It will be okay," one of the women says as she kneels in front of Koepp. Her hand reaches for his arm and with a gentle stroke, attempts to comfort him. "It will be over before you know it."

"Will it hurt?" Koepp peers at Nix, unfazed by his injections but also only receiving half of that which sits before Koepp. As far back as he could remember, Koepp had never received any vaccinations, nor had a needle ever broken the skin on any part of his body. The only syringes he had seen were not ones the doctors would approve.

"It's just a pinch and then done."

"Well, if that's all it is."

"Let me walk you through what each one does so it will seem less scary." The informant beckons her partner over. She retrieves one of the tablets and hands it to Koepp. "First, take this my chewing it and swallowing every bit. This pill helps to boost gut health so any bacteria in resting water you may come into contact with won't enter and eat through your intestines."

Koepp grabs the pill and puts it into his mouth, chewing ferociously as the consequences of not taking it seemed far worse than the awful taste.

"Now, close your eyes and I'll explain the others to you."

With every explanation, she injects a vaccine in Koepp's arm. He focuses on chewing the pill and listening to her words, not even flinching as the needles enter and leave.

"Okay, now open your eyes and we'll get started."

Koepp opens his eyes and notices the empty needles on the tray. The informant cleans away any blood and wraps up his arms.

"See that was easy. Just one more tablet and I'm going to stick this one," she points to the patch, "on your back. It will slowly disperse an anti-toxin through your body so your immune system can learn a proper response when faced with the actual toxin."

Koepp smiles and follows her instructions, swelling with pride at his bravery.

Botalia bites her bottom lip, curious as to why no informant with a tray approaches her. Her eyes discover Merwyn, Cefni, and Mairo mumbling to one another, occasionally glancing toward her. After a brief discussion, they approach Botalia.

"Hello, Ms. Ulton. Allow me to properly introduce myself. I am Mairo Phillips, Council Member of the Magistrate Association and Scholar of Pharmacology and Chemistry. It is an honor to meet the daughter of the esteemed Ultons, whose experiments and studies have revolutionized an entire generation's way of understanding the sciences."

Mairo holds out a hand, inviting her to a handshake.

Botalia turns her head to the ground and rubs her thumbs together.

Mairo retracts his hand and clears his throat.

"While testing your blood, we were looking and waiting for reactions to any number of bacteria, virus, or toxin that may be a hazard while in Qoterra. Checking for any missed immune responses, or any reaction that failed to occur to stop the spread."

Botalia bites her lip, understanding where the topic heads. The monstrosity that is her DNA never fails to amuse others, especially those most interested in the works of her parents. The information was widely available to magistrates of his caliber, no doubt a study requirement to achieve his position at such a prestigious institution. The council members who remembered her exile, those who now learn of what she is and what she has done, the minds of many will be influenced to judge her on her DNA over her own achievements.

In their minds, she is her parents' experiment. She is no human and therefore not worthy of being treated any more than a laboratory rat. And in their awe of her, a dehumanization of her agency manifests. Awe and fear drive their judgements, no doubt those who were impressed by her aura and DNA would never question exiling her had they been there ten years ago.

Mairo hands a manila folder to Botalia. She accepts and opens to a page of tests run on her blood. She glances up at him then quickly back down again. She flips through the pages, some of the tests she knew were not even needed for traveling to Qoterra, as such bacteria thrived in hot, dry climates, quite the opposite of the island they traveled to. She questions how much blood they must have drawn to conduct so many tests. She questions how cautious her parents must have been, the weekly physicals and check-ups making more sense, though at the time she deemed them excessive. Her parents had prepared her to take on the world.

"To summarize those results, you are already immune to any possible disease to be encountered in Qoterra."

Botalia closes the folder and hands it back to him. No doubt he would store it somewhere to show his colleagues, beaming with pride to encounter a specimen such as her.

Tenebrant marches up to the group and hands a tray of emptied syringes to Cefni. With a smirk, he turns away and joins Lenora as she calls for his assistance.

Cefni passes off the tray to an informant and reaches into his pocket. His phone vibrates. Nodding, he whispers to Merwyn and leaves the library, following behind Mairo and his team.

Botalia distracts herself by leaning into the texts once more, the journal the most fascinating. It starts with the history, or myth, surrounding an ancient altar which leads to a realm, wholly created by the life force present in the staff itself. The tales of the divine power of the staff far exceed the abilities of any person who has ever wielded life force. As the supposed history grows more unbelievable, credibility of those observers and historians transforms into a legend, myth, of storytellers from cultures of the Second Era.

And yet, whether it be her dream from before they set out, whether fabrication or genuine article, what she experienced was far beyond her comprehension. The sights and the sounds transcended the world around her, a premonition in her unconscious state. The emotions that riddled her were not her own. She fell into a trance, the staff called to her. Its immense power singing out, hoping for someone to wield it.

Whether the song be joyous or malicious, Botalia fears the power it possesses rather than desires it. But what scares her more is an understanding that not many would react in a similar fashion once in its presence. Desperate people fall to a hunger for power when temptation presents itself.

In the text, the staff is depicted in a variety of ways in the sketches and pictures provided. Only a few resemble the staff she saw: a tall, yew staff with a gnarled head. Though most of the stories appear quite similar, one tale in particular catches her interest.

Written like a journal, the tale gives elaborate details about the traveler's expedition and experience with the altar and staff. The story begins with the man and his team arriving at the "door," the supposed entrance to an alternate world. A conversion of mass amounts of energy is used as the key to open the door, specifics not given.

Once they arrive on the other side, the traveler takes very detailed notes of the environment: a sky covered by ashy clouds, a ground composed of alkaline soil, a vast plain with only low-lying shrubs and weeds, ancient ruins constructed of marble with wearing from strong winds, and across the way a tall plateau with a stone brick staircase running up it. The altar is assumed to be at the top of this staircase, as if the gods oversee it themselves.

As the travelers march through the ruined city toward the plateau, they report strange hallucinations and disembodied screams and humming. However, this evidence is hard to back up as no two members of the team experience the same event in tandem. Some members feel nauseous while others fall to the ground, already affected by the illness they've only just encountered. Ancient birds of prey circle above and the ground tremors beneath their feet. They trudge forward and their paranoia kicks in. The entire team searches desperately for the eyes that seem to spot them, however, the mention that the shadows themselves are watching seems the most accurate.

The travelers arrive at what used to be a flood plain, separating the city from the mountains. The ground under them quakes and they run back as they see titans rise from the earth. Many are not fast enough, the titans' stride and strength unmatched. The titans' rising wakes other beasts of the realm, most unnamed and ill-described in the panic that settles over the team. The author of the journal exits through the door, the lone survivor of the journey. He returned at a later time with another team, only then getting a glimpse of the altar and staff atop the plateau. However, the illness he contracted on his second voyage killed him within an hour of leaving the realm, the journal found with near the ancient altar. Nothing is known as to if any other returned from the second journey

Botalia closes the book and gulps. The tragedies to pass the team of explorers present an additional layer of fear. Her greatest anxiety about the mission of reclaiming the altar piece includes the inevitable altercation with Tanten and a possible army of his followers. Having to step foot into an alternate realm should it come down to it takes a close second on her list.

Merwyn steps to the boys, leaning over to observe their studies. With a chuckle and a statement, Koepp and Nix jump up, wide eyes and endlessly moving lips that demonstrate excitement.

Botalia closes every book, stacking them up. Her eyes pass the text of the altar and staff, her fingers lingering on the cover after closing it. She scans the library, seeing how Merwyn distracts the boys, how Lenora points out directions to Tenebrant and him begrudgingly following every command. Botalia slides the book into her satchel before standing and joining Merwyn and the boys.

"Hello, Ms. Ulton. Cefni is preparing flight accommodations as we speak. It shouldn't be much longer now," Merwyn states, a slight grin forming on his face.

Botalia notes his posture, rigid, perhaps from his age, though she has her doubts. His face, dark brown skin with soft features, gives nothing away. As she examines his aura, she notices movement of that of a calm lake, tranquil waters with no surface disruption. The council member had seen many tragic events in his life, his youth as a magistrate and disciple full of examples of his heroism. From assisting after natural disasters to singlehandedly sculpting a wall to divert a landslide from destroying a developing region in south Arydden, this mission would be but another to add to a long list of accomplishments.

"Are you nervous?" Koepp asks as he stares up at Botalia.

"Um..." Her eyes bounce between the three of them, the question alone enough to accelerate her heart. "A little. But we have something they don't."

Nix, who had been staring at his fidgeting fingers, looks up.

"What do you mean?"

"We have the element of surprise. None of them know what our team is capable of."

"But if they're strong, it doesn't matter," Nix responds, crossing his arms. "If they're stronger, they'll win every time."

"Not necessarily," Merwyn chimes in. Nix glances at him in surprise, perhaps intimidated by his presence. "Those who have a plan will always outperform those with none. The element of surprise is quite a strong advantage indeed."

Merwyn shares a smile before clearing his throat.

"I believe it's time then. Gather your belongings and wait near the door, transport will be taking us to a nearby airport. The time has come."

Koepp hops in place, grabbing Nix's arm in an attempt to get him to join in. A smile slips through a forced frown, Nix batting Koepp's hands away. Botalia glances about, ensuring she has left nothing behind.

"Did I hear correctly?" Orphacia shouts as she sprints from a nearby office, arms struggling to contain the folders in her grasp. "Take these, take these." She hands a folder to each of them, the remainder going to Merwyn. "It is every tidbit of information you should need once you get to Qoterra, put together by myself and my team."

"Thank you, Dr. Glatz. We will ensure our team goes over these on our journey to the island."

Tenebrant marches over to the crew, ignoring every request from Lenora to lower one more book, lift one more chair, move one more shelf. Merwyn offers him a folder, his reaction no more than a chuckle.

Botalia follows at the tail of the group as they leave the library. She takes a deep breath, hoping it will not be the last time she'll step foot into the space. The next time, hopefully she could do so as an informant or disciple.

Chapter Two

A s they sit in the waiting area, the two young boys anxiously rock back and forth, glancing from time to time at the door to the airfield. Koepp attempts reading his study materials, sliding his finger along the page in the folder given to him by Orphacia. Nix helps, quickly growing frustrated that Koepp asks about every other word. Koepp, understanding his friend's irritation, closes the folder and stands to examine the aircraft out the window.

Tenebrant sits apart from the group, legs crossed, eyes closed, wishing to be elsewhere.

Botalia reads over the notes. All data regarding the altar, from witness testimonies to the folklore surrounding it, are outlined in the folder. She notices some passages cited from the book she had been reading earlier, the one adding weight to her bags. Much interest has been taken in these objects, not only the staff but the altar as well. No explanation can be given to how an inanimate object possesses a life force of its own, the only suggestion is that the objects themselves have developed sentience. That is perhaps the greatest mystery of all.

A door clicks as it opens, Cefni Medina and Merwyn Giacobbe entering the waiting room. Atheas Maynard pokes his head through the doorway and observes the team with stern expression before shutting the door.

Koepp and Nix jump from their chairs, their boredom starting to make them jittery. Botalia stands and slips the folder into her bag, licking her lips as the anticipation sets in. Any to observe her aura would notice the slight tremble, but perhaps only after the awe of its magnitude and movement passed.

"Our business here is finished," Merwyn states, eyes passing from face to face. "Let us head out."

Merwyn leads the way, exiting a door to a set of stairs descending to the tarmac. Koepp and Nix race to the door, pushing and shoving the other playfully to get in front. They both try to squeeze through the door at the same time. Though not as agile, Koepp's build is more muscular than the ex-assassin, and he succeeds in getting through first. A smile springs to Koepp's face as Nix crosses his arms. Botalia holds up a hand and gasps, imagining one or the both of them toppling down the steps in their efforts.

She glances back at Tenebrant, the necromancer having not twitched the slightest since the announcement of their departure.

"Are you coming?" Botalia questions, her voice uncertain as to his response.

Tenebrant sighs and rises. Without a single word, he passes her by and descends the stairs.

Cefni and Botalia lock eyes, hesitation evident with both. Memories of the past always surface when one glances at the other, and when both pairs of eyes connect, neither is safe from their mind. No matter the current environment, no matter their present emotion, sorrow and dread find them both. Cefni gestures for Botalia to exit before him. She nods and takes a deep breath, reality melding with all that could happen. There was no turning back.

Once on the tarmac, Koepp and Nix explode in excitement, racing around, circling Merwyn as they go. Questions bombard the senior council member, though primarily all of them coming from Koepp. And, with great patience, Merwyn answers every single question, often interjecting tidbits of his knowledge that may interest the boys.

Botalia focuses her hearing and grins fascinated by Merwyn's expanse of knowledge. Though not a Scholar by trade, he could fool any who held conversation with him. Professionals weren't thought of as being the most intelligent, but Merwyn certainly defied anyone to suggest that the case of all life force wielders.

Tenebrant marches along silently, his face reading boredom, his aura something much different. His fingers twitch, a muscle in his arm spasms. He wonders how long he'll be able to maintain his composure. His urge to fight only heightens in the presence of numerous council members, their hatred of him like fuel to the fire.

"I hope you learned quite a bit, though I know it wasn't much time to absorb all the information." Cefni speaks in a voice only Botalia can hear. "You read the journal, didn't you?"

Botalia nods. Her fists clench, the images carved into her mind of the nightmarish creatures and unpredictable illnesses of the explorers passing through the portal to the realm created by life force.

"Its findings would concern me as well if more evidence led us to believe it." Cefni scratches his head then covers his eyes with his hand to observe the sky above. Cumulus clouds fill the sky, an exhale of relief. "We can't find any sources to validate the tale. Any number of possibilities exist, but no matter what we encounter, we must face it head on."

"What's the difference between us and them?" Botalia questions, staring at the ground as she walks. "Whether selfish or selfless we are both risking our lives and for what? An object that may not truly exist?"

"Whether the object exists or not is insignificant," Cefni responds. "The fact that people are willing to kill over said object is enough for us to take action against them."

"Do you believe a staff of the gods exists?" Botalia glances up, observing his expression to read any truth she could find.

"We know an altar exists. And that chunk that they found somehow possesses a semblance of life force."

"It is life force," Botalia assures him. She bites her lip, the thought of life force being sentient haunting her. "There is no doubt about it. The power it contains is life force."

"You should listen to her," Tenebrant shouts back, fingers clasped against the back of his head, elbows high in the air. "She's the strongest wielder you'll ever meet. If she says it's life force, it's life force."

"I don't believe I presented an invitation for your opinion. Better you just keep that aura in check, don't go assuming we haven't yet noticed."

Tenebrant scoffs and turns to face them, walking backward as they go.

"What is your goal? What is it you're fighting for, Cefni Medina?" he asks.

Cefni attempts to lock eyes with Tenebrant but finds the task impossible. Rather he peers at Botalia before diverting his eyes to the sky. He sighs.

"I'm fighting to protect the only world I know, necromancer," Cefni replies, his final word leaving in a hiss.

Tenebrant laughs and turns to face the front and shakes his head.

"Unbelievable," Tenebrant's whisper meets their ears.

Cefni glares at him, anger building, regret at allowing his accompaniment ever growing. Botalia stares at the ground, hoping regret would not engulf her any time soon.

Merwyn curiously glances back, releasing a profound exhale before returning his attention to the boys.

The team arrive at a set of steps, ready to board their airship.

Koepp and Nix race to the stairs when they no longer can contain themselves. Nix wins and climbs with great speed, his agility even after the lack of sleep impressive. Koepp trudges upward as he admits to his loss. Merwyn follows close behind them, a corner of his mouth lifts, amused by their excitement but guilt consumes him for that which their innocence may encounter in the days to come.

Cefni makes his way to the front of the line, pulling out a keycard and scanning it at the door pad. The metal door opens in, and they enter.

Botalia climbs the steps, takes one last glimpse around, and sighs. Tenebrant stares at the clouds, his attention focusing on smoke rising in the distance from the ongoing attacks to the city. Gunfire rings out for a moment before silence consumes the day, not even the birds daring to let their location be known.

"You're coming, right?" she yells from the top of the stairs.

Tenebrant glances up, squinting as the sun peeks through. He glances back to the smoke, scratches his head, and then sticks his hands into his pockets and shrugs.

"I've come this far, haven't I?"

As he places his hand on the rail to the stairs, he pauses.

"You're not afraid of heights, are you?" Botalia questions, a playfulness in her voice. He laughs and climbs to meet her.

"This mission is not meant for those controlled by their fears," Tenebrant states. "Flying is mere child's play. The real fun is going on out there." He points to the distant warzone, close enough that the effects are within eyesight.

Botalia sighs, wondering if their mission is really more important than the assistance they could offer to the people in cities affected. Tenebrant views it differently than her, but undoubtedly taking out any fighter would be helping the Association he claims to hate. Perhaps his only reason for joining them, for any amount of fun could ensue.

Botalia's jaw drops as she enters the airship, a spacious area inside appearing as living quarters. Unlike a regular airship with parallel aisle seating, this airship has four couches sitting in a square as a conversational setup. The area in the back of the airship has a few bunk beds, bathroom, and kitchen area. Koepp and Nix busy themselves touring the ship, opening every drawer and cupboard, experimenting with their hiding places.

"We will be departing. If there are any objections or problems, please state them now before we lift off," Cefni states over the loudspeaker, taking the pilot position in the airship. There is silence. "Very well."

The ship slightly shakes as it begins its ascent. Nix and Koepp race toward the window to watch the ground below them get further away.

"Look down there, Nix! The people look like ants!" Koepp giggles. Nix crosses his arms to act cool and collected, but a smile slips through.

Merwyn and Botalia take a seat on the couches. Merwyn pulls out a notebook and writes. Botalia observes him. Focusing her eyes, she sees a majestic and tranquil aura. Merwyn's aura glows and dances like a calm lake with a subtle breeze disrupting the surface. His control over his immense life force seems effortless. Merwyn is most certainly an amazing life force manifester, probably the strongest in existence. She admires his good heart and recognizes his incredible power and intelligence. She knows he can feel her gaze, yet it doesn't seem to bother him.

Cefni exits the cockpit, the airship in autopilot now that it is in the air at suitable height. Cefni sits on the last empty couch and sighs. He leans his head back and closes his eyes. Koepp and Nix join the group, sitting next to Botalia. Everyone sits in silence. Koepp and Nix continuously glance at one another then at Botalia, holding back laughter. Pulled from his work by the suppressed chuckles, Merwyn, with cocked eyebrow, looks up at the boys. They drop their heads, their shoulders deceiving them in the hiding of their laughter. The boys glance up to see Merwyn pointing behind them. Koepp, Nix, and Botalia turn to see vibrant, colorful fish, constructed by his life force, swimming in the air. The three smile at the spectacle. Botalia turns to Merwyn and grins. The corners of his mouth raise, and Merwyn returns to his work.

Koepp and Nix lean over the back of the couch, stretching out their arms in an attempt to touch one of the life force fish. Botalia walks to the center of the swimming fish. As they swim around her face, Botalia examines each of them with a smile. She gestures for Koepp to walk over to her. She gets down on one knee and holds out her hand, Koepp accepting it. She clasps his hand in hers and closes her eyes.

"Focus," she whispers.

Koepp tightly squeezes his eyes shut. Botalia can feel his concentration. She wanders through his present thoughts, her life force flowing through him in the same way it did when she saw his dreams and the hallway of his memories. In this moment, she solely focuses on helping him manifest his current wishes. She notices he wants to add to the school of fish, including his own variety. Unfortunately, his life force has never been tamed and cannot stay materialized for long, even with Botalia's help. The best way to bring his wish to life is to use his life force to condense the moisture in the air around them. Her life force slowly pushes his along, leading it in the right directions to best achieve what he's focusing on.

Everyone watches from their seats. Tenebrant, Cefni, and Merwyn focus their eyes, realizing what Botalia is doing. They see her life force flowing from her and into Koepp through the connection in their hands. Her life force carries his outside of his body and helps it to transmute the air around them. They notice the drops of condensation as they grow larger and begin to take shape. Botalia's life force instructs Koepp's life force in the sculpting of the water, making it appear as a fish. The fish begin to swim around in the same manner as Merwyn's. Nix drops his jaw in awe.

"Open your eyes," Botalia instructs.

Koepp listens and smiles from ear to ear as he witnesses his creations swimming around. Botalia grins. She lets go of his hand and stands. The moment she lets go, his life force returns to his body. However, Botalia helps his fish maintain their shape with the assistance of her life force. Nix and Koepp run around in circles, watching the fish as they move, pretending to swim alongside them every so often. Botalia returns to her seat and shares a smile with Merwyn. Tenebrant chuckles and closes his eyes. Cefni continues to gaze at her as he shakes his head.

"She's not the same girl from years ago," Cefni thinks. "There is no way one could undergo such a transformation. How is she able to smile? Is her smile a false front? Maybe the monster is trying to trick us? Do I distrust her so much as to question her happiness?" Cefni's thoughts tear him apart. He glances at Koepp and Nix. They continue to admire the fish, attempting to focus their life force and create more. Nix is able to manifest a small fish, but it quickly vanishes. Koepp squeezes his eyes to focus his life force, however, his efforts aren't enough to even move his life force from his body, though his life force appears to be forcibly pushed and pulled.

"Keep trying, Koepp, you'll get it eventually," Botalia states, though not looking at him. She pulls the binder out of her backpack and opens it. She pretends to read the information, knowing she's too distracted to actually digest any of its contents. Skimming over the page time and time again, she picks up certain words and phrases, but none of them form complete thoughts. Botalia sighs.

Her thoughts wander in the same direction as Cefni. Despite the problem becoming increasingly larger between them, the air growing thicker with the time that elapses, they cannot discuss the past, eye contact alone forcing despair and grief. They fear asking the inevitable questions, reminding one another of a past they both think the other hoped to forget. Neither can focus due to the distraction constantly taking a hold of their thoughts. They know they must address the past before arriving in Qoterra, for it may interfere with the mission, and yet neither can bring themselves to do so.

Nix and Koepp quiet as their energy depletes for the first time in the past day. They head to the bunk beds and lay down. Merwyn releases the fish and Botalia follows suit, dispersing the water fish little by little. The boys slowly relax themselves, needing to be recharged. They appear like zombies, their crash hitting them in an instant.

"Hopefully they'll get some rest before we arrive," Merwyn says. He closes his notebook and returns it to his bag. He locks eyes with Botalia. "So, Ms. Ulton, what class of life force user do you consider yourself?" Merwyn asks, his blue eyes gleaming with interest.

"Um... well. I don't really practice any category in particular..."

"Then how do you train? I ask because your life force exhibits incredible control, yet flows swiftly, as I noticed when you wished for it to travel into Koepp's person. There appeared no resistance. No friction. I wonder what type of training allows for such freedom and control." Merwyn gazes at Botalia. Merwyn understands the storehouse of her life force came from a sacrifice or ritual of sorts, but her ability to control it continues to amaze him.

Many people who perform rites or sacrifices for power often find themselves overwhelmed with the stress a sudden flux of power exerts on their body. This stress often crushes them from the inside, many cases leading to hospitalization or death. Also, these people find they can no longer utilize their life force, as if it's been chained, for life force never truly leaves a living person. As Merwyn looks at Botalia, he knows she is different. She is no different than those people in terms of procedure, however, her intentions contrasted heavily.

Often, those who perform the rites desire power for their own selfish and power-hungry purposes. And as a result, they reap what they sow. But Botalia's case differs. Merwyn agreed with the President when he predicted she'd grow strong. Though more powerful than he imagined, Merwyn was always certain of one thing. She wouldn't gain power to fulfill her own desires. She had no selfish intentions, no want to become powerful. She sacrificed something else and gained power as a result, without wanting it. A curse, not a gift.

Botalia taps her finger to her cheek, answering after some thought.

"I believe the freedom and flow of my life force is a result of not limiting myself to one area of utilization. While I enjoy manifestation and current creation (a term used to describe creating a connection for life force to flow into other beings, namely plants, creatures, and people; it's how she helped Koepp's life force exit his body; named for electric currents), I often exercise other types such as manipulation and transformation.

"I don't often think about classifying my life force. For me, it's about exploring the possibilities, which are infinite. My imagination is my only hindrance when it comes to using my life force; nothing else holds me back." She laughs. "I guess I'm kind of lucky in that I don't have to study a certain branch of life force. I'm free to experiment with it as I like."

Merwyn accepts her answer and turns to Tenebrant, who obviously listens to their conversation. "And yourself, Mister Mortu?"

Tenebrant opens his eyes and raises an eyebrow at the council member.

"I believe we can address one another on a first name basis." Tenebrant replies. Merwyn grins.

"Of course."

"I will only answer your question because I feel it's not to my advantage to keep it hidden," Tenebrant starts. Cefni scoffs at his statement and shakes his head. Tenebrant grits his teeth, refusing to make eye contact with Cefni and releases a sharp exhale.

"As a Mortu, I'm well learned in necromancy. It's in my blood."

A sharp pain stabs at his chest like a dagger. Tenebrant closes his eyes and feels himself trembling. He raises his hand to pull at his shirt's collar. He knows well the length of their journey before they arrive at the destination. He understands suppressing his violent habits may be the death of him. Though not requiring his full energy yet, Tenebrant knows the longer he waits, the more difficult it will be to control and mask his aura. In the meantime, his best diversion is to shift the attention away from himself.

"Botalia, I see you're at approximately sixty-five percent."

"Yeah," Botalia responds.

His diversion works for both Cefni and Merwyn turn to Botalia. Whether truth or not, they see Botalia's strength has increased since they began their journey. Merwyn and Cefni think along a similar wavelength. They wonder what she must have done prior to arriving at the Association to have expended her storehouse of life force. What circumstances surround the usage of such an immense amount? They both wonder yet refuse to ask for the time being.

Everyone disengages from the conversation, seeing as it had plateaued. Cefni returns to the cockpit. Merwyn desired to create bonds with his new team members and evaluate their strengths and weaknesses. However, he realizes how difficult such a task is when dealing with the team he's been presented. Not knowing what the team is fully capable of threatens their chances greatly. Every second in battle counts, and if they so much as hesitate, their mission may fail. Merwyn knows well that Cefni will not allow traitors like Atlas and Tanten to defeat them, and considering himself Cefni's longtime ally, Merwyn will not suffer failure.

Ten hours after their departure from the port, the airship begins to descend. Dark clouds fill the sky as if imposing gloom and despair upon the team, acting as a bad omen. The falling rain creates a melodic sound on the sides of the airship.

The deciduous mountain range comes into view as the airship sinks beneath the lowest layer of clouds. Amidst the rocks and trees, Cefni finds a flat area large enough for their landing. Hoping not to draw attention to their ship in the night, he decides not to activate the flood lights but rather the headlights simply to see the spot as they land. He notices the wind pick up as the land senses their entry. Hands on the wheel, he focuses his eyes and sends forth his life force. His life force acts as a cloak covering the ship. The cloak stiffens and acts as a rigid boundary between the ship and the ongoing weather. The instant the rain touches the barrier, it travels in the opposite direction, returning to the clouds from which they came. The wind hits the barrier and curves around. Though previously shaking with the torrential storm, the airship steadies and carefully descends. Cefni checks the pressure gauges and watches the radar as he lowers the ship. When the airship touches down, it slightly quakes. Cefni releases a sigh of relief all while cursing at his luck for the weather turning grim.

Cefni leans on the pilot's headrest, rubbing at his temples as he anxiously shakes, his nerves and fear of failure setting in. The unknowns of their mission swirl about his head. The risk of being jumped by the team with the altar piece and the possibility that an army awaits to counter any attempt to retrieve it, force curses under his breath of their unpreparedness. Their team is small, experience in combat minimal. A strong strategy may prove insufficient if they are overwhelmed by numbers. The assumption that Tanten Flynn is incapable of finding allies to agree with his selfish intentions may be shortsighted.

Cefni exits the cockpit once calming his aura. As he pokes his head around the corner of the door, he observes the team. His eyes meet Merwyn's.

"I suppose there will be no problem waiting until morning?" Merwyn asks.

He gazes at the back of the ship where Koepp, Nix, and Botalia lay, then looks up to Cefni.

"Allow them to rejuvenate, for they'll be weak if they don't."

Cefni sighs. The time they have is precious, resting does not seem a fit way to spend it.

Merwyn continues, "Besides, the weather would only serve to dampen our spirits."

Chapter Three

As the sun rises, a still day greets them, mist along the ground as the condensation rises from the night before. Cefni and Merwyn step out of the airship and survey their surroundings. They mark their maps, having landed on a flat area of rock on the south end of the continent. They must travel northeast to reach their destination. To get there, they will need to cross rough terrain and navigate through dense forests.

Cefni and Merwyn eye the markers on the map and peer at the key. Tribal territory lays on many sides of the route used by the scientists and informants of the Magistrate Association. Small sections of great biodiversity were claimed and are protected by the Magistrate Association for wildlife and ecosystem conservation purposes, the tribes hostile toward any to wander outside of agreed upon boundaries. Merwyn remembers the outline of the treatise presented to the tribal chieftains of the groups they were able to come into contact with on the continent, and those who chose to participate in such an agreement. While a greater majority of the groups understood the desire to research and preserve, others felt it a criticism of their ability to do so.

An ancient runic symbol marked an area on the map shown in darker hues. An area where elevation rises and then drops. A caldera, the marker in the center, where the druids of past eras held their rituals. Perhaps their strongest ritual yet was performed at this site, opening a portal to a different realm. Cefni hopes their mission to reclaim the altar piece occurs before they draw near the site, the ancient land feared by even those whose blood ancestors sacrificed to the power. Their team feared the unknown that was to come. The druids feared the portal for they knew exactly the horrors to await should one enter. Those who knew possibly possessing a stronger fear than those who did not.

"When landing, did you notice lights on the ground?" Merwyn questions. Cefni shakes his head.

"Nothing out of the ordinary," he responds. "The tourist spots and observation cabins with their lampposts were the only lights I could locate. However, the weather played a significant role in my vision of the land. It wouldn't be hard to not be seen here if one doesn't want to. The question is if those who are hidden saw us."

"The time we collide is insignificant. A battle between teams is inevitable."

"Hopefully fortune is in our favor."

"And do you believe luck will be the deciding factor? Fortune is all Tanten Flynn depends on typically, strategy a foreign object to him. If luck be the winning key, we may be short of victory."

"Tanten may be egotistical, stubborn, and a whole other number of things that should make him the underdog, but he is a strong life force user. Not to mention, ruffians of all sorts attract to him. And even if they're not strong, we cannot underestimate Tanten's ability." Cefni chuckles. "He may even be more of a threat if he fights us solo. He wouldn't hold back, just unleash total hell and chaos."

"Tanten wouldn't hold back even if his team were there," Tenebrant chimes in.

Cefni and Merwyn turn around, surprised by the necromancer's appearance. They look to one another, the shock of the other apparent in the glow of their eyes. Being hardened magistrates, Cefni and Merwyn are well practiced in the detection of life force. They are able to sense presences within a thirty-meter radius of themselves, the radius even greater when their senses are heightened. To march through the circle in their direction, undetected by both Cefni and Merwyn, requires elite skills in concealment of aura and life force.

Tenebrant returns a wide grin, stops concealing his presence, and continues. "Sorry, for listening in. I was simply curious."

"No matter," Merwyn responds, returning the grin. "Your skill for concealment is quite impressive."

"I accept your compliment, but shall we return to the discussion?" Tenebrant asks.

"What do you mean when you say Tanten won't hold back?" Cefni questions. He locks eyes with Tenebrant and senses Tenebrant's hostility. He doesn't need to focus his eyes to know Tenebrant's aura slips from his control now that he is no longer devoting his energy to concealment.

"Tanten Flynn only withheld before because he was a part of the Council and would have been removed from his position if he acted how his intrinsic nature intends. He was eager to hunt first class bounties, whether for alliance or rivalry's sake. If anything, his ex-team of official magistrates with their strict guidelines held him back. But here, on this mission, there are no rules. Tanten has nothing to lose but the prize. He'd willingly sacrifice his entire team if it meant he had better odds in achieving his goal. But even if it didn't, he couldn't care less. Caring is an emotion Tanten Flynn will never be capable of." Simply saying Tanten's name, Tenebrant feels his aura spike. He understands Cefni cautiously watches him, but knows Cefni will not attack, even with his own hostility visible.

"If there is any we should fear as we traverse Qoterra, it is none other than Atlas Lurio."

"Atlas? How do you know he's interested in the altar piece?" Cefni asks. Tenebrant puts his head in his hands and shakes his head, his shoulders raising and dropping in amusement to Cefni's surprise.

"I tell you in truth that Atlas is on his way or already here, hoping to reclaim the altar piece. However, his intentions with it are far different from our own. From what I understand, he leads a strong and cohesive team of life force users. And," Tenebrant pauses and squints, looking around. He steps toward Cefni and Merwyn and lowers his voice. "I know Atlas is the only one to fully comprehend his opponents. All of them."

"What do you mean?" Cefni whispers, squinting at the necromancer.

"He knows about us. Atlas knows of our team."

"How did you come about this information?" Merwyn asks.

"Let's just say I have an ally on the inside. But tell me, did you know Atlas was leading a team?" Tenebrant understands the two Council members had to keep some information regarding their quest confidential, but not revealing possible adversaries could have proven deadly for them all. Cefni and Merwyn look to one another and sigh.

"We assumed he was in on it," Cefni replies. For the first time, Tenebrant sees some of Cefni's hidden shame shine through. "We also suspected Atlas's allies within the Association remained loyal to him even after his resignation. If he hadn't have found out about our team, our mission, it may have come as more of a shock."

"Do you believe Atlas to be more of a threat than Tanten Flynn?" Merwyn directs at Tenebrant.

"Despite his psychosis, Atlas is charismatic and powerful, in appearance and status. It would not be hard for one to follow Atlas as if he were an idol. Once they pledge loyalty it's as if he can do no wrong." Tenebrant pauses to allow the words to sink into the Council members' minds. They worked alongside Atlas for fifteen years. However, not many can deduce Atlas's character or motives, even after a lifetime of knowing him.

"Also, Atlas is a master strategist," Tenebrant continues. "He knows the most effective method in all scenarios. As much as I hate to admit, Atlas would make for an incredible ally but for his insanity."

Tenebrant's heart violently pounds for the praise he offers to Atlas. He shakes his head and backs away from Cefni and Merwyn. Though forced to be on their team, Tenebrant does not consider them his allies. He remains skeptical about the existence of the staff and believes the true prize of joining in on the mission is the war bound to occur between the teams. Tenebrant hopes not to miss a battle. Not a single one. He shakes simply thinking about the amusement he may find. After a minute of silence, the group collectively sighs.

"The sun continues to rise. We must leave before it begins its descent," Merwyn states. Cefni nods in agreement. "I'll wake the others and make certain they're well fed. Cefni, you make preparations for the journey. Carefully read the itinerary and survey the surrounding area. Tenebrant," Merwyn pauses as he looks at Tenebrant with a grin. "Don't hurt anything."

"Don't tempt me," Tenebrant responds.

"If you dare-" Cefni begins, a rage forming within him.

"No worries. I won't do anything," Tenebrant replies. Cefni frowns and quickly turns away. Merwyn sighs and returns to the airship. Tenebrant sits on the ground and leans his head back to view the sky above. "What a lovely day."

Botalia and the boys are already awake and eating their breakfast as Merwyn enters.

"Good morning," they all greet one another. Botalia stands and walks over to Merwyn.

"Are you ready?" Merwyn asks. He senses her nerves, her aura well within her control but her expression betraying her. She peers at the boys, desperation and shame present in her eyes. "We're a team. We won't let anything happen to them."

Botalia releases a nervous, breathy laugh. "If anything could trigger the monster, it would be harm coming to either of them. My instincts would take over and that's the way I know I'd respond." She scratches her head and crosses her arms. Staring at the ground, she shakes her head. "They mean so much to me. I... I know the mission is to reclaim the altar piece, but their safety is my top priority. I just... I don't want them to suffer. Not after... I can't even talk." Botalia hides her face in her hand and feels a pressure on her shoulder.

"Remain in the present. Not the past, not the future. To think about such times will only cause more suffering and heartache if you continue to utilize them in such a manner. Remember the positive and continue to reach for happiness. If you don't, you'll only find eternal pain," Merwyn whispers to Botalia. She lets out an audible exhale.

"No matter the path I choose to climb the mountain, eternal pain will always be at the top," Botalia replies. She looks at Merwyn, tears forming in her eyes. "It's the mountain I chose. Now I must live with it." Botalia wipes her hands across her face and fights to reclaim a steady breath. She's surprised her emotions escaped her grasp but feels relieved knowing Merwyn understands her concerns. Though, as she gazes into his eyes, all she can see is pity. "Well," she begins, with a new tone in her voice. "When are we departing?"

"Soon," Merwyn responds.

The airship door opens and Cefni walks in, a bag in his arms. His eyes move from the young boys to Merwyn and Botalia, pausing on her a moment as he notes her watering eyes and blushed face. With a sigh, he quickly enters the cockpit.

"Excuse me." Merwyn follows Cefni and Botalia walks to Koepp and Nix, who are no longer eating but talking.

"But what if you miss?" Koepp asks Nix, his curiosity spelled across his face. Nix laughs while simultaneously throwing his head back in an overly dramatic form of amusement.

"That's why I practice. So I don't miss," Nix answers.

Koepp smiles but doesn't seem satisfied with the answer. He squints and finally Nix sighs.

"But if I do miss, which I don't, we're supposed to wait for another opening."

Nix reaches for the last animal cracker, but Koepp snatches it off the plate and shoves it into his mouth. A wide grin covers his face and Nix furrows his brow with a pretend rage. Koepp's eyes widen and they are about to commence their chase when they see Botalia standing behind them. They quickly assume their most proper seated positions and snicker quietly. Botalia puts a hand on both of their shoulders and lowers her head between them.

"Are you boys about ready to leave?" she asks. They turn to her, nodding vigorously. "Gather your belongings, we'll wait for the others outside."

The boys rush to their bunks and grab their backpacks. Their excitement emits from them, their auras bouncing. She senses no nerves in them, only pure joy. "It's amazing, truly," Botalia thinks. "It's as if the only thing they fear is returning to what once was." She peers at the cockpit but rapidly decides she must gather her belongings.

She exits the airship behind Koepp and Nix. Each carries their own change of clothes and packed food. They also bring other survivalist tools and weapons for their trek. However, being life force users, not much is necessary outside of the amenities.

The boys find a spot adjacent to Tenebrant. He chuckles at their lack of fear of him and rolls his eyes. The sun heats up the flat rock on which they sit, the area about the forest growing misty from the evaporating water from the rain the night before. The humidity added to the thin air at the high elevation makes breathing difficult, especially for Botalia as her lungs were accustomed to the sea-level island.

Taking her seat next to Koepp, Botalia gazes out at the forest below, knowing their journey will take them in that direction. Negative thoughts reveal themselves once again, constantly echoing in her ear. Her senses heighten in this foreign environment, and she prays they will not overload her in the days to come.

"Botalia," Tenebrant voices. He doesn't look at her but rather the ground. He kicks around a pebble in front of him, his embarrassment slipping through. Though searching for words, Tenebrant finds none in his vocabulary fitting of the situation. Botalia understands and closes her eyes.

"This team has to remain intact," Botalia states. "We can't afford to lose anyone. Just... don't mention it."

Botalia returns her gaze to the forest and follows the horizon to the mountains. The sound of footsteps arrives behind them. The team stand and circle up. Cefni calls out the checklist, Koepp and Nix loudly proclaiming when items match up. As they search through their bags, checking items off the list, Merwyn approaches Botalia and Tenebrant, who have wandered to the edge of the flat rock, peering out at the forest.

"Do you feel any presences?" Merwyn asks.

Botalia shakes her head, and Tenebrant continues to scan.

"We may have arrived before any others. Whether that gives us an advantage or not is yet to be determined, but I'd say it gives us the upper hand. What say you, Tenebrant?"

"Being the first to arrive, I'd say we're at a definite advantage. We'll be able to see or hear anyone who plans on arriving by air, which is the most effective way to travel noting the distance between this landmass and any others," Tenebrant responds. Tenebrant turns to face Merwyn. "Arriving first means we set the rules."

"I hope you are correct," Merwyn replies.

The three return to surveying the area. The stillness and tranquility resonating from the forest have the opposite effect on

Botalia. Her nerves continue to grow and her doubt in her own abilities parallel. Something lurks there, deeper, hiding. Of all Botalia read about the continent, growing complacent with its extravagant appearance and biodiversity could not only be dangerous, but a death sentence.

Cefni whistles to get the attention of Merwyn, Botalia, and Tenebrant. The three turn around. Cefni holds a map with other navigational tools such as a compass and sextant chained to his person. Holstered on his hip is a revolver, though its form is not equal to any market sold models. The barrel appears longer and thinner than current makes of revolvers and a strange inscription lines the frame.

"We're moving out," Cefni orders.

Koepp and Nix high five one another, their wildest dreams becoming tangible. Merwyn, Tenebrant, and Botalia walk to them, ready to embark. Cefni examines his team and continues.

"I'll lead the pack. Koepp and Nix, you two will follow behind me, and Botalia and Tenebrant closely after. Merwyn will rear our team. Any concerns need to be addressed now. Once we leave, there's no turning back until we've completed our mission." Cefni nods as he sees the resolve on each of their faces.

Botalia focuses her mind, taking a mental photograph of the environment around her. She focuses on every sound, scent, and feeling of standing on the rock in this location. She senses her life force probing the ground. The metamorphic rock stands stable, its surface practically frictionless for Botalia's life force. As it travels downward, like roots reaching for the core, a strange sensation tingles in Botalia's fingertips, the point of release for her life force. She feels a slight pressure press against her fingers and slide into her palm. A sudden jolt strikes her body and Botalia gasps for air. Her life force instantly retracts.

The team shocked by her choking noise, turn to her in panic. No one speaks. Botalia examines her hands, opening her palms to the sky to check for markings, bruising, anything. Nothing appears. All stand in silent observation for a moment longer than makes Botalia comfortable.

"Are we going?" she asks, masking her fear of the sensation previously felt.

A collective exhale leaves the team, Merwyn looking to the skies, as if it were an omen. Cefni licks his lips in anticipation, nods, and begins his march. As the team falls in line as Cefni previously dictated, Tenebrant glances at Botalia, his confusion and curiosity causing anxiety rather than excitement, knowing that if she, or the monster within her, feel something, then they should all be worried.

Cefni leads them down a steep path, mountain to their left, cliff to their right. The sheer cliff drops about eighty meters from where they began, but the path continues to descend. Every so often, little pebbles fall at their sides, or they hear rockslides occurring underneath them. They figure the rain from the night before may be causing mudslides and erosion. Small puddles on the ground, the group cautiously tries to avoid them, whether for fear of slipping or leaving footprints. Tailing the pack, Merwyn does his best to cover their trail, however, the giant airship provides a giveaway to their arrival point.

The rocky path winds about the mountains, their descent lasting several hours. Their energy slowly deteriorates in the hot sun and humid air, those who can utilize their life force doing so to assist the physical strain of a constant downhill climb. Every so often, Cefni steps the team into the shade of the eroded mountainside and pretends to read his map, for Koepp's and Nix's sake.

Though young, Koepp and Nix hide their irritation, boredom, and fatigue well. Nix underwent much training in his childhood in preparation for even the most tortuous of conditions, so he understands the need to pace his energy. Koepp is acclimated to working in the heat of the day, and he's learned not to complain; he will be a burden to no one. Botalia follows close to the boys, watching their every footstep. The heat doesn't bother her as much as the humidity, however, her thoughts continue to be a distraction for her. She seeks an answer for the sensation she felt earlier, her fingers rubbing at her sweaty palms.

Tenebrant eyes the skies, head constantly swiveling in hopes to find Tanten or in the least any signs of human life. After all, he agreed to join in the mission with that sole purpose in mind. He couldn't care less if they find the altar piece, he simply wants to fight, and to fight Tanten would be the prize. Tenebrant stares ahead, glaring at who he believes to be the only obstacle in his quest. Although, he wouldn't mind getting in a fight with him either.

As evening approaches, the team reaches the tree line. Cefni pauses and looks around. Though exhausting, their trek down the mountain was not a difficult feat, gravity greatly assisting. Cefni peers into the dark woods, unable to assume the dangers that await them, knowing not to underestimate the wilderness of Qoterra.

Many creatures live on this continent, many of them not known to people on the mainland. Not accustomed to visitors, Cefni took this into consideration and long thought about the best course to take through the forest. One path leads to a cave system through the mountain, and while considered an easier path by the Biological Scholars of the Association, the path would add four hours to their travel time. If they wish to arrive first to the caldera in an attempt to intercept Tanten, adding time to their travels could be the deciding factor on their success.

The path through the denser wood of the forest, though more likely to run into any hostile native species and perhaps tribal land, is the shorter path to reach their destination. Also, they will be able to hear if any team arrives by airship or any other mode of transport that produces noise pollution.

Cefni clicks his tongue as he looks at his map then up to the sky, noting the time of day in his decision. He knows which path Merwyn approves of, and that which he was warned by many Scholars against taking. Time is of the essence. They can reclaim ground, they are formidable wielders of life force should any danger present itself, but time cannot be reclaimed. Cefni knows which path he would choose, his eyes glancing to the crew to note their current state.

Koepp and Nix sit to relax given their short respite. Nix stares into the darkness of the forest, and Koepp flinches at every insect to walk or fly near him. His fear of the particular mention of the blood moth forces his eyes to move unblinking about the surroundings. Nix can't help but giggle as his friend squirms at the stem of a leaf thrown in his direction.

Merwyn clears his throat and marches over to Cefni. With low tones, they discuss their options.

Botalia senses tension in the air as Merwyn passes. Her eyes follow but quickly turn away when met with a heated glare from Cefni. His worries fit him like anger, wrath blooms in his anticipation of failure. There is a slight tension between the two Council members, a disagreement Cefni wishes to end on the right side of.

Tenebrant taps his foot as he leans against the cliffside. He grows increasingly impatient with the amount of traveling and stopping. Peering into the forest, Tenebrant notices the limited light. As the sun sets, navigating through the dense forest, even with light sources provided by their life force, will prove difficult. Any substantial light they create will beckon attention to them. And, for anyone outside of perhaps Botalia, sustaining a substantial light source for a long period of time can drain one's life force quite quickly. Should they ask he take a turn in doing so, he would do no more than scoff, wanting to be at full charge when he meets Tanten.

The necromancer glances at Botalia, who stares intently into the forest. He senses a strange flux of aura and focuses his eyes. Her life force, especially the concentration in her chest, appears to pulsate, trying to escape, like it has a mind of its own. Her eyes are wide, and she pays no attention to anything around her, only the forest.

Botalia scratches at her ear, trying to ignore the sensations and forget the sounds she heard on the way down the mountain, blaming what she considered schizophrenic tendencies on her fatigue. However, sitting in front of the forest only confirms her suspicions.

Her heart races. Staring into the darkness, of never-ending shadow, the canopy robbing all light from below, part of Botalia wishes to run in, as if some secret lie waiting for her. The dialogue of the forest calls to her, inviting her to join them. Instinctively, Botalia understands no one in the team can hear the forest's invitation. A monster's instinct. It's a language only she can comprehend. The pressure grows on her chest, her life force causing a fluctuation in her aura as she fights to suppress it. She bites her lip. Usually, Botalia has no problem controlling her life force, but the longer she peers into the void that awaits them, the less power she feels she possesses. As if something stronger will unravel her sanity, claiming control of her physical being for its own.

Botalia examines her hands, curling her fingers to her palms, and places them on her chest, the feeling, the energy all too intimate and familiar to her. Her heart wishes to betray her to act on impulse; an animal instinct to return home.

With a profound inhale, Botalia brings her hands together, as if to pray, and closes her eyes. She squats down to the earth and separates her hands, placing them on the ground. Her life force quickly accelerates through the soil and roots, and instinctively travels through the forest, knowing the path to take. A large creature with shaggy hair and long limbs comes into view. It appears a quadruped at first, but after a few seconds it stands on its hind legs. It's powerful and hostile. She examines its physique and movements and slowly realizes what makes this creature incredible. In that moment, the creature senses her life force in the area and emits a pulse of its own. Botalia's chest contracts and her life force instantaneously retracts. She seizes at her heart but loses the battle. She blacks out.

Tenebrant notices Botalia's aura jolt in his peripheral vision and rushes to her aid. She collapses, his arms extending with just enough time to prevent her head from hitting a boulder with force. Despite her weight proving no worry to his strength, the contact between the brush of her skin on his causes him to wince. With care, he drops her back and neck from his hands to the earth and steps away. A quick glance at his hands and arms reveals a series of blisters and rashes.

The others gather around in urgency, the young boys panicking. Cefni bends down to Botalia's form, hovering a hand over head, understanding the reaction on Tenebrant's skin to not be a one-time fluke. The sizzling of his palm, a pain etched into his memory, not only for the surprise it caused but for the curiosity it garnered from those who cured him, remained with him more than a decade later.

"Is she dead?" Koepp asks, tears forming but dammed back by his own shame.

"No, she's just unconscious," Cefni answers, emitting short and quick life force pulses but none able to pass through the shield surrounding her.

Tenebrant scoffs and shakes his head. "And not even a week has passed since the last."

Cefni glares at the necromancer. He licks his lips and sighs, not even able to maintain an aura of hostility in this moment. His desire to appear threatening is surpassed by the fear of Botalia's current state.

"How long before she woke?" Merwyn questions, folding his hands in front of him, directing his question to no one in particular.

"About two days," Tenebrant responds with a venom laced to his tone, eyes unmoving from Cefni.

"When we first met it was four days unconscious, an additional two in paralysis."

Koepp gasps and tugs at Nix's shirt.

"Who's gonna protect us now?" he whispers as Nix swats away his hand. Nix clenches his jaw and the muscles in his core, a tremble courses through his aura.

Both Professionals eye the forest, wondering if there to be cause in its depths to her current state.

Merwyn glides forward and leans down. As his hand hovers above her head, a heat meets his palm. Merwyn holds his palm steady and emits his life force. It slowly encapsulates Botalia as it travels across the rough surface of her aura. He conjures up a guardian, a golem made of the very earth they stand on. The golem lifts Botalia, its arms protected by Merwyn's shield around her aura. Rocks and sediment fall with every movement of the creature, Merwyn's life force sentient in its repair of the being.

With Botalia in good hands, Merwyn removes his bag and takes out a vial of clear liquid. He walks to Tenebrant, who has attempted to conceal the burns on his hands and arms.

With a gesture of his hand, Merwyn asks Tenebrant to offer up his wounds. With hesitation, the necromancer obeys. Dripping the contents of the vial into his palm, Merwyn waves his free hand and murmurs a chant. The contents change texture, from fully liquid, to a gel-like substance. Tenebrant clenches his jaw and, as the salve casts about his arm, a stinging sensation reverberates through his body, a heat followed by an extreme chill.

"Which route, Cefni?" Merwyn questions, wondering if the situation cleared his mind of his doubts.

Cefni glimpses at the map while fully understanding it will not make the decision for him. Any glimpse of Botalia in his peripheral vision flickers with a hue of red, distracting his thoughts by pulling them to a distant memory, though not as distant as he would like.

"We continue on through the forest," Cefni responds.

Merwyn sighs and nods his head in resignation. Tenebrant glares at Cefni, understanding during their preparation the forest path to be the dangerous one of the two. Not only have they lost their most valuable weapon, but protecting an incapacitated teammate may prove even more deadly to the group. Cefni shrugs off the seething glare of Tenebrant and bites his tongue, withholding any insult or threat, praying that he will have made the right choice. The clock ticks.

Cefni marches into the forest, Koepp and Nix closely following as their senses have heightened due to current events. Merwyn instructs the golem to travel behind the boys. He gazes at Tenebrant, who continues to glare ahead at the leader of their pack. Tenebrant addresses Merwyn's eyes with silent concern and wrath before they enter side by side into the shadows of the forest.

Chapter Four

The dense canopies of the oak, elm, and sweet gum trees prevent most light from entering the floor below. Mountain laurel and other shrubs cover much of the ground, stretching wherever light manages to slip through, along with dead leaves and twigs, cracked and clawed at by the many species. Worn paths embed themselves to the land for the creatures who created them, a warning to the team of which directions they should tread lightly.

With little ability to gather direction from the movement of celestial bodies, Cefni uses a compass to lead. With swift chops of life force to any obstacles in their path, he creates a road the team can travel without concern. His eyes constantly scan the surroundings, recalling the images of any poisonous vines, ivy, or insects that await them in this deadly environment. They trudge through mud, unable to dry from the frequent rain and lack of heat to reach the ground. Pulling their boots from the sludge puddles, frustration and fatigue grow at a much more rapid pace. The mosquitoes arrive in swarms to their group, as if an open invitation buffet traveling straight to them for their feasting pleasure.

Merwyn, utilizing subtle orbs of life force to swat away the pests, glances at Tenebrant.

"You've seen something like this before, haven't you?"

"Yes. The last time it happened, she collapsed due to an extensive loss of energy. I can't think of what may have thrown her into shock this time," Tenebrant replies, cursing at the bug swarms under his breath and spitting one to the ground that found entrance in his talking.

"I believe it's a defense mechanism in response to losing consciousness," Merwyn states. "Though illogical and contradictory to the teachings of many Professionals, I believe her aura protects her of its own accord. The concentration of life force in her chest releases in her unconscious state, and her body reacts by creating a shield using her aura as a boundary and her life force as a weapon. Anything to cross said boundary is considered a threat, and her life force attacks the threat, like a mother protecting its young." A silence falls between them. Merwyn drops his tone to little more than a whisper. "I don't know your relationship with Ms. Ulton, and I won't enquire about any further information on the subject. However, curiosity strikes me. Are you aware of what she is?"

Tenebrant chuckles and looks to the ground. He nods.

"Which makes your theory all the more probable. Even stranger than knowing what she is, is admitting she acts more human than others, emotionally and psychologically. Probably not what her parents were expecting. Yeah. She's definitely... different."

"The Ultons were a great many things. Not that I should say I aligned with all their practices, some questionable hypotheses made it through grant collection. However, Ms. Ulton exhibits quite a many features I do not doubt would cause question within the scientific community, and were her parents still around, no doubt they would be the most curious minds of them all."

Merwyn's lips draw together to a frown, his eyes unblinking, listening with full focus. Tenebrant notes the reaction, the silence of Cefni's footsteps bringing the group to a halt as his senses alert him as well. The distant roar of an engine breaks through the dense canopy to their ears.

"What's going on?" Koepp questions, looking around the team as rising anticipation inhibits their ability to form words.

Nix peers at Tenebrant and senses a wave of bloodlust. Though unable to focus his hearing to the same extent as the Professional, he can easily deduce the situation.

"Someone else is coming."

Koepp panics and bites his lip, his fingers fidgeting as his feet mimic running about. Nix holds a finger up to shush the anxious mumbling of his friend.

"It's an airship. I can't quite tell the model from the hum. Maybe a Ptera 3120, but I can't tell. No doubt it left from either Dominia or Divesregio," Cefni reports, his observation bringing him no further comfort.

"No doubt an excellent distraction should there be any others already landed," Merwyn states. He glances at his side, feeling the wisps prick at his aura. "Rein in your life force, Mr. Mortu. Emotion related to events not yet transpired is an awful waste of life force usage."

Tenebrant gulps and clenches his fists, exerting control over his life force tendrils. The necromancer hadn't realized the escape in his excitement. As if a present delivered straight to him, he wishes to know what is inside. Who is inside...

"Time is ticking away. We must keep going."

Cefni resumes his march, pulling others to attention with the sounds of foliage hitting the ground. He rounds about trees and larger bushes, not wishing to waste his life force in absolute deforestation. Fortune arrives from the inability to tell midday from night. The misfortune arrives as the creatures who prowl in the dusk leave their burrows and dens, ready to make their presence known.

He ducks under a low hanging branch in their path, apologizing to those behind for his decision to skip over cutting it. As he raises his head on the other side, a flying creature dives at him. The beat of the flapping wings is deafening as it occurs near his ears. The residual ringing forces his hands to cover his head, hoping whatever it is to not have sharp talons.

"It's coming again!" Koepp screams, pointing through the branches above at the beast.

Black plumes ending in red tips, heated embers, and wavy air signatures visible across its body. The wings fold in four layers, unveiling a massive wingspan as it dives from the branches headfirst before opening to glide toward the target. A talon scratches at Cefni's hand, hissing as hot metal meeting water. Cefni curses and swats at the bird, sending it back to its branch above.

"A volcanic eagle," Merwyn states, focused on the creature's movements. "They form their nests near magma, safe from predators or any other threat to their eggs. Nocturnal creatures, they hunt as the sun sets, listening for sound rather than relying on vision. The heat of the lava near their nests would render any mucus to surround and saturate eyes useless."

The eagle dives at the team again, a strange glow forming at the tip of its beak. Cefni wraps life force about his arms to shield himself from the next attack. Before the sharp talons meet his flesh and the wing beats signify flying away, the head of the eagle, severed from its body, lands at his feet. The bird's body erupts into flames as it falls to the earth. Nix lands at his side, a disgusted grimace as he eyes the singed sleeves of his shirt.

"I hate birds," he mutters.

Merwyn laughs at the response, no one else quite sure how or if they need to respond. Cefni sighs and cuts through the next obstacles in their way.

Despite the abysmal levels of light to enter during the day, nighttime travel through the forest proves all the more dangerous for the team. Visibility sinks to nil and staying on course grows difficult, even for the most studied of them all.

Merwyn emits orbs of light that accompany them and swirl about the forest, scouting any odd noises or sounds Merwyn believes he hears. A small orb hovers over Cefni's compass, another always a few meters in front of him.

Koepp scratches at the bites on his face, the pests of the forest showing no mercy to the one who lacks the ability to defend himself but with his hands. A shuffle in the bushes nearby causes him to panic.

"What's that?" he screams. An orb floats in the direction he points, Merwyn emitting a stream of life force to shake the bush and possibly force whatever hides there from its cover. Nothing reveals itself.

"Just calm down, Flynn," Cefni calls back, huffing as he grows exhausted from the constant utilization of energy.

"Can't blame them for being jumpy," the necromancer shouts ahead, the irritation in his tone causing Cefni to roll his eyes. "Many would feel such paranoia after walking through a dark space for hours. You do know that sightless isolation has been deemed a form of torture by the Magistrate Association, correct?"

"I don't need you teaching me on what the Magistrate Association has or has not deemed torturous. I signed and sponsored most of those papers."

"Then you should also know forced sleep deprivation is on there as well."

"I know!" Cefni yells, stopping in his tracks to allow his glare to find Tenebrant. "I would understand and appreciate your concern much more if you weren't a serial murderer, necromancer."

Tension fills the air, the sounds of chirping and whistling insects eliminating the possibility of silence. Tenebrant swats at a mosquito on his arm, promptly squashing it, but his eyes do not disconnect from Cefni's. They maintain a steady glare until the golem steps between them, blocking their vision.

"The sooner we arrive at the cabin, the sooner we can rest," Cefni responds, not wishing to give in to Tenebrant's desire for discord.

"We wouldn't have had to wait to arrive at the cabin if we would have taken the path through the cave. There was a suitable position within for a respite. This forest and its oh so many pleasures will not allow a break."

"Sometimes there are things more important than life's comforts. We have a mission."

"One that we'll easily fail should none of us be rested. We're down our strongest player. You don't think we're already at a huge disadvantage for it?" Tenebrant's tone fills with venomous fury. He growls and punches a nearby tree, his life force willing for some form of escape. With a deep breath and bloodied knuckles, he finds better control of the swirling winds about him.

Merwyn licks his lips and sighs. His hand reaches for Tenebrant, but the necromancer swats him away.

"Let us return to our hike. We draw attention to ourselves."

Cefni sighs in resignation and cuts down the next bush with more life force than necessary, however, the release allows him a breath of relief. As he gazes on, he notices shadow darker than the blackness surrounding them. The trunks of the trees are larger, roots raising from the ground as they search for paths not taken by another. Shrubs grow sparse, the canopies of the older trees in this part of the forest denser than in the previous section. An odd glow of bioluminescence occurs, revealing in its glimmer a family of mushrooms at the mossy base of a formidable blue oak. Cefni gulps, their nightly venture growing more dangerous with every step.

"Whoa!" Koepp whispers, observing the glowing antenna of an angler beetle. Nix pulls him back by the collar before Koepp's finger becomes a meal to the beetle, the glowing orb dangling in front of fangs inviting the boy to touch the bait.

"Do not touch anything," Cefni instructs with stern tone, paranoia rising in these parts. Humidity increases as the heat from geothermal vents fails to pass the canopy. Thick and misty, the air extracts their sweat and paints them in it. Thirst grows in the team, vision blurring even with the orbs of light.

Tenebrant mutters curses as the dangers of Qoterra present themselves in such a guise. Distracted by glitters in the branches above, as if eyes reflecting their light, Tenebrant accidentally steps on a vine crossing their path. He panics, believing it to possibly be a snake or salamander. The reaction causes a cough from a bulbous fungus blooming from a tree trunk to his side. It releases a puff of red smoke, life force particles interspersed with the toxic fumes. Tenebrant covers his mouth and nose and quickens pace.

Cefni slashes through a vine, ready to continue, but the plant mends itself in an instant, utilizing life force to pull the cut ends back together and seal the wound with a rancid smelling, white ooze.

"Damn," Cefni mutters.

He glances about to find a path this vine ceases to cover, not wishing to simply nudge it aside for any other possible abilities it may have. Cefni steps over a few paces and hears a crunch beneath his feet. He bends down as the object captures his attention. A handcrafted arrow.

"Merwyn, take a look at this."

Merwyn joins Cefni, observing the object and attempting to date the piece. The task proves impossible for the two Professionals, wishing in this moment that a Scholar had joined them. Merwyn takes the arrow in his hands and moves his life force through it. He hopes his little knowledge of psychometry assists in knowing their present danger level.

"Why is there an arrow here? Is someone hunting?" Koepp asks with a shiver up his spine.

"No doubt. And if they are hunting, we're probably the prey," Nix responds, his eyes no more than slits as he scans the surrounding forest. Koepp gulps.

A dash of life force lifts from the arrow and flies in a single direction a short distance before disappearing.

"That is the direction in which it was crafted, whether in the previous era or yesterday. Either way, I suggest we avoid tribal territory."

"Don't have to tell me twice," Cefni responds, marching in the opposite direction of which the sparkle of light headed before clearing more of a path.

Tenebrant, who analyzes Botalia's aura periodically in an attempt to sense the progression of her state, notices an erratic movement occurring as it fights Merwyn's containment shield. The mist darts with force to be rebounded from the shield back to the normal confines of its flow. Life force leaves her fingertips like needles, slowly chipping a hole through the shield. Like a chisel to marble, though more so as one encased in the marble attempting an escape, her life force hopes for a release. A patient yet determined sentience of one accustomed to imprisonment and the slow race to freedom.

The necromancer opens his mouth to inform Merwyn of their problem when running footsteps sound in the shadows behind them. The two turn in urgency, Merwyn commands a series of orbs in the direction, casted like fireworks to light the space as quickly as possible. As he does so, another noise occurs above them as if a creature jumping in the branches. This sound causes Nix to peer up, alert demanding life force to his hands should he need to react quickly. Tenebrant mumbles and emits a smoky curse above, forcing whatever life it hits to betray all presences within the area of the smoke. No more than a glowing outline of fungi and an array of insects shine with the curse.

Cefni, unaware of the noises the others experience, mutters at his compass. The orienting arrow points in one direction for a few seconds, then quickly spins to another, repeating as so every couple of seconds to pass. Cefni taps the glass as he steadily points it in one direction. The spinning arrow causes an anger to boil within him, lack of rest with their long travels surely not helping his lack of patience. With a hint of an idea, he focuses his eyes. Panic sets in.

Roots of life force flow through the ground all around them. Each grows almost undistinguishable from the others, forming a net carefully woven about the area in which the team stands. The pure concentration of life force causes his compass the inability to connect with the fields it uses to function.

"Merwyn, the ground!"

Merwyn's face grows grim.

"These strands derive from no living being."

Orbs find their way to the perimeter of the net, their light flashing on trees with symbols etched into the bark. Tenebrant chuckles.

"Of course. We're in a ritual circle."

"What does that mean?" Koepp murmurs, eyeing the symbols in a confused fear.

"It means we stepped right into their trap," Nix snarls and prepares a defensive position.

"Son of a-" Cefni starts when shuffling occurs on all sides of the team. He licks his lips and turns to slash away at whatever obstacle can get them out of the net they find themselves in, but all the vines surrounding the way forward heal a moment after the slice.

His free hand flies to his neck as a pinching sensation hits. His fingers find a quill of a Pine Mouse. As he extracts it, he notices the tip has been manipulated, filled with a substance other than the sedative naturally created by the creature. Drowsiness hits and without warning, Cefni collapses.

Koepp cries out and Merwyn commands the orbs to explode in a burst of light, revealing all within this area of the forest. A collective fear hits as hundreds of eyes stare back at them. A pinch hits Merwyn's shoulder from behind, sending him to the ground. Nix falls next. Koepp panics and tears fill his eyes before the quill pricks him and sends him into a deep sleep.

Tenebrant stands with a thick smoke surrounding him. Every quill attempting to penetrate his shield deteriorates before it can reach him. He summons his kris and enshrouds it with a curse. As he does so, the golem carrying Botalia crumbles, large chunks of rock rolling to his feet. He jumps to avoid the rubble, a quill pricking his ankle midair. His kris dissipates in wisps and he falls to the earth, muttering curses. Before his eyes close, he sees the tribe draw near. They hold no weapons, only rope.

The tribe are protectors of the land. Their team are no more than trespassers in the tribe's eyes.

The ritual circle fades in and out as it loses power, the tribe arriving in time to apprehend the life force wielders before they were the ones at a disadvantage.

Chapter Five

He looks out the window of the airship and down on the forests and mountainous terrain of the dangerous continent. They fly above the birds, no more than small dots he crushes in his mind. The layer of clouds underneath the ship coats the mountains in a mist, daunting and mysterious. He fidgets in his seat, excitement and anticipation for the moment he's long awaited as it slowly comes into frame. His eyes betray his desire to appear calm and collected. A slight pressure lands on his shoulder causing him to flinch.

"Tanten," the woman's voice calls him to attention.

Syrenne rolls her eyes as she senses his irritation for being pulled from his fantasies and removes her hand from his shoulder. She continues.

"We're set to land in one hour. What shall we do to prepare?"

Tanten Flynn returns his eyes to his view out the window and sighs. He taps his fingers on the arm rest and looks back at the troops with a grimace.

"Gather your belongings, what else? Take another head count, though I don't expect anyone could escape from this airship successfully. Not even my team would have the capacity of an atomic shift. Just make certain they haven't killed one another yet."

Tanten swats her away before leaning forward, elbows on his knees, and retires to his fictional reality. Syrenne glares at him as she departs.

"His lack of respect and selfish desires will cause the fall of our team," Syrenne mumbles once Yasmine joins her side. Yasmine places a massaging hand on Syrenne's shoulder and offers a quick peck to the back of her neck. Syrenne monitors her breathing, relief in her allies not all being absolute pricks.

Tanten taps at the arm rest of his seat as anticipation grows. The moment the ship begins its descent, Tanten jumps from his seat and pats himself down, ensuring every weapon and tool are in place and secure. He furrows his brow and glares at the team preparing their own equipment. Some carry multiple bags of survival tools, food, liquids, and comfort items. The very thought causes Tanten to scoff.

"They dress for a camping trip. Yet none brought a shovel to dig the other's grave," Tanten mumbles.

With a slight quake, the airship touches down. Tanten pushes past the team, wishing to be the first to observe what awaits them in Qoterra.

A cool breeze meets him as the door opens. His hand raises to block the rays of the setting sun, viewing the mountains in the distance, the base of the forests quite far from the point of their landing. No immediate dangers present themselves. Any grazing animals surely fled as the airship descended. The chirps of birds overhead and calls of insects leaping through the long grass and patches of wildflowers create a serene mood. Tanten licks his lips.

"This deadly continent tries to deceive us so soon. No doubt its charm will work on some of these bastards."

"Mr. Flynn!" Reece rushes down the steps of the airship and stops next to Tanten, breathing heavily. "Syrenne's... Syrenne has given the okay... Her troops are ready... to move out... whenever." He pauses and tries to catch his breath. "What are your orders, Mr. Flynn?"

"Assemble the team. Time is of the essence and wasting time is the worst mistake we could make."

Tanten focuses his eyes into the distance. Their first and only destination lies to the west, awaiting them: the gateway to the lost realm. Reece marches to the command, but Tanten stops him in his tracks.

"Oh, and Reece. Don't act so careless while carrying the altar piece on your back."

"My apologies, Mr. Flynn," Reece responds before returning to Tanten's earlier orders.

Tanten smiles, devious and confident. No one suspects his plan.

"Everyone believes my desire for the staff is too great to abandon them. Fools. I'm not one to share the prize." Tanten chuckles.

"Tanten."

He flinches, having not heard footsteps approach from behind. Syrenne releases a breathy laugh at his reaction, having not concealed her presence in the slightest. She pauses in front of him, map and compass in hand.

"I've assigned one of each of our members to carry the crate with the altar piece. Does that satisfy you?" She asks, the sarcasm barely hidden in her question. Tanten rolls his eyes.

"Compromise is compromise, I suppose."

"Well then. Do you wish to lead?"

Tanten sighs and scratches at the back of his head, his scruffy black hair seemingly growing at an unprecedented rate since making physical contact with the altar piece. The thought passes him, a curiosity crossing his mind, and one he had not thought of previously. Syrenne's heated glare hits him and pulls him back to the present. He shakes his head.

"You're the one with the map. You lead and I'll tail. Is that acceptable?" Tanten asks, mimicking Syrenne's earlier tone.

She pokes her tongue from the side of her mouth as she bites down and nods. Her hands fall on her hips as she turns toward the airship. The last of the troops exit, the others with their bags in the grass already laying down or stretching out their cramped limbs. Some pick the flowers from the fields and inhale the sweet scents.

"Let's move out!"

Syrenne slowly turns away, a hand raising to rub at her temple as a headache sets in. Yasmine whistles and brings all to attention, motioning for those already forgetting of the line up.

As Syrenne takes a step toward the troops, Tanten calls to her.

"Syrenne. We have to succeed. There is no other option."

Syrenne closes her eyes, his words echoing in her ears as her own brain puts an emphasis on his choice of words. *We.* She gives a slight nod and marches toward the team.

Syrenne rotates her torso, waiting on the arrow of the compass to align. She ignores Reece's mumbling behind her, his abilities honed to direction by the fields he utilizes for his life force. She refuses to rely on him, a devout follower of Tanten, as her sole tool on this mission. The arrow steadies. She orients herself west, and they begin their march.

Yasmine rushes to the front and grabs the compass from Syrenne, placing a water bottle in her hand.

"I might need something stronger if this doesn't end quickly. I can still hear him swearing behind us."

Tanten curses as they trudge through marshy spots of the fields. A torrential downpour passed them as they approached, causing turbulence, but he had hoped the earth would absorb it by the time they landed. He was no Scholar, so the best he could do was hope.

Reece and Tanten tail the group. Tanten carries several small weapons on his person, not too intimidating if it weren't for his life force. But nothing he carries is more important than a dagger with an inscription on the grip. Reece marches beside with a large travel pack on his back, hunched by the weight of it on his shoulders. He tries to compensate with life force, but he is unaccustomed in the utilization of reinforcement.

Upon entering the forest bordering the plains, visibility drastically drops. One of Syrenne's team members crafts luminescent orbs the size of beetles to in the least keep the group together. Tanten scoffs at the effort but refuses to summon his own source of light.

Many eyes fall on the team as they trek deeper in the darkness. The eyes of hidden creatures observe, territorial, hostile, and cautious. Insects swarm about them, attracted to the light emitted from the orbs. Some members continuously spray repellant at the air, others use their life force to shield their skin. A blood moth lands on Tanten's arm, and he crushes it with life force within a split second. He releases a breathy laugh.

A shrub rustles behind. A small mammal with large feet and ears, its entire body covered in thick fur, emerges. Tanten taps Reece's back, and he turns around and smirks. Tanten kicks a pebble toward the rabbit-like animal, the rock landing no more than an inch from it. The creature arches its back and hisses at the pebble, its hair standing on end. It lifts itself on its hind legs and glares at Tanten and Reece, with wide, red eyes. Tanten smiles.

He focuses his eyes on the creature, amused by its tenacity. In that moment, the creature's limbs fall from its form, and the creature cries out in agony, causing some of the other members to turn and look. Blood flows from the creature, pooling on the ground already saturated with water. After a few seconds, the head of the creature flies off into the darkness of the forest. The shouts of joy from the scavenger species echo from the trees. The decapitated body lays on the forest floor, fur matted in its own blood.

"Is that the scariest you've got, Qoterra?" Tanten whispers.

The members rotate and race to catch up with the group. After several hours, a dim light filters in through the edge of the forest. The area opens into a glade containing a small pond, cattails, and long grasses scattered around with frogs and other animals humming and singing as dusk approaches.

Syrenne allows the team to refill their flasks and rest their legs and backs. A collective sigh of relief leaves them, collapsing to the earth and catching their breath.

Tanten, irritated by their stop, bites his lip and mutters under his breath. He kicks at a wildflower and finds a boulder to sit on. Swatting at the pestering insects in front of him, Tanten attempts to focus his eyes onward, scanning their path for any dangers. Reece walks toward Tanten, flask extended.

"Would you like a drink, Mr. Flynn?"

Tanten locks eyes with him for a moment before accepting the drink. He hands the container back to Reece.

"How are you holding up?"

Tanten examines Reece's person, which does not appear fatigued after their hike, despite his lack of conditioning. Reece picks at his earlobe with eyes focused on the ground. He licks his lips and drops his tone to almost a whisper.

"I don't feel tired at all, actually. I've been using my life force to strengthen my legs. Also, I created a life force chamber that acts as a vacuum inside of my bag. It makes all contents within it almost weightless. I-"

Tanten raises his hand and Reece stops talking immediately. Tanten grins and gazes above. The sky is a deep shade of navy, the stars glimmering as their ancient light arrives to them. Not something that could be seen in the city.

"I'm glad to hear you're okay. And while your physical stamina is of concern, I'm more interested in your psychological state." Tanten leans in. "Back when the team was excavating the piece, it's said that several of the assigned excavators with long periods of exposure slowly went insane. They began hallucinating, grew paranoid, and fell into unexplained depression. They didn't realize the true horror until one of the team leads committed suicide by jumping off the scaffolding and into the excavation site.

"If you say you're fine, so be it. Just don't want you to meet that tragic fate. The altar piece is an ancient piece of magic. I'm not sure how well life force will protect you from its power."

Tanten leans back. Reece gulps and scratches at his arms, the feeling of a thousand legs of insects crawling across his skin. With a deep breath of resolve, Reece adjusts the bag on his shoulders and peers in the direction they will be heading. The technomancer only cares about what lies ahead, never regretting the path he decided to take when he chose to follow Tanten Flynn.

"I won't disappoint you, Mr. Flynn."

He never had, not disappointed him but perhaps frustration verging on doubts rose within Tanten at times. But there was never regret in those eight years since, when Reece passed the Magistrate Assessment. Reece hadn't known what to do next. He didn't want to return home as that meant he'd be going back to a life he wanted to leave behind. His parents were politicians, and, like most politicians, strongly disliked the Magistrate Association. However, Reece had been determined to become a magistrate because of his adventurous and curious spirit and the innate abilities his type of aura allowed him. Passing the exam, which so many before him failed to do was all the proof Reece needed that the path to his future was built differently than his family's bloodline would suggest.

After receiving his license, Reece sat outside the Association building, indecisive about his next move. He felt worthless, lost, he doubted his purpose and whether his parents had been correct all those times before. But Tanten Flynn saw potential in Reece, the potential for greatness. His intelligence, strength, and loyalty proved Reece's worthiness of being his student. Reece became a disciple under Tanten and regret never found him again.

"Tanten! Reece! We're leaving!" Syrenne yells, pulling Reece from his reminiscing.

Tanten stands and readjusts his clothes. He connects eyes with Reece, who nods. The line forms, and the team heads into the forest. Tanten, who memorized the itinerary for this trip months back, understands the team will not reach the caldera before dawn, hoping that in the least they are ahead of any other group already on this continent.

As they enter the shadows of the forest, Tanten ponders the story of the origins of the altar. Constructed of marble, lined with gold and sapphire intricacies, it is revered as an object of fear, not of fortune, by the druidic tribes. Perhaps the piece Reece carries on his back was never meant to be restored to the altar, broken away from the original in hopes none would be able to open the doorway again.

But they hold the key. Tanten will restore the altar to its former glory. Countless sacrifices were performed in the space, countless lives lost time and again whenever any would travel to the alternate realm. The waste of that energy if the staff were never to get the chance to be wielded by man. By him.

One question still shrouds his mind. A puzzle he has been unable to solve. The doorway does not simply appear upon restoring the altar, that would be too easy. From stories and accounts past, an activation ritual is required. An immense amount of energy and possibly sacrifices are necessary to open the gateway. Tanten glances about their current environment, hoping for an idea on how the team will source energy. He shakes his head as one idea after another fail in his imaginary simulations.

"We have to get this right, the first time."

As his thoughts distract him, a jolt of an energized aura strikes him. Reece freezes at his side. The technomancer focuses on the ground in front of him. Tanten pauses but refuses to draw attention from the rest of his team.

Tanten squeezes Reece's arm, pulling him from his frozen state. Lifting a finger to his lips, Tanten signs for Reece to remain silent.

With another gesture, the teacher instructs his student to calm his aura, Reece's spinning about him as an electromagnetic field affected by a surge of flux. Reece inhales profoundly and follows his teacher's direction, despite the nerves that refuse to leave his stomach. Tanten observes the environment around them and continues forward cautiously.

They catch up to the group, no further disturbances outside of the bothersome insects and latching vines as they reach the edge of the forest. Hours have passed and the bright stars glimmer in the reflection of a lake in the clearing. Lighter shades of blue enter the sky on the horizon, the sun threatening to cast its light so none may remain hidden. A mist sweeps across the lake to them, a shiver rising up many of their spines.

Syrenne allows the team another respite. Sighs of relief and whispers of joy spring across the team. Those carrying the crate with the supposed altar piece set it upon the grass, other members rubbing their shoulders for their sacrifice of energy to carry such a divine object.

Syrenne approaches Tanten with the map held out in front of her. He chuckles.

"You look like this is nothing more than a walk through the park. But I assume your kind don't need beauty rest," Tanten jokes. Syrenne glares at him before rolling her eyes. She shoves the map at Reece, who takes the map in his hands.

"We're here," Syrenne states, pointing to their current location on the map. Tanten puts his hands behind his head, pretending to listen to Syrenne. "I believe if we take the northern route around the lake, our travel will be less difficult. The signs of a heavy rain mean the plains along the southern route will most definitely be flooded due to the rivers stemming off this lake in that direction."

"Why are you telling me this?" Tanten asks.

"I thought you'd want to know my plan."

"Why?"

"Well..." Syrenne feels taken aback by his question. She wants to believe Tanten trusts in her judgement, though her gut tells her he probably doesn't care how they reach their destination. She clears her throat.

"Well then. If you have no objections, we'll move out immediately."

Syrenne takes her map, turns her back, and begins to walk away.

"Six hours," she calls out. "Six hours and we'll be in the center of the caldera."

Tanten sighs. He surveys their surroundings, breathing in the fresh air. He shakes his head.

"It's like the calm before the storm," Tanten whispers.

Reece chuckles and readjusts the bag on his back. Tanten heads toward the group, and as Reece takes a step to follow him, a sudden dizziness hits. The ground beneath him quakes and a strange pressure radiates throughout him. He shakes his head, as if to dislodge the origin of the pressure. Once he regains stability, he joins the line by Tanten's side.

The sun rises over Qoterra. The different species awaken and the air around the lake thickens. Tanten understands the difficulty of taking other paths in comparison to the route they now walk, but he would have preferred a path that did not expose them. They travel out in the open, an opportunity any predator would take advantage of. Their chance of escape is incredibly limited.

"Mr. Flynn?" Reece mumbles.

His heart presses against his chest in an attempt to escape. The closer they draw to the altar, the more potent is Reece's sense of danger. His instincts scream at him to hide, but, because no one else feels the same way, he continues on. He perceives several sets of eyes on him, not from one specific direction, but from all. Reece gasps for breath through the saliva build up in his throat.

Tanten squints at Reece and firmly grips his shoulder. He takes the bag and swings it onto his own back. An expression of shock covers Reece's face.

"But, Mr. Flynn..."

Tanten doesn't look at Reece but follows the group once more. Reece stands in utter shock for several seconds, his disappointment in himself eating at him. Tears form in his eyes and the negative chants echo in his head. Words like "useless," "failure," and "disappointment" being thrown around. Reece, paralyzed by his thoughts, gazes at Tanten, who continues to walk forward.

"I won't disappoint you, Mr. Flynn," Reece whispers. "Even if I must die, I will never abandon you."

He runs to catch up to the group.

When Reece joins Tanten's side, Tanten grins.

"Glad to have you back," Tanten states.

Reece smiles, feeling unworthy of Tanten's welcome. There is a silence between them for a few seconds.

"Do you hear that?" Tanten quietly asks, not changing the expression on his face. He wants to ensure only Reece hears his question.

Reece focuses for a moment before hearing the low rumble of a distant airship. With a grin, the technomancer focuses, noting the sounds of the wildlife in the forests and mountains behind and beyond. Though, he must quickly pull himself from his senses for a ringing in his ears start up. It's an annoying, shrill tone similar to the audible frequencies given off by some electronics. Reece often hears the noise, a reason why he chooses not to focus his senses in most situations. The tone can be disorientating, especially in a large city with plenty of devices giving off such frequencies. However, Reece did not expect such sounds on this continent.

"Who do you suppose?" Tanten questions. Reece widens his eyes, wondering if that is an order, but Tanten shakes his head slightly. They peer at the group ahead, no one paying any attention to the sky. "It's safe to assume they don't know," Tanten comments. "What an incompetent crew. Luckily, Syrenne is too focused on that stupid map to pay attention to our surroundings. If she wasn't, I'm sure she would have heard it."

Tanten gazes at Reece, who continues to stare ahead while fully focusing on the environment around them with his other senses. Tanten grins and follows suit.

Tanten releases small fragments of his life force and allows them to travel through the ground, though he did not send any ahead, for fear the team would sense it beneath them. He individually controls each small fragment and experiences the information they collect simultaneously. The fragments heading to the north pulsate as they feel concentrated life force. Following the path further north, Tanten's life force lands in a minefield in the form of life force utilizers. Not simple species but humans. He disperses his life force, slowly calling it back to his pores.

"You've known for quite some time, haven't you?" Tanten asks. Reece, still focusing his eyes forward, nods. "I felt it, too. Tell me. How many do you suppose they have amongst their ranks?"

"Exactly thirty-one."

"Hmm... so-"

"But that's just to the north. I'm getting a faint signal to the south, but I can't quite determine the number. The life force is quite concentrated, too concentrated to distinguish one person from another, especially at this distance."

"Your detection range never ceases to amaze me," Tanten compliments. Reece feels a bounce in his heart and tries to suppress a smile by biting his lip.

Tanten looks down at the ground, their shadows shrinking in front of them as the sun rises higher. Tanten chuckles.

"You know... it may be about time we leave this party. Though, I wouldn't mind sticking around for a while. After all, in no more than an hour, this ground will be a battlefield."

Chapter Six

The group marches forward, eventually arriving at the opposite side of the lake. Syrenne observes their surroundings. Ahead of the team lies a rocky flatland, and further in the distance the hot springs.

Syrenne's paranoia and doubts grow as, to Tanten's irritation, they march in the open, no signs of cover for themselves from those who may pass over above or from a mountainous vantage point. In the least, this scenario also deprives all predators of a sneak attack. Her life force dances on her fingertips, the time for such conflict drawing ever nearer.

Every so often, Tanten focuses, noticing the enemies move closer every minute.

"There's no question. They're preparing for an attack," Tanten whispers. He glances at Reece, who also pays close attention to the movement of the infringing group.

Reece clenches his jaw. The pain surging through him is distant. Too far away to attack, but too near to escape. His head rings and his body shakes at the pressure he suppresses. With every passing moment, weakness and fatigue slowly wash over and consume Reece. He shakes it off as no more than psychosomatic symptoms. After all, the preparation for this mission and the multiple sleepless nights left him distressed and anxious. But he feels as if his body is crumbling under some unknown weight. His legs go numb, his ears ring out, his hands tremble. He senses something strange. His eyes widen as fear takes over, wondering why she hides as much as they do.

Syrenne, though wearing a stoic expression and strutting forward as if no thoughts distract her, releases discrete stems of life force into the ground. She conceals the stems so well that not even Tanten can detect them. These stems shoot toward the forests, tagging every target.

"Tanten underestimated her," Reece thinks. "She knows we're being watched, and she's probably got a better idea of their strengths than even we do."

Reece glances at Tanten, who continues to focus on the troops who draw near. He wonders whether he should warn Tanten of Syrenne's awareness. Reece decides against it, not wanting to worry Tanten, but also hoping Tanten will get the satisfaction from figuring it out on his own, that is, if he figures it out.

Tanten focuses on projecting small fragments of his life force to determine the troop's exact position, paying no attention to his own team. His life force moves through the ground at a high velocity, twisting and turning to avoid objects that will cause a greater resistive force. As his life force draws near the edge of the forest, it hits a wall. He recognizes the sensation of the aura, his fragments scurrying away and traveling to him with this information.

The moment it arrives, he instantly dissipates his life force and flinches as he walks into the back of the person in front of him. The line stopped moving. The piercing glare hits him and sends a genuine chill down his spine. Syrenne focuses her rage as he has never encountered before. He mumbles a curse.

Syrenne opens her mouth to yell, but the enemies beat her to it. Reece pulls on Tanten's sleeve. Chaos unleashes. The team draws their weapons, preparing their life force to utilize it instantaneously. Their adversaries run at them from the forest to the north. The sounds of bullets firing and the whirring of life force projectiles cause the team to raise their defenses, though most of them prefer the offense. Tanten panics. Syrenne notices Tanten's hesitation at giving orders and decides to take charge.

"Sculptors! Create a shield! Projectors, take the offensive with a barrage!" Syrenne screams as she marches the line. They assemble themselves according to her orders. She stops in front of the two soldiers carrying the crate and watches as the infringing army draws nearer. "You two, stay back. We can't let them have it."

She finds difficulty in swallowing. Her heart calms after the rapid acceleration from earlier, handling her stress as any Professional should be able to under such conditions. Analyzing their enemies, Syrenne's fear manifests as quickly as the life force on her fingertips.

The Crusaders rush them, some falling to the barrage of life force projectiles, others doing their best to make the battle in close quarters. Once within range, there is no escape. They must fight until the other team is dead or until their very bodies give out. A fight of honor.

Syrenne clenches her fists every time an allies scream reaches her. Their dedication to the mission becomes the hope she needs. In honesty, a life force utilizer like Syrenne excels in close quarters combat. Her life force drastically weakens when not in direct connection with her body. Up close, her life force is far superior to many. Though frightened of battle, she is determined to come out the victor.

Syrenne glances around, analyzing with every bit of focus to determine weaknesses of those about. Her eyes widen, a strange void opening in her stomach, as the realization hits her.

"Tanten... Reece..." she mumbles, noticing neither are to be seen.

She breathes deeply, trying to calm her once more excited heart. Syrenne jumps as she hears the first clash of weapons. A splash of blood hits her face and her eyes glow, a combination of her rage and determination shining through.

The screams of both sides ring out. Life force flies in all directions. One team member summons strange metal creatures to do his bidding. The enemy responds with a transmutation of moisture and other atoms of the air and ground, utilizing their life force as the energy needed to create hydrofluoric acid. The acidic wave melts the metal beasts and aims to attack the conjurer. The acid burns through the member's skin. The enemy raises her pistol and finishes him off with a bullet to the head.

Another fight occurring simultaneously is between two physically fit men. They utilize their life force to enhance their physical and weapon's material strength, making their bodies harder than steel armor to resist any blows to get past them. One with broadsword and one with cleaver, the two exchange swings. After only a minute, both bleed from cuts on their arms and legs. The enemy soldier also has a slice across his chest.

They grunt as their swords clash. The team member draws back. The enemy slices downward, seeing an opening. However, his reaction time is slowed by his exhaustion. The team member thrusts forward his broadsword, which pierces the chest of the warrior. He falls to the ground. The team member unsheathes his sword from the corpse and searches for his next opponent.

Meanwhile, Syrenne makes her way through the ranks. She moves fast, her agility and flexibility giving her a great advantage, not to mention her energy levels are much higher than anyone on either team. When the enemies recognize her, their hesitation is their downfall. She grabs hold of their arms, her life force quickly flowing through them, attacking their brains. Her life force manipulates their actions, causing them to kill their own allies.

Her methods prove brutal, as the enemy, fully aware of their actions in killing their own team, cry out for mercy because of their inability to stop their betrayal. Screams of begging for death, the soldiers hope to maintain their pride and honor to the grave. They

squeeze their eyes shut, though their bodies robotically follow
Syrenne's orders and kill all who she considers her enemies. She
commits this act multiple times, enemy forces falling rapidly due to
her effective method. She eliminates them not only by controlling
them, but by having them kill one another thus sparing her true
team.

Among the fray, Syrenne spots Jevid, the leader of the Crusaders.
She makes her way over to him.

He summons his life force spear from the head of one of her
team members, like a magnetic pull back to his palm the spear darts
through the air. He senses her gaze and chuckles, understanding
her betrayal to the Crusaders. However, he understands her level of
power outweighs his own.

Jevid throws his spear, its speed too fast to be dodged by most.
With incredible focus, Syrenne easily dodges the spear and continues
her run at Jevid. His smug expression drops as fear takes its place.

He quickly summons his spear and throws it time and time
again, more so in an attempt to prevent her from getting near. Jevid
knows if he wastes time aiming, he may have no time left.

Syrenne continues to flip and bend around his spear, a smile
slowly spreading across her face. Once a few meters from one
another, Jevid grasps his spear tightly, eyes focusing on Syrenne,
awaiting her next move.

Though he must think of a strategy, Syrenne trusts in her
instincts. She won't allow herself to be the prey. This time, she claims
the role of predator.

Syrenne lunges at Jevid who jabs the spear at her chest. She grasps
the spear under the head in her left hand and grabs onto Jevid's
neck with her right. Syrenne pauses a moment, adrenaline pumping
as her muscles tense to prevent the spear from penetrating her. The
force behind it disappears. Jevid does not resist. He understands if

he tries to fight back now, it's asking for death, and he believes by surrendering, his life is secured.

Syrenne observes Jevid with a straight face. She feels herself trembling but does her best to conceal it. The battle continues all around them. No one dares interfere with the fight between the two leaders. Syrenne and Jevid lock eyes, allowing the background to fade away. She doesn't loosen her grip around his neck despite the perspiration sliding down his face, slight moisture meeting her hand there. Jevid expresses a half smile.

"I didn't know another team out there treated you better," Jevid comments. Syrenne maintains her straight face.

"They didn't."

"They were the highest bidder," Jevid states, nodding his head toward the crate. "How many times did you switch before discovering where your loyalty lies?"

"I'm tired of being a puppet."

"Surely. You make a magnificent puppeteer. Unfortunately, it's come to this."

He coughs as Syrenne tightens her grip. She glares at him, examining every pulsing vein in the whites of his eyes, her own glowing with pupils no more than slits as a huntress with her prey dangling by its tail. Jevid sees no regret, no fear, only her determination. However, Syrenne's next move remains blurry, even to her.

"What next?" Jevid asks, his confidence growing the longer he lives in her grasp.

Syrenne turns her head to look at the battlefield behind her. The sun continues its rise in the sky, providing flawless illumination to the bloody scene. Her own team and robots holding their own against the enemy, the number of forces on both sides dwindling. Syrenne returns her gaze to Jevid, who appears relieved of his earlier fear. She never loosened her grip, the situation has not changed, yet his aura lives completely within his control. He mocks her.

"So, Syrenne? What kind of leader watches her team fall?" Jevid asks.

"One who believes in their abilities to overcome."

Syrenne pauses for a moment. She analyzes Jevid's face, his expression spelling his surprise at her response. She continues.

"I've taken plenty of risks trying to impress both teams. I ate my disgust at the selfish leaders and their lack of care and compassion, willing to throw away the lives of others and then claim the prize for themselves. Building a team to use as their shield. All I saw were clueless puppets obeying their malicious puppeteers. Soon, I realized I was no better. But, as I said earlier," Syrenne tightens her grip and delivers her deep glare, "I'm sick and tired of being a damn puppet."

Quintessential fear strikes Jevid in an instant. Syrenne's life force flows from her hand gripping his neck and hacks his brain. She releases her grip and steps back. His life force spear slowly grows corrupted in his grip as a new, stronger power envelops it. He looks at it in distress, trying his hardest to resist the movements of his arms but unable to do so. His body trembles and his heart screams for an escape.

Jevid takes the spear with both his hands and stares at the sharp point. In a moment, he forces the spear through his chest. His screams break through Syrenne's control, though, she could have prevented it if she so pleased. Jevid falls to the ground, blood spilling from front and back, the spear having fully penetrated his body. As he hits the ground, the spear disappears in a mist, his life force fading away as he takes his last breaths.

Syrenne watches the life leave his body. She turns to face the fray, the battlefield covered in corpses and blood. Focusing her eyes, she sees only five enemies remain while eight team members and three of her robots continue to fight. Four left. Despite realizing the possibility of winning is slim, the enemies continue to fight with every fiber of their being. Unfortunately, the numbers and power outweigh them on the balance of the battlefield. The last four fall to the hands of the team members.

Syrenne focuses her mind on those she manipulated. Each of the three commit suicide in a way tailored to their combat style: one slits their throat with a conjured life force dagger, another suffocates themselves in a concentrated toxic smog of life force, and the last places the barrel of their gun under their chin and shoots. The three collapse, Syrenne relinquishing their lifeless corpses of her life force.

The remainder of the team stand, motionless, gazing upon the living nightmare of the conquered battle around them. Unlike the rest of her team, Syrenne appears emotionless. The eight remaining members express a combination of relief, exhaustion, and shock. They take deep breaths, attempting to calm their hearts and auras, though trembling with adrenaline and despair at the knowledge of their fallen comrades.

Syrenne examines the bodies on the ground. All on the soil find their resting place there. Syrenne analyzes the wounds the team sustains. None of their injuries appear life threatening. She releases a sigh of relief.

Her next priority is to assure the altar piece is safe. She marches to the crate. Bullet holes, singe marks, and blood splatter cover the wood. Though beaten up, it is whole. And unopened.

The team surrounds the crate and carefully opens it. A pit drops into Syrenne's stomach a moment before she sees it. As if she was aware all along, but wished against and denied it. As they slide the lid off the crate, a large chunk of rock is revealed in the cloth meant to protect what they carried. The team members gasp, one member takes the rock out and looks underneath the packaging material.

"What now?" Emiri, the man with the broadsword, asks Syrenne.

"Now that I think of it, where did Tanten go?" one of his original team members asks. The other members search around, not seeing his body amongst the mass of corpses.

"Tanten and Reece both. They're gone," Yasmine replies while another bandages her arm.

"No doubt they have the altar piece," another comments.

"What are our orders, Ms. Tyrney?" Emiri questions.

The remainder of the team looks to Syrenne, their loyalty to her command evident. Syrenne's face changes for the first time since the end of the fight. It expresses her shock at the resolve on their faces.

From the time she joined the team up until this point, she's never truly given her own orders. She's always relayed orders or commanded while thinking of other's desires. Whether Bysciw, Jevid, Tanten, or Atlas, she considered them her superiors, despite her feelings toward them. She submissively obeyed all their wishes, putting their best interest before her own. Syrenne attempted to impress them, but they never expressed amazement, for anyone. Except the girl... But, no matter their treatment of her, Syrenne wanted to prove her worth to the people others idolized. They were like kings among men, born leaders, intelligent and strong. All Syrenne desired was a paralleled confidence. She threw away her morals and her pride, an act she quickly regretted. However, in this moment, Syrenne can begin to correct the mistakes of her past and atone for her sins. None of the kings are around and the villagers standing in wait look up to her as their queen, asking her for their orders.

"This whole time we've pretended to be heroes though helping the villains. Now is our time to do what is right."

Syrenne examines her team and can't help but grin as they nod in agreement. They keep silent, awaiting her orders.

"Our mission is this: Stop the others from reaching the staff. We all know how difficult this task is. Though Tanten has the altar piece, he and Reece are not a great threat. Worst case scenario: We collide with Atlas's team."

"But we still don't know what's become of Bysciw's team," Yasmine states. She rotates her bandaged arm around her shoulder and closes her eyes as she stretches. "Unless we assume the airship earlier was them."

Only half of the team appears shocked with her statement. The others act as though they were well aware of the airship. Syrenne lowers her head and chuckles.

"Professionals indeed. You all hid your knowledge of the airship quite well. I'm impressed, though not surprised," Syrenne remarks.

She looks to the west and notices no signs of movement ahead. She closes her eyes to think and falls into their surroundings. She senses nothing; no threats, no suppressed hostility, nothing but the calm air and the sun bathing them in its rays. Running her hands through her hair, Syrenne raises her head to the sky, attempting to calm her loud thoughts.

"We head to the hot springs. There we eat and wash up. After, we must find a vantage point from which we can see the crater. We enter through the gateway only after ensuring its safety. Understood?"

The team members assume their soldier stances and bow, accepting Syrenne's orders.

AS THE BATTLE CRIES ring out but before the first explosion of life force, Tanten and Reece race to the forest, retreating to a position south of where the enemies exit. Reece grits his teeth, as every strike and death cry from the battle rings in his ears as if those fighting stood adjacent to his person. Tanten slows as Reece falls behind, licking his lips but refusing to look back to the team they've abandoned.

They enter the security of the forest, its shadows enough to hide them as focus is pulled to the fields. Tanten pauses for a moment and watches the scene unfold, several members from both sides falling to the ground, nothing more than corpses now. Blood saturates the thirsty ground, leaving more than a feast for any scavengers circling overhead or observing from their holes below.

Reece hunches over, fighting to catch his breath, bile rising up this throat. He gazes upon Tanten, who bites his lips and tenses the muscles of his bicep as his fists clench, no doubt upset at not participating in the fight. A light reflects in his eyes, the same as that of an arson who watches in admiration as a building burns to the ground.

"What next?" Reece pants, his question slipping through as he exhales.

"We run until we reach the hot springs. Try to keep up."

As if issuing a challenge to test Reece's worthiness, Tanten takes off within seconds of his command. He races through the forest, jumping over any obstacles on the floor, ducking from any low-level branches and vines, ignoring any pest to bump into him as he goes. His agility and proprioception are extremely acute. He focuses on arriving at the hot springs before any others using his natural talent and instincts to lead him. The weight of the bag on his back doesn't add to the difficulty of his run, as if it didn't exist.

Reece kicks from the ground and follows behind his boss. A stabbing pain issues from his sides, but he watches Tanten's back, not wanting to lose his leader. He bears his jaw and swings his arms across his body to cut through the air. His ankle twists below him as he hits uneven ground, issuing no more than a curse as his stumble transforms into a sprint once more.

After several minutes, Reece senses a shift in their environment. He peers around, gasping for air, unaware of what has changed. He focuses his ears, his eyes, his nose, his aura, anything he can, hoping for a clue. The sound of his and Tanten's feet hitting the ground, the birds and beasts of the forest singing and communicating, insects buzzing, their wings flapping nonstop, enter his ears. Reece peers about the forest. The trees, the animals, every displaced speck of dirt reacts to the shift. His eyes move to focus on the plains. The absence of many presences has shifted the entire field of Qoterra.

"Tanten!" Reece calls out, quickening his pace to catch up. "Tanten!"

"What?" Tanten yells back, still racing forward at fast speeds.

"They've stopped!" Reece screams. "The battle... it's over. Man... it smells like blood."

When Tanten and Reece reach the tree line, they halt their journey and strategize how to cross the remainder of the plains without being seen. As they deliberate, life force flows to their eyes to zoom in on the graveyard that was once a battlefield. Tanten relies on Reece, his disciple's abilities honed to gathering such intel.

"It's Syrenne and eight others. Unfortunately, I lack the energy to hear what they're saying. There's so much residual life force seeping into the ground, filling the air. It creates a field of its own that's hard to penetrate."

"No matter," Tanten responds. "I wonder if they've noticed."

Reece takes a drink from his canteen then offers it to Tanten, who shakes his head. Tanten peers at the bag he placed on the ground for their temporary respite.

"The crater is approximately twelve kilometers that direction. If we make it before evening, we should be first to reach the altar and, more importantly, safe from harm for the time being."

"Have you determined the best method of energy supply for portal creation?" Reece asks, having no ideas of his own to share. Tanten sighs.

"Well, the plan I had developed is no longer of use to us. That is, unless we have terrible luck."

Reece curiously looks at him, wondering what the original strategy could have been. Tanten scratches his head and takes a final look around.

"Are you ready?"

Reece nods and they run once more. Out in the open plains, under the heat of the sun, the two head in the direction of the crater. Tanten keeps his eyes forward, refusing to look back. However, Reece continues to check behind him, his paranoia causing his nerves and partly to blame for his exhaustion.

As Tanten runs, he listens to the strange melody of his heart, as if it skips a beat every so often. He squints, trying to determine if what he sees are mere hallucinations or genuinely occurring features on the plains. Images appear to be drawn into the soil on the ground, like hieroglyphics. The symbols among the ground include swords, stick figure men, and strange creatures that appear on a different scale to all else due to their enormity. Tanten cannot make out the scenes as he runs, but he quickly disposes of any thought that they may foreshadow their encounters to come. He blames the heat of the sun for his hallucinations, hoping nothing else will appear.

After passing a glyph that looks like a crescent moon, Tanten stops, his body frozen in place. His head forcibly turns to the left. He sees a tree quite a distance away, an obvious mirage for it did not exist prior. Though he wants to escape this reality unfolding before him, he is not in control. From behind the tree steps a young boy with a frightening resemblance to himself. Tanten holds his breath, intuitively knowing what will happen next. The arm of an instinctively familiar man reaches out and grabs the boy around the neck with a heavily ring-adorned finger. The boy struggles and is pulled behind the tree, vanishing forever.

Tanten jumps as a slight pressure falls on his shoulder. Tanten and Reece lock eyes for a second, but Tanten turns back to whatever captured his attention earlier. The mirage has disappeared. He releases a sigh of relief.

"Let's move on," Tanten commands.

"Mr. Flynn... I-"

"Never mind it."

Tanten adjusts the bag on his shoulders and starts to run once again. Reece sighs before following.

Tanten and Reece grin when they see a geyser shooting out of the ground ahead of them. They stop next to it, not getting close enough to be splashed by the hot water, but close enough to know they've made it to the springs. Immediately after stopping, Tanten removes the bag and carefully sets it on the ground. He grabs one of the canteens from Reece and quickly satisfies his dehydrated self.

"What now, Mr. Flynn?" Reece asks.

Tanten glimpses around and, seeing no signs of life, assesses their current situation.

"I'd say we have time to rest up a bit. However, our first priority should be devising a plan on how to transfer a large quantity of energy to the altar. Without that, the rest will be pointless."

Reece nods in agreement and sits on the rocky ground. The gentle breeze often carries a watery mist in his direction. Tanten walks a few meters away and looks at the sky. He scratches his head furiously. Reece hears him mumbling to himself, the only words he can make out being "stupid ants."

Chapter Seven

He jumps as the sounds and sensations meet him, a fog filling his mind as he awakens from an unconscious state. The smell of smoke and cooking meats finds his nose before his eyes adjust to the shadows. Cefni's stomach growls, his groan audible, his frustration at their situation growing the longer he considers all the signs that could have warned them.

A weight shifts on his leg. His eyes focus to see the form of a young boy laying there, not yet awoken from the quills' potent drug. Scanning about the dark hut, he notices Merwyn propped against the wall, staring at his view of the tribe, firelight dancing in his eyes.

Another of the larger forms on the ground flinches as the person comes through. With a muttered curse, Cefni understands it's none other than the necromancer. A sigh of disappointment sounds from the Professional at the thought that the group still remained wholly intact, having wished that at least one particular member would have been lost to the forest.

Nix lays on the ground, breathing in and out in deep concentration as his fingers fight the ropes to free his hands. After several failed attempts, the ex-assassin sighs and rolls into a sitting position. He finds a space near Merwyn, the slits his eyes form and furrowed brow enough to understand the irritation and wrath may be a mask for his fear.

The final form lays near where Tenebrant shifted. The necromancer peers at her, not moving from his position as if willing to use his body as a shield to protect her from any who may enter.

Cefni listens to the voices outside the hut, unable to comprehend their language. Judging by their tones and shouts, none seem too concerned of the group they've taken hostage.

As he adjusts his position, Cefni bites his bottom lip as the rope binding his wrists cuts into him. Tight and secure, the rope has been used to bind the entire party's wrists and ankles. Attempting to focus his life force, a burning sensation courses through Cefni. Like fire spreading across his skin, acid running through his veins, he clenches his jaw and stops his attempts. Merwyn turns to him at the muffled sound of his grunt.

"Attempting to break these bonds of our own accord will only cause more damage to ourselves," Merwyn states, his voice at normal volumes as if not caring to hide their status. "And the tribes would not be pleased if we did manage to break them. I could only imagine the time and talent it took to form them."

"They're inscribed with an ancient curse," Tenebrant chimes in, peering out the opening in the wall to examine the tribe's activities. "Actual strands of life force woven into the fabric to form a certain formation of words. The words mean nothing. It's the tribe's intention behind those words that holds the power. They must know we use life force. It's the only reason they would have chosen such a spell."

"Of course a necromancer would recognize it," Cefni mutters under his breath. He shakes his head and adjusts his arms, the rope searing through his skin at every movement. A sudden realization strikes. Cefni scans the space. None of their items appear to be around. The hut they sit in is empty, fabric banners with unrecognizable symbols hang about them.

"What do those symbols mean?" Cefni asks.

Tenebrant chuckles.

"Yes, Mr. Mortu?"

"I simply find it amusing is all. To think I would be the one who had the knowledge to save us."

"What are you on about?" Venom laces Cefni's words as he furrows his brows.

"Those glyphs. They dictate time of day and form of execution. Probably why this hut is empty. Time of day, sun rise. Execution style, devoured by spirit wolves. Druids aren't too different from necromancers you see. They capture the essence of the dead in a different way. As their own perish, they perform rituals to absorb the life force into certain objects or vessels. Then they have rituals of release to pull life force from these vessels or activate objects in order to perform certain actions."

"Well, that all sounds kind of grim," Cefni remarks.

He observes the stars in the sky from the sliver of outside within his range of vision. The crooked woman constellation falls over the tree line, the brightest star in the sky making up the hunch of the back. Sunrise was not too long away. He sighs.

"But you said you could save us," Nix mutters, his irritation in the necromancer's presence almost equal to Cefni. Not even those raised in the business of killing could accept the lawlessness and arrogance of Tenebrant.

Tenebrant licks his upper lip and attempts to suppress his malicious laugh.

"Yeah. But why should I?"

"Always a fucking tease, aren't you, necromancer?"

Cefni's movement in his frustration forces the burning to course from his wrists up to his neck, causing a cramp like none he had ever experienced. He mutters curses and turns to Merwyn, pleading with the aged Professional to try to get through to Tenebrant.

"Mr. Mortu-"

"That's not my name."

"Tenebrant. If these symbols show no more than that which will come to pass, how do you suppose we may escape such a fate?"

"Oh, I don't actually know what they say. I was just making stuff up."

"You jar of piss," Nix mutters, catching the eyes of all who are awake for their surprise of his language. The necromancer glares at the young boy.

"I wasn't lying though. What the druids are doing with their life force does not differ far from the necromancers of certain groups. It's all very ritualistic. The best chance for escape will be when they start to perform their rites. To perform the ritual, they'll be focusing their life force elsewhere. They don't know how to control it without words and movements of the collective. We overpower their rites, we can escape from this hellhole."

"We wouldn't even know what direction to head. They took our things, including our bloody map. We may as well run right into the hands of another tribe."

Cefni is overcome by the urge to fidget, to attempt to escape the bonds, but the fear of the burning prevents him from doing so. He leans his head back and considers their options. They could brute force through the bonds, hoping the pain caused would not exceed their abilities to rapidly heal after. Or they could wait, as Tenebrant suggests, hoping to overpower the tribes while their attention and life force is focused elsewhere.

"That bastard's gonna open the portal before we even get the chance to see what the altar piece looks like," Cefni mumbles, agitated at his weakness in the moment.

"I would like to trial diplomacy with these peoples. There are agreements between these tribes and the Magistrate Association. Perhaps we could recall a piece of the treaties signed to barter for our release."

"Oh, so now you also speak in their language?"

Merwyn purses his lips and stares at the necromancer.

"No, actually. My hope is that they would have a translator within this camp."

"Well, that certainly would be lucky," Tenebrant whispers, a venom lacing his tone. "But luck doesn't exactly seem in copious supply these days."

A hand grasps about the entrance of the hut, no more than fingers ringed with bone jewelry and tattoos from fingernails to knuckles reveal themselves. A young woman enters with head bowed, a lantern, suspended by a bamboo pole in a harness worn on her back, dangles above her head. The hand of the elder leaves the doorframe and loops through her arm as she guides him into the hut. An older woman dressed in silk robes, tassels dangling with furry mammals' feet and the cracked chrysalises of blood moths and shells of cicadas, and belt with many transparent flasks of powders, follows behind the elder. None of their eyes meet their hostages, their attention focused on the one of the two among them that had not yet awakened. The older woman, a shaman priestess to the community, kneels at Botalia's side.

Tenebrant clenches his jaw, noticing Cefni's eyes also going wide. The bonds burn as he struggles. The young woman at the elder's side turns in alert. Their eyes meet.

The shaman places a hand above Botalia's forehead. It hovers there for a moment before scanning over Botalia from head to torso. A red glow emanates from the bonds, Botalia's differing from that of her team. Rather than ropes tightly constricting her ankles and wrists, leather bands strap across her chest and thighs. The inscriptions of the bands smoke as the life force within them is awakened to keep her captive, fighting against the life force of another. However, Botalia is seemingly unconscious, even now.

"You must be careful with her," Merwyn speaks, keeping his voice low to offer vulnerability in place of intimidation.

The elder glares at Merwyn before glancing at the young woman. He murmurs a language unfamiliar to their ears. She nods in response.

"Who are you?"

Merwyn grins, the glitter in his eyes directed at Tenebrant who scoffs and shakes his head.

"We are from the Magistrate Association. We have been sent here by them on a mission."

The young woman's jaw drops, a twitch in her fingers enough to understand her fear. The elder tugs at her shawl and the young woman translates to him what Merwyn spoke.

"Your group are outside of agreed upon limits," she states, the elder continuing alongside her words and she doing her best to follow. "Lines were drawn despite the land being ours. We gave up much in an agreement as per threat it was deemed necessary for our own survival. You..." Her words drowned out despite the elder vehemently expressing anger at the team for their actions. The young woman bites her lip and blushes, uncomfortable to fully translate that which the elder speaks in his raspy voice.

As the elder calms down, the shaman stands. She marches to Tenebrant's side and gazes upon his form. Squinting at the thin outlines of the curses engraved into his arms, those which have been used more often deeper and darker than the rest, the shaman mutters to the other two in their language. Cefni shakes his head, wondering what issue Tenebrant's presence will cause them in this instance.

"You are from the Magistrate Association?" the young woman asks, her question directed at the necromancer.

Tenebrant chuckles and licks his lips.

"Yes, he is," Merwyn answers, met with a glare by the shaman.

"This is true?" the young woman presses, the elder pinching her arm requesting the answer from the necromancer.

"By association, you could say that," Tenebrant frowns, trusting that Merwyn understands the best route to take with their answers. The young woman tilts her head, as if not fully comprehending what was said.

The elder spits at the ground and roars out a supposed insult. Tenebrant furrows his brow and fights the bonds, grinding his teeth as the ropes burn at raw skin. The shaman jumps back.

"What did he say?" Tenebrant forcefully presses the young woman, whose eyes grow wide.

"He said," she gulps, "he said you are a traitor to tribal peoples. Those marks are for warriors who protect tribes with the mana of their fallen kin. You use it to protect those who do harm to your own."

"Impressive," Tenebrant smirks. "That answer is not so far from the truth. However, my tribe, or whatever you want to call it, doesn't need the energy from the dead. We use it, sure, not for very noble deeds but it's there so why waste it. No, we've learned to cultivate energy on our own."

His tattoos flare as he exerts an extreme release of life force from his person. His wrists and ankles burn at the contact of life force meeting life force, smoke surrounds him. Wincing and moaning can be heard until all stops. As the smoke clears, sweat drips from Tenebrant's brow and his chest heaves in and out. The ropes have not been damaged in the slightest. The shaman snickers.

Before the smell can dissipate, Koepp awakens. All turn to the poor boy who twists and turns and cries at the burning of the ropes. The young woman steps to assist, but the elder holds her arm back. She hesitates to obey, biting her bottom lip as the light glimmers from the water pooling in her eyes.

"Koepp, calm. They will burn the more you squirm," Cefni instructs, his voice trying to sound as paternal as possible.

Koepp's movements stop instantaneously, his whimpers muffled as he presses his face to the uneven ground they sit on. His tears hit the ground, muddying the clay.

Smoke fills the space once more. The shaman mutters, staring at Botalia with fear spelled across her face. Her bonds burn as her life force overpowers that which restrains her. Despite stronger than their own bonds, the straps turn to ash, Botalia unmoving as it occurs. The aura finds escape from the curse that bound it within and extends from her person.

The shaman bends down to place her hand where it hovered previous. She flinches as the heat finds her palm. Words leave in a whisper, fear now present in the eyes of both the elder and the young woman.

A scream rings out from the outdoors. People begin to run past the opening, the excitement not from celebration but unwanted surprise. The shaman opens her palms to the heavens and issues a prayer. The screech of an animal can be heard not too distant from the edge of the camp, not distressed but full of wrath.

The elder tugs at the young woman's arm, pointing at the banners as if to use them to block the door from the invaders.

"We can assist to protect if you would just untie us," Merwyn suggests in their moment of panic, knowing full well that if they fail to protect their tribe, the captives themselves would also fail to see another day.

The elder lashes out at the idea.

"You wish to help but have brought an *iseuo*, a curse, to our lands. Your friend is a vessel, and she has summoned the divine creatures to punish us."

"What creature?"

"The korokos."

Cefni and Merwyn peer at one another, the name familiar and yet too distant to remember why. The screeches echo throughout the camp, arriving at them from all sides. A small group of men sprint past the opening, a creature's long slim legs leading to a hairy muscular torso gives chase in the firelight. The young woman gasps.

The team all find it within themselves to slightly struggle once more, the burning not enough to surpass their survival instincts. When they understand their task is futile, they each formulate the scene in which they will meet their end.

"Botalia," Koepp cries, still lying on the floor, trembling. "Botalia, please hear me. Please wake up."

As the echo of his plea leaves the air, drowned out by the screams and prayers of the druids' attempts to protect their camp and one another, Botalia stirs. The shaman's prayer stops, the acidic heat from the aura transforming to a less hazardous state yet gaining power. Botalia's eyes open slowly, adjusting to the light that had not met them for days.

Their hope may have arrived too late. Long, thin fingers wrap about the doorframe. As tall as it stands, the creature bends down to peek in, revealing a snout the length of a horses with ears like a rabbit protruding from the skull, eyes no larger than marbles. And, despite being unable to focus their eyes to view it, the team understands this creature to be no regular mammal. It possesses an ability supernatural, or as the druids believe, divine. This creature can manipulate its life force.

The druids jump back, using their captives as their shields. Cefni fights to move in front of Koepp, wondering how it ever came to be that he would be willing to sacrifice his life for a Flynn. Merwyn flinches as a different sensation crosses him, small fingers working to unweave the ropes, hiding in the shadows just enough that his movements go unnoticed. However, Botalia's movement is more pronounced than the others, being free to move her limbs, her life force charging at extreme rates.

Unaware of the current threat they face, Botalia stands. The creature lowers itself, appearing to take a defensive stance. It wipes its long fingers in front of its face, communication or no more than an itch none can say, and takes a step forward.

"Botalia, watch your back!" Tenebrant shouts, pulling the attention of both Botalia and the koroko.

Botalia eyes Tenebrant with curiosity, saying nothing and reacting as if his words are empty. Her arms swipe to the sides and her fingers climb the air like spiders through a web. Her head swivels to the koroko, no surprise in her expression, as if understanding it to be there all along.

As the bonds fall from Merwyn, his aura slowly takes form as the ability to use his life force comes back to him. The Professional focuses his eyes, the aura surrounding Botalia different than he remembered, and gulps.

"Tenebrant, that's not Botalia."

The aura about her swirls in unison with that of the koroko. The creature screeches and lifts a leg to take another step. Botalia lifts her hands and forms a gesture with her fingers across the air, forcing the koroko to freeze. It screeches at her. Botalia opens her mouth but finds she does not possess the ability to speak as needed. Her jaw clenches and the movements of her arms become more extreme, moving quickly, life force sparking at her fingertips.

More padded footsteps approach the hut, blocking out any firelight that may have been able to enter. The hairy bodies of the tall beings shimmer in the lantern light coming from the young woman. The screams have all but died out, no more rampaging battle cries from neither druid nor koroko. Botalia continues in her movements, the concentration of life force growing in her palms.

A whirlwind sweeps through the hut, tearing the banners from the walls and lifting the wooden panels from the ground. The first koroko to have peeked in steps back but finds itself unable to for the wall of bodies behind it. The sigils on the banners burn bright and slowly change shape as they fly in circles about the enclosed area. A burst of light flies from Botalia's chest and the walls lose form, falling outward. The thatch roof turns to ash, quickly blown away by the artificial wind before even the smallest speck could fall upon any of those who were within. The air stills and the banners glide to the ground.

The sun rises in the distance, the last visible stars settling over the forest canopy. A fresh breeze takes the place of the humidity they had only become to grow more acclimated to, and silence meets them.

All eyes land on Botalia. She falls to the ground, supporting herself on a knee with her fingers digging at the hardened clay beneath her. A sound unique to their ears originates from the korokos, clicking their tongues to communicate with one another. One of the tallest members of the korokos steps forward and gestures at Botalia. She fails to respond.

With that, the korokos bend to be on all four limbs and jog back to the forest. As the last disappears into the shadows, the druids slowly reveal themselves from their hiding places and start to clean up the mess made by the surprise attack.

Nix races to Koepp's side and quickly unties his friend, Merwyn moving to Cefni to do the same. The druids do not stop them. Koepp rushes to Botalia's side and embraces her.

Nix and Merwyn meet eyes, glancing at Tenebrant and debating internally which of the two will free him. Nix crosses his arms and closes his eyes. Merwyn smiles and attends to the necromancer's bonds. As he removes them, Merwyn notices the damage done to the necromancer through his attempts to escape. Raw to the very bone, Tenebrant winces as the ropes fall, as if they were the only thing to prevent his skin from melting to the ground. Tenebrant pulls up a banner from his side and rips strips of the fabric to wrap about his injuries, hoping it will be enough.

The young woman removes her harness, the lantern light no longer needed as they sit within reach of the sunrise. She collects a banner from near her feet and gives it to the elder. His fingers rub the fabric, sensing the change in the threads from which it was made. The fabric falls to the earth.

"You are free to go," the young woman translates. Relief hits the team with these words.

"What about our things?" Cefni asks, concerned more for his map than their wellbeing.

"I will gather them for you. We ask that you stick to your route and do not stray. We do not wish another summon of the koroko on our land."

Botalia lifts a hand to her chest as sympathetic eyes meet the young woman. Resolve crosses the druid woman's face as she leads the elder away.

Intent ears listen as birds call out and distant screeches reach them. No hum of airships finds them. Cefni bites his lip, tapping his foot as he watches in the direction the young woman went.

The shaman approaches Botalia, hesitant with a glimmer in her eyes. Koepp steps away, his eyes moving between the two. The shaman stops in front of Botalia. She places a hand on her forehead.

"*Iseuo koroko*," the shaman mutters, a tear streaming down her cheek. Life force leaves from her palm in a sharp pulse. Botalia struggles to inhale and collapses to the ground. Tenebrant flinches, itching to attack the older woman, Merwyn holding out an arm to block such an act.

"Tenebrant, do not be rash. It is a misunderstanding."

The necromancer growls and crosses his arms, averting his eyes to the forest. Koepp and Nix meet Botalia on the ground, Koepp wrapping his arms about her bicep in an attempt to help her up. Botalia catches her breath and meets eyes with the shaman. Botalia pats her chest, mimicking the beating of her heart in quick succession.

The shaman straightens up and steps back, understanding the movements despite their inability to communicate verbally. She snaps off a furry foot from one of her tassels, sprinkles a powder from one of her flasks over it, issues a prayer, and offers it to Botalia. Closing her fingers about the trinket, Botalia grins and stands. The shaman walks away.

"What was that about?" Tenebrant asks, breathing heavy as anger fills him the longer they remain in the camp, muscles twitching to fight.

"It was just a misunderstanding," Botalia mumbles. Her legs tremble under her. Koepp and Nix each offer a shoulder for her to rest an arm on. She smiles.

The young woman returns to the group with their things. Cefni meets her, quickly pocketing his compass and checking that it is indeed his revolver.

"May you be safe in your mission," the young woman states.

Merwyn smiles and nods.

"Thank you for your hospitality."

"Enough of this. We've lost enough time already. Now which way..."

The young druid woman points. Cefni squints at the map and then to her.

"Um, yes actually. That way."

The woman smiles and walks away.

Sipping at their water and finding their food stores untouched, the group replenish themselves and step to the forest, new fears sweeping through them on their quest.

Chapter Eight

Anticipation and anxiety grow among the team. The fear of the unknown and inevitable conflict only make the journey last all the longer. Fortunately, the ocean breeze creates a tranquil atmosphere in the sun's rays as it beams down with its full fury. Their ship swims onto Qoterra's beach and the team climbs down a series of ropes, carrying the supplies onto the shore.

Atlas wanders to the edge of the forest and listens intently. He analyzes every sound, every movement, whether creature below or birds above. Whether specks of sand blown by a breeze across the beach or the winds that disturb the canopies above. The continent exists through a rooted network, the flora and fauna, even up to the vapors in the air connected to a complex unit as if all part of one living, breathing machine. In that connection that transcends the human senses, Atlas feels as though the balance tilts, the environment slightly out of equilibrium. He sighs, realizing his mistake, hoping it will be his last. For, despite their early departure, their arrival seems all but too late.

Keniph approaches Atlas, the others in the team forming a line behind him.

"Are we ready to move out, Red?" Keniph asks.

Atlas grabs his bag from Keniph's hands and swings it about his back. He nods and leads the way, no map or compass needed. They march at a quickened pace, Atlas attempting to compensate for the time wasted on sailing. He believed avoiding detection from the other teams should be first priority, however, every other group seemed to have prioritized reaching the altar.

"Whose airship do you suppose that was we heard?" Keniph questions.

"Instinct says Bysciw," Atlas replies. He tries to determine the times they need to reach each of their checkpoints, his fingers meeting as each number crosses his mind. Unfortunately, frustration interrupts his mental math. "I cannot explain through scientific means, but I know Tanten is already here, as well. And I smell blood."

Keniph peers behind, ensuring no others hear or react to Atlas's whispers.

"They say a true Professional's instincts are rarely wrong," Keniph assures his partner. "I trust in your instincts. And our fears can't be helped when so many are obsessed with this mission. We have to go for it. Hesitation or surrender would be abandoning all we've given thus far."

"I suppose so," Atlas concedes.

They continue their rapid march in silence, closely examining their environment, hoping not to give a chance for ambush. As Atlas focuses in front of him, he notices a stretch of plains meeting the tree line of the forest. Tall grasses and wildflowers block the view due to the slight incline of the forest floor. Ascending the mound, Atlas bites his lip as he notes what the wild grasses attempt to hide from view. An airship.

Sitting in the middle of the grassland, with no signs of the team who offboarded from the Dominian military branded machine, Atlas listens to the wind to learn when it was last disturbed. His focused hearing finds the songs and squawks of the wildlife a distraction, but he manages past the noises he had not accustomed to prior. What he fails to prevent interrupting him are the murmurs of his team as the airship comes into their view. Atlas sighs.

With no desire to stray from their path, and no presence of danger near, the team marches directly to the airship. As they near, Atlas notices the footprints imbedded in the muddy ground. He holds out his arm, and the team freezes. Atlas steps carefully examining every footprint their enemies failed to conceal. With a smirk, he shakes his head and beckons the team forward.

"Disappointing the precautions we've put into place when they have not the same level of care. As if intruding a house by simply knocking on the front door and demanding entrance. Fools."

Atlas marches across the plains and to the forest opposite of that which they just left, knowing full well they travel the path of those who arrived by the airship. The life force concentrated in his eyes outlines every footprint. Though attempting to contain his excitement, Atlas expresses a slight grin. He had hoped for this opportunity and now he has locked onto the one he most wishes to find. The one he most wishes to drag to defeat, hear him begging, pleading for forgiveness, surrendering and admitting his arrogance as that which led to his demise. Tailing the team, Tanten's footprints were the last to pass and therefore the most visible to any who stumbled upon the path. Atlas notices a second pair of prints to follow beside.

After marching for some time, Atlas cringes at an unfortunate pile of fur and blood laying in the path. The corpse of this creature has already provided a meal to another. Atlas knows this creature met its end by a person's hand. By the hand of a life force wielder. The quartered limbs of the creature have been removed flawlessly and some residual life force of the murderer is left on them. In Atlas's eyes, the color of the life force glows in the same wavelength as the footprints he follows. Unlike the other team members who look at the carcass in disgust, Atlas views it as a hopeful sign.

They reach the glade but don't stop for rest nor hydration. Without so much as a pause to catch their breath, the team marches into the next section of forest. When they arrive at the lake, many of the team scrunch their faces, their life force swimming to those places where they are most comfortable utilizing it, their auras trembling. A strange smell fills the air.

Atlas leads the team around the lake, still following the footsteps of Tanten and his team. Approximately three hours have passed since they arrived on shore, and this is the first time Atlas feels they may need to stop. Whatever scene lies ahead will be unpleasant, or so the wind whispers to him.

Atlas gulps. The remains of the bloody battle enter his vision, the scent carried by the breeze not long after. Most of the team shutter and gag at the gore left by the outcome of this war. Signs of residual life force and weaponry litter the ground around the bodies, slowly fading as the environment consumes that which is rightfully nature's gift to man.

Though his heart quakes as it fills with rage and misery, Atlas shares no expression of emotion, his eyes blank with apathy. He must appear calm, uncaring, stolid for the team's sake. However, his guise slips as he recognizes many of the faces lying around, men who willingly gave their lives to accompany the wicked Tanten Flynn on his selfish quest for an almighty power. But where did Tanten stand in this fight? His body is not among the fallen, though many lay unrecognizable in the long grasses of the field. A breeze brushes his face, carrying the rancid smells but also secrets left behind from the truth the dead learned too late.

His focused eyes follow the footsteps of Tanten, and who he assumes to be Reece, that travel back to the forest. The time signatures of the prints versus those scattering the ground from the battle reveal the grim truth.

"Coward," Atlas whispers, noticing Tanten left before the battle ever began.

His eyes find another set of footprints, presumably the survivors of the battle. A group of nine people. They were cleverer about their approach after the battle, no doubt heightened senses forcing them to grow paranoid about every movement or sound to meet them. Not to mention, they no doubt understood the betrayal they faced by the time the last enemy fell. This group covered their tracks once they took off, Atlas unable to figure where they may be at this point. Squinting, he scouts the area. Though safety is not a feeling he will allow fool him on Qoterra, he can't help but feel the small group of survivors is no current threat.

An opened wooden crate sits amidst the graveyard. Atlas steps carefully toward it, wondering if it may be some sort of trap for those who may be curious of the battle or try to loot those who are no longer in need of their earthly possessions. But, with a quick scan, Atlas notices no tripwires nor mines in the ground nearby. Stretching his neck to get a peek, Atlas sighs, whether in relief or disappointment he can't quite be sure. The inside of the box contains packing materials and a slab of rock lays next to it.

"What's that?" Keniph questions as he approaches Atlas. Keniph peeks inside, only to dissatisfy his curiosity. "Empty, huh? I bet I know what they were carryin' in it. Only question is: Who has it now?"

"I'll have to disagree with you, Keniph. I don't think this crate had anything of value inside. It was more of a red herring than anything else," Atlas turns to the forest and squints, hoping to see movement in the distance. As expected, he sees nothing and continues. "Though the answer to your question would intrigue me. However, I feel as though we all know the correct answer." As Atlas examines the battlefield, he notices Jevid's body and chuckles. Atlas shakes his head. "I should be grateful for his efforts, eliminating the majority of our greatest adversary's team. However, their goals were similar, so his demise brings me relief." Atlas smiles as his head tilts, continuing to examine the dead body from where he stands. Keniph gazes at Atlas, unaware of how to respond.

"Shall we move forward? It seems most of the team is on the verge of passing out due to the overwhelming stench of blood. Well, except for that new guy you brought along." Keniph looks at the black-haired, young man, who appears rather intrigued by the scene, almost as if trying to recreate every killing motion in his head. Atlas doesn't respond nor acts as if he even heard the question. "Red." No response. Keniph raises his tone. "Atlas."

Atlas jumps, startled. He had fallen into his thoughts, all his curiosities of the opposing teams brought forward with a newfound excitement. He opens his mouth as if to speak but promptly closes it, not knowing what to say at first.

"Forward it is," Atlas replies. Blinking his eyes several times, he looks to the west. "No need to follow their trail anymore. We'll simply follow the sun's lead."

As they begin their journey toward the hot springs, Keniph believes he hears Atlas mumbling to himself. Keniph closes his eyes and shakes his head.

"This mission is driving him to insanity," Keniph thinks. "Though he may have been crazy all along. He's incredibly strong physically and mentally, but maybe there's a break psychologically... Look at me, thinking these things. I must be exhausted."

Much like Keniph, Atlas finds his own mind flooded. "Tanten, Bysciw, Cefni, and presumably Syrenne. They and their teams are all that stand in my way... Stand... Tanten and Reece are more like sitting ducks. And their total strength may be equivalent to Syrenne's team at the moment... Part of me wishes to reach the staff without conflict, but the other part would prefer a good fight. It would keep things interesting, no doubt. Like good versus evil, the cliché of every tale. When I hold the power of the staff, the legend will rightly depict myself as the hero, and Tanten will be the villainous scum whom I execute... Such tales and legends intrigue those too simple-minded to understand the facts, the truth."

"Atlas."

The voice calling out causes Atlas to flinch. A smile forms on his face, Atlas catches the eye of the young man. Inviting him to join their expedition may have been his greatest idea thus far.

"What is it, Naht?"

"I've finished analyzing some of the mental snapshots I took and found something I thought may interest you," Naht answers. "The footsteps we were following, they slightly changed shape and depth. I noticed along the lake path the sudden change. This leads me to believe Tanten Flynn took something from the one walking alongside him. Whatever was transferred was extremely light physically speaking, but the residual life force in the footprints says different."

"The altar piece."

"Yes, that is my assumption." Naht pauses. "Also of note, Tanten Flynn and his comrade headed to the forest approximately three and a half hours ago. The other nine left the scene of the battle forty minutes after. All who lay on the field were dead before that time. However, it appears Tanten Flynn and company fled before the first fell."

"As I imagined, my suspicions confirmed by an elite," Atlas mutters, more so to himself than to Naht.

"If you want me to analyze those who died in battle I will. However, I feel as though that would be time wasted, for examining the amount of corpses will take hours, not to mention a tremendous amount of life force. I-"

"I trust in your judgement." Atlas interrupts. "You are a professional after all, even if the Magistrate Association would require some extraneous exam in order for the title to be legitimate." Naht nods his head in gratitude of the compliment.

"I would rather determine the persons who survived the battle. Based on the database you provided, I..."

Naht freezes his speech but continues to march forward. His face grows serious and his eyes focus ahead. Though looking forward, he relies on his peripheral vision to find what he searches for. Atlas senses the slight change in his aura. What was once calm now is highly alert. Naht's concealment impresses Atlas, for Atlas knows he can only sense the change due to marching adjacent to Naht.

Atlas focuses his own mind and chuckles.

"You feel them, correct?" Naht questions. Atlas nods.

"But I cannot determine the direction. It's as if they surround us but are invisible to our eyes."

Atlas glances behind him and sees no one else has noticed, or they hide it well if they have. The sensation he recognizes as being seen by others may pass off as paranoia. Atlas's eyes sweep the area, but his search fails.

They march forward, attempting to hide their awareness from those who watch as well as the team.

"Naht?"

"Yes?"

"Tell me, honestly. I have no fear of three of the existing teams, but the fourth team seems to be a threat. I've worked with Merwyn and Cefni for years, and their strength places them as a fraction of the top ten life force users in the world. Little Flynn is of no fear, and I trust you can handle your brother. However, Mortu's and Ulton's power remain unknown and unspecific in my mind.

"So, tell me. First, I wish to know of Tenebrant Mortu's abilities," Atlas inquires.

While talking, he does not make eye contact with Naht, who directs a slight glare in his direction. Naht exhales, attempting to script the answer in his head before responding.

"Tenebrant Mortu is a strong fighter, and he rarely relies on his life force as a form of combat. Therefore, he is unpracticed in fighting when it involves life force. Also, he is unaccustomed to fighting those at a level similar to his own," Naht replies. "As all Mortu's, he's a necromancer. And there is naught more dangerous than an unpracticed necromancer." Naht pauses and lowers his head to the ground. "That being said, he despises failure."

"Don't we all," Atlas laughs and tilts his head to the side. His eyes shift to glare at Naht who stares at the ground.

The further they march from the lake, the dryer the soil becomes under their feet, hiding their steps all the easier. The grass becomes sparse, and a slight steam rises from the earth. The sun descends routinely to the western horizon. Though not complaining, the team slow their march which has had little respites on their trek. Some of their legs tremble, whether from dehydration or exhaustion. Atlas senses their fatigue and, having arrived at their checkpoint, allows them to rest. He pulls Naht aside, his questions not fully answered. Keniph watches from afar, a frown worn on his face.

"What of Botalia Ulton? From what you've told me, you had the opportunity to fight her one on one. What was it like? What are her strengths? Weaknesses? Anything of note you'd be willing to tell me?" Atlas questions. A sinister glow illuminates his eyes, his inquiries seeming like an obsession. Naht locks eyes with Atlas, remaining expressionless.

"You know of her immense life force, quantifying it is near impossible. It would require more experience than my own."

"You humble yourself." Atlas reveals a grin, but Naht's expression remains unchanging.

"Whether outside of or in combat, she harbored no ill will towards my siblings nor I despite our attempt to assassinate her. We were an empty threat. When we later fought, I became further impressed by her abilities. Like an animal, she listened to her instincts and adapted to my fighting style. I... well..." Naht pauses and lowers his head, unable to find the words, certain that the words crossing his mind should stay there. Atlas's expression grows serious.

"Well, what?" he presses.

"I... I couldn't..." Naht blinks several times at the ground, hyper focusing on a pebble smoothed by waters long drained. He has thought many times about their fight, the sensation he felt, the way his supposedly insurmountable strategy failed him. He never came to a proper conclusion. No theory seemed complete, therefore he did not accept them. He thinks, "The only possible theory is- but no, that can't be. She stated she'd been alone for ten years. She was alone on that island. She was fully capable of using her own life force. How-"

"Naht." Naht faces Atlas. "You specialize in manipulation, correct?"

"Yes."

"So, in your fight you planned to manipulate her?"

"Yes." Naht hesitates to speak, believing Atlas to be reading his thoughts anyway. Atlas smirks.

"It didn't work, did it?" Atlas tilts his head. His eyes don't read curiosity or intrigue as they had prior. They express amusement. A strange urge arises in Naht as he feels his heart accelerate. The flood of thoughts in his mind disappears, and Naht says nothing. Atlas glances toward the team, who appear to enjoy the rest. Atlas licks his lips and continues. "You've provided a strength, but what of her weaknesses?"

"Her weakness?" Naht expresses half of a grin. "She's human."

"Botalia Ulton is not human."

"She is. More so than ourselves. A functioning human, with emotion. Where there is emotion, there is a weakness. As an assassin and manipulator, I've learned how to determine emotions which affect my targets. Most all my targets in the past succumbed due to fear, pride, or greed. However, my targets often include corrupt, underground parasites. Botalia... Her emotional weakness became evident the moment I stole a glimpse of her. The boy."

"Little Flynn?" Atlas places his head in his hands and laughs. Many of the team members turn to the pair, confused by Atlas's reaction in comparison to Naht's blank expression. "A multipurpose hostage. An ideal bargaining chip. Wicked. Immoral... Perhaps necessary." Atlas strokes his chin and looks to the sky, surrounded with new ideas. He turns to Naht. "How would your brother react? They are friends, after all."

"Nix has no friends. Our father believes he's being manipulated."

"Do you believe that?"

"I have not the authority to disagree with my father."

"I see. However, I sense a flaw in this plan, this plan of using her weakness against her," Atlas states. "Let me say again: She is not human. Her DNA is a hybrid of human and a creature found on this very continent. Having rational and animal instincts makes her personality quite contradictory. But her emotions may play as a greater strength than weakness. Just as a mother with its young, all animals become protective and self-sacrificial when combating those who harbor ill will. Do you know why Botalia Ulton was exiled to the island those ten years ago?"

"No, I cannot say I do."

"Because she's a monster. Through an act of revenge, she slaughtered a gang of underground, high bounty, organ traders and left without a scratch on her person. She's exiled to an island for ten years and her aura and life force magnified exponentially. Her weaknesses are a contradiction to her strengths. Little Flynn as a hostage will prove a great trick but getting him without Botalia's knowledge will prove more difficult," Atlas responds with a stern tone. He deeply inhales the fresh air of the springs. Slowly, he calms his racing heart. Closing his eyes, Atlas feels himself root into the soil, attempting to communicate with the surroundings, as if hoping they'll deliver him news of the enemies or gift an omen of good fortune. A soft breeze brushes his red hair from his face and he smiles. "The wind tells me fortune is in our favor. We'll not worry presently. I trust in this." Atlas shares his smile with Naht, brimming with a newfound confidence.

"A strange thing to say from feeling the breeze. Atlas the austromancer. A fickle science, in my mind," Naht whispers to himself. He returns to the group who prepare to move onward.

"To Praecantatis Tepui!" Atlas shouts. The resounding cheers of the team erasing all doubts of their determination.

Chapter Nine

C efni peers out the window of the observation cabin, hoping not to see any possible threats in the vicinity. His toes tap on the wooden floorboards, the rhythm matching that of his racing heart. Despite being out of the woods and far from the grasp of the tribes, danger never looms too far.

The cabin sits in the middle of the forest, a small garden in the corner of the plot of land cleared for the Association along with a well for water and geothermal vents for energy supply. Within, many tools and pieces of equipment, not incredibly high-tech, line the walls and fill the drawers of desks and hutches. The magistrates who carry out experiments and studies in this location always seem to bring plenty and never take much of it back, working on the Magistrate Association's coin never causing them to worry about returning to ask for an upgrade. Much of the heavier equipment and hardware are concentrated on the upper platform of the split-level cabin, the lower portion acting as a living space with an open floor plan to the kitchen and dining area. Drawings, pictures, diagrams, and commonly used equations hang in frames, most often left by the informants of those to have reached such historical conclusions and findings. The sheer quantity of clutter forces Cefni to shake his head, wondering how those deemed intelligent could also live several weeks in such disrepair.

Koepp and Nix sit on a muskin rug in the living area, adjacent to the sofa Botalia lies on, recuperating her energy little by little. They don't speak often, whispering when they do decide to relay a message, still shook from their run-in with the druids and the magical creatures to attack the encampment.

Nix bites his lip in frustration, wondering how such events could overwhelm his emotions. His fingers play with the hem of his pants, every now and again his fingernails digging into the sides of his fingers. Perhaps he was a trained assassin, professional in every sense of the word. But that never felt real. In fact, he had never felt anything. His eyes land on Koepp. His hairs raise on end as the sight of his friend, bound and thrown to the floor, defenseless, crying and afraid sears into his memories. It was so real. And he, one who trained for every possible scenario, preparing for every possible outcome, was useless. In such a situation, his father would have suggested to any other assassin to taste the poison, to find a way to sacrifice themselves to preserve the name of the Kufuta clan. And yet, coming out on the other side of it all, Nix starts to realize that fear is something else entirely when wielded by another, even more reason to never return to the family business again.

Tenebrant sits on the ledge between the lower and upper level, staring at the wall, though his vision focuses on nothing. His facial expression is blank, quite the opposite of his mind which swirls as memories, distant yet not enough for his sake, pelt him and torture him. His fingers tap the wooden steps where he sits, cursing that the druids were not stronger.

The back door of the cabin opens. Merwyn enters. Calm and collected as always, his hands fold across his abdomen. The Professional sits at the dining table endless thoughts running through his mind just as the rest of the team.

"Are you ready?" Cefni asks.

"Yes, I believe so," Merwyn responds. A slight tremble accompanies his voice, as if fear unable to find his expression could not be masked by his tone.

Koepp and Nix hesitate to approach the table, Botalia placing a hand on each of their shoulders as she guides them with a solemn grin. They remain silent as they pull their chairs out and sit down. Tenebrant approaches and wears a serious expression as he stands behind Botalia, arms crossed, his eyes unmoving from Merwyn. Cefni also chooses to remain standing, perhaps the nerves getting to him as he finds himself pacing already. He finds a hutch nearby to lean on, eyes finding the necromancer more often than his counterpart.

"As you all may have guessed," Merwyn begins, willing his voice to remain even, "I sent out five familiars to scout the area to the north where I assumed the other teams would be. As expected, they came across a group of life force users. No druids, but others on an expedition, presumably for the altar piece."

All eyes widen and curiosity piques. Though all understand they were not alone in this mission, others hoping to accomplish that which their own team sought to prevent, the thought of being so near forces bumps to raise on their skin.

Cefni snaps. "Is that all you know?"

"Cefni," Merwyn starts. "We need to remain calm and-"

"We don't have time to waste calmly discussing the enemies!" Cefni raises his voice, using a stern tone. "The enemies aren't far from here, we're down a key player, and they will likely reach the altar before nightfall."

Botalia bites her lip and observes the pine tabletop in front of her, understanding her inability to be their downfall as they rely on her capabilities for so much of the latter part of the mission. Guilt finds her and Cefni for different reasons. Cefni rubs his face with his hands, wrinkles stretching and creasing as he stares at the table.

"Cefni, please trust in me," Merwyn states in a soft, delicate tone. His voice sounds melodic, the tune enough to slow Cefni's previously racing heart. Cefni takes a deep breath then locks eyes with Merwyn. They look at one another for a moment, as if communicating telepathically. They reach an understanding and Merwyn continues.

"The first scene one of my familiars came across displayed the results of a bloody battle. My intuition tells me one entire team was wiped out as well as a majority of the victor's team," Merwyn says, pausing to allow them time to process the information.

"The remainder of the victorious team were out of sight before my familiar arrived, however, I could feel strong presences in the surrounding plains. The familiar traveling northwest happened upon a traveling party, though the mass was not injured in any form, leading me to believe they did not partake in the battle. It kept its distance, but two of the party instantaneously raised their guard as it focused on them."

Everyone continues to listen intently to Merwyn's familiars' excursions. Though it sounds a storyteller creating tall tales at a camping site, the team are continuously reminded of the reality around them being that which they listen to. Merwyn peers about, taking in the still environment, the distant beeping of the equipment kept at the cabin and monitors no more than the metronome of their final march.

"Knowing you, I suppose you caught a glimpse," Cefni remarks. He understands Merwyn is willing to take necessary risks even though he attempts to take the least dangerous path possible in all he does.

Familiars, if destroyed, which can only be done by life force users, lose all value and purpose. Though connected to a person through their life force, a familiar that leaves no track to the user can only reveal information once reconnected. The game is one of patience. Much like Merwyn's personality, his familiars are similar in that they take the path of least risk first in most all scenarios. Not only cautious but determined to complete their assigned task. Cefni knows Merwyn's familiars returned with news of more worth than what he reveals to them.

"Yes, though I doubt the answer will surprise you," Merwyn replies.

Tenebrant's heart accelerates as an answer of the encounter may finally fill his mind with the joy he has awaited. The face he so longs to see, to destroy, may finally be within reach. A familiar excitement returns to him.

"Atlas and his team are on Qoterra. And they do not lie far from here."

Tenebrant's excitement quickly dissolves. He glances at Nix then returns his eyes to Merwyn, hoping the Professional does not reveal too much information.

Tenebrant was unsure before about the senses one must possess to sense one of Merwyn's familiars, seeing as he only knew they existed from watching Merwyn sculpt them. If he hadn't seen them, Tenebrant is unsure if he would have felt their presences in this harsh environment. Any who sensed the familiars must have keen senses. If two felt them, with Atlas surely being one, Tenebrant can think of one possibility for the other, despite solely knowing about Atlas's team from the information conveyed to him. Though perhaps in appearance he is unknown to Merwyn, any description may tip off Nix, and possibly Koepp and Botalia. Excluding the Council members, every other person in this room knows the youngest generation of the Kufuta clan.

"We must get moving then," Tenebrant improvises in an attempt to sway the conversation from more talk of Atlas's team. "It would prove disadvantageous to arrive at the altar last of all the groups."

"Maybe not," Merwyn states, his thumbs rubbing one another. "It seems far from reason that we will be the first. At this point, one would best hope that any who do arrive fail to open the portal."

"Wouldn't that mean a war at the altar?" Cefni asks, doubting the plan he believes Merwyn to be concocting.

"Not necessarily. If the goal is the staff, my thoughts are the other teams would wish for another to open the veil to the tepui. From all my research and that handed to us through the teams of Mr. Robinson and Dr. Glatz, there was never good explanation as to what is needed to open the gateway."

"Immense power," Botalia mumbles. She licks her lips and picks at the skin about her fingernails.

Every word circles through her head, trying to hypothesize what they even mean. As Merwyn states, it is very unspecific. *Immense power.* It isn't necessarily what these words would mean to them, but to the druids.

"I've been contemplating what that could mean, reading through the stories for any sort of hint as to how the first explorers managed their way through. If one knew that, they could try to replicate those events," Merwyn states, folding his fingers into one another.

"We are talking about druidic magic," Tenebrant states, as if reading Botalia's mind. "Ancient magic."

Cefni rolls his eyes and lets out a sigh.

"Yes, why would we not have asked our resident expert, the necromancer, before trying to draw our own conclusions," Cefni remarks, clenching his jaw and fists as rage builds within him.

"Now, Cefni," Merwyn interjects, noting the speedy gusts of Tenebrant's aura. "We may be Professionals, but that does not mean we are above learning."

"Tenebrant's right," Botalia states, forcing more volume to her voice. She can almost see Tenebrant telepathically sticking out his tongue to Cefni. "Life force is wielded by the druids much differently than by us. Life itself is power."

A pulse issues through Botalia and a hand flies to her chest. She hopes no one has noticed, but looking up sees all peering in her direction. She gulps.

"Unfortunately, I can only think of one way..."

Tenebrant chuckles, catching a glare from Cefni for his reaction.

"Of course you know. You've done it before. Well, not you."

Tenebrant bites his lip, regretting his words the moment they leave his mouth, wishing to take them back. Botalia still clutches at her chest, eyes turning to the table as visions of the brutal attack remind her of that which the druids feared.

Though not accomplished by many, lycanthropy is revered by the tribes of Qoterra. Yet, the Hymn of the Beast functions in another way for such practitioners. Whereas it allows them to transform without giving up their humanity, controlling that beast that they create within themselves, the ritual allowed Botalia to do something much different. It wasn't only about control, it was fear. Fear that the beast would escape again. Despite saving her life more than once, Botalia feared that if it took control, if it took over her faculties and mind, it would refuse to give it back. To wander, subconsciously within herself, no more than a captured sentience. For all the good she wished to do for humanity, she knew the beast would always hold her from being viewed as an equal. She fought to cage it, to ensure it would never come out again.

But the druids saw it. They knew without the beast, the koroko, needing to make its presence known. Her body did not shapeshift when it took over, true lycanthropy not an ability she ever wished to obtain. But they shared a body, nonetheless. And even a magical creature like the koroko knows, the best source of life force is taking it from other living beings. Just as the druids, capturing the essence of life as one of their own dies. As they sacrifice an animal for their feast, leading any undispelled life force to a vessel.

Heightened emotions expand the storehouse but don't fill the battery...

The druidic rituals conducted by the tribes were full of emotion, whether fear or grief, even joy and loyalty as they gifted sacrifices to some almighty power. As so, they expanded the storehouse of the vessel, whichever object it was they so chose. To fill it, they would channel life itself there, leading the life force as it spilled from whatever being could no longer sustain its power.

The easiest way to fill an environment with life force, which was an immense and mystical power of its own, was to take life.

The necromancer knew long before the rest of them the only way to open the gateway was to provide a suitable sacrifice. The altar itself was created through such a means, the life force it possesses not its own, but captured from the souls to have lost their lives by the hands of those who knew how to channel that life into an object. The druids gave the altar sentience, they gave the altar power. And now it thirsted for more blood as the price for its labor.

"So, if we show up too early, we become the means to power the gateway," Cefni mumbles, his voice low yet enunciated enough so all can make out his words. He mentally works through the situation as he speaks. "If we show up too late, others will have already made it through, with many lives lost to do so."

"That is correct," is all Tenebrant can say. His eyes rest on the back of Botalia's head, her aura spinning like a chaotic electromagnetic storm about her.

"So, do we show up to fight, ensuring the gateway never opens to begin with?"

"Any life taken in the vicinity of the altar will be collected by it. We may unintentionally open a portal should we choose that as our battleground," Tenebrant responds.

Koepp and Nix cross their arms, understanding the danger of this mission to be more than they anticipated. It seemed there was no winning. Success was not merely defined as those who win, but by those who lose the least. And no matter which equation they'd choose to run, they would not be as successful as they once hoped.

"Can't Botalia just teleport us there?" Koepp whimpers, trying his best to help brainstorm in their time of despair.

Cefni and Merwyn squint, understanding the suggestion but knowing it outside the realm of possibility.

"Sorry, Koepp," Botalia whispers. Due to their proximity, all can make out her words despite the low tone. "I unfortunately need to see the destination in order to ensure a safe atomic shift. I cannot do that here."

Koepp releases a profound exhale and returns to playing with the wrinkled fabric of his shirt. He couldn't prevent himself from the internal name calling and bullying to follow his suggestion, wondering why he even bothered to speak up in the first place.

"Why not mask our auras and try to get as close as possible without blowing our cover?" Nix questions, a hint of confidence finding him aided by his friend's courage to speak up.

Merwyn smiles.

"That might work. My only fear is the caliber of life force user we are facing. How will we know we have masked our auras sufficiently to go unseen?"

"I also appreciate the suggestion," Cefni mutters, rubbing at his chin. "However, I fear that to mask to that extent for such a period would require an immense amount of life force, a quantity we will not be able to regain when we should most need it."

"The longer we sit here discussing this, the closer they draw," Tenebrant states, eyes no more than slits as he glares at Cefni. "My thought: We let them open the portal. Then we face them before they are able to get the staff."

"If I wanted to know your thoughts, I would have asked," Cefni states.

"Always the team player." Tenebrant smirks and rolls his eyes.

"Listen, you. I'm not risking the life of this team by entering a different world full of creatures we know little of. At least we know of our enemies in this world. In there, it's too much of a risk."

"Please calm, you two. Mr. Medina, I understand your concerns, believe me, but we have vowed to stop them no matter what it may take. If they do manage through the gateway, we must follow them."

"I'm not disagreeing. I simply see that as the last possible resort should we be able to help it."

Silence falls between them. The cogs spinning in each of their heads are almost visible. For so long, they believed their group to arrive at the altar first. Since this no longer seemed possible due to their detour, brainstorming an idea they could all agree on seemed almost impossible.

Botalia places both hands on the table and uses them to push herself from the chair.

"It's not worth bickering any longer. Every team is no doubt of the same mind as we are with our worries and fears. Our best bet is to head out."

"Botalia..."

"We are still miles from the springs," her eyes meet Merwyn and her tone elevates in her anxiety. "There is no part of me believing that any group already there is looking behind. No. Their attention is focused ahead. We must leave now. Even if it becomes a stalemate, that is honestly the best possible outcome at this point."

"Tanten does not care what he must sacrifice," Tenebrant retorts. "There will be no stalemate. This is about power and those who seek it. He is loyal to none but himself."

"Though it may not surprise you, I disagree with that," Cefni mumbles, his voice more passive than aggressive as he stares at the floor. "Tanten is loyal to his own person and to that which will grant him power. He will listen to the altar. Give it the blood it requires.

He will expect that in exchange he will be easily granted the Staff of the Gods. He is committed to this quest. Willing to risk it all for fealty to legend."

Merwyn sighs and rises.

"I believe we all have come to an accord. We depart now."

Each member rushes to gather their belongings. Koepp and Nix trudge to their satchels, dark circles about their eyes as despair comes to find them once more. They had begun to find relief in the safety of the cabin, hope that they could abandon the mission and remain within the sanctuary of wooden walls and scientific equipment fluttering in the distance.

Botalia glances at their somber expressions and tugs at Merwyn's sleeve.

"They can't stay here?" A pleading tone strikes at his heart.

"I am afraid not," Merwyn answers, his volume low so none other may hear. "It is unfortunate, but we will be better for having them should the gateway be opened. There are certain creatures that are told to avoid prepubescent humans. Whether true or not cannot be verified, but all other tales seem to have some validity. We would not have accepted their help otherwise."

"So you figured all along that the final battle would be fought on the other side? You had to use them and their innocence as a shield for your own fears?"

"It was suggested by a council member specializing in druidic rites and history days before you turned up to the Association. Children are sacred to such tribes, their innocence and natural connection to the world a much stronger power than our practiced life force in their eyes. Why else would you imagine that children are off limits from sacrifice? The power to result could crumble the entire island and everyone on it."

Botalia exhales and steps outside behind him. Her eyes focus on their surroundings, yet her instincts tell her there is no reason to memorize any detail about this place. If anything, she wants to forget it. Kneeling to the ground, she threads her fingers together and looks to the sky through a crack in the trees canopies above. She hesitates to pull her hands apart. Though she wishes for her life force to guide them on the best path to the springs, the thought of finding another koroko in the wild sends a chill up her spine. She does not need the beast within her to fight back again. Not now.

A hand falls on her shoulder. Koepp peers down at her, tired eyes begging her to make it all go away. To take them home to their math lessons and jellybeans. To wish upon the streaking meteorites overhead, observe the stars from a place of tranquility, where one wouldn't need to peer over their shoulder every other second. The songs of the birds and beasts were different on her island. Melodic and welcoming. Even she missed their music. On Qoterra, the screeches and calls sounded like instruments in a swirling tornado. Chaotic and raising paranoia. The disastrous symphony to accompany their death march.

Botalia pulls her hands apart and places them on the dirt path. Life force shoots from her hands in the direction they will soon travel. As it meets the steamy, geothermal activity near the springs, a pressure counters her life force from advancing any farther. As if a shield created of life force, fortified and unwelcoming, prevents such a discrete tactic for strategy. Like a taunt.

"If I wish to see what lies beyond, I'll have to use my eyes," Botalia whispers.

"Sense anything?" Cefni asks as he stops at her side.

"There's something in the way. As far as our path is concerned, there seems no present danger."

"That is the best we could hope for."

Cefni places a hand above his eyes and squints through the tree's canopy. Grey clouds race to cover their white counterparts.

"It seems rain may hit again."

"It may be an omen," Tenebrant states as he passes, a smirk growing on his face as he awaits Cefni's sarcasm which always hits when his opinion enters conversation.

"Or just weather," Cefni responds. Tenebrant chuckles as the Professional becomes too predictable for his own good.

The team march into the forest, sore muscles in their legs and backs screaming for a longer respite. Koepp and Nix march side by side, their fatigue preventing even the slightest paranoia from taking them. They stare at the dirt road, worn by the many journeys of the informants to the springs.

Cefni observes Botalia's aura. It envelops her closely, masking its true strength. He wonders if their time resting gave her sufficient ability to recuperate that which was lost. Many memories ricochet about his mind, his pessimistic internal voices claiming that he would need to make amends before they meet their death. He sighs.

"I wonder sometimes why people are willing to sacrifice so much for power," he mumbles. Botalia glances at him then quickly averts her eyes to the ground.

"Are you talking about me?" she whispers.

"Not really," Cefni responds, clearing his throat. "Flynn, Lurio, and the plenty that are like them. Those two are already so strong. I can't help but wonder what more they believe they could gain."

"Maybe they feel they aren't the strongest. They want to be on top."

"Can't say I know the true extent of their power. Just know I really wished I would never have to find out." Cefni chuckles and anxiously checks his compass, despite the path already being carved for them.

"Tanten and Atlas, they both know about me and what I've become," Botalia whispers, a tremble in her tone. "If it comes down to us versus either of them, they won't hold back. And I won't either."

She bites her lip with resolve spelled on her face as she stares at the path. Cefni rests a hand on her shoulder, the two of them pausing in their tracks.

"Just don't do anything rash," he pleads, a paternal expression carved into his face like the begging eyes her father once gave when she escaped the house at a young age to play in the rain. Her father had been terrified others may assume animalistic qualities in her, not understanding that most children enjoy bouncing in puddles and the sensation of water droplets on their heads.

Botalia's eyes connect with him.

"Why would I when I have everything I could ever want already?"

A grin slowly spreads on his face.

A gust blows past them and the screeches and calls of animals blare throughout the forest. Scuffling and digging sounds occur on every side. The day darkens as charcoal clouds cover their grey friends. The air shifts. An odd static forces their hairs on end. Botalia, Merwyn, Cefni, and Tenebrant all have the same idea. They shoot strands of life force into the ground, trying to better read and understand the drastic alteration of the environment.

A boisterous clap of thunder sounds at the same time as the clouds illuminate with a bolt of lightning to travel from Qoterra to the heavens. All life force exhausted springs back to them with a snap, fear and panic shaking them more than the icy breeze.

Botalia shakes her head as the echoes and callings of that ancient voice returns. A pounding on her chest, which she wishes was just her heart but is actually another screaming for an escape, forces her hands there. A shrill tone rings in her ears, life force lingering on her fingertips in preparation.

"It's opened."

Chapter Ten

Azriel stares through the large window from her office in the Magistrate Association, scanning the city below. Clouds sweep in from the north, grey and looming. An omen, menacing and threatening, as if challenging the loyalty and pride of these fair-weather warriors.

"Any rain may serve to wash away the devastation and destruction below. Put out our fires for us," Azriel mumbles, her expression soft, contemplating as if in a daze. "No. It's a metaphorical lie that rain washes the problems away. Only a flood could alter the course, at this point."

The Schism was a virus, a stain on her record as the one who had to step up when the President was killed. Multiplying and finding life through a group of susceptible hosts. Close mindedness, selfishness, stupidity... it was a plague. Even those who knew nothing of the matters began choosing sides. It spread at a rapid pace... this desire to choose a good and an evil, the dream to be hero, a patriot, and put an end to villainy and terrorism. It was not concentrated to their municipality, to their province. It was an international pandemic.

The fissure separating the Scholar from the Professional branches started on Dominia, the continent being the home of the Magistrate Association. When the Schism spread to other lands, Vayl began to understand the scope of the situation. The belligerents weren't solely fighting for supremacy but for the sake of fighting. It was not a challenge directed towards the enemy, but the Magistrate Association. Despite the threat of attack and an agenda to tear the

Association limb from limb, it withstood the trial. Unscathed and standing tall, the Association building demonstrates the stability of the higher ranks of the organization to work together to prevent such intimidation tactics. Only the altar piece was lost to them, perhaps the greatest regret of all.

Azriel Vayl sits in her chair, fingertips tapping the window, finding every drop of rain to hit the glass. She traces their path down the pane, pursing her lips as the water droplets combine on their way down, gaining speed as their mass increases. The rain patters drown out the intermittent shouts and explosions from below, their melody slowly speeding up overtime. Azriel sighs.

She swivels her chair to face her walnut desk, cluttered with many files, few of which she's read, many of which she's skimmed. Vayl picks up a manila folder labeled "Ulton, Botalia R." She bites her bottom lip, eyes and ears intent on determining her solitude, and opens the folder.

Name: Botalia Rhoda Ulton

Sex: Female

Date of Birth: 21.1.327.4

Date of Death: [Blank]

Parents: Chezland Costelloe Ulton [deceased] and Rhoda Anise Noble-Ulton [deceased]

Siblings: None

Status: (The words Registered Citizen of Dominia are crossed out) Exile

Magistrate: [Checked yes]

Class: [Blank]

"But why exiled..." Vayl whispers.

She flips through the pages discussing the Ulton's Last Will and Testaments, listing the bequeaths unto Botalia. The log of the Ulton's Last Will revisions reveals an update every other season, causing Azriel to pause. The only reason to update the bequeaths so frequently could only mean massive change to accounts or assets at such intervals. The consistency of the revisions leads Vayl to suspect some form of foul play or illegal activity. She scans the assets. Vayl raises her eyebrows as she notices most residences were crossed out and seized by the government, all happening shortly after Botalia's exile.

"Interesting."

She turns a few pages and sees the minutes of the Council meeting discussing the exile of Botalia Ulton.

Members Present: President Daigoneisson R. Magus, Vice President Atlas Lurio, Ormus Alloway, Rhys Champney, Roltan Demich, Tanten Flynn, Hanish Frey, Merwyn Giacobbe, Neculai Hennes, Dalschun Igoe, Norlea Kendrick, Atheas Maynard, Cefni Medina, Walpurga Ohle, Gwyn Sanoba, Femryck Sherrard, Ibovel Sobiski, Evangeline Stursa, Ashika Sukel

The minutes include ten pages of discussion, so Vayl skims the text, looking for any details of interest. The last page paraphrases much of the arguments for effective voting.

As previously stated, the incident concerning Ms. Botalia Ulton and the Class S bounty group of organ traders prove her dangerous and enhanced mammalian instincts in connection to such situations. Despite her hybrid nature and manufactured DNA, an earlier vote by the Council allows her to be protected under human law. Punishment for homicide to this extent, twenty-eight known dead by her hand, qualifies Ms. Botalia Ulton for execution. Given the circumstances of defensive combat, her maximum punishment, decided by the Council, could result in a relinquishing of citizenship. When stripped of citizen status, Ms. Botalia Ulton will be escorted by Cefni Medina to Videcrea Island, owned by the Ultons. An annual check will be forwarded to ensure she follows the terms laid out.

Vote Results:

For: O. Alloway, R. Champney, R. Demich, H. Frey, M. Giacobbe, N. Hennes, D. Igoe, N. Kendrick, D. Magus, A. Maynard, C. Medina, W. Ohle, G. Sanoba, F. Sherrard, I. Sobiski, E. Stursa, A. Sukel

Against: A. Lurio, T. Flynn

The President, Vice President, and Council accepted the results in a unanimous ruling. Hanish Frey made a motion to accept. The motion was seconded by Gwyn Sanoba.

In accordance with the Constitution of the Magistrate Association, that which says the Magistrate Association may involve themselves with the status of an official magistrate if the predetermined conditions, set out by the bylaws of the Constitution are met, Ms. Botalia Rhoda Ulton is hereby exiled.

Should the exile not respond to an annual checkup:

A. a warrant will be issued to search the entire premises

B. a fine will be set (determined at time by majority rule of Council)

Punishment should the exile be broken:

A. a fine will be set (determined at time by majority rule of Council; seconded by President and Vice President)

B. a permanent revoking of citizenship

C. execution

Signed,

Atlas Lurio

Vice President of the Magistrate Association

"Tanten and Atlas both voted against..." Vayl whispers in a drawn-out manner. When her phone rings, she flinches, lost to time and space by her echoing thoughts. Azriel places the documents on her desk and answers. "This is Vice President of the Magistrate Association, Azriel Vayl speaking. How may I help you?"

One of her secretaries responds, "Dr. Entzia Weaver is on line 2 and wishes to speak to you."

"Alright, thank you." Vayl presses the button for extension two. "Mrs. Weaver?"

"Hello, Ms. Vayl," answers Entzia in a relieved tone. An excitement appears to break through her voice as she continues, "You would never believe the hybrids Ms. Ulton concocted on this island! It is incredible the variety of plants and creatures, most of which are unknown to the scientific realm, but which Ms. Ulton keeps detailed records of."

"I'm a busy woman, Mrs. Weaver," Vayl states, her care for hearing of Entzia's tales being nonexistent. "I'm thankful all is well on your end, but-"

"Ms. Vayl. It's one of the plants," Entzia interrupts, a strong urging in her voice. Her tone raises concern in Vayl.

"What about the plant?" Vayl questions.

"It stores a tremendous amount of life force. Exponentially more than any we, in the scientific community, have ever witnessed."

Vayl attempts to determine if the news excites her or not. Her eyes circle the room then return to the files on the desk. She moves the files and notices a folder that catches her eye. The folder is labeled "Mortu, Tenebrant K."

Entzia continues to ramble in the background, but Vayl cuts her off. "Mrs. Weaver, I need to go... important business. Take care." Vayl hangs up the phone and returns her attention to the file.

Since the early morning, her mind lived in a fog. Her attention span is certainly shorter than most days, however Vayl cannot determine the cause. The only information able to pique her interest includes the contents of the files. Through her research, she learned much that perhaps she should have known as Vice President of the Association, data that the late President and Atlas knew about, but never thought to include in a syllabus for up-and-coming leaders (granted, both of their exits were quite unexpected). Vayl knew little of the dangerous underground organizations (learning of them never having been a priority for her as a Council Member), of the Ultons and their immense collection of research and experimentation, and of the secrets contained within the Magistrate Association, most often kept hidden from those outside of the department they belong to (but certainly information the President and Vice President should be made privy to).

Vayl returns her attention to the file of the notorious Tenebrant Mortu. His name is known well among magistrates, especially bounty hunting Professionals, who hope to bring him to justice, more so for the reward than the "greater good." Vayl cannot comprehend how he and Botalia came to ally with one another, but their relationship is of no significance to her. She sent Cefni and Merwyn to take care of her concerns among the group who claim their goal is to reclaim the altar piece. However, in Vayl's mind, the party appears quite dysfunctional: two Council members (one a sympathetic artist, the other a depressed wizard), an exile, a criminal, an assassin, and a Flynn... Vayl weakly slaps herself in the face realizing her drift from her main tasks.

She opens Tenebrant's file, and it reads:

Name: Tenebrant Kristoph Mortu
Sex: Male
Date of Birth: 26.4.326.4
Date of Death: [Blank]
Parents: Gommin Pyke Mortu [deceased] and Xiomara Synn Mortu [deceased]
Siblings: Ina Matus Mortu [deceased]
Status: Wanted Criminal

The rest of the first page appears blank, missing data including but not limited to health, occupation, and contacts. Vayl squints at the blank lines, questioning how not even Professionals were able to uncover this information.

The next few pages were taken from school records, which appear questionable due to the lack of delinquency from him. Vayl chuckles as she examines his good grades and attendance record, that is, up until a certain day in his tenth year when he stopped attending school altogether. Comments from his teachers taken from interviews after his murder sprees express their disbelief that the exemplary student they knew could be accused and responsible for such crimes.

The last thirty or so pages include his criminal history, most of which are homicide cases. Often Tenebrant's fights with others turned into their death sentences. Disagreements and simple jabs quickly transformed into the spilling of blood in Tenebrant's presence and the drawing of a crescent moon was his sigil to mark such occasions. He never attempted to hide the murder scenes nor pin the blame on anyone else. He had no need to. Evading Professionals became a game for him, and after approximately five years of chasing him, many hunters gave up and began hunting for those they had the possibility of catching. Vayl counts the murders committed by Tenebrant: twenty-seven. Vayl reads many of the gruesome accounts of the murder scenes and begins to feel nauseous. She closes the folder and places it atop the pile.

Head in hands, she leans on her desk. Her thoughts appear sidelined to some other issue, an issue invisible to her. If only she could determine the cause for her drifting attention. Someone knocks on the door. Vayl sits up straight, startled by the sound.

"Come in," she says. Vayl quickly straightens the piles on her desk, swiftly moving Tenebrant's file to the bottom of the pile. The door opens and Turin Vitas enters. "You're late."

"I swear I left early this time," Turin responds, scratching his head.

"Perhaps you should learn how to perform an atomic shift."

"Even Merwyn would have trouble covering that distance. I had to travel at least four kilometers to get here," he replies. He looks around the room and walks up to the desk. Casually glancing at the desk so as to not let on to him being nosy, Turin takes a seat across from Vayl. "You've been busy?"

"Haven't we all," Vayl raises her eyebrows and expresses her fatigue in her voice. She grins and locks eyes with Turin. "What is there to report?"

Turin gazes over his shoulder, perhaps his paranoia of being overheard or guaranteeing his escape. He sighs. "Well..."

"Do not act as if you've accomplished nothing. I gave you one task-"

"It's not that we've accomplished nothing. We've simply had some... setbacks."

"Explain."

The air in the room grows thick. Turin shifts his eyes, hoping the right words will find the way to his mouth. Vayl's stare pierces him. She does not move her eyes from Turin. Though she funds many projects through the sponsoring of the Magistrate Association, she's entrusted many of her closest allies with heading them. Turin, being an ally of Vayl, was entrusted with one such project.

"Since the altar piece was stolen, we've not had sufficient energy to power the MantiCore Drill. We underestimated its supply of raw energy and cannot find a suitable replacement. The drill draws massive amounts of energy, but if we up the voltage from the city's main power plant, we may face a city-wide blackout, which would set us back further," Turin says with a resigned sigh.

"First problems with financing, now this," Vayl mumbles, tapping her fingers on the desk.

"Hopefully, the team you sent will restore the altar piece to us soon enough."

"If we are truly fortunate, they'll return with the staff, not the altar piece."

"The staff of legends? Even if it does exist, do you believe any team could be capable of such a feat?"

"Perhaps I am being optimistic," Vayl replies as she turns her chair to gaze out the window. She stares at the navy sky, the clouds covering the sun above. The raindrops continue to play their tune against the glass panes. Her heart matches the rhythm, though the tune is not one of tranquility but a pounding, unrelenting anxiety. She reconsiders Turin's comment.

Did I ever truly think they would be capable? Despite aiding Atlas, I never thought he and his team could attain the staff either. I also assumed he'd never keep his promise of granting me the staff anyways... though his connections are quite a benefit from our relationship. Hmmm.

Turin stares at the back of her head, discerning her inner dialogue. He again peeks at the files on her desk. He notices the top file is labeled "Magus, Daigoneisson R." and the one underneath it "Flynn, Tanten D." He shakes his head and returns his gaze to Vayl. He focuses his eyes, examining her aura. It appears much as Turin expects Vayl's face to look, full of conflict and doubt. The room remains quiet for a few moments, the only sound deriving from the raindrops against the glass. Turin decides to break the silence.

"Ms. Vayl, it does not much to worry about matters outside of your control. I'm sure progress in the other divisions, though I know not of their works, will provide us with much needed information to our energy problem."

"I suppose you're right," Vayl responds, rotating her chair to face him. She understands Turin's desire to draw out information on the other projects under her control, however, she has her reasons for not revealing information to those not in the designated division. It concerns her word may spread about the individual divisions and their projects before she has readied the proposal sufficiently to reveal it in a contained fashion, but if information has leaked, no one has let on as of yet. Within the Magistrate Association, it is best not to be an enemy of those in power and keep the secrets of the Association and one's allies close by. Vayl hopes the advances in scientific and sorceric fields will impress the magistrates and its reach will spread even to the common citizens and residents across the globe. Her name will gain recognition for the projects, enough that she will be elected as the next President of the Magistrate Association. Atop that pedestal, nothing will be impossible.

Turin coughs, pulling Vayl from her thoughts.

"Thank you for your report (though I'd have preferred better news)," states Vayl, the latter comment she keeps within her thoughts. She sighs and leans her head back to look at the ceiling. It never changes, but she feels as though she looks up often anymore. After a few seconds die away, Vayl rises and walks to the other side of her desk, Turin rising to meet her. "Well, all I can hope is the MantiCore Drill construction is complete before our timeline expires."

"I have no doubt we'll be in the green by then. Sooner if the team pulls through." Turin turns to leave the room, but after taking a few steps, he promptly turns back. "It would be a shame to lose members such as Merwyn and Cefni... We'll need to have faith in them for the present." Turin leaves the room, closing the door behind him as he exits.

Vayl stares at the door, her expression displaying her solemnity. Though she knew death was a possibility from the beginning, it felt no more than an imaginary consequence. Much like the living youth who feel immortal to the harsh ways of nature, Vayl considered all fighting in this battle would see the end result, despite knowing the impossibility of it. In the past days, she's watched people warring over the Schism, bodies filling the morgues, and refugees getting mixed in with the violence. Many citizens have lost their lives or family members in the battles. Even watching Death himself strike down those on the ground below her, the scene never felt real. Merely an act of fiction, a production, where people would return to their normal lives the next day. Death, from the multitudes to a single person, in Vayl's eyes was an occurrence outside of her understanding. Almost as if she couldn't accept a life simply ending, slipping out of existence. Not denial, but incomprehensible and not discernable in her mind.

She shakes her head as if snapping out of a hypnotic trance and returns her attention to the files. Vayl sighs. Noticing the file of President Magus on top, Vayl rubs her face and retires to her seat. She's previously skimmed the contents of his file on multiple occasions, each time hoping she'll learn new information about him.

"With the staff, I'll be more powerful than you ever dreamed," Vayl speaks aloud, as if the President can hear her. The sound of the rain against the windows slows to a stop and the sun breaks through the clouds. Vayl sees the shadows become pronounced on the ground and chuckles. "I won't let you down, teacher."

Chapter Eleven

The team quicken their pace, Botalia bolting out in front of the pack. Like running toward a blazing fire, they race for the altar, abandoning all rationale and letting their instincts take over. Botalia's heart sinks to her stomach which sinks even further as the gravity of the situation pulls her toward the core. Her body trembles, and she struggles to find a normal breathing pattern, the uneven lands with its variety of surfaces threatening to cause her to stumble.

Cefni follows not far behind her, the rest of the group doing their best to keep up, with Merwyn hobbling at the back due to age and for the benefit of protection. Cefni's background in investigation and hunting down criminals has accustomed him to stressful, life-threatening situations. His ability to conceal the rising pressure coursing through his blood stream to his racing heart proves useful. An odd comfort finds him in performing dangerous tasks where his life is on the line, knowing that the punishment he'd receive if he so fails would be the only acceptable end.

The dark skies remain ominous, foreboding what lies ahead. Loud rounds of thunder echo through the forests, the calls of the creatures seldom slipping through the roars. They run full speed toward the altar, hoping chaos has not yet been unleashed. Hoping the Staff of the Gods is not yet claimed by those who entered the gateway. However, if someone had managed to get the staff within their grasp, surely they would know the moment it occurred. Botalia cannot help but envision the staff in the hands of one who would abuse its power and what may become of life if that should come to pass.

Tenebrant clenches his jaw, feet barely leaving a print as he sprints. The gateway in the caldera opening does not excite him like he expected it would have. The opening would mean inevitable conflict. Battle. Blood. He does not understand the sensation, but he assumes the feeling must be nerves. Fear. Tenebrant cannot deduce whether the fear derives from not arriving at the portal before any others or feeling, for the first time in so long, his own life may be hanging by a thread. He's always needed to prove his own strength to himself, but that often meant strategically picking fights he knew he would win. Understanding their present predicament and those they may face, anxiety tears him to shreds with its bullying calls of fragility and weakness. The echoes nostalgic and ones he'd thought long erased from his memories. A constant internal battle tearing him apart and degrading his confidence, whether it was real or false in the first place. Yet, he hides behind the façade of immaculate power and strength, no fear or nerves to be found.

Tenebrant peers at Koepp, who struggles to breathe the longer they run. Koepp slows his pace, holding onto his sides which scream in pain. The boy fights to keep running, staring at the back of Botalia, hoping to find inspiration in following her. However, his exhausted physical state catches up to his fragile mental state.

Koepp is fully aware he is the weakest of the team, in strength of body and mind. He knows he's not well versed in adventure or combat. He understands the probability (now understanding what this word means) of his death is extremely high. He is the weakest link and, if the time comes, he should be the one to fall. After all, he is a burden to them. Though he never wanted to fall into the position, it's where he presently finds himself.

Looking around, Koepp notices everyone else on the team is in fine condition to keep running, but he feels himself shake as his energy threatens to deplete. He finds difficulty in swallowing and breathing and hears himself forcibly screaming a prayer within the exhausted confines of his mind. Though he accepted death before, he does not now. He desires to live, wishing it above all else. He's found friends and happiness, and though a nightmare lies ahead, he hopes the dreams will return soon after its end. His willingness and stubborn attitude lend to his desire to live, and he pushes forward with every fiber of his being, absorbing strength from the environment around him. He focuses his eyes and pushes onward.

The team reach the edge of the forest and, without hesitation, keep their speed through the plains, entering the hot springs within seconds of seeing the steaming earth. All sense the presence of others to the north, others to the northwest near the center of the ashy clouds. As they race toward the altar, they experience strange sensations across the surface of their bodies, much like encountering strong electromagnetic pulses.

"What is that?" Koepp winces, believing an attack to be infiltrating their very beings.

"The gateway must have a highly concentrated electromagnetic field maintaining it," Botalia yells back, clenching her fists as her aura swirls about her.

The pulses hit them in a rhythmic pattern, headaches and dizziness threatening to make the race to the altar all the more difficult. A few minutes pass, and they hear the shouting of orders ahead. Botalia freezes, the others following suit. They listen intently to the voices but cannot make out any words.

"It's a woman," Botalia whispers, unable to register if this is a team partaking in this mission or on an excursion of their own. Were there more teams they didn't know about? "There's Tanten, Atlas, presumably Bysciw... but I thought that was it..."

She listens intently but her scattered breathing after the long run takes priority as it fights to calm. Everyone around breathes heavily while carefully trying to mask any sounds, understanding that on the other side of the caldera wall is the location of the gateway. Botalia places her hands on the ground to read the presences around. However, as she does so, the presence of someone within the caldera vanishes. An aura that once filled that space is now gone. No subtle dissipation as if life leaving a body, but displacement of particles as if an atomic shift occurred. The reality of the current situation strikes her. While reading of the gateway, she understood it was meant to transport whoever enters to another realm. However, part of her remained a skeptic, not believing such a mechanic to be viable within their world. The energy required to open such a beast now makes sense, though her understanding does nothing to quell this new fear.

"What do we do?" Cefni murmurs, eyes staring at the wall of the caldera as if wishing to bore a hole through the stone. Particles of life force spark at his fingertips, wary and anxious. Life force roots form beneath his feet, their veins unable to stretch as they are met with the resistive force of the altar.

"Presumably we wait for this other team to enter, give it a couple of minutes, and then follow behind. There is no safe way to go about this. We must enter if there are others already on the other side," Merwyn states. The Professional's aura wraps about him as a whirlpool surrounding a ship. From his position within it, he remains calm, though any to observe the spectacle would fear the potential of such a wielder.

Botalia eyes Tenebrant, who stares at the ground, focusing on his other senses above sight and life force usage. He listens to the world about them, smells that which awaits them when they enter the caldera. His fists clench at his side, the necromancer fully aware that this sort of opportunity for him to practice his skills are few and far between. The heightened tension between himself and Cefni Medina proves greater than his desire to jump at the chance to utilize his life force as best suits him. Though it could give them the edge in the battles to come, misfortune placed him on a team that values ethics above absolute victory. A furrowed brow expresses an attempt to convince himself that his moment will come. Another chance may yet arrive.

Koepp squeezes his eyelids shut and bites at his lip with quivering jaw. His fingernails dig into his palm. As Botalia focuses her eyes on the young boy, she notices the small wisps of life force escaping from his pores, barely visible to even her despite looking for it. And yet, perhaps the wisps are no more than pure illusion, the landscape already playing its game and attempting to trick those too near. A primal instinct within her refuses to bow to a sentient object, yet her amazement at its capabilities remain, especially if it is able to pull life force from those not practiced to summon it themselves. It requires more energy. It thirsts for it. Botalia knows the longer they wait, the more it will drain from them. But how many more must enter before they can risk it?

Nix's malicious aura hits her with an oppressive, looming sensation, forcing her hairs to stand on end. A demonic glint is visible in his eyes. Despite the resistance of the altar to utilize life force to check for life within the caldera, small slivers of his life force head back the way they came. Botalia thought not to look behind, her worries centered on the unknown to lay ahead. But Nix, trained to be aware of all corners of a location, feels something more than they can. The acute paranoia of the assassin senses other presences looking on.

As time progresses, the voices and movement of those once within the caldera vanish. Botalia, her heart racing and her fears progressively taking control, listens to her instincts. She places her hands on the wall of the caldera, fingernails scraping down the rock as she mumbles words of confidence to herself. Stepping into a notch on the wall, Botalia pries herself up and peeks over.

"They're gone," she whispers, her voice barely reaching those below. However, her expression reveals more than these simple words would. Shock, surprise, relief, yet overwhelming anxiety flood over her. An odd mixture of fear and desire force her heart to an odd beat. The pressure of being watched from all sides, as if the air itself possessed the thousand eyes of an insect, seeing them through all spectrums and searing through them with omniscience and omnipotence, sends a chill down her spine.

A shuffling occurs as a woman stands from behind the altar. She had been kneeling there, as if observing the carvings, trying to interpret the writings, as if attempting to charge her own life force from the battery that powered the portal. The woman sighs. Botalia wishes to keep watching the woman, but the call of the gateway pulls her eyes.

Atop the altar, a portal resembling a black hole, the inside no more than a void, wavers, static in the space. No light or sound escape. In the pits of its darkness, Botalia fights her sight, doubting the movement that occurs beyond. It is not alive... or is it? Masses darker than the starless midnight floating there come in and out of view. A strong presence and energy resonate from the void, providing an ominous and cryptic aura.

The woman climbs atop the altar, hesitating before plunging herself through the depths. Nothing of her remains as she passes through. Her blonde hair pulled back and her blood-stained clothes, all vanish just as she does. The portal does not tremble. The ground does not quake. Lightning does not strike where she previously stood. The nothingness to follow haunts more than the vanishing act.

As if forgetting the others stand in wait below, Botalia pulls herself over the wall and slides into the caldera.

"Botalia," Cefni calls after, noting her trance-like state as she does so. Without a moment to pass, he and Tenebrant race to follow her.

The group unites within the caldera, expressions of disbelief and disgust covering them. Tenebrant cracks his neck and gulps, life force dancing on his fingertips. Bodies pile up near the altar, blood pooling on the ground. Many faces appear scorched, body parts severed from a forceful blast.

"Must have planted some sort of life force explosive. Arriving to the altar must have triggered it," Cefni states, observing the corpses. "All that life, taken in an instant. Like a supercharge to the battery. Wicked, but surely the best way to achieve their goal."

"What a pity," Tenebrant murmurs, his focused sight not finding any residual life force left in the air. "One could never conjure an army in such conditions."

"You wouldn't have dared," Cefni grumbles, a threatening glare resting on the necromancer.

Tenebrant thinks to speak, to provoke yet another argument, but he bites his lip. All eyes move from the bloody site to the portal.

Botalia leans near the altar, her finger tracing its marble, skating to wipe across the sapphire and gold detailing. One corner appears quite better preserved than the rest, no doubt the piece restored to bring wholeness. If she were to break it away, remove the piece once more, she wondered if the portal would shut. Would that solve all their problems?

"We're near the gateway, but now what?" Tenebrant states, a hostility in his voice. "We can't go in there without a proper strategy, and how are we supposed to strategize when we haven't the faintest idea what we're up against? It's a lost cause."

"I'm sure we'll think of something," Merwyn responds, hoping to sprinkle optimism into the group.

"Why can't you admit we're not strong enough for this?" Tenebrant forcibly responds. He vehemently grabs a hold of Merwyn's arm and points in the direction of the altar with his free hand. "Do you really need further explanation of what had to be done just to open the portal? A necromancer would never be able to bring these bodies back. They're less than hollow shells at this point."

Cefni squeezes his hand around Tenebrant's wrist and piercingly glares into his eyes, which share the same look. "You dare..."

At this Tenebrant grins, Cefni realizing the necromancer does so simply to frustrate him. Unable to overcome the rage building within him, he throws Tenebrant's wrist from his grip and gazes at Merwyn, whose calm composure finds him but fails to quench the hunger for blood.

"A woman," Botalia mumbles, fear lacing her voice. All faces turn to her in confusion. "There was a woman. She... she went t-to the other side. Whatever that means." Botalia's eyes remain fixed on the altar, the glyphs pulling her further into madness.

"Botalia, what-" Merwyn begins before being cut off.

"I-I didn't think it was real. I mean, I had visions and premonitions and that dream... and I felt its power and I-I couldn't, no, I didn't want to believe it existed."

Botalia trembles and buries her face into her hands, sobbing uncontrollably. Koepp places his hand on her shoulder. She locks eyes with him, upset to realize the glint in his eyes derives from a fear no longer able to be suppressed. Botalia wraps her arms around him.

"What are you doing here? Why did you have to come?"

Nix averts his eyes from the scene, whether unable to watch his friends crumble to fear or if something else calls his attention. The twitch of his fingers grabbing at his pant legs suggests a mixture of the two. His nose scrunches at the stench of the rotting corpses, decaying faster than a body should. The chemical vapors of the springs floating into the caldera may be the cause, yet they all feel a greater power preying on the nutrients of which it had been so long deprived.

Merwyn peers at Cefni, pleading for the Professional to assist Botalia. Cefni had been the one to help her in the past, the familiarity may be what she needs now. Yet only he and Botalia know the words she spoke to him on the way to the island...

I won't do anything. How can I when I have nothing? ...I'll do nothing.

She was no more than a hollow shell, emptied of every emotion and memory to protect herself from the trauma. If any understood self-preservation, it was the hybrid created in the lab to perform who-knows-what in the instruction of the creators. She lost everything before... And it risked happening again. New bonds formed. New family found. And once more the line between life and death was so fine one would need a microscope.

They all stand before the altar, before the gateway. It pulls at them, calls to them, its voice ancient and melodic to some, to others it hisses and croaks. Cefni gulps. He tiptoes to Botalia, her face buried in Koepp's chest as he eyes the portal with distrust and rage.

"Listen," he starts, his voice little more than a whisper. "We have come this far. We have faced incredible challenges and have overcome. This is the final phase. We get the Staff of the Gods and we go home."

Botalia pulls herself away and aggressively wipes the tears from her eyes.

"Don't act as if one can just go home after nearly dying. A person loses a part of themselves, a part they'll never get back," Botalia says, choked words forcing themselves through.

"What do you mean 'get the staff'? Aren't we just supposed to not let the others get it?" Koepp asks, eyes still unmoving from the void hovering before them.

Botalia's eyes grow wide with jaw falling agape.

"You..." Her words leave as a breath. "You always wanted to get to this point. The real mission was to get the staff all along. Wasn't it?" Rage filled every syllable as realization struck. "You liars!"

"There were several plans in place," Merwyn interrupts, not wishing the situation to escalate further. "Unfortunately, many have become obsolete as we see what transpires in front of our faces."

"Yet this was probably the hope all along," Tenebrant snickers, shaking his head with a glare shooting between the Professionals. "Your greedy council wants that staff for the Association. No doubt that kind of power excites them."

"The Magistrate Association fights to protect all!" Cefni proudly exclaims, rage filling him at the slander the necromancer spews.

"Fights? That's not a very peaceful word. What happened to diplomacy? To compromise? Is war the best answer nowadays? Surely the Schism was only the start to the changing views of the Association," Tenebrant states with venom in his tone.

"The Magistrate Association never wished for a schism," Merwyn responds.

"Yet their very council members were the ones to orchestrate it," Tenebrant bites back.

"That bad fruit fell from the tree," Cefni says, eyes turning to the ground.

"Fell. Voluntarily. Not removed for their unethical approaches and warmongering desires," the necromancer says.

"Our bickering will not stop the staff from falling into the wrong hands," Botalia interjects. "We have no choice now. We can fight about this when we make it out. That is... if we live."

Silence encapsulates the group. Merwyn beckons Cefni to his side and they step from the team, avoiding body parts and other debris as they refocus their attention on their mission and come up with a plan. Nix joins Koepp's side and forces his friend to look away from the gateway. Their eyes scan the caldera's wall, searching for possible opposition to meet them there. Botalia wanders to Tenebrant's side.

"I'm sorry I dragged you along into this," she starts, a tear threatening to form.

"My schedule was free. I had nothing better to do." A smirk crosses his face, but she refuses to find the humor. He continues, "This is what you wanted, no? Save the world? Help humanity? Well, now's your chance to make history. To be a legend."

"And you? You'll be in the books alongside our names," Botalia manages a slight grin.

Tenebrant sighs.

"I do not intend on helping the team with this mission." He pauses and scans the area before locking eyes with Botalia. "I have my own reasons for accompanying you all to this point, but to assist the corrupt and undignified Association, the same which hunts me, any further would be to betray my ideals."

"The ideals of a murderer must be fickle," Botalia jabs, his comments being of no surprise to her. She hoped and wished he would change, perhaps she still wishes to see a different light shine in his eyes, a transformation of gaunt expression. But there was always hostility in his aura. The winds always blew about him as if disturbed. It was nothing like the boy who once sat on the stoop beside her.

"What happened to you? Why are you so-"

"Different? Not who I used to be?" Tenebrant finishes her sentence, wearing a frown and glaring at Botalia. "I guess people change when there's nothing left to do. Isn't that right, Botalia?"

"I'm sorry," she mumbles, eyes refusing to unlock with his. "I can't change what happened, to either of us, but I hope that one day that weight will not be so heavy on your heart."

"I don't need the past to change," Tenebrant whispers, his enunciated syllables sending a chill up her spine. "I just wish it would leave me alone."

Tenebrant raises a hand to his temple and rubs at them. He slicks back his silver hair, greasy and unkempt, and shakes his head.

"I was stupid to think they could kill you at the island, erase the last part that existed. And yet, something within me cheered you on, wanted to see you win. Like taking on a bully, taking on someone who wants to see you suffer. We all want the underdog to win, right?" He laughs. "But most of us will never have your power. Most of us can only win against the underdogs. But that doesn't mean we're not tempted to take down those bullies."

Guilt washes over Botalia as she notices the slight quake to his voice, the trembling of his knees that slips his control. Perhaps he had assumed she knew all along, never having trusted there to be any honest persons left in existence. But she couldn't pretend to be honest. She had done exactly what he assumed. She thought making the trade, helping to expel some of his hostility toward their team, would make up for her guilt of exploring his memories, those shared with her through a touch of the hand. That painful slideshow, tragic, and yet she expected no less. But she had to know. Curiosity was her greatest weakness. She had to know: Why did Tenebrant resent her? Why, after ten years, he didn't look at her like an old friend but as an old enemy? The sense of nostalgia was present when he arrived at the island, she felt it in his aura. His revelation as to that odd mix of energies she felt that day causes a pit to drop in her stomach. Some curiosities may be better left unsatisfied.

Cefni and Merwyn march over and call for all to gather around. Tenebrant doesn't think twice before heading to their imaginary circle. Botalia hesitates, the call in her heart, in her soul, forcing her to doubt the reality that presents itself. Her eyes find the void, tempting and inviting. Does it trick them? Or does it force truths that would serve to break bonds? Maybe it wants more violence, more death. Its hunger has not been fully satisfied. She licks her lips and trudges to them, wishing to be outside of its gaze as quickly as possible.

"We can't remain at the location we're transported to after we enter the alternate dimension," Cefni states, a serious, level tone almost calming. "We must also pray encounters with the other teams and the beasts we've learned of within the dimension are minimal. Heck, we may as well pray the beasts are mythical."

"What if it's trapped?" Nix asks, no tremble or fear evident in his tone. "On the other side of that portal," he says, nodding his head toward the void acting as a gateway, "Isn't there a chance the first team in trapped it?"

"Certainly the possibility exists," Merwyn begins, a weary expression worn as he gazes at the void. His final word trails, revealing his hesitation as the thought had not passed him previously. With a profound exhale, he shakes his head. "We must hope their focus on the staff calls to them more than employing tactics to delay others."

"Sounds like a lot of hoping and praying that things just happen to go our way," Tenebrant states, picking at his fingers and eyeing a corpse with arm and leg blown from it, a burned face that none would be able to identify.

Cefni grunts and crosses his arms, eyes turning to the mountainous, grey clouds swirling above them. The ominous shapes seemingly revolve at the point directly above the altar.

"I suppose we must not hesitate any longer," Cefni grumbles, resigned to their fate, whatever that may be. He strides toward the wall of the caldera they previously slid down and places his navigational tools carefully on the ground. Ensuring he is far enough from any spilling blood and foul scents, Cefni slips off his backpack and empties out all objects he does not consider a necessity into a pile besides these tools. Testing the new weight of his gear, Cefni rises and addresses the group.

"As we all know, time is of the essence, and we don't want to walk in as the team who claimed the staff is on their way out."

Cefni Medina rubs his hands together, and his life force accelerates. As he marches to the marble altar and places his hands atop, Botalia's speech halts him.

"Wait!"

Botalia places a hand on his shoulder and urges him to move aside. She climbs onto the altar, trembling knees and racing heart pleading her to turn back. The marble altar feels different compared to the uneven earth they'd been traveling the past few days. Solid, heavy. No give to comfort her sore feet and legs. Yet, as she rises to stand with back straight and head up, the feeling becomes overwhelming. As if standing on the mountain peak peering down at the world below, the calls and screams of distant echoes begging her to jump. Begging, pleading with her to give herself to whatever may exist below the layer of clouds that hides all beneath it. It may as well be a void.

Botalia's aura races about her and the concentration of life force in her chest grows as she fights to control the beast within her. It senses the life force from the sentient object attempting to break through her aura, attempting to manipulate and gain control of another. No person would be able to exercise their life force as so over Botalia, the beast within a roadblock to any manipulation techniques. Yet the ancient magic of the altar exists outside the understanding of humanly life force. It may be capable of much more than any could possibly imagine.

Botalia swallows the buildup of saliva in her mouth, hoping her fear to disappear with it. She loses her focus to the call of the gateway, the portal as deep and dark as a midnight sky with no stars. It exerts its powerful presence, looming and oppressive around the limits of her aura. It constricts, or perhaps tightly embraces... Botalia clenches her fists and stomps a foot in unconvinced readiness. Her eyes find her team and her thoughts return to their reality.

"I'll go first. What Nix proposed is not unrealistic. If the portal is trapped, I'll stop it. Give me a few seconds, and-"

"These are elite magistrates we are dealing with, Botalia. Some traps even you will not be prepared for," Merwyn responds.

"Then I'll come out after I've guaranteed its safety-"

"Botalia-"

"I have to do something. I've been of no help thus far," Botalia replies. Her eyes squeeze shut as she feels the tears threatening to break through, reveal those emotions and thoughts she wishes to remain hidden. A calloused hand grips around her ankle. She opens her eyes to see Cefni, a fatherly pleading lining his expression, tears threatening to break through his guise as well. She sinks in her position and, with delicate touch, lifts his fingers one by one until his hand slowly drifts down to the marble. Her voice leaves in little more than a whisper. "Please. I deserve whatever happens to me. Please, let me go."

Silence encapsulates the team as the weight on their shoulders increases. The gateway tugs at Botalia, its impatience growing the longer the presences around refuse to satisfy its hunger. But physical pressure is only one of its tactics. The altar sparks and a slight tremor shakes the earth, forming a thin crack in the soil that points south. They understand the line it draws to be a warning. Others are coming and they have entered the field of the altar.

"Is it to be trusted?" Botalia mumbles, a new fear striking as the possibility of another bloody battle looms in the horizon.

"We don't know how many entered the gateway before we arrived," Merwyn scans the walls of the caldera, attempting to catch a glimpse of the smallest movements. "It is not outside the realm of possibility that another team will arrive soon."

"Can we go already?" Tenebrant asks, aggressive and hostile. He rolls his head as if he's in pain. "We're not the last team to enter that dimension. There's another team approaching from the north, and they're not far off. I would have said something sooner, but I thought you were Professionals."

"Right," Botalia responds. She gulps and fills her lungs with as much air she can hold, scrunching her nose at the stench, before releasing it. "I'll go first, you can follow in any order. Trust me. I'll stop anyone who attempts to trap us on the other side. However, I can't say the same about the native inhabitants of the land. Tenebrant is right. We've wasted enough time. Let's go."

Botalia places a hand on her chest, gripping the fabric of her shirt in a moment of anxiety, and plunges into the void of the gateway. She falls through space, weightless, as if in a vacuum. No air forces her hair back, no wisps of chill nor heat, as if the temperature about her matches that in her core to the very tenth of a degree. Nothing exists in this space but her. She starts to question whether she is even falling or simply levitating. Her aching sore muscles and grumbling stomach, the aches passing through her head and chest at the stress, all disappear. As if she were a ghost and no longer a physical being.

It reminds her of when she touches someone's hand, accepting their suffering to convert into raw life force, the experience evanescent. However, unlike those moments, she does not feel saturated in emotions. She feels nothing. The amazement and awe she experiences in the transport to the alternate realm leave her aura in a tranquil state, one she has no control over. The space around her envelopes Botalia, however, the feeling is of weightless fabric against her skin. A strange sensation, similar to an atomic shift, courses through her, and she closes her eyes and focuses her mind. As she inhales, an acrid smell, like smoke from an unknown fuel, enters her nose. Solid ground forms under her feet. Her eyes remain closed. She moves her fingers, pressing them against her palms to check that she is still alive. Nothing but the foul aroma hits her. Botalia tilts her head back, an honest relief to feel life. Botalia whispers to herself, more relief to be found in hearing her voice.

"Let's do this."

Chapter Twelve

B otalia tiptoes away from the gateway, life force sparking at her fingertips and probing the surrounding area for possible traps or other life. She holds her breath. Curious eyes scan the small, barren room, examining the disturbed grains of sand on the stone floor, a myriad of footprints leaving no doubt in her mind that others were already here. Not that she doubted. She had seen the woman enter through the gateway. But it didn't stop her from wondering how many possible exits there could be. Understanding the footprints to be fresh, with no precaution taken to cover them, many doubts seemingly disappeared while others formed.

No longer able to hold her breath, and in no current state of danger, Botalia allows the stale, dry air of this ancient room to fill her. She rotates to examine the state of the gateway, its appearance identical to the one she stepped through on Qoterra. Its veil does not quake but the echoes have quieted. Botalia licks her lips, tempted to step through and see if she falls back to Qoterra. However, she feels a distant tug attracting her like a magnet. A sharp, shaky exhale leaves her.

Botalia takes another step into the room, testing the floor beneath her. She places a hand on the wall, the gritty marble carved and positioned centuries back by those who once lived here. The thought of any living in such an environment with such creatures she'd read of in legend sends a shiver down her spine. Light from the outside world streams in through a carved-out doorway. On the other side, shining in the bright light of this realm's sun is a dry, rocky soil, devoid of life and losing another top layer of sediment with every passing breeze.

She presses with greater force on the wall, every part of her palm meeting the rough marble, and allows her life force to flow. To her relief, Botalia senses no presences in the immediate area. No threat of creature or environmental disaster enter the field her life force projects from her. The silence of this realm causes her uneasiness to spike. Yet her curiosity does the same. The doorway into the outside world tempts Botalia, but she resists. "Not until they get here."

Approximately two minutes after her arrival to this realm, she notices the gateway void waver in its place. The outline of a form appears, his dark skin and dirtied clothes gaining color and dimension as each atom finds its place in the puzzle. The figure gently floats to the ground, tapping his feet to feel the solid land beneath him. His eyes glow with admiration, an appreciation of such ancient magic and technology that goes well beyond how the engineers of today combine the two. He moves away from the portal and locks eyes with Botalia, who beams seeing his calm and unharmed person.

"We appear to have made it," Merwyn says, an enthusiasm evident in his voice. He looks toward the gateway, waiting for the others to appear. "The method of transportation is questionable... I don't know if I've ever felt the sensation prior."

"I believe it utilizes a technique similar to an atomic shift," Botalia replies, though not wanting to press her knowledge on Merwyn. He gazes at her, not amazed she knows about shifting but an amazement that never ceases in understanding she knows what it feels like.

"Yes... now you mention it-" Merwyn responds before pausing his thought to witness the one arriving through the gateway. The small shape materializes before them and stumbles onto the ground. Koepp hits the dusty floor, ensuring its safety and sturdiness before standing. At the sight of Botalia, he gets to his feet and runs to her side.

"I did it," Koepp states proudly, brushing the dust from his knees then hands. His smile expresses his joy in the accomplishment, though, whether the gateway was meant to prove as a hindrance or a simple door is unknown. "I just focused my mind, just like that one time."

Merwyn blinks as if waking from a dream and squints with curious expression between Koepp and Botalia, not understanding if he heard correctly.

"You... He has experienced an atomic shift?" Merwyn questions with a smile creeping to his face.

"Only twice, as far as I can recall," Botalia says matter-of-factly. Merwyn releases a breathy chuckle and shakes his head.

"Youth these days..."

Merwyn marches toward the door carved out of the stone. Peeking his head through the opening, he carefully examines the land, analyzing all footprints visible in the dry soil. His awe of the gateway appears to have faded, his mind quickly adjusting back to the task at hand.

Unlike Merwyn, Botalia cannot so easily be pulled from her fascination of the gateway. When faced with a new discovery or mechanic before unknown to her, Botalia cannot settle or lose interest until the concept is fully dissected for her personal understanding. Though she deduced the energy is similar to an atomic shift, she cannot provide a rational explanation as to how the portal would work for one who has no idea as to what an atomic shift is. The portal, though ominous and forceful from the other side, acts tranquil in this dimension. It's as if the portal is sentient. Being capable of transportation through the use of an external energy and a complex system of forces must mean the gateway has a mind of its own.

The next to drop from the gateway is Nix. He squints in confusion and clenches his fists. Blinking a few times to help his vision focus, Nix's expression lines with shock and doubt at the tranquility upon entering this realm. He joins Koepp at Botalia's side, eyes never resting on one position for too long as paranoia haunts him.

"Wasn't that fun, Nix?" Koepp asks, smiling at his friend. Nix stares at Koepp as if he's some eccentric antique before closing his eyes and crossing his arms.

"I mean, it was okay. Too easy if you ask me," Nix begins, his coolly overconfident persona leaking from his person. He sighs. His head turns to the ground, though his eyes remain closed, and his cool attitude grows solemn. "I did not expect to pop out over here and be fine."

Botalia giggles with a nervous tremble at their conversation, easing a small fraction of her anxiety. However, her thoughts continue to flash the images from her dreams, the creatures, the barren wasteland, and... the blurred figure. Her animal instincts kick in and she senses the seismic waves before she feels them. The ground quakes beneath the team. Looking around in panic, they cannot decide whether the quake is artificial or natural. Botalia's heart accelerates, quickening her breaths.

A few seconds pass and Tenebrant steps out of the gateway. His face expresses irritation as he stomps away from the portal and fails to acknowledge the existence of his team standing before him. Botalia pleads to have his eyes connect with her own, widening them with a paralleled shock the quake brought. His aura swirls around him like a whirlwind, his anger tangible. Life force seeps from him as wrath fights to manifest from his pores. Tenebrant's sole focus remains on the door, uncaring to prepare himself for that which may meet him there. No roots to detect presences. No sculpted beings to play sacrifice. He does not even focus his senses in the way one would when entering a dangerous, foreign environment. As if relying solely on a hostile aura, one of an apex predator while hungry or enraged, Tenebrant marches for the door with the whirlwind surrounding him as his only shield. He fails to exit before Botalia calls out.

"She'd never be happy... knowing what you've become."

Tenebrant freezes in place but refuses any urge to face her. He releases an aggressive exhale and his fingers twitch. A wave of Tenebrant's hostility and anger directs itself at the team in a strangling mist of life force. It hits the lungs and constricts their breathing for no more than two seconds. A warning. He says nothing verbally, but his aura speaks volumes. Tenebrant cracks his neck to one side and marches into the streets of the ruined city. He does not attempt to conceal his presence and he does not look back.

Botalia bites her bottom lip in an attempt to prevent her eyes from watering, but a tear manages to slip through her defenses. Her body shakes much like the ground had and her breathing grows shallow. The reminder of Tenebrant's slideshow, the audio and video she deceitfully infiltrated without his permission, covers her in guilt and shame. "His suffering, his trials, have led to this. And I'm partly to blame..." Botalia thinks, beginning to hate her ever active and ever punishing conscience.

"What was that all about?" Koepp asks in little more than a whisper, terrified the necromancer may hear and return to kill them.

"Probably just itching for a kill," Nix answers, no attempt to conceal his disgust in his voice. "To think some people enjoy the touch of blood. Sick."

"Kufuta by name but not by design, I see," Merwyn says with light tone, breaking up the tension in the air.

"They tried," Nix says. "But not all kids want what their parents want for them. I wanted something else." Nix's eyes fail to connect with any as his hand raises to grab his arm, crossing in front of him as if internally cursing for revealing a weakness.

Cefni glides through the gateway and his body and clothes take form. A mixture of emotions grows evident in his aura. With brief examination of the team and their surroundings, Cefni adjusts his jacket and marches for the door.

"We're moving out," he orders, a gruff tone cutting through.

Without another word, despite the questioning expression of the group, there is a telepathic understanding of a refusal to give any explanation as to what happened while the two were on the other side. Botalia gazes at Cefni with a glimmer in her eyes, wishing to know the truth. Merwyn sighs and obediently respects Cefni's orders, ushering the young boys forward.

The sun's heat strikes down on them as they exit the protection of the room housing the gateway. The stark change of environment that they trekked not even a day before, damp, humid jungle to dry, arid wasteland, forces a twist in their stomachs and a painful pulse in their heads. Dust covers the marble and sandstone ruins which are all that remain of the city. Some buildings, with better structural integrity, stand tall above the fallen pillars and crude walls. One such building stands on the opposite end of the city, more elegant and stately than the other buildings, more than likely a place of great significance to the druids given the size. A variety of living and dead shrubs grow from the soils and streets, which have been worn from years without repair but have held up well for being an ancient concrete mixture. Soil, sand, and marble rubble run across the roads with the breeze. Every so often, crushed and flattened debris stick to the concrete surface, disturbed by the weight of someone... or something.

Cefni and Merwyn huddle and whisper to one another, no detailed map of the ruined city provided in their training. Traversing an unknown city is dangerous enough, but lacking understanding of its inhabitants creates all the more risk in traveling the streets without a plan. Merwyn raises an arm and points south, the distant peak of the tepui in view above the ruins. Cefni motions at the footprints.

"We all understand the direct path would be the quickest, but obviously given their paths each team already agreed that it was not the safest. Whether for fear of an encounter with another or those creatures that call this city home, I can't be sure," Cefni says, wiping and wrinkling his nose as the dust sweeps by.

"My understanding would be they had just faced an altercation and wished to conceal themselves and heal before a possible second, or even third, battle commenced," Merwyn says. Unlike Cefni, any paranoia is not apparent in his expression nor in his aura. Small, barely visible orbs float from his fingertips in all directions, blending in with the sand swept into the air as it collides with the walls. Merwyn continues, "The most sensible for any team sustaining injuries would be to take that path less traveled."

Botalia gazes in the direction of Praecantatis Tepui. The hum that fills the city, a tone so low some may not even pick up on it, originates atop that structure. Sore muscles scream as she gauges the distance. About three kilometers. The flat terrain of the wastelands and flood plains provide for a less strenuous hike, however, the other challenges of these lands cloud her thoughts.

Paranoia grabs her attention as a shadow moves in her peripheral vision. As if peaking about a building, Botalia jumps at the sight. Even as she turns to see nothing, Botalia understands. They are being watched.

Koepp places a hand on her arm and opens his mouth to question her reaction, but not before the ground trembles once more under their feet.

"Perhaps an aftershock," Merwyn suggests, clearing his throat as his voice cracks and lets slip his doubts.

"That was not the first you felt?" Cefni asks, furrowing his brow and one hand finding the revolver at his side.

"We did feel one earlier. Stronger. Whether natural or..."

"Manmade," Cefni finishes, gulping down the saliva building up in his mouth. Merwyn sighs.

"I cannot be sure."

"I think we both know the answer."

"It may not be made by man," Botalia mumbles, eyes scanning their surroundings. "But it may be made from that which was made by man."

"Hmm," Cefni responds, eyes focusing east.

Instinct tugs the team as they also peer down the same street as Cefni.

"What is that?" Nix asks, eyes growing wide and stepping back slowly.

A dark mass gathers on the ground and accelerates in their direction. No clouds overhead disturb the light in such a way. The shadows move of their own accord. As it draws near, the team freeze. It is no solid mass of shadows but a stampede of several hundred shadowy blobs racing across the ground past their feet. Botalia jumps at the slight pull of the ground under her as they travel by. Every shadow rushes in the same direction, all heading west. They bend around the corner of a building, disappearing behind the ruins of the city. Botalia's eyes follow the path up and notice the temple sits in the direction the shadow creatures head.

"No doubt there's a team there," Botalia whispers, the marble landmark standing tall above all the city. An excellent vantage point should any want to know the other team's movements without utilizing significant batches of life force.

"Were those things alive?" Koepp asks, tucking into Botalia's side.

She nods and places a hand on his shoulder.

"Why didn't they attack us?" Koepp whimpers, the tremble in his body apparent as Botalia grips down.

"They're not hostile," Nix answers, squinting at the building they curved about. "Those things are scavengers. They don't have the energy to form their bodies so they stay like blobs on the ground. They're hungry. And I don't think they've had anything to eat in a long time."

"Scavengers?" Cefni questions, whether rhetorical or not is unclear. "That would mean their movement could predict bloodshed. Possible death?"

Nix nods and scrunches his nose, fingers rubbing at his pant legs.

"How curious," Merwyn murmurs. He seemingly ignores their conversation and observes a line of spiders crawling due south. Thousands of the creatures form an organized queue as they scurry across the sand.

"We can note the wildlife some other time," Cefni states, licking his upper lip as he's tempted to squash some of the spiders running past.

"Scientific records show animals can perceive things humans cannot," Botalia says, curious eyes watching the spectacle. "Perhaps another quake or some other disaster is about to befall these lands."

"Then we better not be here when it's time to find out," Cefni says.

Koepp tugs on Botalia's shirt.

"What's that?"

He points at the gateway. It waves in space and warps about the circumference.

Botalia's jaw drops.

"Someone else is coming through. We need to go. Now."

"Which way?" Cefni asks in a panic.

Merwyn points east.

"We have seen scavengers move west and we do not wish to take a direct path to the tepui. East is our best option if not our only one."

"East it is."

Cefni leads the pack in a sprint, life force stemming from his feet with every landed step. The roots spread like a lightning strike and retract with any contact with the dry earth. Botalia emits a life force field. It will not only conceal all of their presences, the field will detect any presences to fall within its radius.

They loop through the ruins, hoping in the least to be out of eyesight to whichever team exits the gateway. They inch further south with every bend. The quiet landscape they encounter heightens their paranoia, every footfall on stone echoing from the marble walls. Labyrinthine passages through the supposed alleyways of the ruined city grow narrow in parts, forming a single file line the only way to squeeze through.

Cefni's aching legs cause him to slow, Botalia bursting to the front to prove her worth. Determined and motivated, she ignores her screaming muscles and pushes her physical abilities to the limit. A tightness grips her chest, as if an internal alarm ringing out, and Botalia freezes.

At the edge of her life force field, Botalia finds the presence of another. She focuses and expands the range, noting that it is not just one individual but a team.

Cefni notes her expression and licks his bottom lip, the salty taste of sweat causing his facial muscles to contort. The others stop, unaware of why they may have stopped. Merwyn, who tails the group, peers behind them.

Botalia tiptoes to the building where she senses the presences and places an open palm on the wall. A jolt meets her in an instant and she pulls her hand to her chest. Her eyes meet Cefni, a static expression revealing hesitation.

Cefni nods. He bends over and scrapes his fingers across the sand. He stands up straight and cracks his neck. Life force trickles from his fingertips and a small disc of sand begins whirling near his feet. Merwyn beckons the team to continue their run and Cefni charges the isolated sandstorm, focusing it about the building where the team conceals themselves. The flurries of sand shroud the walls on every side. Had they been willing to attack, they would first need to quell Cefni's sandstorm.

After several minutes of running and no attack to find them, the team seek shelter in a marble house with walls still mostly intact. They catch their breath once inside, Botalia closing in her radius to only include concealment of their presences within the space.

Nix kicks a pebble at the wall, biting his bottom lip. Several furrowed brows meet him.

"Why didn't we take them?" Nix growls through gritted teeth. He finds another pebble and launches it with the tip of his shoe. "We had the advantage. Why didn't we snuff 'em out while we had the chance?"

"An enemy now could be an ally down the road," Merwyn says, a tranquil tone attempting to calm the young boy. The words fail to take effect.

"Or they could be the ones to kill us."

"I did not sense hostility in them," Botalia says, voice firm. "They were strong. I'll give you that. If they do come after us, we will be at a definite disadvantage. That one... she would have taken control of me in an instant if it wasn't for who I was. Her life force was dancing, anxious to manipulate any to dare come upon their presences and reveal their location. I don't think they're looking for a fight. Judging by their numbers, I'd say they'd already been in one."

"What? On the other side by the altar?" Cefni asks, his interest piqued with her observation.

"I don't think so. That was the team that went in right before us. I recognized her. She's the strongest of the group. We need to hope they find the others first... Or that the others find them."

"I don't think anyone's backtracking," Cefni says, peeking about the doorframe where he stands guard. "It's currently a game of capture the flag, and each team seems to be taking a tactical approach. No one's rushing for the staff, but they've all got their eyes on it."

"Why wouldn't they just run to get it?" Koepp asks, pulling his knees closer to his chest as he sits up against the marble wall. "What could be worse than another battle?"

"That's the problem. We don't know," Cefni says. He sighs and scratches his neck. "Battles are brutal. Life force users of this caliber are beasts of their own breed."

Botalia releases an audible exhale and crosses her arms, looking away from Cefni. He closes his eyes and bows his head, regret for his words instantly finding him.

"Let me rephrase." His voice cracks. "In Qoterra, the lands and creatures are treacherous, but the biggest threat was always going to be other life force users. Here, well, we don't know that to be true. In fact, we believe it quite the opposite."

Koepp rests his head on his knees, the dust sticking to his pants and rubbing on his sweaty face not bothering him.

"Think of it this way," Merwyn says, marching to the young boy's side. Nix steps over, glaring between the Professionals and takes a seat by his friend. Merwyn sighs. "We may hide from each other, but we are also hiding from whatever may still be hiding from us. The unknown is unknown until it is known. But no one quite wants to be the one to discover it first."

"Then, the shadows and spiders aren't the only things living in this city?" Koepp asks.

"According to research, no. Unfortunately, with so little information, there may be much more here than we anticipate." A silence encapsulates them for a moment before Merwyn continues. "Cefni, let us use our combined efforts to search the city to locate any others. We must determine if we are truly secure in this place or should we move out with haste."

Cefni nods. Botalia waves her hands in front of her.

"Hello? I'm here, too," she says, clearly agitated that they've ignored her despite her power. "Please don't leave me out of this. I want to help."

Merwyn motions to Cefni to dictate the final decision. Meanwhile, he sculpts dragonfly familiars, gleaming with bright, emerald scales. The green glow shimmers from his dark skin as they fly about him, landing on his shoulders, arms, and then wrap about his head, awaiting their instruction. With gentle hand movements, as if weaving the air in front of him, the dragonflies disperse, exiting through the windows and the doors, any cracks in the structure they can find.

Cefni marches to Botalia, the two connecting eyes.

"I'm going to get my eyes on that team we passed. My hopes are they aren't closing into our position. You think you could locate any other teams that may be around?" Cefni asks, not wishing his question to sound as if he doubts her abilities. Botalia smiles, causing his facial muscles to relax.

Botalia places her palms together and squats. As her palms pull apart, threads of life force cling and stretch from her hands. She slams her open hands onto the dusty surface of the stone floor beneath them. Life force shoots in all directions. Like the cracked seedling called to sunlight, her life force travels toward any other sources of life force.

Her first find is those they had passed. Their position had shifted, nine individuals total, but they traveled further west, no doubt having discovered their own team to have run east, Cefni's power enough to force them further away. A jolt strikes her as another of her stems of life force finds a large group, twenty-seven individuals accompanied by ten conjured beings. She gulps. This team is not far from the gateway, but she is nonetheless intimidated by their numbers. Her life force travels southwest, in the direction of the towering, marble structure that overlooked the city. The auras are blurry, getting an individual count not reliable from such a distance. As if trying to capture radio frequencies from wavelengths that have lost their potency, the static of their collective auras reveals heightened senses. Fear? Or possible hostility? The shadow creatures had moved in that direction, they may be the cause... or they were the effect of some other missed calculation.

Just north of the structure, her life force experiences greater interference. But the size of the interfering field is small, no more than three individuals could fit within the space. Her life force pulses like that of sonar. The two individuals must not understand the full capabilities of life force, concealing only those spaces where they exist, not understanding that a realm made of life force would easily reveal those spaces without. Two individuals. Botalia pulls in her other stems, committing greater strength to determine who these two may be. A blazing aura with black and white memories causes her to recoil her life force stems. She promptly stands and her eyes grow wide.

"I found him," Botalia mumbles through hollow breaths. "Tanten. I found him."

Cefni remains focused on his search, his meditation not a purposeful means to ignore her. Merwyn's expression grows solemn, and he shakes Cefni's shoulder.

"What?" Cefni asks, slightly irritated as his life force ricochets back through his hands.

"She's found him. Where? Where is he? Did you find others?"

Botalia's eyes find Koepp, who squints at the grains of sand on his boots. The young boy's aura, untamed and outside of his control, glows like the cooling embers of an extinguished fire. She bites her bottom lip and faces Merwyn.

"I counted four separate groups. Four teams if we're to assume none have split up."

"So Tanten's team made it through?" Cefni exhales as his jaw clenches, shaking his head all the while.

"They may not be the threat we expected," Botalia quickly adds, noting the fear and doubts flooding Cefni's mind. "It's only him and one other. Though we should not doubt their strength, I'm certain their numbers play to a disadvantage."

"And Atlas Lurio? Any signs of him?"

"There was a very large team to the north, but I didn't sense him there. I've only experienced his presence once a couple of weeks ago, the first time in a decade, but I know he's not with that team. But the group in the temple. Their auras all mixed together, as if the one concealing understood total concealment by each individual was less effective than a concealment field. I wouldn't doubt that he's among that team."

"But why choose a place so obvious?" Cefni asks, rubbing at the stubble on his cheeks and chin. "It's the tallest building in town, an obvious lookout but also the first place bound to be attacked."

"And they may have found that reality earlier than they expected," Merwyn interjects. "The shadow scavengers no doubt found them there. And due to their hungry movement, an attack had already hit them."

"Four teams? Who is the fourth?" Cefni asks. He squints at Merwyn who shrugs and peers out the window.

"I... I don't know," Botalia mumbles. Her mind fills with a twister of thoughts, wondering if there she would find any clues as to the unknown adversary. "Each individual's strength proves no insurmountable power, however, their numbers are what truly terrify me."

"Well, we should move out before the others choose to do the same, now that we know their positioning," Cefni says. He marches to the door and peeks out into the quiet wasteland of ruined marble structures. "Our best bet is to find shelter in a building nearer the floodplains. From there, we'll have a clear sight of the tepui and any teams seeking to cross. Arriving first will be of great advantage to us."

"Agreed," Merwyn nods.

Cefni mirrors the action and beckons with a hand wave for the others to follow behind as he exits. Botalia races to his side, biting her tongue in anticipation of the words that may slip. She peeks back to notice the boys slog a distance back, Merwyn attempting to coax them forward at greater pace. With the space between them, her eager words escape.

"So the plan is to wait, and then what? When a team begins to cross the floodplains, what do you plan to do?" Botalia whispers in a forceful question.

Cefni peers down at her without moving his head and sighs.

"At that point we'll have no choice but to attack. We can't let them reach the staff."

"And should every other team fall before the staff is attained? Do we just leave at that point?"

Another telling exhale leaves him audibly.

"To ensure it will truly not fall into another's hands, we will have to retrieve the staff ourselves."

His words, though steady, cannot shed themselves of the guilt that he fights within him. Botalia bites her bottom lip and her head bobs.

"It seems the mission we've been fed is ever-changing. And though we may have once agreed, I don't think our goals align any longer."

"Well, I suppose we'll have to fight for what we, as individuals, wish to protect."

Botalia gazes at Cefni, a solemn expression worn, before nodding in agreement. She knows her only wish is to protect her allies, sacrificing her own life or taking the lives of others if need be. However, a hidden wish begins to reveal itself, a desire she's had all along. The resonating hum returns to Botalia, the melodic tune communicating with her. Its magnetic pull grows stronger and, despite her intentions to do what is right, she wonders if she'll be able to when the time comes.

Hesitation could be her downfall.

Temptation could be the world's downfall.

But who other would be able to control such a power if not the fantastical, hybrid creation of the famous Ultons? Her heart pounds, pains at her ribs growing as if the pulse tries to push all other organs away. The beast within yells at her to return. But Botalia must see it for herself. She refuses to leave until the yew presses into her palms and their powers become one.

Chapter Thirteen

Atlas Lurio observes their landing as they exit the marble ruin containing the gateway. A previous journey to the druidic realm documented the positioning to be in a different location. Atlas does not doubt that the cartographer was accurate in their scaling of the realm, assuredly utilizing life force to map the region as they traveled through the ruined city. Atlas pauses to wonder if the landscape shifts when no one is present. Or perhaps it moves under their feet in this very moment.

"I've located Tanten and Horne," Naht says, fists clenched and squinting in their supposed direction.

"Back down. We're not continuing the chase," Atlas says, his tone cold and authoritative.

"What do you mean, Red? They just killed some of our troops. We can't..."

"I said back down."

Keniph straightens his posture and solemnly eyes the wounded from the attack they faced before entering this realm. He forces down the bile leeching up his throat and sighs. Naht releases his fists and stares at the ground, redirecting his life force to other matters.

Atlas bites his bottom lip.

"Damn..."

He rolls up the map, no longer viable in the ruined city they've found themselves in, and replaces it in a pocket of Keniph's bag.

"Red, we can't just back down," Keniph whispers, his words meant for only Atlas's ears. "Their loyalty to our mission will slowly fade if they feel we've given up on the fight."

"And should a fight come, I'd rather have rested and recharged troops as opposed to injured and anxious ones." Venom laces Atlas's voice as his eyes, showing through no more than the slits his eyelids make, find Keniph. "And I would think my second-in-command refuting my orders would cause a greater effect on their loyalty to the mission. Wouldn't you say so, Jet?"

Keniph bobs his head and steps back.

"Assist Leda for the mean time. We must move out immediately."

"Aye, Red."

His greasy, blonde hair droops over his eyes as he leaves Atlas's side. As he follows his general's movement, the burned flesh and singed skin of those injured enter his vision. Atlas quickly turns away, eyes closed.

"That bastard," Atlas whispers.

He focuses his hearing as a breeze brushes by them. Debris dances by its command, sand, dirt, and marble grains mixing with other sediments of the landscape. But the wind does not speak to him. No message can be found in its current. Atlas exhales profoundly and peers about. It is not a simple breeze. It is a breath. The realm is breathing.

"Though some may hear a hum..." Atlas mumbles and attempts to identify direction. But it's all about them.

"Do you hear something?" Naht asks, noting Atlas's focus as he approaches.

"This realm is alive. There is no space within that exists without life force. It may as well be an intricate mirage."

Naht expresses a short-lived grin and peers at the troops assisting one another at the door of the gateway.

"This may not be the best place for that," the assassin nods in their direction. "We never know when another team will enter. Undoubtedly any nearby heard the explosion and rushed to the site."

"Tricky isn't it," Atlas sneers at the path of two sets of footprints in the midst of undisturbed soil. With every breeze, the shape loses form. "I assumed the man too dimwitted to open the gateway even if he could obtain the piece of altar. Nowhere in any text was there mention of a field surrounding the site where life force would fail to be utilized."

"Before the altar piece was in place, that field did not exist," Naht corrects. "Restoring the piece must have been the trigger, so to speak. You seem to have forgotten that we could sense their presences within the caldera before they placed the piece. As we prepared our attacks sliding inward, there was no friction. But when the piece was replaced, the altar restored..."

"It overpowered us," Atlas mumbles. "The resistance was too great, and our plan was left in shambles."

Atlas shakes his head and peers above. A harsh sun beats down on the ruins, the arid wasteland proving even sparse clouds refused to leave their waters within these lands. The light intensely reflects from the marble buildings, which were no more than a scant collection of walls.

"Bringing land mines to a war may not be short-sighted, but it is certainly lucky a life force user as strong as Tanten Flynn would think to rely in such explosives," Naht states. "And to plant them before placing the altar piece was not something any of us could have anticipated."

"I wonder what other tricks he has up his sleeve," Atlas murmurs and watches in the direction Naht revealed their presences to be found.

A moan fills the air as Leda wraps the arm of one who had been too near an explosive when it detonated. Flesh peels from them as red sores form, raw and bloody, covering their arms and face. Those killed at the site had limbs ripped from torso, faces burnt beyond recognition. Quick deaths, surely, undoubtedly excruciating pain right before the end. Others who are uninjured but clearly shaken by the experience of it all, bore holes through the ground with stares that reveal a trauma they will be forced to relive with every firework or popped balloon.

Atlas points to the temple overlooking the town.

"We head for that structure."

"It seems the most obvious place to be in this ruined city," Naht says, his expression refusing to show emotion.

"Exactly. Should we control it first, we have a great vantage point for all. Not to mention, your exact line of thinking is what I hope all teams believe and will strive to avoid it. We rest up and develop our strategy."

A shadow shifts in his peripheral vision. Atlas jumps at the sight but realizes no one nor things cast such a shadow. He squints.

"We move out now."

"You help him up. Ilric, sculpt up a walking stick... I don't care that your focus is on weapons of war, just do it," Leda instructs as she helps a woman with injured foot stand. With a wet towel, she pats the head of another member, beads of sweat forming faster than should naturally be possible, as if the water they drank seconds before leaks from their skull. "Anyone have the slightest elemental ability. Ice. We need some ice."

Atlas takes his flask of water in his hands and channels life force through it. The chill kisses his palms, and he passes it to Leda. She blows strands of brown, frizzing hair from her face and shares a quick grin.

"Thank you, Mr. Lurio."

With a long band of fabric, she straps the ice pack on the nape of the man's neck, pressing against his skin to relieve the extreme heat coursing through him. Their march for the temple begins, their pace more similar to a trudge. Atlas and Naht lead, both eyeing the shadows slinking along the walkways after them.

The temple stands tall as a three-story complex, a small courtyard of stone and weathered statues before a set of stone steps leading to unharmed wooden double doors. The metal along the doors is gold, while dull still shining brilliantly in the sun. Marble columns, more than may have been sufficient upon construction but has assisted in holding the temple upright despite the rest of the town decaying to ruins, hoist a fine marble roof above the structure. It was undoubtedly a religious site for the druids. Perhaps the engineering of the build was not all that withstood the trial of time, a deeper strain of magic also at play. Atlas smirks and turns to his team.

"We'll hide within. Jung-lei, Lorena, Naht, we must search for a staircase to the parapet above," Atlas points to the roof. "From there we will conduct our search of the town, with eyes on both the gateway and the floodplains."

Murmuring voices float to his ears from the distance, echoing from marble walls with insufficient pronunciation to make out what is being said. No others reveal in their expressions to have heard anything. However, Naht's expression never reveals anything at all. Their eyes meet and Atlas itches at his ear. Naht delivers a subtle nod.

"Keniph." His general furrows his brow, his glare delivered with a focused eye while the other drifts, reflecting the temple behind him. "Jet. Take Beck and Metmah and secure the perimeter. All others will enter the temple, assist Leda in her care to the injured."

"Can Targe not come with us?" Keniph asks, looking from Beck to Metmah who nod in unison to his suggestion.

"Artoria needs to stay with Leda. Her shield will be the best defense for the larger part of the team should an attack occur."

Keniph sighs and nods his head in understanding.

Atlas marches the steps to the temple, leaving behind the three to investigate the direct area surrounding the structure. Rusty hinges made of a different type of metal creak as the doors swing inward. Light streams in through cracks in the marble ceiling above, reflecting from the dust and debris floating through the air. Rows of wooden benches travel up the sanctuary within, the first ten rows constructed of stone. An altar sits centered down the aisle, its make and style a replica of that which sat in the caldera on Qoterra. From the paths to the furniture, Atlas easily discerned the ancient from their newer counterparts. The druids undoubtedly attempted to repair their temple tirelessly while the remainder of the town fell to ruin, abandoning homes and forming a commune within their temple with those too faithful to leave. The breath was a hum to them, slowly leading them to insanity and their inevitable downfall.

In the corridor lining the main sanctuary, stairs ascend to the upper levels. Atlas beckons the three previously chosen to follow. The stone steps, covered in grains of sand and marble rubble, stand as a proud testament to the resilience of the people once living here. A different air finds Atlas as his head surfaces above the stairwell to a flat portion of roof. It whispers of movement, and not that of his team. Atlas grins.

Naht, Jung-lei, and Lorena march to the banister overlooking the courtyard below. From their vantage point, the entire ruined city sprawls out before them. Atlas marches to the opposite banister, not as interested in what they have already seen, but what they have not. Chunks of marble and walls of sandstone, a material not used within the city they had traversed, are constructed behind. He squints at the structures, their pattern not one of a typical town with roadways. Understanding hits. It's an expansive cemetery.

Movement occurs in his peripheral vision. Atlas tilts his head to look down upon Beck and Metmah. They march about the corner of the temple, attempting to keep their wits about them despite the inexplicable placement of shadows. They make note of the structures and approach a sandstone mausoleum with roof intact. They shelter in its shade while they utilize life force webs to scout the area.

"Atlas," Naht pulls Atlas from his pondering. "Others have arrived since our trek here. I waited until our arrival at this temple to be certain, but you were correct. They have positioned themselves in an area quite far from here."

"Movement! There!" Lorena calls out as she points toward the structure housing the gateway. Naht and Atlas jog to her side.

Naht releases his life force like vines scaling down the marble walls of the temple and through the ground. Atlas sends his life force disguised as particles in the breeze. The intensity of the auras within the structures causes his heart to speed up. Naht, who also senses the power, retracts his life force immediately should their direction be discovered. Their eyes meet.

At that moment, the ground quakes below them. The four step back from the banister, not wishing to fall from such a height. As the tremor settles, Naht's gaze looms toward the tepui. Atlas thinks differently and urgently marches back to his previous position. Beck and Metmah are no longer in the shadow of the mausoleum, but he fails to find their forms amongst the structures. His life force releases in a rush of air and he notes they are no longer on the grounds below. The particles drop to the earth and seep through the arid soils. The particles are met with the life force of those he seeks. Were they buried by the quake? No...

Atlas recalls the particles and absorbs their info. They had not been buried. They found and entered a tunnel system.

"There are tunnels under this temple," Atlas says, cursing that he'd left the map with Keniph. "I don't recall any mention of such a system within this city. That makes everything we do all the more dangerous."

"Do you think any others came across such information in their research?" Jung-lei asks, his hand finding the grip of his dagger at his left side.

"I'm not certain. We must remain vigilant."

Naht does not break his stare from the tepui in the distance, its peak above a thin layer of clouds, unmoving despite the light breeze of the air.

"Can you see it?" Atlas whispers, Jung-lei and Lorena too far to hear his words. "Can you see the staff?"

"No," Naht mumbles in irritation, as if the brief distraction broke a possible chain of information. "It shrouds itself. That fog, it's like a visible aura, to be seen by the unfocused and untrained eye alike. But it fails in hiding, the mist enough to give certainty to its position atop the tepui."

"The druids could have made several artifacts. We've no evidence nor deniability that the staff is the only object created to contain life force."

Atlas's eyes glide from the landmark to the floodplains below, separating the ruins from the tepui. Focused eyes observe the dried wild grasses and crackling land.

"Do you believe the titans still rest there?" Atlas asks, nerves creeping through him as he hesitates to move particles of life force through the floodplains should he waken them.

"Yes," Naht answers without a moment lost. "There is no doubt there are beings there. Note the odd mounds peeking out of what was once a riverbed. Layers of debris may cover them due to a long slumber, but overcoming the weight atop their chests will be mere child's play for a titan."

A screech rings out in the skies above. A shadow briefly casts upon the roof of the temple. The large vultures, webbed flesh where feathers should reside, circle overhead.

"Where did those come from?" Lorena calls out, her voice cracking as fear hits.

"They look like prehistoric condors," Jung-lei says, focusing his eyes to get a better look at the beasts.

"Phantom sand birds," Atlas responds, fists clenching at his sides. "Acute sense of hearing and smell, hence the long beaks and pointed skull, ear bones large and infused to the skull for support and shorter neuron transmission. Carnivores. Hunters. They must have been roosted until our entrance, the quake stirring them from further rest."

One swoops at the rooftop, Atlas sending a swift breeze into its wings to rock its course. The sand bird flaps to return above, preparing for the next attack. Another bird makes its attempt. Jung-lei rubs his hands together and as he pulls apart sends a small missile of life force at the creature. It squeals and returns to the skies.

After a minute, their circle shifts away from the four on the rooftop. Atlas believes it must see his men below. But as he leans over the banister, Atlas sees no one. He peeks down the stairwell opening and notices Keniph is within the sanctuary assisting Leda. Beck and Metmah are not present.

Atlas focuses his life force into small bubbles, forcing them through the soil and into the tunnels, traveling until hitting an aura and then commanded to return. Several bubbles find Atlas with information of the whereabouts of Metmah, another coming a short time later with that presence of Beck. And then, with a jolt of shock, another aura is revealed to him.

A quake trembles the earth once more. Caught off guard, Atlas, Lorena, and Jung-lei fall to the ground. Naht slides out his stance to better hold his own. A screech rings as the sand bird finds their opening and swoop down. A taloned foot latches about Lorena's arm, dragging her across the roof. Atlas shoots a concentrated gust of air, ripping a hole through the flesh webbing of the wing. Its unable to lift her weight with the injury. Jung-lei performs a kip-up and sprints for Lorena. The creature, intimidated by the move, releases her and takes off.

Lorena whimpers and clutches a hand to her arm. Her eyes blink in sporadic movements, eyelids undeciding and unable to commit to being fully opened or fully closed. Her whimpers gain greater fervor as beads of sweat form on her face. She releases her bleeding arm and swats at imaginary beings that supposedly exist in front of her.

"What's going on?" Jung-lei asks, placing his hands on Lorena's shoulders and dodging her hits. She does not acknowledge his existence nor his words.

"Their talons are venomous. More than likely a countermeasure to especially strong prey. The hallucinations must tire one before their exhaustion makes them unable to fight the beast," Atlas says, brushing bits of marble dust from his clothes. "Get her to Leda immediately. If the venom spreads too far it may cause irreparable damage."

Jung-lei attempts to lift Lorena but she struggles against his touch. He sighs and binds her hands with life force, throwing her over his shoulders before descending the stairs.

Atlas and Naht glance at one another, Atlas furrowing his brow.

"You know something. What is it?" Atlas questions, closing the distance. Naht doesn't react, his expression blank.

"You already know. You are stronger than I, Atlas Lurio," Naht says.

"Know what?"

"Beck and Metmah are not coming back. Another has found the tunnels."

"Yes, but who? That aura, it was not Tanten Flynn."

"I am a manipulator. My life force works best at close range. I'm afraid I cannot satisfy your curiosity."

Atlas licks the corner of his mouth and peers out at the ruined city. He notices debris kick into the air, forming an isolated sandstorm about a structure in the distance. Atlas steps nearer the banister and leans over the marble. A swarm of shadows gather at the base of the temple. They take the form of creatures as they rise from the ground, shaped as three-dimensional beings in the air. Several shrieks ring out below.

Atlas darts for the stairwell but freezes as his eyes find Naht. The assassin stares with tilted head at the mausoleum. The focus in his eyes shines with expression his face had not yet betrayed, nonverbal communication. Telepathic communication. Another shriek.

"Come, Naht. We will need to leave this place at once."

Naht nods and follows Atlas down the stairwell, silence filling the space around him for the remainder of their time at the temple.

Chapter Fourteen

Tanten rubs his hand across his face, feeling the grime and sweat to meet his palm. His mind swirls in a relentless fog, the ringing of his ears from the explosives not helping with a search for clarity. Reece presses his open hands to the earth, not typically one to utilize sensory life force in such a way for sensitivity, but also unable to focus his hearing for the events to have passed not long before. The technomancer breathes heavily as he fights to identify their numbers, despite the temple not being far from where they hide. His concealment slips slightly as he emits a pulse of life force in all directions. Reece's vision blurs and he retracts his life force, leaning against the marble wall for a rest. Shadows move along the stone path, passing the building with their focus on what lies ahead.

"I wonder what killed them," Reece says as a shadowy figure manifests outside the doorway. "Debris from the quake? Illness? Those dinosaur birds flying overhead? Or a person perhaps?"

Tanten licks his lips and tilts his head back. He sits on the dusty ground, trying to sort through his thoughts, Reece's annoying worries adding to the ringing in his ears. Screams had rung out, the creatures were waking, or rather the realm itself was waking. Tanten squints about, every grain of sand that moves in the breeze a possible sign of something drawing near.

"Perhaps no more than a lingering injury from the explosions finally taking another," Tanten replies, deciding to cooperate with Reece rather than feud with his only ally.

The slideshow from the mine blasts plays again and again in his mind. They buried the mines before approaching the altar, understanding another team not to be far behind. It was lucky they had thought to bring such technology, as the field of the altar created an almost insurmountable friction to conjuring anything with life force. Thunderous bangs and clouds of dirt filled the air. At that moment, lightning struck with a blinding light and the portal formed as if a dagger had sliced through the air to wound it. Spectral and celestial all at once, it sang and called to Tanten Flynn, an invitation to enter. An invitation to the chance of obtaining the staff for himself.

"If Atlas believed others to be nearby, he would evacuate the team immediately to a more open space. Surrounding oneself with walls on all sides is a great defense but a poor offense should any tactics or strategies need employed. My assumption is this defense was meant to allow them the chance to rejuvenate as best one can in this realm before marching to the floodplains."

"It's just... I thought I felt..." Reece's words drag and turn to no more than a whisper. His aura slightly trembles as life force dances on his fingertips for his fears. "There were mentions of otherworldly diseases in the journal... You don't suppose we've been infected?"

"No, and shut your mouth for a moment," Tanten orders.

Rested and ready to follow the alluring voice of the staff once more, Tanten releases small orbs of life force into the ground. Focusing on their concealment, Tanten commands the orbs to scout the surrounding area. While he waits for their return, he continues brainstorming.

"Being down a few members, do you think Atlas will lead his men into the floodplains any time soon?"

Reece's eyes widen. He hesitates with a response, not wishing to displease Tanten with what may be taken as a wrong answer. "Uhh... I'm not sure."

"The question was a matter of opinion. A theory," Tanten crossly responds.

"Oh. Uh..." Reece finds difficulty in swallowing, delaying his answer to Tanten even more. Beads of sweat form on his brow as his trembling hand reaches up to wipe them away. He doesn't want Tanten to regret forming an alliance with him or, greater yet, regret choosing him to be his disciple.

"Never mind," Tanten mumbles as the orbs return to him.

Tanten closes his eyes and digests the information learned by his life force. His life force orbs successfully located two identifiable teams, Atlas and Syrenne being the leads. A strange phenomenon occurred in a different direction, a barrier blocking his orbs from seeking entrance to a building they attempted to scout. Atlas and his team are still within the temple, though Reece could have told him that much seeing as they believe they've discovered all entrances and exits to and from the premises. Syrenne and the remainder of the team are to the southwest, hiding in a small house much like the one Tanten and Reece seek refuge in.

"We need a team to reach the floodplains to lure the titans out of hiding. If they're preoccupied with another team, reaching the staff should be less of a problem. The truly difficult task is ensuring the teams do not start the war within this city. If that's the case, we may never reach the staff." Tanten stares at the floor as if the images in his head vividly display themselves.

Reece examines Tanten's aura, which appears the opposite of the state his own aura takes. Since they entered the portal, perhaps earlier, an overwhelming anxiety fights within Reece. The droning hums and distant echoes of bodiless voices send his senses into overdrive. His abilities always worked well to identify origins of shifts in the natural fields of the world. Within this realm, a presence exists and disrupts the space around them in ways he cannot describe. The only explanation he lands on is the Theory of

Simulation to be far more real than leading scientific Scholars deemed capable.

Reece sighs in resignation, understanding his abilities to be useless to his teacher, the Professional to lead him to this realm for no reason other than trust. Undoubtedly Tanten Flynn, one of the greatest life force users in the world, would have attempted this alone should he think of none capable of assisting him. But not only did Reece get invited to join the team, he was also the one to withstand the great betrayal they committed on Qoterra, Tanten trusting him to keep the secret of their departure from the team days before. And even now, the Professional shows no signs of slowing down. Tanten's aura is calm and composed, as if nothing out of the normal occurs, the tranquil flame of a candle on a cloudless night.

Tanten, uncaring but entirely aware of Reece's observation of him, quietly mumbles to himself to the point Reece no longer tries to understand. Reece reserves his energy and focus on his first duty: keeping lookout. Reece returns his attention to the outside world, but it's not long before he is recalled once more. Tanten snaps his finger as one does when faced with a brilliant idea. Reece turns to him and, to his surprise, he sees a brimming smile on Tanten's face.

"We'll simply kill Syrenne and her team before they run into Atlas," Tanten states, as if the plan is infallible. As if there is no way he and Reece could lose. Reece's eyes widen in horror of the suggestion, almost believing Tanten may be intoxicated from the ashy air.

"Mr. Flynn?"

"Yes?"

"May I ask how two people simply kill nine?" Reece locks eyes with Tanten, a concern rising in him.

Reece wipes his brow and notices the shadow beasts no longer move in the streets. Odd placements of shade where the sun should not have it cast are motionless.

"So quickly they consume the dead?" Reece questions, a chill coursing up his spine.

"This realm is odd, surely, but there is no saying whether the absence of death in this current moment is supernatural or not. We should move before they wake again," his words ringing with the tune of suggestion with room to counter should Reece not have already understood his position.

Tanten rubs his hands together, expressing his excitement of the upcoming battle, life force waking in every pore on his body.

"And as to your concern with numbers," he continues, a furrowed brow expressing his disappointment of the young man's doubt, "I believe the element of surprise is on our side."

Tanten Flynn confidently strides from the building, no hesitation in passing through the doorframe without further probing with chance of detecting another. Reece suppresses a gasp, despite knowing should an attack occur immediately he would be to blame for failing as lookout. A burst of flaming aura erupts about Tanten as he expands a life force detection ring, sending out sensors in all possible directions. None are near, and none follow their movements via their own channels. At least for the time being.

Weaving through the ruins of the abandoned city, Tanten stalks his prey with speed and efficiency. His movements are silent, and he focuses on his life force scouting as a reliable indication of where each step should be placed. Reece follows his footsteps carefully, not wanting to be the reason they get caught. Tanten scowls as he feels the shadows watch him, hoping their slight shifting does not give hints to Syrenne and her team.

Tanten pauses and cracks his neck. His left hand fidgets at his side, his fingers tapping against themselves. A distant voice echoes through the walls and finds their position. It had bounced from so many walls to find them in what was little more than a whisper, indistinguishable to Tanten but all too clear to his disciple. Tanten uses a single hand to sign to Reece. From his peripheral vision, Tanten watches as Reece signs the letters: B-Y-S-C-I-W. Tanten shakes his head, a frustrated grin cracking his level expression, before continuing forward.

Tanten slides up behind a marble wall, the only left of the building it once helped to form, the others having since crumbled. He places a hand on the cool marble, coated with layers of dust and sand, and probes about them for the presence of others. Bysciw and team are near to where Tanten and Reece departed from not long before, a position near the temple fitting for the man who undoubtedly wished to be the center of the world's devotion, drawn to the most magnificent building in the town. Unfortunately, or perhaps not, Atlas and team are no longer there. Tanten fails to find them.

Reece stares at the wall but does not need his life force to detect those nearest. He hears their footsteps, their whispers, their breathing. Syrenne and the other eight are no more than thirty meters away. Being so near, as if able to reach out and grab one by the shoulders, Reece trembles. That which he deemed as once probable was now inevitable.

Tanten opens his eyes as he recalls his life force probes. His hand does not move from the wall, rather he rubs his palm against the marble, bits of debris falling away. Tanten pushes on the surface, exerting a light pressure. His life force does the rest of the work, slowly cracking the wall into several pieces and carefully ensuring the process occurs quietly. He masks the wall in his life force, holding it together despite being broken into multiple pieces. Tanten pokes his head around the broken stone division and stares at the building the opposing team hides in.

"We need a lure," Tanten says, his eyes not leaving the building.

He slowly creeps toward the house. Reece pursues but senses a strange presence approaching behind him. Turning slowly to face it, his eyes widen. Tanten, unbeknownst to the presence, focuses on not being noticed by those in the house. He starts to project his life force, creating a glowing spike with the intention of blasting through the entrance as a surprise while he enters through a carved-out window at the side of the structure. As the spike takes shape, Tanten hears a scream from Reece.

"Mr. Flynn! They know!" Reece yells.

As Tanten turns, he sees a large, transparent blue golem with a club. The golem swings at Reece, but not quick enough to land a blow. Reece rolls out of the way and Tanten sends his spike toward the front door of the house. The team members about to run out the door must quickly dodge to avoid the spike. Unfortunately for them, Tanten freezes the spike at the entrance and initiates a detonation which creates a barrier of marble with the explosion of the life force. The exit Syrenne's team were planning on using is now blocked.

The golem glimpses Tanten and, realizing the threat, rushes him. Reece, instincts beating out his fear, holds up his hands in the direction of the golem and opens his mouth. No sound can be heard by those on the outside, for the frequency exceeds a human's hearing threshold. The golem freezes in place, the high velocity sound waves increasing the thermal energy within the golem. Reece keeps the waves extremely compact and focuses his power with the thought of saving Tanten, the only motivation he needs.

As the golem disintegrates before his eyes, Tanten's instincts force him to the ground, as a waltz of swords flies at him. The sabers disappear where they would have intersected his body and the life force returns to the caster, giving away their position. Tanten points his right arm in the direction of the caster and launches a life force projectile. It curves around the corner and Tanten hears the death cry of a young woman. His eyes widen as he feels the deadly presence of someone behind him.

He turns to see a man with a broadsword preparing for a strike. Responding to the threat of the sword, Tanten uses the life force containing the marble wall to pull the pieces rapidly toward their location, the elasticity of his life force accelerating the marble fragments. The first fragments to reach the swordsman force him to the ground. Tanten rolls out of the way and, getting to his feet, launches a spiked life force projectile through the man's skull. Tanten grabs hold of the broadsword, which is heavier than he first expected, and charges toward the back of the building where there seems to be an exit.

Reece joins Tanten, hoping to accompany him in destroying Syrenne's team. Tanten commands the remaining marble wall pieces in his control to smash into the back wall, giving them the opportunity to turn the corner before enabling their attack. Reece places his hand on a marble wall and uses his life force to compress the building. The wall he touches slams into the wall opposite, crushing the two people who were still within the shelter.

The dust in the air provides an opaque screen, vision not useful for a few seconds. Fortunately, magistrates can easily cope with the loss of one sense. Reece relies on his hearing, unlike Tanten and Syrenne who rely on gut instinct to win the battle. Reece hears two members leap from the pile of rubble caused from the parts of the wall being directed at them.

"Reece!" Tanten yells and tosses the broadsword in Reece's direction. Reece grabs hold of the sword and, using his life force to manage the sword's weight, pushes off the ground and slices through the air, the two bodies falling to the ground beside him. He feels one body hit his leg as it falls which is enough to put him off balance. As he drops to the ground, the first second is used to center himself.

An enemy, realizing the opening, lunges for Reece with a conjured falchion. Tanten points the index and middle fingers of his right hand at the member and a small, but tightly concentrated, life force projectile shoots through the chest of the member. Reece gasps as the body falls in front of him, the blade scraping his right arm as it falls.

In his peripheral vision, the glitter of sun bouncing from blonde hair meets him. Tanten leaps toward Syrenne, but his eyes widen as the figure he thought was her disappears. His head spins in all directions, understanding he fell into their trap. As he hears the step behind him, he catches a glimpse of a smiling face. The person, only using one arm for the other arm is heavily bandaged, raises her hand to the sky as if to call an elemental power to finish him off.

"Mr. Flynn!" Reece, his fear exceeding Tanten's own, utilizes every ounce of his life force to bolt himself forward. The pulse he causes pushes the woman back, knocking her out of her center of gravity, however his efforts were futile. Tanten watches a knife fly past, so near to him that the air it severs brushes a strand of black hair from his face. Reece knows his fate before it hits him.

The knife cuts through his neck, filling his windpipes with blood. The technomancer quakes as his body hits the ground, gargling noises leaving despite his attempts to silence himself. Streams of blood flow from his mouth and pool beneath him, a few salty tears mixing with it. His eyes water as his memory of life, of what life was and will cease to be, flashes before him.

He repaid Tanten Flynn with the only thing more valuable than any magical artifact they could retrieve in this realm. He repaid with his own life, what he believes the highest bid. For Tanten trusted in him, believed in him, from the beginning. The look in Tanten's eyes when asking for him to become his disciple made all the difference. The truth was evident. Tanten, a man who portrays himself as cool and uncaring, took him in, a young novice who felt his own life was worthless. But Tanten saw potential, and that was all Reece needed to gain confidence and trust in himself. But who now would take his place? Tanten Flynn, a true savior, will be left alone with the world against him. A world that will never see Tanten as Reece did. Perhaps that was Reece's only regret: not helping Tanten achieve the recognition and praise he deserved.

The sun shines down with full intensity, the strongest rays seemingly finding them.

"Even these skies have found their light in the end," Reece thinks as he feels Death coming to greet him. Blurry vision finds Tanten, unable to make out an expression. "Hopefully, they'll be able to experience the light for a while... just like me..."

As he lay there, his final breath leaving him, his eyes remain open, hoping to keep watch over Tanten until the end.

The background sights and sounds fade away as Tanten watches Reece fall. A numbing chill overcomes him. A strange sensation with the effect of consuming all feeling and emotion courses through his body. His aura flares like a fueled conflagration, full of rage and hate toward the one causing him pain. His life force, mimicking his aura, explodes in a fury.

"Syrenne!" he screams at the top of his lungs. The explosion of his aggression sends a mix of dust and rubble into the air, masking his vision, though his vision is already blurry. Dragging his hand across his eyes, he feels moisture, muddying the dust and dirt layering on his skin. Dark shadows fill the space around him, and they rise out of the ground and sculpt themselves into mobile creatures.

As the haze clears, Tanten fails to find any sign of Syrenne or Yasmine. Rational thought says he could use his life force to track them down and finish them off. And yet the emotion that grips him refuses to listen to anything rational. Rather, the first thought to pass that he acts on is racing to beat the shadow beasts to Reece's body.

Tanten flips Reece to his back and removes the knife from his neck. A trembling hand hovers over his disciple to stop the blood flowing from him, as his hair was already matted with the red liquid, which also paints his face and clothes. His hovering hand lowers to the boy's chest, hoping to feel what has long since stopped. A shaky exhale leaves Tanten, silence overpowering his thoughts.

Tanten picks Reece's head from the soil and cradles it in his palms. He trembles, his calm and cool composure gone, not even salvageable in this savage environment. Tanten wishes to escape into his imagination, change the reality he's set in, but he can't. His mind only focuses on the scene before him. Though it may be gruesome, it was the reality he wished for... the reality he was excited for. What does he regret? That his wish didn't go exactly as planned? Or that his overconfidence may have killed his only ally? After all, Reece was right. Being two to nine, they were at a major disadvantage, yet Tanten dismissed the thought due to his own arrogance.

The shadows loom closer to Reece's body. Tanten closes his eyes, unsure of what he wants. The answer calls to him out of the darkness, a mystical sound that resonates a powerful energy. Hitting him the moment he asked the question, the moment he felt a semblance of regret for traveling to the dimension. The image of the true prize displays itself to him. A grin spreads across his face.

"The staff," he states, his foggy mind growing clear. "The staff... My mission is the staff. It's all I care for... all I need." His love for the object turns to obsession, the traumatic scene molding his thoughts. The power corrupting his ill intentions further. An act of revenge would be the minimal penalty from Tanten the executioner. With the staff in his power, he can not only kill those who have harmed him in any way, but... he may be able to save a life.

The shadows pull at Reece's feet, attempting to pry the body away from Tanten. Tanten rubs his hand over Reece's head one last time, his hand dyed red from the blood, the drying liquid painted over with a fresh layer.

"For victory," Tanten whispers. He uses his fingers to close Reece's eyelids, so he does not have to witness the horror of his body being devoured in the afterlife. The shadows tug harder, their hunger never properly satiated despite the number of corpses.

Tanten places Reece's head on the ground and stands. Backing away from the corpse, the shadow creatures attack. Tanten extends his right arm and chants a prayer for Reece. A spiral of flames rises into the air and ignites the body. As the body burns, Tanten calmly walks toward the floodplains.

The silent streets allow him to compose his thoughts. Thoughts of the staff, the other teams in the surrounding area, and how he should go about reaching the altar circle in his head. A different reality to the one he was set in a moment ago. All thoughts of the battle seem to have vanished, as if he no longer remembers. As if he forced himself to forget.

Tanten eyes a marble house nearby and chooses a rest for his life force to be the best tactic for the time being. Before approaching, he gazes up at Praecantatis Tepui in the distance, at its peak rests the altar and staff.

"Only for victory," Tanten mumbles.

His stride reveals his confidence as he continues for the structure. He marches the once unfamiliar street as if he's lived in the ruined city his whole life. His aura retakes the shape of a tranquil flame, and his heart sets the pace of its flicker. Images of Bysciw, Atlas, Syrenne, Botalia, and any who have denied him his due praise, slowly burn in the fire in his mind.

"I will not fail."

Chapter Fifteen

L oud bangs and screams ring out in the distance. A swarm of dust rises from the ground, and, upon further examination, a strange glow tints the horizon. The shadows around them race toward the position of the conflict, the absence of nonsensical shadows and ever watchful eyes lessening the anxiety brought on by the environment. The sky grows darker the longer the teams linger within the town. Botalia bites her lip, hoping the realm isn't preparing an attack of its own.

Merwyn leads the way as the team zigzags between the ruined buildings. As they near the floodplains, a grimace finds the Professional's expression. The structures in these parts contain only a fraction of their walls, and the cracks expose a weakness that refutes any argument for a safe place to hold defenses until further notice. In this part of the city, eyes would easily spot one from many sides. Merwyn observes the piles of rubble and stones lining the ground, wondering if with life force he could construct a building in which they could hide. However, such a sight would most definitely catch the attention of any surveying the area, as if finding a house untouched in the middle of a tornado's path. They must settle for hope, that those around these parts have their eyes on one thing and one thing alone: the staff.

Botalia, picking at her fingers as they walk, pauses in awe as she gazes down the road. No structure nor wall obstructs the path leading to the temple, its size and magnificence all the grander than she presumed from their distance earlier. She had not often laid eyes on religious buildings, her parents never being fond of acknowledging some omniscient, omnipotent beings who were worthy of more respect simply for "existing," but she could not deny the majesty of the marble structure and the care with which it was crafted. And it was by some odd power indeed that the largest structure within the town was also the one left most intact.

A bolt of life force leaves her like a lightning strike, her curiosity growing. Her life force shoots through the temple and bursts into tiny roots scouting the grounds. Botalia senses no presences. She bites her lip and catches her relieved exhale before it leaves. It was a mercy that no team stood atop and took note of their position, luck indeed. However, if the team was no longer there, where could they be?

"In here," Merwyn whispers, beckoning the distracted Botalia into a nearby structure. She twists her head, realizing she was the only one left on the road, and sprints indoors.

She assumes the building chosen was once a workshop. Many slabs line the ground by the walls and even separate walkways within. Weathered walls are supported by the stone workbenches, holding them upright despite any strong winds to sweep through the lands. Botalia dusts off a spot on a slab with a gust of life force and takes a seat.

"Botalia, scout the surrounding areas for teams and let us know what you find," Cefni says. He removes a handkerchief from his pocket and wipes the sweat from his brow. Sweeping his hand through the air, he condenses any moisture lingering there and wets the kerchief before wiping again. Pale marble debris sprinkles the stubble on his jaw, falling to the ground as he itches away at the irritation. A frustration reverberates through his aura, as if impatience surpasses anxiety. Botalia stares at him in silence.

Cefni meets her expression and drops his tensed shoulders with an audible exhale.

"Apologies for being so brash," Cefni lowers his voice and tries again. "Could you please assist with locating the other teams? Merwyn and I are going to plan our defenses and our way forward."

"Yes, I can do that," Botalia says, averting her eyes from Cefni. Her sights sweep past Koepp and Nix, lingering there too long for their own good. A tear slides down Koepp's cheek, his lip revealing a slight quiver before he wipes at his face with his dirty shirt. Nix avoids gazing upon his friend to save him the shame and embarrassment he himself would feel to lose control of such weak emotions. Guilt hits Botalia with an intense pang in her chest. The ground seemingly sways beneath her, but she knows it's no more than her frail body's doing rather than the actual earth waking.

Her palms rub together, and she splits them apart as she folds her legs to the ground. As she pulls her hands apart, the web of life force clings between them. The strings dart through the soil the moment her skin touches the cold stone. Immediately her life force finds the residue of a battle, markings of life force usage splattering the walls and the ground, particles of life force still floating in the air, insufficient in quantity to manifest, despite the realm's wishes. A singular presence is not far from the site, a raging aura with not the least bit of concealment. Tanten's flames are no stranger to Botalia, his wrath all too infamous and prevalent. But he is alone. No longer does another accompany him. Lost to the battle?

A chill courses up Botalia's spine. She scrunches her nose in discomfort and follows her life force in a different direction. It travels towards the floodplains, a powerful presence dimming with every attempt to control a level field that matches the realm. Atlas's group, undoubtedly, with greater distraction and anxiety than prior, move forward.

Another group still lingers back, not having moved far from the portal since their arrival. Perhaps they focus on being defensive and taking every precaution over a rush to the staff? Or perhaps they realize they've already got a checkmate, simply waiting for the opponent's next move. This thought fills Botalia's mind with the most awful of images. She's seen many cruel and unfortunate sights through the memories of others and her own past. She will never cease to hesitate when the opponent is a competent life force wielder. And, with ever growing knowledge of how incredibly life force can be utilized, fear constantly consumes her since removed from her isolation.

And yet, of all the presences, Botalia fails to find the one she most seeks.

"Where is he?" she mumbles, frantically scouring every surveying life force line with hopes to sense even just a hint of his aura.

"Where is who?" Cefni asks, concern and urgency lacing his tone. "Are you unable to locate Tanten?"

Botalia hadn't realized the volume of her plea. She stumbles.

"Oh, uh, I found Tanten. But he is alone. His partner, whoever that may have been, is no longer with him."

Cefni scoffs and shakes his head.

"No doubt Tanten initiated that fight we just heard. It doesn't matter how weak the opponent, two people taking on a team is bound to not turn out well. The numbers game is just as valid, even if the scales seemed tipped toward power."

"Assuming he is alone, Tanten may no longer be our greatest threat. I assume Atlas's team has pushed ever closer to the floodplains. I sensed the temple to be empty of any presences, and we assumed previously his to be the team there, yes or no?" Merwyn asks.

"Yeah," Botalia nods, her word leaving with her breath. "They've pushed forward. But something is very visibly affecting them. Whoever fights to conceal their presences, or should I say blend their auras into that of this realm, is struggling due to the team's own inability to control their individual auras. It's not confidence or anger, it's fear."

"Interesting," Merwyn taps a finger to his cheek. "Atlas always prefers scouts to soldiers. They may be cohesive and strong as a team in any sort of bonding exercise, but a military force they surely are not."

"He just breaks raw potential, that's what he does," Cefni pokes his head through the doorway before sheltering back inside. "Lurio has never changed. Train people to be as powerful as they can, then shatter them so they'll never achieve greatness. Can't say Flynn's much better."

Botalia glances at Koepp, who plays with a marble pebble with the tip of his boot. Eyes droop as a hopeless frown covers his face. *Tanten wouldn't know potential if it slapped him across the face.* Botalia thinks.

"Gyah!" Nix screams and swats a spider from his jacket, using a life force projectile to squash it against a stone slab. "Stupid spiders. They're everywhere."

Pulled from their thoughts, Botalia, Cefni, and Merwyn look about them, jaws dropping in tandem as they hadn't realized the number of creatures crawling about the workshop. The spiders scale the walls, racing across the floor and through every visible crack, as well as some spaces seemingly too tight a fit.

Botalia bends over and cups a palm as she scoops a few spiders into it. She observes the creatures up close, the strange sensation of their furry legs running about her skin causing a slight tingle to reverberate up her arm.

"These aren't arachnids," Botalia murmurs, focusing her eyes. "They're arthropods. Look." She shoves her hand by Cefni who jumps back in disgust of the creatures. "They don't have eight legs. They have hundreds of them. And a bunch of little antennae sprouting from their head. Ouch!"

She shakes her hand and drops the creatures to the ground. One of the feelers had poked through her palm, a small droplet of blood filling the hole it had made. A slight dizziness overtakes her, but Botalia quickly shakes it.

"Venom," she whispers. She pushes the contaminant from her blood with her life force, a procedure she'd done countless times with her experiments. "Undoubtedly that would paralyze a much smaller creature. But what in this realm could they possibly eat that's so small? I haven't seen nor sensed any creature of such a size..."

Shuffling steps occur outside their building, the sound of an army tiptoeing ever nearer.

Every eye in the workshop widens at the sudden realization they'd been snuck up on. A surprise attack.

Cefni silences his steps with life force and marches to the wall nearest the origin of the sound. He places his palm on the marble and releases a quick pulse. Bangs sound violently as a rainstorm of rocks hit the opposite side of the wall, Cefni attracting them there as an attempt to incapacitate their opponents. But no human screams cry out. Rather a vicious roar with the echo of a hiss fills the air. Fear sweeps over them.

"Follow me!" Cefni screams and races out the door.

They exit the workshop in a rush, heading down the road away from whatever creature lurked outside. Curiosity gets the better of every member as they turn back to the origin of the awful cries. The dust parts and a gargantuan creature with thousands of legs and tentacle-like antennae lunges from behind the wall where it had been attacked.

"It doesn't look hurt," Nix says as they run. "It looks pissed."

The creature sprints after them, its speed far exceeding what their exhausted forms could achieve.

"We have to fight it!" Botalia yells, life force swimming to her hands. "It's too fast. It's going to catch us!"

"I've got a plan," Cefni mutters through parted breaths, visibly tired and sore.

He leads the way, and they weave through the ruins. Twisting around walls, jumping through windows and doors of weathered structures, ducking and diving under piled debris and fallen archways. Yet they fail to quiet their panting and silence their footsteps as their energy drains. They manage to find their way back to the main road and accelerate as the temple comes into view.

Their pace slows to a jog, curious eyes turning back to judge their distance from the creature. Botalia, at the back of the group, pauses, listening intently for where it may be. A loud crash occurs, and a gust of dried soil rises into the air as another wall falls, knocked over by the force of the creature locating them.

Botalia stretches out her arms and sends her life force like webs to attach to walls on either side of the road. As the creature approaches, she rubberbands her life force and the walls break from the ground and smash in the center of the road, sandwiching the creature between them. The others freeze to witness the sight, wondering whether she'd done it. A struggling movement is heard through the cloud of dust and debris, another roar fading into a wail. Cefni directs a hand at the haze and mutters. A field encapsulates the dust and a fire erupts within. No smoke nor cries find their way from the sphere.

As his life force fades away, the fire extinguishing with lack of fuel to keep it burning and a swift breeze, a crisp charcoal mass reveals itself below the broken rubble.

"That couldn't have been the only one," Cefni states, wiping his brow. "We've got to keep moving. We head for the temple. Whether stupid or not, it's the only building with protection from all sides. Let's go."

With a quickened pace to their walk, the team march for the temple, sore, shaken, and riddled with anxiety of what lays behind every corner in this town.

When they arrive, the magnificent size and state of the temple magnifies within their minds. The marble columns leading to an intact roof with its semi-weathered, decorative architectural parapets above lends a vision to all that this city once was. The sand and dried soil about the cobblestone has been disturbed by many footsteps, an obvious sign another team had already been there. Koepp traces the footprints with his eyes, counting how many unique ones reveal themselves. As the number grows, his eyes lose their light.

"We'll shelter here until we've rested a bit," Cefni says, chugging from his water sack, an audible note of satisfaction releasing after the hydrating drink. "But, as always, we need to ensure the perimeter is safe before we corner ourselves within. I'll check the back. Merwyn, Botalia, check the inside and roof. We don't need any more surprises."

Botalia and Merwyn nod. Cefni rubs at his arms, itching the grimy debris from the hairs, and scans the horizon in the direction of the tepui. His eyes grow solemn.

"We're almost there. We're almost to the end."

His words are met with silence. Not that a response doesn't fill every single one of his team members' minds, but they are too exhausted to speak aloud every intruding thought the image of 'the end' should bring. Cefni sighs. He removes his revolver from its holster and holds it close as he sneaks about the side of the temple.

The remaining team stand in the courtyard for several moments, observing the weathered statues about them, occasional glances peering at the doors leading into the sanctuary, worried at any moment they may open to reveal a team.

Koepp trudges to the stone steps and takes a seat, eyes locking in on a weathered marble limb broken from one of the statues. Nix notices a metal button on the ground, undoubtedly from any group who had walked there before them. He kicks it across the stone and the metallic ping rings as it collides with the marble base of a statue.

"This is so stupid," he mutters, anger and frustration seething through his barred teeth. "That thing almost killed us and we're just gonna keep moving forward like nothing happened."

"Nix," Botalia starts in a soothing tone, but her words fail to stop his rant.

"And now we're in the most obvious place in the city. Assassin 101, try to blend into the environment. Right now, we're basically calling more danger to ourselves."

"Nix..."

"And sure enough..." Nix grunts as he clenches his fists. "They're already coming."

Botalia and Merwyn exchange glances, each with a subtle nod to confirm that the ex-assassin's senses had not deceived him. Botalia fought to hide her worry, surely Merwyn doing the same as he pondered what their next move would be. And surely Nix had felt the presence behind the temple as well. They are surrounded.

"Mr. Kufuta, your abilities are very impressive for such a young life force wielder," Merwyn says, his tone low and level. "Please, do your best to assist Botalia in anything she may need, and the young master Flynn, of course."

"What do you mean?" Botalia asks, furrowing her brow. "You can't possibly..."

Merwyn closes his eyes and lowers his head. With a pulse of his life force, the doors to the temple fly open.

"Go. Hide within. I will keep guard out here."

The small team composed of eight men and a manifested creature round the corner of one of the buildings. Their eyes burn intensely, casting away their fears and replacing it with the hate of those they will challenge. Those who recognize Merwyn Giacobbe, the famed Professional and long time Council Member of the Magistrate Association, clench their jaws, rage and excitement escalating at getting the chance to take down one so worthy.

"Go."

"But..."

Botalia's feet slide across the stone as Merwyn's life force pushes her back. He no longer faces her but their adversaries. The strong force persists, Botalia not wishing to disrespect him by overcoming it, but also not wishing Merwyn to take on the crew alone.

"Merwyn, that's not all of them. The team was much larger," Botalia forces a resisting step through his force. "Something is not right."

"Go!" Merwyn commands with a deep voice, the strength of his life force thrusting Botalia back.

She balances herself before turning and grabbing both Nix and Koepp by the arm and pulling them up the stairs. Nix bats her hand away, biting his bottom lip while life force rushes to his fists. He races past them and scans the sanctuary for any signs of life before turning and beckoning them forward.

When they arrive at the doors, Botalia turns in time to block a life force arrow aimed directly for her. The shield catches it no more than a meter from her chest. The arrow dissolves.

"Get inside. Get inside," Botalia mutters as she forces Koepp through and thrusts the doors shut.

She utilizes her life force to lock and secure them, her eyes quickly searching for any other entrances the enemy could utilize.

Nix also races about, checking under every bench and lighting every shadow filled corner to ensure they are truly alone. He groans as he notices fresh puddles of blood on the ground near the stairs leading to the rooftop.

Koepp trembles and sits on a bench, terror lacing his expression. As Botalia and Nix regroup near him, Koepp lets out an unexpected whimper.

"Nix... Botalia... When the battle starts, don't worry about me."

"Shut up," Nix mumbles. He closes his eyes and puts his hands into his pockets. Botalia's jaw drops as if to say something, but all words escape her.

"I don't want-"

"Just shut up!" Nix yells. He turns his face away from Koepp and Botalia. His body shakes. Koepp looks to the ceiling, light catching the tears he prevents from streaming down his face. Botalia folds her hands and takes a deep breath.

"Everything will be okay," she whispers, as unsure of the words she speaks as they are. "We'll be okay."

Bangs and thuds continue outside the door. Screams and indistinguishable shouts fill the air. It is no more than a torturous lullaby to those inside, awaiting the result.

Chapter Sixteen

Botalia, Koepp, and Nix sit in silence, each with their own haunting thoughts as to what the future holds. Grunts, shouts, and explosions occur on the other side of the door, no more than five meters from where they sit. Botalia wishes to surround herself in a shield of life force, blocking out the sounds that penetrate her aura and send a chill of fear through her. She glances at the boys. Expressions of resignation rest on their faces, as if they no longer possess the energy for fear. Yet, Nix's aura swirls with the wrath of a monsoon, prepared to destroy any and all things in his path. Botalia is certain this is what the assassin was taught. When in times of ultimate danger, surrender is forbidden. One must fight until their last breath, fight for their right to survive. If they cannot manage victory, death is the only acceptable outcome.

But... Nix is not an assassin. Despite years of attempting to chain him to the code, the ties easily snapped when faced with choices he could not be so certain of. Not even his siblings forfeited their lives when they understood Botalia could not be defeated despite their mission. The great Kufutas were not all monsters. There was still part human in them yet. Just like her. Just like their enemies.

"They're just human," Botalia whispers, life force springing forward to her fingertips. "We can win this. We just need to find the others."

Botalia places her hands on the ground and focuses her mind. The varied array of life force utilization occurring on the other side of the door acts as a magnet to her life force, pulling its attention.

No doubt this team's intention. Her fingers press firmly against the stone, and she fights to defy the magnetic pull. Her life force splits away to the corner of the temple. Presences linger there, so subtle they mesh with the life force of the realm. They learned the secret. But the blob is large, greater than just one or two individuals occupy that space.

"But they can't be in the wall... They must be..."

Her eyes widen. Before she can say anything, a loud thump shakes the large doors behind them. Botalia leaps to her feet. Koepp and Nix stare at the doors, fists clenching as they prepare.

"Not there," Botalia says, back to the doors. "They're trying to pull our attention. It's a-"

Her life force senses a sharp vibration from the marble wall in the corner of the temple. Botalia throws out her arms and creates a barrier of life force as the explosion occurs. Pieces of the marble wall fly in all directions, the dust and debris filling the air. Botalia shields Nix, Koepp, and herself from the rubble detonation. Through the dusty haze, figures march into the temple, confident and fueled by adrenaline.

The life force strands and roots of the enemy find their location. Botalia holds her breath.

Deafening clashes and crashes erupt as life force projectiles and gunfire hit Botalia's shield. She struggles to hold the rapid fire back, her barrier covering the three of them and her energy reserves draining with each missile she dissolves. The enemy is no more than a blur through the fireworks hitting the barrier and the dust floating and reflecting the strands of light streaming in. Her feet slide back as a particularly large explosion occurs dead center of the shield.

With gritted teeth, she glances at Koepp and Nix. Nix places himself in front of Koepp, life force flowing through his hands, ready to jump when directed to do so. Despite a trembling aura, fear does not find his expression.

Botalia removes her hands from the shield, hoping the remaining durability lasts long enough to execute her plan. Palms facing upwards, Botalia sculpts long blades made of her life force. She hands the katanas to the boys.

"Do not let them touch you and do anything to survive. Nix, you don't often go up against life force users, so don't be hasty. This is a new battlefield, for all of us," Botalia states, her attempt at a pep talk falling short.

A loud boom rings out and a visible hole appears in the barrier.

"I'll attack, you defend. Simple as that."

"Defend what?" Nix asks, an iron grip about the katana, irritation evident in his eyes.

"Each other," Botalia answers, pleading with him through her expression. "And you need to have my back as well. I'll take the brunt but a surprise from any side could be the end of me. I trust you can manage that?"

Nix nods and focuses his eyes on the enemy.

The figures keep shooting from a distance, understanding the barrier to be wearing down. Botalia stares forward, understanding what she must do to stop them. Her chest pulsates. A balance in strategy is necessary. A balance between rationalization and instinct. A contradiction perhaps, but the only way Botalia operates.

She closes her eyes and whispers to herself, "Are you ready?"

Not a nanosecond later, Botalia absorbs the life force from the remaining shield and lunges forward. Botalia draws the fire of the enemies, becoming their target as she charges into their ranks. Her body moves like water between the troops, knocking down those unprepared and defenseless. Against the shield encasing her, she feels the barrage of the projectors, the attacks of the conjurers, and the sensation of manipulators. Unfortunately for them, their overconfidence in the face of an enemy leads to their downfall. Their infallible plans become fallible. The obvious advantage becomes a disadvantage. An innocent exile protecting two young boys becomes their worst nightmare.

The manipulators grow confused as their abilities prove useless against Botalia. Projectors and conjurers alike attack sporadically, hoping to hit her at least once, hoping to slow her down. Their skirmish slows as fellow team members begin to realize her motive. Self-destruction. Many of the fallen members are a result of friendly fire. Botalia smiles and cracks her neck to the side.

"Survival of the fittest," she thinks. "Adapt like water."

Botalia claps her hands together and, as she pulls them apart, materializes a fan. Small enough to sculpt quickly, compact enough to prove no hindrance to her movements. The opposing projectors shoot their life force at her for the moment she's preoccupied sculpting the object. Her lightning reflexes fan out her weapon and twirl it about her in a spectacle, dissolving her opponent's attacks the moment it touches the life force fabric.

The manipulators, realizing their abilities have no effect on Botalia, direct their attention to the young boys. Botalia gasps as they rush Koepp and Nix. A shiver courses through her. Nix's killer instincts may be all they need to survive. Or so she hopes.

Nix stands ready to fight, his eyes glowing like the demon within him has been awakened once more. He slides his hand along the blade gifted to him by Botalia, imbuing his own life force within it. Scowling at the enemies as they approach, Nix the ex-assassin leaps into the air and lets out a battle cry. His motion defies gravity, seemingly kicking off the air to propel himself forward. He descends in a spiral, slashing through the unfortunate souls preparing their attack below him. His feet hit the ground and an exhilarating rush courses through his system. He no longer fights for the client, or the business, or his father. He fights for himself.

Trembling as he holds the sword, Koepp knows he'll be unable to maneuver like Nix. For a moment, he believes Death is waiting for him. However, seeing Nix and Botalia fight, not to kill but to protect, motivates Koepp to focus his strength cutting down the enemy. A man rushes him from the side, dodging Nix's attack and aiming to kill Koepp. Koepp takes a deep breath and firmly grasps the katana. He feels Botalia's life force course through the blade and flow like a current through him. The man lunges for Koepp's arm, in an attempt to manipulate him. Koepp's reflexes are instantaneous. He raises the blade above his head and slices down. The motion intrinsic in his muscle memory because of a past consumed by carpentry and manual labor. His eyes widen as the man falls to the ground, blood pouring from the area between his neck and shoulder. He's never killed a man before this moment. He'd never hoped to nor wanted to. But survival overtook his moral compass. Perhaps he was more like his father than he would have wished to admit.

Botalia continues to wield her fan, an uncommon weapon for a warrior, but her weapon of choice for this battle with numerous sculptors and conjurers. The fan is sculpted from her own life force, inscribed with the same pattern written on the floor of the arena back at the island. It's specially made by Botalia to absorb and slice through life force. The greatest weakness of a life force wielder is a weapon that nullifies that power. Her fan does exactly that. It shields from projectiles, dissolves materializations of all shapes and sizes, and experiences no friction from objects or people enhanced with the help of life force.

A woman who specializes in alchemy transmutes a bubble of air into poisonous gas and pushes the bubble toward Botalia. Botalia recognizes the technique, for she's accustomed to performing transmutations, and dives out of the wave. She casts a bolt of fire in the direction of the toxic air, which causes a combustive reaction. The woman dodges the firestorm and pulls out a shotgun loaded with her own life force ammunition. Infinite possibilities arise when it comes to life force ammo, whether it be conjuration, manipulation, transmutation, or other areas of study. Botalia knows she must be careful, for it is not easy to detect the form of life force concealed in a shotgun shell.

A roaring shot travels through the air, Botalia as the target. She holds up her fan, hoping the acceleration of the shot won't be enough to rip through her life force. Luckily, Botalia underestimates her own ability. Her life force engulfs the shot and shoots pellets of energy back at the woman. Finding their target, the compact life force, composed of an acidic solution, hits the woman between the eyes. She lets out a shrill scream as her skin starts to burn. The woman sinks to the ground, anguished expression easing to emptiness.

The smell of blood and pressure of life force surrounding her as it leaves the bodies and is absorbed by the realm, catches up to Botalia with a pound on her chest. Black dots cloud her vision and a dizzy spell hits. Ears ringing and the beast within her crying out, Botalia fails to realize the fight had not yet ended.

A man whose presence towers over her, pulls the collar of her shirt to him. Before she has the chance to defend herself, the shock delaying a response, his hand grabs hers. Excruciating pain courses through her and a white light blinds her. The slideshow races past as her exhaustion precedes her ability to concentrate on who the enemy may be. A face she doesn't recognize appears time and time again. The words spoken, cried, screamed, are mere staccato notes in a performance, their meaning unrecognizable yet the emotion they hold too tangible. Too painful. A steel grip about her neck, lifting her from the ground, pulls her from the slideshow, the beast within forcing her back to the outside world as its own instincts understand the danger.

The man turns her to face Koepp and Nix. Koepp sits on the floor of the sanctuary, injured but alive. Nix stands in front of him, sword extended, defending Koepp and himself from two well-equipped men, one with life force racing through a scimitar, the other with two single-hand crossbows pointed at Nix.

All parties freeze, as the slightest twitch of a muscle could be the beginning of the end.

Botalia's heart races. Her body shakes. Consciousness threatens to leave her. Botalia begs and pleads in her thoughts, unable to form words with the hand enclosed about her vocal chords.

Nix, though standing, bleeds from lacerations all over his face and arms. Dirtied clothes are ripped in multiple sections, a heaving breath betraying the resolve on his face.

The two men wielding weapons before the boys appear more powerful than the frontline of soldiers who entered the sanctuary first. Was that their plan? Send in their weakest members for the sacrifice to prevent their strongest men from being injured early in the battle? Botalia, hypnotized by her desire to cut down any threats to the boys, never realized others entered the arena. She struggles in the grip of her captor, more so to breathe than to act as if she's resisting.

"Stop squirming or the boys die," the voice of her captor orders. She immediately stops all movement, hoping her trembling body won't give him an excuse to hurt Koepp and Nix. Botalia never caught a glimpse of his face outside of his memories nor does she have any idea who he could be. She closes her eyes, but he interrupts her thoughts. "I felt your little spark earlier, though I don't think it had the effect you'd have liked it to. If your life force extends, even a little, we won't hesitate."

Without gazing at his aura, Botalia cannot determine his true strength and without that information, she cannot know if she has a sufficient supply of life force to initiate an attack while concealing her aura from them. Her thoughts race as she thinks through any and all possible strategies, but none find her, or in the least, not any that wouldn't risk the lives of Nix and Koepp in the fray.

The man grasping her neck addresses Nix. "Put down the sword, boy, or the girl dies."

Botalia's eyes widen. She tries to express to Nix not to follow his orders, but Nix's eyes remain on the enemies standing before him. Nix, realizing Koepp is in a bad state and knowing Botalia may be their only hope for escape, grits his teeth and places the sword on the ground. She closes her eyes, not disappointed in Nix, but fearful that both he and Koepp are unequipped should these men betray their word and attack anyways.

Botalia gazes at the door, hoping Merwyn will enter and save them. But the noises outside have faded to nothing.

"Your friend isn't coming to save you," the man states.

Botalia prevents her eyes from widening.

Friend? Singular? He must not know about Cefni. But where is Cefni?

"So, you're Merwyn Giacobbe's allies? Interesting choice," he examines Koepp and Nix, the young fighters intriguing him. As he looks at the ground, he notices the loss his team has faced. A total of eighteen bodies lay before them on the stone floor of the sanctuary. His eyes move to Botalia, the primary cause of his team's loss. As he strengthens his grip about her hand, he senses her incredible power. Her aura twists about her as violent as a magnetic field experiencing flux, her life force pressing the bounds she sets for it. A tremendous storehouse of life force despite what must have been expended to take down the life force users at the front lines of the attack.

Botalia winces, the position she's in growing painful. He holds her right arm tightly to his chest as his right hand pulls hers to an extended position. Her left arm hangs limp, the sensation of an acrylic arm band etched with a runic language pricking at her skin. Her body is pressed firm to his, the hand about her neck forcing her against his pectorals. Botalia understands, despite back pressed against him, his massive size in comparison to her own enables him the confidence to see her as prey. An ember of rage lights at the thought.

"Excuse me. I feel as though I'm being rude." Botalia rolls her eyes at his statement. "We haven't met before, have we?" No one responds. He tightens the grip on Botalia's neck before loosening it again. "When someone asks you a question, it's rude not to answer, girl."

Botalia looks to the ceiling, praying help will arrive, that this torture will end soon.

"We've never met," Botalia replies.

"Are you sure?"

"I'm sure."

"Then allow me to introduce myself," the captor continues. "My name is Bysciw." Botalia feels a sharp jolt hit her as he reveals his identity. Her body gives away her rise in apprehension. Sensing the change and seeing the fluctuation in her life force and aura, Bysciw presses on, interested in her knowledge of him. "So you've heard of me? Hmm... Who might you be?"

When she doesn't immediately answer, he squeezes her neck once more. Botalia closes her eyes and chuckles. Bysciw furrows his brow.

"Answer me," Bysciw orders in a deep tone.

"I'm your greatest mistake," Botalia answers, realizing psychological warfare may be their way to victory. Her mind adapted. No longer were physical attacks the best strategy.

"What are you talking about, girl?" he asks, the irritation evident in his voice.

"Not only did you inform me of this mission, but you failed to kill me. Well, maybe I'm being unfair. Not you specifically, just your team."

As his grip loosens from confusion, Botalia uses the chance to breathe profoundly. She must calm her heart should she clear her mind. This new strategy, one she has read about in the books and studied in psychological studies, is outside her realm of comfort. One does not get many chances to manipulate with words when exiled to isolation, after all.

"I'm Botalia Ulton."

Though she cannot analyze his aura, moving her own life force to probe a sure death sentence for her and the boys, the twitch in Bysciw's grip makes it apparent he remembers her name. How much he knows about her, she's unsure, however, her name instills a form of fear or shock in him. His grip tightens.

Wait...

Botalia finds her own fear rising again with her mistake.

This isn't fear, it's excitement.

Bysciw laughs, his boisterous bellow filling the walls of the sanctuary as a ghastly chorus may have once done. When it comes to mental manipulation, he may well have her beat. She wouldn't expect any less from a man who once commanded Tanten Flynn and Atlas Lurio.

"Well, well, well... This changes things, doesn't it?" Bysciw rhetorically questions. "See, I was going to kill the three of you after our nice conversation, but I don't feel I should anymore. We've got ourselves quite a conundrum, haven't we, boys?" He directs this to the two members cornering Koepp and Nix.

Stagnant air fills the room as Bysciw audibly ponders what to do. Botalia calms her breaths, gathering herself to focus on her senses since life force is not an option. Her eyes find Nix. He grits his teeth, his fingers twitching at his sides. Botalia squints. Nix's focus is not on the two men in front of him despite watchful eyes glowering at them. His foot taps on the floor, slow and purposeful, his knees slightly bent as if expecting to jump backward. Botalia knows his expression and body language. Nix senses another.

Botalia clears her throat, knowing she must draw the men's attention so they do not find what Nix senses. If it is an ally, Cefni or Merwyn, a surprise attack may be their chance to escape with their lives.

"If you're not going to kill us, what do you plan on doing?" Botalia asks.

"Do you know the lengths some evil people will go to in order to obtain power, Ms. Ulton?" Bysciw questions. When he says the term "evil" a chill runs up Botalia's spine, a malicious drawl lining his tone, venomous, ravenous. She understands he's referring not only to himself, but to Tanten, Atlas, and everyone else who participates in this quest. Bysciw chuckles and answers himself. "Of course, you know the lengths, the pull of desire, the call of the beast. I can tell just by looking at you. So, tell me, what did you sacrifice? Money? Loved ones? Humanity?"

"Happiness," Botalia answers. Saliva builds in her mouth, rage and exhaustion combine to form an impenetrable wall of hopelessness about her mind. A tear escapes and slides down her cheek. As Bysciw speaks of power, of attaining power, his aura surges with the force of a tornado, herself in the peaceful eye of the storm with full understanding of what awaits. The one Nix senses, who hides in the shadows, may be too late to save them.

"You and the staff alike are both valuable prizes, Ms. Ulton. A power beyond the comprehension of most men. However, your power appears much less dangerous and self-destructive, wouldn't you agree?" Botalia makes no moves. "Ms. Ulton? Wouldn't you agree?"

"Yes," Botalia responds, her voice monotone.

"Happiness seems like a small price to pay. If I'm being honest, that much power would make me quite happy."

Botalia gazes upon Nix through a blur crossing her vision. His foot stops tapping and his head turns to a statue atop a semicircle fountain attached to the wall. But the fountain contained no water, the marble statue with its features long weathered. She controls her gasp. A shadow rises from the depths of the fountain base. Her eyes meet the stranger, masked by the shadows.

"The price varies," Botalia states, gulping down her fears and counting down with her heartbeats. "You'll definitely pay."

"With what?" Bysciw scoffs and tightens his grip.

"With your life," the booming voice leaves the shadows and echoes off the walls of the sanctuary.

Bysciw drops his smug expression, shock washing over him. Botalia tilts her head to the side. She hears the dagger cutting through the air, and it pierces Bysciw's forehead, slicing through his skull as if it's water. After a few seconds, his grip loosens, and Bysciw falls to the ground.

Botalia's life force fan dissolves, and she stumbles to the stone floor. Her life force flows from her fingertips and into the ground, taking hold of her life force katana laying on the floor and slicing through the men in front of Koepp and Nix before they're able to respond. Blood flows from the men, sprinkling onto Nix who grimaces in disgust of the texture on his skin.

Botalia darts for Koepp and Nix, her arms wrapping them in a tight embrace as her heart races. The man in the shadows has made no moves, but that does not prevent Botalia from building a barrier of her life force about them. She rubs her hands on Koepp's skin, whispering and letting her life force flow through him to help his wounds heal with quickened pace. Nix wipes the specks of blood from his cheeks and the sweat from his brow while simultaneously glaring at the man in the shadows.

The man steps from the fountain, no longer concealing himself in a wall of shadows built by life force. His steps are sure, his expression devoid of fear, rather covered in amusement. His hair and clothes are more unkempt and dirtied than usual, the trip surely as tough for him thus far as it had been for them. Yet, exhaustion does not cause his knees to quake nor his aura to tremble. The tranquil flame ebbs and flows from his being, powerful, bountiful, and completely within his control.

"Tanten," Botalia calls out. He walks past them and bends down to Bysciw's form, placing a finger on his neck to check his pulse. With a chuckle he rises and meets her eyes. "What are you doing here?"

"Well, I thought it was obvious."

He steps about the corpse, bends over, and retrieves and cleans his dagger with a torn piece of Bysciw's clothing. He wipes the blood away, examining the clarity of his own reflection in the blade, smiling all the while. He gazes at Botalia, his eyes then move to Nix, finally pausing on Koepp. He sheaths his dagger and opens his arms, a gesture of peace over hostility, yet Botalia refuses to believe it for a single moment.

"Outstanding teamwork. Wouldn't you say?" Tanten joyously smiles, despite the drear environment backgrounding the bloody battlefield. The three stare at him, Koepp and Nix not understanding the current situation. Koepp glares at the man that looks similar to himself, hoping it to be some mistake, that this is not the one he longed to meet. Botalia cannot find words. She locks eyes with Tanten, unaware of her next move.

"You know, after you rejected my recruitment, I felt that someway, somehow, you'd find a way to involve yourself in this. Call it instinct, I guess," Tanten states, his sardonic tone beginning to shine through. "Then again, you wouldn't be an Ulton if you didn't." Botalia bites her tongue, wishing to release her rage but still finding herself in a daze of all that transpired in such a short time. "Strange how I'm the only Council member who didn't get what he wanted out of this deal. First you were exiled like the majority wished and now, as Atlas originally hoped, you're no more than a government dog."

"I won't stand for this degradation," Botalia says, fists clenching at her side. Nix and Koepp repeat her action, as if prepared to fight should she give the command. Tanten smirks at their movements.

"How sweet. Your apprentices seem quite loyal to you."

"Yeah. They're wonderful students with infinite potential."

"Glad you seem to think so. Well, if that's how you feel, you should be thanking me."

"Why? And if that's the case, should I also thank you for the assassination attempt?"

"That wasn't on me. Honestly, I was upset Bysciw even thought to waste your incredible potential. Not that anyone could touch you, let alone kill you. After all, you're truly a monster."

"You disgust me."

"Can you blame me? After what you did to those organ pirates, surely you can't think anyone would ever see you as anything other," Tanten peers about the sanctuary, inhaling the fresh aromas of war and scouting the shadows for any movement. Nothing draws his attention. "I knew there was still a beast there, deep, deep, down behind the eyes of the human girl. Maybe being a protector, territorial, is what brings it out to play. He lived a meaningless life up until I sent him to you, so it couldn't hurt to try, I thought."

"How dare you."

Botalia's fingernails dig into the palms of her hands as her rage grows. A gentle caress finds her arm, the calloused and sticky hand of Koepp. His eyes plead with her through her peripheral vision, begging her not to give in to his games. Conflict with him wouldn't end well for any of them. Tanten Flynn was no more than a ticking time bomb at this stage, willing to go to any lengths, as Bysciw stated, to achieve ultimate power. Koepp, though young with much to learn, could easily read the rabid body language of his father. It was a look he'd seen several times before, of those bosses and contractors that took advantage of his and other children's labor time and again because of the imbalance of power. Tanten believes himself the most powerful, despite acknowledging Botalia's strength. As if he believes she would sacrifice herself with no hesitation for the boys. Tanten uses them as a bargaining chip. Botalia knows this. Koepp accepts this, as he had been thrown to the curb by this man years ago. Nix's expression hides nothing. Fire burns in his eyes and life force sparks at his fingertips, the temptation to attack, to protect, growing within him.

"Where are Merwyn and Cefni?" Nix asks. Tanten, who had been ignoring Nix up until that point, turns to him with a malicious grin.

"Who are you?"

"Nix. Nix Kufuta."

"An assassin?"

"Not anymore."

Tanten chuckles. "I didn't know one could simply quit that business... It may interest you to know-"

"Where are Merwyn and Cefni?" Nix's tone does not change. He heard his own father, Aurelius Kufuta use this voice when speaking with those employees who led failed assassination attempts. He did not accept skirting about the issue. Direct answers only, or else.

"I can't help you," Tanten answers, furrowing a brow at the disrespectful tone of the ex-assassin. "My target was Bysciw, so I'm not concerned."

"What happened to your ally?" Nix continues to ask questions, not out of genuine curiosity, but to spite him. Tanten glares at Nix and takes a step forward but senses Botalia's aura accelerate. He freezes and clears his throat.

"I could ask you the same. Despite the obvious of Merwyn Giacobbe and the fragile Cefni Medina, I thought there was another who tailed along. What happened to the delinquent who followed you around?"

Botalia inhales profoundly, noticing the new shadows accompanying those of the sanctuary. Many presences take form on the other side of the door, the reasoning of these creatures far beneath their senses and instincts. Soft thuds occur against the doors and walls, having manifested too soon and unable to enter the feast lying on the floor of the sanctuary, though they may have already gotten their fill outside the temple if Merwyn succeeded in eliminating the enemy. Or perhaps he is among them, his corpse unable to be identified after the shadow beings devour his features for their meal.

"If you speak of Tenebrant," saying his name alone causes the hairs on her arms to rise and a pain in her chest. "I thought he was headed for you. Apparently not."

Tanten smirks and examines the room. He sighs as he observes the pile of corpses, wishing he could be responsible for more than one of them. Shaking his head, he locks eyes with Botalia. "I can't say I'm surprised he betrayed your alliance. He is a Mortu."

"He's nothing like them. And you're no better," Botalia snaps.

"I never said I was. But while I manipulated the minds of the many to think I was always the hero, Mortu will never be any more than an infamous criminal who not even the lowliest would aspire to.

"But maybe you're right. I'd say he's worse than the cruel Mortus and the lot of necromancers I'd hunted throughout my time at the Association. He's an arrogant, selfish child who never matured and continues to play the victim when in reality, he's no more than a cold-hearted murderer."

Tanten grins and moves his head in time to avoid a curse cast in his direction. The life force spirals, hitting a decorative pillar and causing the top portion to crash to the ground, the point of contact turning the marble it touched to dust. The caster steps into view, entering through the hole in the back of the temple created by Bysciw's team. His expression does not show disgust or shock at the sight within. Rather he wears a smile.

"It's rude to talk about someone who's not around," Tenebrant jests, his tone light.

Behind him stand beings unrecognizable to his ex-team members. Their presences are faint, and they have a likeness similar to humans, however, they do not possess a life force of their own. Botalia's jaw drops as she realizes a new form of power, a supernatural and cruel power, something she's read about but never imagined how disturbing it truly is. The ability to resurrect the dead, rather create puppets of their physical beings, and command them without sympathy or pity. Utilizing life force to awaken those who are meant to rest, forcing them to operate without soul or spirit. Mindless, reanimated corpses. The power of a necromancer.

"I'm glad you could make it," Tanten grins, his back to Tenebrant as a show of disrespect and utmost spite for one many would deem his nemesis. "Unfortunately, I have other business I must attend to, so if you don't mind waiting."

"Botalia," Tenebrant calls out, his tone still light despite the heat and rage bottled in their last interaction. She locks eyes with him. As Botalia examines him, she notices his aura, while full of hostility, trembles for he does not have the energy to hide his exhaustion. Burns and blood cover his person, his clothing singed in places, and remnants of ice crystals in his hair. She feels numb. Tenebrant licks the blood intruding on his upper lip. He moves his eyes from one person to the next, and to Botalia's dismay, his expression never changes nor do his eyes offer any hesitation. Her heart tries to escape.

A hollow frame. That's all he is. "I'm glad to see you didn't rip him apart before I got here. Though, I doubt you would have done so in front of..." he nods in Koepp's direction.

"You all can have this conversation later," Tanten says and raises his hand as if the gesture alone would stop all other conversation and bring the attention back to himself. He stares at Botalia and waits for her eyes to meet his. "You have too much potential to waste on these lowlifes. Do you not understand the significance of infinite power and knowledge? Sharing what you've learned, studying what you've become? The world will progress in all fields. Power is not evil-"

"Not convincing coming from an evil, power-hungry, traitorous bastard," Tenebrant interjects. Tanten furrows his brow but refuses to turn around.

"Know your place, delinquent."

Tanten Flynn takes a step toward Botalia, and once again her aura flares. She does not wish to take the offensive but will not hesitate to defend should she need to do so. Time ticks away in the background.

They should have been back by now... They should have been here...

Botalia placed roots of life force through the stone what feels like ages ago, but they had yet to extend beyond the inner sanctuary, the distractions and overwhelming emotions washing over continually. She wishes to know, to find an answer and not be it those golems standing beyond Tenebrant, despite what features they still possess being far from those she searches for.

"Tenebrant... W-Where's..." Koepp mumbles, Botalia's and Nix's thoughts becoming tangible with the words he attempts to form. Tenebrant saves him the humiliation of sounding fragile. His face grows serious, and he glares at his ex-teammates.

"Leave," he commands, the word leaving simple and brief and stern.

Botalia pulls herself from her senses and notices the sudden change in the air. The hostility present multiplied within a matter of seconds. Tenebrant's aura gains speed as it wraps about him, Tanten's aura growing as a flame given fuel. And then another force hits her: The aura of Koepp beside her, the transformation of a small flame becoming an inferno. His life force appears concentrated in his hands, as if he's ready to attack.

Koepp's moved his life force...

"You killed him! Didn't you!" Koepp screams, tears breaking through his defenses. He lunges forward, but Botalia grabs onto his shoulders and pulls his body into her own, restraining his movement. He resists her prison, a rage Botalia did not know he possessed begins to escape. Nix's eyes widen and his mouth opens. Seeing Koepp in hysterics causes his own body to quake. Tanten gazes at his son, sensing, for the first time, a fiery spirit within the young boy.

"Go," Tenebrant again orders, the harsh tone fading into a breathy syllable. He closes his eyes. Botalia gazes upon Tenebrant, catching a glimpse of the one she used to know. "If you go through the hole, I scared off those shadows. Turns out they don't like fire. Just... leave."

Botalia nods. She holds on to Koepp and the three walk to the back of the temple, passing by Tenebrant and the reanimated corpses as they go. Tanten makes no moves. He stares at the ground and smiles, a maniacal and irritated smile.

They exit the temple and find a path back into the city. Traveling until the shadow creatures are out of sight, Botalia, Nix, and Koepp settle themselves in a marble structure, the roof and one wall destroyed but sufficient cover, and rest and rehydrate themselves. Botalia leans her head against a wall and, looking up, notices the dark clouds rolling in. She mumbles the lullaby, the only thing she can think to stop the monster's escape.

Chapter Seventeen

She'd never be happy... knowing what you've become.

The words echo time and again in his head as he leaves the building housing the portal behind him. His entire person shakes as anger and rage threaten to consume him, to turn his vision red and commit acts even he may come to regret.

Tenebrant shakes the thoughts, the tattoos on his arms twitching with his muscles underneath, the ink darkening and symbols not once noticeable protruding from his skin. His aura trembles and his fists clench. A sharp pang in his chest sends Tenebrant to his knees. His hand clutches at his shirt, gritted teeth holding back the scream. The drum beats and beats and beats within him. The reverberations of its rhythm accompany a vision of flames and corpses. Death. The sight of death. The smell of death. The sound of death. A mix of life force screaming to manifest as it escapes those who have come to know death. Its power a taunt, a lure, feeding his every motive to learn how to control it. At that time, he couldn't. But now, in his wrath and overwhelming apathy for those he faces, this could be his redemption.

Tenebrant steps into a marble structure, wishing to find an opponent, any opponent to test his abilities. As his life force springs from his fingertips, he senses the pressure of a thousand eyes watching him. He quickly withdraws his life force and produces a shield about himself. But an attack never occurs. No footsteps stir, no heartbeats nor breaths pass through any space near him. After a few calming breaths, he tries again.

His life force leaves him, but the pressure returns. However, this time, despite his attempts, Tenebrant fails to recall his life force. As if manipulated by another, his life force snakes across the dried earth and seeps into a nearby stone tile before disappearing.

Tenebrant glances at the stone, curiosity surpassing any fear of what may have possessed him. He steps to it. He bends over to rub his fingers along its surface, small runic inscriptions reside in the corner. Tenebrant licks his upper lip. An idea strikes him. He digs his fingers beneath the stone tile and lifts. Without much fight, the tile obeys, a musky air escaping from underneath feeling like an inhale by one strangled from breath for so long. The echo of distant laughter rings in his ears.

Placing the tile to the side, Tenebrant ducks his head into the space and notices a series of tunnels. Tenebrant smiles. He jumps through the hole, feet hitting solid stone as he lands. A faint light illuminates down the way. Saliva builds in Tenebrant's mouth. His hunger mounts and the ruined city responds, just in time to satisfy his hunger.

He walks for no more than five minutes when the murmurs of prey fill his ears. Life force encapsulates his hands and forearms, the tattoos now dancing in delight. A smoke forms about him and the kris manifests in his hand. Two men. Their words leave them in whispers, their auras skittering with their paranoia. They had found their way to another entrance of the tunnel. Tenebrant needs to lure them within.

He releases small glowing orbs of light, floating like mystical fairies to the daylight streaming in. An excited voice spots the life force creatures. Tenebrant beckons the orbs to return, hoping the men will follow. Their footsteps give away their movements, no attempt made to even conceal them.

"Poor souls," Tenebrant whispers, a fairy orb twirling in front of his face before vanishing. "They won't even know what's hit them."

Tenebrant issues a silencing curse to consume their screams. The earth trembles beneath as the magic takes shape, as his minions take shape. Tenebrant pricks a finger with his kris and draws a crescent moon on the wall, his blood an offering to the city that provided for the necromancer. Not the success he wished, but far from the failure he expected.

Tenebrant lurks at the back of the temple, watching as Atlas, Naht, and the others leave the area, heading toward the floodplains. Whether marching for the altar or simply advancing, Tenebrant could not be sure of their objective. Naht told him earlier that Atlas doesn't have a strong desire concerning the attainment of the staff and its power. Atlas is more obsessed with his twisted ideal of justice. The thought makes Tenebrant chuckle.

As Tenebrant scales the deteriorating marble columns of the temple, he takes care to conceal his aura. His ability to conceal his aura and life force make him near impossible to spot. Not even Naht steals a glimpse, whether because he sensed it was Tenebrant or discovering the presence was outside of his own ability as well.

Tenebrant watches as Atlas's team heads north from this new vantage point, examining how they cope with the loss of two team members. Grief takes many forms in humans, yet resilience, or in the least faking it, takes a drastic toll on the mind. Not even the soldier on the battlefield can maintain a stone composure after the retreat. That is... unless the mind morphs... no longer fully human.

He grins and glances down at his minions below. Developing a strategy to lure the members from their group proved rather tricky given the heightened climate of fear. Tenebrant could not fault them for showing courage until the end. Taking life grows easier every day for him. Granting them life from his own hands, reanimating the corpses, was complex, the outcome never up to his standards of satisfaction. His necromancy skills were rusty, fully manipulating the corpses was no simple task. Giving a corpse back its own spirit was a skill he had not achieved, yet.

In the distance, Tenebrant notices Cefni leading the group in the direction of the temple. The necromancer quickly hides behind the dome, windows either shattered or stained from centuries of buffeting sandstorms. Hostility grows within him as he gazes upon the Professional, Botalia beside him. Using his life force as a buffer between his feet and the ground, Tenebrant jumps off the temple roof. He commands his undead allies to follow him, his thoughts unstable. Fighting... killing... the rush of excitement, seeing his strength, feeling Atlas's apprehensive aura... the combination of these experiences puts his mind in a flurry. He wants more. More excitement. But the ones nearest him are also the members of the team he betrayed... Does betrayal have a limit?

His minions limp after him, his pace too fast for them to keep up. Tenebrant scopes out the area, wondering where to hide himself or if he wants to adhere to that option at all. His mind tells him to let the group be, but his body refuses to listen. Standing approximately fifty meters from the temple, Tenebrant stares at the building, frozen to the spot. Around him lay marble slabs, some buried within the ground while others protrude. A cemetery.

His face turns to the sky as a soft laugh thanks whichever druidic gods must be on his side. Demented and as sadistic as him. His life force seeps into the soil and feels the remnants of creatures, or perhaps humans, who were laid to rest, their corpses long decomposed. Tenebrant closes his eyes as the dusty breeze caresses his skin. The wind carries voices to his ears, begging for his regenerative life force to wake them from their long rest.

Tenebrant grows alert to his presence before he sees him. An enraged and aggressive aura, laced with bloodlust and revenge. A foolish and immature mixture of emotions. Why would people wish to give in to something as lowly as revenge?

Without placing eyes upon his adversary, Tenebrant turns and strolls away. He smiles as the man pursues him. The necromancer and his undead allies create a maze in the marble ruins of mausoleums, obelisks, and weathered statues. Tenebrant loops left, right, then right again. The man quickens pace to close the distance so as to not lose sight of Tenebrant.

Tenebrant swiftly ducks behind the corner of a marble division wall and pauses. The corpses had taken a different path through the maze of ruins, waiting for their master's command. This man paid no mind to the minions, intent on his pursuit of Tenebrant.

The presence disappears. Tenebrant pushes a palm against the marble wall and searches for a heartbeat in this field of the dead. He detects nothing. Peeking his head around the wall, Tenebrant sees no one. He successfully evaded the enemy. With a shake of the head, he sighs.

"I thought you'd put up a better chase," he disappointingly mumbles.

The loud bang of a shot fires.

Tenebrant leaps into the air, fast as an eagle taking flight, and lands atop the wall he had been leaning against. Not a second later, the marble wall shatters into thousands of small shards, launching like shrapnel in all directions. Tenebrant had catapulted himself into the air as the bullet made contact, leaving him with no more than superficial scratches from the marble pellets. Where the wall once stood lay a burnt and smoky foundation.

Tenebrant studies the surrounding area, attempting to use the angle of incidence to determine the origin of the bullet. However, he realizes the ineffectiveness in doing so, for another bullet already targets him. He launches and somersaults to the side. Despite the dodge, the bullet, encapsulated in its own aura, tracks him. Tenebrant grins, amused by the challenge.

He runs around the ruins, not only evading the bullet but assembling his allies. Finding a marble slab, Tenebrant lifts it with his life force to act as a shield. The bullet strikes and the shield disintegrates. His vision blurs and the city rotates about him. A concussive shot. He lowers himself, placing his hands on the dry soil and closing his eyes to return to equilibrium.

"You're not giving up already, are you, coward?" Cefni Medina questions. Tenebrant chuckles, Cefni's hostility fueling his strength.

"You ask as if I would surrender to the pitiful likes of you, Cefni Medina."

Tenebrant opens his eyes and stares at the rough presence of the Council member before him. Cefni aims his revolver at Tenebrant's chest. Though powerful, Tenebrant knows the previous two shots were not set to murder him. The Magistrate Association deems Cefni one of the best life force users in the world, and Tenebrant does not deny that claim. Tenebrant knows the limits of his own strength and intelligence, which gives him an advantage in most battles. Granted, he's never met an adversary as worthy or respectable as Cefni Medina.

Cefni feels no fear in the face of Tenebrant. A stone wall. Both mentally and physically on the battlefield. Tenebrant's raw ability means little to his years of experience. Cefni patiently waits for the moment to reveal his true strength both to his opponent and himself. That is, if his true strength even warrants revealing itself.

"Arrogance is a pretty shade on no one."

"Nor revenge," Tenebrant flashes a devious grin. "But it seems a natural fit for you."

"Why would I seek revenge against you?"

"Not specifically me... I simply assumed you have a hard heart set against all murderers and criminals... Considering your past..."

Cefni cocks the revolver. "I'm not gonna warn you again. The Association would have no qualms if I ended you here."

"You don't have to be kind," Tenebrant laughs. His face grows solemn in a flash. "No one would."

Tenebrant and Cefni stare into each other's eyes, though Cefni carefully pays attention to the reanimated corpses in his peripheral vision. He steadily aims the revolver at Tenebrant. Cefni's heartbeat is as tranquil as an undisturbed pond, but his mind swirls as if in the outer ring of a hurricane. Tenebrant tilts his head to the side. He observes Cefni's aura, appearing like a star experiencing solar flares and coronal mass ejections.

"What are you fighting for?" Tenebrant inquires. His eyes do not deviate from their position, slowly breaking through Cefni's defenses. Finding the weakness his body and aura attempt to keep hidden, but his eyes and soul cannot hide. Cefni understands Tenebrant's state of hostility and psyched aura cannot be quelled until he kills others. Until he encounters an attempt to bring back life before the spirit finds its way from the body. Until he can prove to those long gone that he will never worry to lose those closest to him again. The pity that no one close remains...

"I fight for the protection of those things still lovely in the world and to squash those trying to damage it," Cefni answers. Tenebrant erupts in laughter. Cefni stands, stolid, his resolve cements itself in his expression. Tenebrant notices and falls silent.

Furrowing his brow at Cefni, Tenebrant remarks, "Liar."

No sounds occur in the environment around them. No rustling of the brush under their feet, no settling of the rubble from the marble ruins. As if the environment understands that only silence can fill the moment. The tension increases between the two enemies.

"You speak of a lovely world, a world we both know ceases to exist in our eyes. Others still see it, some will never see anything but. Many who lose that image deny its reality to begin with, as if a false projection was torn down to reveal the cruel world we live in. They reject the idea of a lovely world for now they see the truth. Or is it the truth? Can we say a lovely world never existed if so many claim to live in it? Can we say they are wrong, that they don't understand because they're blinded by a false pretense?"

"Is it so wrong to hope for a lovely world?"

"No. Not if one wishes to suffer. Hope is but a sad excuse for exerting a belief we know borderlines reality and imaginary. Scholars cling to the hope for a panacea to save the world from disease, yet understand it to be outside the realm of possibility. Many hope for worldly happiness and peace yet understand humans would cease to exist if the world were to come to that. Hope is a tortuous artifice used to destroy the soul. To prove the world is not a lovely place. Because those who rely on hope know the world is cruel. Hope is the first step in a cycle of suffering. You hope for a lovely world, but your hope is another's suffering. To protect your so called "lovely world," someone has to take the fall."

"Those attempting to destroy-"

"Isn't that subjective? Your lovely world will never be everyone's lovely world and therefore will only live as it exists today. Your lovely world is devoid of what you deem evil acts, your hope a smiling fourteen-year-old girl who embodied your ideals of eradicating those who do wrong."

"The world has no need for murderers."

"And yet someone must if the world is to be rid of them. No matter the way you approach the situation, she's a killer. You're a killer. I'm a killer."

"Don't compare yourself to us." Cefni's frustration is evident as his aura experiences more frequent disruptions than before.

"We're more alike than you know," Tenebrant quietly mutters. He closes his eyes, feeling their exchange of conflicting ideals to be dissolving his excitement and hostility. However, he refuses to find despair in his new emotions. With his bloodlust gone, his mind is clear to discern why Cefni is a true enemy.

Superficial disagreements. The two words perfectly encapsulate Tenebrant's reaction to every felony of his involvement. Eradicating narrow-minded, weak, arrogant, unintelligent, ignorant weeds became a job to Tenebrant. It reaffirmed in him his own strength, his abilities. No one could bully or overpower him. He wouldn't allow it. He had control. Always. Whether it be the psychological lure or the physical strikes, Tenebrant began to find little satisfaction in killing those who were no more than weeds to society. They weren't even comparable to the colossal weeds that never seem to die, for those are a greater pain than those he murdered. His hostility and excitement assisted in his killing sprees. If not for a rapid flood of emotion, he would not find satisfaction whatsoever. But, in the face of Tanten and Cefni, he finds a contorted obsession. As if winning a fight against either would solve his internal conflict. He wishes for that control, for that strength, to reclaim himself.

Tenebrant cracks his neck and sighs. He glances at his allies then back at Cefni, who appears unwavering in his stance.

"How about we settle this?" Tenebrant questions. He slides his right hand along his left arm, revealing a glowing language tattooed on it. A necromantic rite inscribed with his own life force, allowing for him to easily command and summon undead minions.

Cefni does not shoot, but rather lowers his revolver, understanding the practice of a fair fight. He prepares his life force, concentrating a large portion into his hands and feet, a small portion moving to his eyes to carefully watch Tenebrant's execution of life force. He's investigated too many cases where necromancers used their life force to conceal curses, therefore rendering the opponent weak, confused, or paralyzed. Cefni glances at the undead warriors, understanding them to be weak but an effective tool for drawing attention and fire away from his primary opponent.

Both men take a defensive stance. They lock eyes, hesitating to initiate the battle.

"Don't hold back," Cefni orders, "If you do, I'll tell the world you died a coward's death."

"As you should," Tenebrant responds with a smile. He cracks his fingers and points at Cefni. "Prepare to join my army."

Cefni chuckles and cracks his neck.

The battle begins.

The undead corpses rush Cefni, their speed, however unintimidating, raises his alert of his surroundings. The moment Cefni removed his eyes from Tenebrant, he vanished. Cefni feels a presence behind him and quickly prepares a shield as he rotates his body. Tenebrant executes a chop to Cefni's core. The makeshift shield rattles and both fly backwards. Though an expert in the use of life force, Cefni's body is not near as nimble as Tenebrant's.

Cefni rises to his feet and throws his arms to his sides, launching a fiery life force projectile at the corpses racing toward him. The beings temporarily fall to the ground, pieces of their flesh peeling off with the heat from Cefni's attack. The damage they sustain lowers their speed, giving Cefni more time to directly combat the necromancer.

However, Tenebrant landed on his feet when the pulse launched him and currently lunges for Cefni. Cefni keeps his revolver holstered, for it's useless in such close quarters combat. Tenebrant directs the palm of his hand at Cefni and curls his fingers inward. A beam of light emits from his hand, glowing cyan and traveling through the air at incredible speeds. Cefni finds he barely has the time to react but manages to create a stronger barrier than the last. The barrier absorbs the curse and gifts the energy to Cefni. Cefni grins when he feels the power behind the curse, a hostility and excitement that fuels his own exhilaration. Tenebrant notes the shift in Cefni's aura and leaps back, forgetting every movement costs time.

Cefni lifts his hands toward the heavens. Simultaneously, his life force exits his hands and feet, forcing the energy into the sky and ground, forming a parallel boundary above and below the battlefield. Tenebrant watches the ground, believing that part of the attack will trap him in place. However, he senses the energy above him and quickly dodges. He jumps back and forth, leaping out of the way of the lightning strikes. Cefni focuses on each bolt, not so much trying to hit Tenebrant but attempting to drain his energy. He understands the difference in stamina, so Cefni uses his strength to weaken Tenebrant.

Unfortunately, while Cefni concentrated on the lightning, the corpses managed to close the distance and swipe at him. One lands a punch on his arm and, though not strong enough to injure him, knocks his arm from his spell. Tenebrant uses the opportunity to charge Cefni. He reaches behind himself and, as if manifested from the air itself, conjures a kris with a smoky aura about it. Tenebrant swings the jagged blade at Cefni's front, but Cefni raises his arm while wrapping it in an icy blanket by drastically decreasing the temperature about it.

As the kris breaks through the ice, a cold flurry sends Tenebrant flying. He shakes his head and attempts to brush the frost from his face. Cefni grunts in anguish and peers down to see the bloody gash in his arm. He quickly rips his shirt and wraps it about his wound, ensuring he does not lose too much blood.

Both he and Tenebrant breathe heavily, attempting to recoup a fraction of their energy without allowing the other enough time to recover. Cefni, showing less wear than Tenebrant, draws his revolver. Before he can aim, Tenebrant leaps at him, swinging his kris down from above his head. Cefni rotates the revolver so the kris strikes the barrel, his gun the only form of protection between him and Tenebrant.

Tenebrant pulls back on his kris and commits to several furious swipes, Cefni blocking each one with his revolver. However, the last strike slashes his finger, the pain forcing him to step back.

Without much thought, Cefni points the gun into the air and shoots. His life force spills down in a firestorm, each packet of flame falling near his body, acting as a temporary shield. Tenebrant realizing he cannot attack head on, once again directs a curse at Cefni. His palm turns a shade of deep purple and the highly energized burst breaks through the fire shield.

A bright flash occurs. Tenebrant turns his head away, for fear of temporarily ruining his vision, but when he peers back at where the shield once was, he sees nothing. Tenebrant, panic-stricken, looks all around him, pivoting in a circle about himself and leaving no area unsearched. He cannot see Cefni anywhere.

Tenebrant extends his glowing left arm and commands his minions, who instinctively attract to living beings, to search for Cefni. Promptly after issuing his command, he lowers himself to the ground so he may touch the tip of his kris onto the soil, for Tenebrant is aware he injured Cefni with his blade. A smoky wisp rises from the ground and follows the minions, meaning both of his abilities have successfully found his target. Tenebrant smiles and attempts to calm his breathing.

Cefni, finding he no longer has the energy or need to support his manipulated electromagnetic field, quickly drops the cloaking. He aims at the wisp first and, with finger pointed at its center, casts an ice bolt at the smoke. Upon contact, the wisp freezes in a spherical clump and drops to the ground, shattering into many pieces.

Tenebrant's minions grab at Cefni's clothing, attempting to restrain him. Cefni disregards Tenebrant and focuses his next spell on the irritating beings, but not before his instincts throw his head backwards. He feels his neck strain and a sting on his cheek, followed by the sensation of a warm liquid dripping down his face. Cefni firmly grasps his revolver and thrusts his elbow upward, knocking away the minion clinging to his right arm. Without hesitation Cefni shoots the corpse to his left in the forehead with an electrifying shot.

The electric jolt renders the being motionless for a short period. Cefni then turns to the other corpse and shoots a fiery shot. However, as he shoots, his arm is pushed downward by Tenebrant who swiftly knees Cefni in the stomach.

The fiery shot hits the corpse's calf, and the being goes up in flames. Tenebrant grimaces, realizing he must deal with his minion before continuing to play with his prey. Cefni catches his breath and wipes his hand across his face, removing fresh blood. To prevent the fire from rising, Tenebrant chops off the leg of his minion and forms a golemic attachment from the earth.

An explosion rings out in the distance, pulling the attention of both Cefni and Tenebrant. They notice the aura shift in the other and launch themselves back into battle. Tenebrant rushes Cefni with his kris, exerting full power into the next attack. Cefni exhales. He aims at Tenebrant and shoots. An icy nova flares from the gun and forces Tenebrant to the ground in a paralyzed state.

The necromancer struggles to move. His heart races uncontrollably as if trying to escape after years of torture. His body trembles, understanding the scenario of predator versus prey. He is the prey. Weak. Helpless. Tenebrant closes his eyes for a split-second, hoping for relaxation, but quickly opens them when the demented images appear. The only words he can think being "This is the end."

Cefni steps near Tenebrant's frozen body, wearing a solemn expression. The paralysis wears away, and Tenebrant feels a sharp pain in his core, understanding the bruises taking form. Every vein in his body possesses a heartbeat. A metallic liquid fills his throat. Tenebrant coughs up the blood and breathes heavily. He continues to lay on the ground, gazing at the cloudy sky.

They lock eyes.

"Aren't you going to kill me?" Tenebrant asks. He half laughs before coughing up more blood.

"Sit up or the blood will keep coming," responds Cefni. Tenebrant shakes his head, but after coughing again, slowly raises his upper half off the ground. He leans forward, not wanting to look at Cefni.

"Just kill me," Tenebrant mumbles, the shame of being defeated, of being weak, seeping in, taking control of his thoughts. Cefni does not respond but looks in the direction of the temple and the explosion. When he turns back to Tenebrant, he sees a shell devoid of feeling, pride, and life. The empty look in his eyes becoming an all too familiar sight.

Cefni sighs. Finishing an opponent is not only an act to display one's victory but also of respect and honor. Yet, Cefni cannot find it within himself to kill Tenebrant. Tenebrant heaves, trying to clear his throat of the metallic taste of blood. He spits to the side.

"Kill me," Tenebrant insists.

"I won't."

"Are you too coward?"

"I-"

"There you two are," a voice calls out from behind a marble mausoleum. "Cefni, I apologize for interrupting your fight, but my news is urgent," Merwyn states.

"What is it?" Cefni asks, as if forgetting about the battle completely.

"Atlas and his group are moving onto the floodplains. Any moment the titans will rise."

"Then we must hurry."

Cefni walks toward Merwyn but notices a sympathetic expression on his face as he glimpses Tenebrant's fragile form. Tenebrant places his hands on the ground, as if bowing to Cefni.

"Please, kill me. I lost," he pleads. "I'm weak."

"No," Cefni firmly responds. "I won't kill you."

"Tenebrant, wouldn't you say by keeping you alive whilst you beg for death makes us the villains? Merciless, apathetic to your pleas, cruel adversaries," Merwyn begins. His face expresses little emotion, for he tries to restrain his sympathy for Tenebrant. "If you cannot remember us as your teammates, then remember us as your enemies. For now, any way you choose, we will have made it so. Cefni." Merwyn gestures and the two begin to walk away. When they reach a series of marble walls surrounding what remains of a crypt, Merwyn glances back at Tenebrant. The two lock eyes. Cefni stops and watches. Tenebrant stands, his body shakes as strange emotions, emotions he cannot explain, fill him.

"What is a man to do when not even his death is granted to him?" Tenebrant jokes. The air lifts, the environment not as hostile or dismal as before. He feels himself slowly rejuvenating, though, he possesses no desire to fight with either Cefni or Merwyn. For the first time since entering this dimension, he finds his mind clear of all thoughts.

"I do believe neither of us were your primary target to begin with," Merwyn comments. Tenebrant chuckles, the answer shining clearly in his mind. He shakes his head, both as a reply to Merwyn's statement and to display his own disappointment in himself for losing sight of his goal. "The temple may be a place to start."

Merwyn bows his head to Tenebrant and walks away alongside Cefni. The two quickly head toward the floodplains, though they briefly stop in a structure on the way to properly heal Cefni's wounds. As Cefni unwraps his injured arm, they discover the kris was cursed thus requiring a necromancer or witch doctor to heal the wound.

Tenebrant closes his eyes, smiling as he thinks about Tanten. He repairs his minions with the soil and hardened clay around him and heads toward the temple. As he nears the back, Tenebrant notices the hole in the wall as well as several shadows beasts sniffing their way toward the makeshift entrance. He marches toward the hole, not alarmed by the beings as they did not harm him earlier. However, as he nears them, the shadows beasts snap their heads in his direction, the smell of death surrounding the undead corpses. Realizing he cannot physically attack a shadow, if that is indeed what they are, Tenebrant decides to fight darkness with light. He sets the ground aflame with his life force, creating walls of fire on either side of him, leaving a path to enter the temple. As he steps nearer, he hears the voice of Tanten Flynn.

The bloody mess within the temple did not surprise him. Tenebrant expected no less in a place that undoubtedly drew all teams to it, whether they wished to be there or not. The greater shock was seeing Botalia and the boys having some sort of standoff with Tanten.

She'd never be happy... knowing what you've become.

"A fallacy... she could have never imagined what I would become. Even I sometimes question who or what I am," Tenebrant's inner voice speaks to him.

With growing exhaustion and mild irritation at his trembling form, Tenebrant does what he can to dismiss his ex-teammates or, as Merwyn may suggest, his enemies. Botalia cannot even look him in the eyes as she passes. They escape from view, leaving Tanten Flynn and Tenebrant Mortu to themselves.

"Seems like we've both been fighting old alliances," Tenebrant remarks.

Tanten chuckles. He rotates his body toward Tenebrant and examines his form. Another breathy laugh. Tanten crosses his arms and shakes his head as his tongue pushes at his bottom lip. Life force sweeps about his legs and feet, demonstrating the equivalent of a stomping toddler throwing a tantrum.

"Why are you here, Mortu?" asks Tanten. His tone is soft and solemn. He gazes at Tenebrant with a straight face, but Tenebrant returns a smile.

"I've been asking myself that exact question. After all, I have no interest in the staff, but the battlefield... a battlefield not yet bloody but will be made so in my own fashion, with the beautiful reds of your blood."

"Your terrorizing speech sounds a lot less threatening than normal, as though it's forced. Granted, allowing the others to escape isn't what I would deem villainous either. What happened, Mortu? You look so... weak."

At that word, Tenebrant's face changes to express rage, suppressing his self-frustration. He conjures his kris and slices the air in front of him, taking a stance to fight. "I'll show you weak when you're begging for life."

Tanten sighs. He sticks his hands in his pockets and nonchalantly approaches Tenebrant. When standing no more than two meters away, he locks eyes with the battle-hungry necromancer and smugly grins.

"I refuse to fight one who's already been defeated," Tanten states. He looks Tenebrant up and down, the injuries apparent from up close. "You're broken... and powerless."

Tenebrant stands frozen in place, not understanding what power holds him down, whether his own or another's. He trembles in Tanten's presence. He wants to attack... he needs to attack, to defeat Tanten. And yet he's frozen.

Tanten walks around Tenebrant and stands in the hole of the temple, the boundary between Tenebrant's goal manifesting and fading. Tanten peers out at the world, the fire dwindling away with the shadow beasts curiously peeking at the great marble structure, waiting for their opportunity to enter. He and Tenebrant stand with their backs to one another, one gazing out at hope and one peering down in despair.

"When you've fixed yourself, come back. I'll be waiting." With those words, Tanten Flynn disappears into the foreign world, heading toward the staff atop Praecantatis Tepui.

The kris in Tenebrant's grasp slowly dissolves in his fingers and he falls to his knees. The corpses once in his control crumble and collapse, no longer forced to live. Tenebrant stares at the ground, broken.

Chapter Eighteen

"Absolute stillness," Naht mumbles to Atlas who crouches at his side. "The noise of the other teams battling can be heard behind, but nothing ahead. Their sleep goes undisturbed, thus far."

"What do you believe will trigger them?" Atlas asks.

The two stare out at the floodplains from the edge of the town. The road and scattered marble ruins fail to stretch beyond this point. The soil appears darker, and a low-lying brush covers large patches of ground across the plains. The clouds in the sky cease to move, creating a thick, ashy blanket between the sun and the environment. In the distance, a cobblestone road takes shape, the path leading to stairs which ascend to the top of the tepui. The clouds rest before the peak, but there is no denying the staff and altar atop it. Its presence radiates with a desire to be known.

Naht taps at the ground in front of him, as if testing to ensure its stability. Any semblance of emotion fails to blossom on his face, his eyes revealing nothing to Atlas as he observes.

"The moment we step foot beyond a specified line, they'll be alert. The problem is determining that point," Naht says.

Atlas sighs. He peers back at the rest of his team, who appear perpetually paranoid and anxious. Keniph attempts to lift spirits and morale but fails to hide his own doubts. Atlas's eyelids grow heavy, wishing to shield himself from the sight. The pressure weighs down on his shoulders, every footstep trudging and exhausting. They are so close... but why does it feel like they've already failed?

Atlas pats Naht on the shoulder, trusting him to reveal any further intel he learns and joins Keniph at his side. His commander wears a grim expression, the wrinkles on his forehead digging deeper and the stubble across his chin and cheeks pocked with grey hairs and grains of sand and debris. Sweat drips from his brow and seeps through his clothes, his running to and fro to assist any team member in any way that he can the last thread that leaves him gripping to sanity he believes is still intact. Keniph huffs as Atlas places a hand on his shoulder, forcing him to stop his racing about. Atlas offers a handful of cooked seeds from a pouch at his side, his commander graciously accepting, for being without a cigar these last few days spikes his anxiety.

"Red, we need to talk." Keniph takes Atlas. He spits the empty seeds at the ground and nods his head away. Atlas understands the words meant for only his ears. They position themselves behind a marble wall, out of direct view of the team. As Atlas locks eyes with Keniph, he discerns something must be wrong, perhaps horribly wrong. Not even the gentle breeze provides comfort, carrying the stiff smell of smoke and dust.

"The team... Red... the team is falling apart," Keniph states with a yearning in his tone. Atlas stares into Keniph's eyes, expressing shock while intuitively not at all surprised. The weight gets heavier.

"What are you talking about, Keniph? Jet?" queries Atlas. The wind, or rather the realm's breath, begins to whisper to him. A malicious hissing of words in another language, the echo of a laugh behind them. Atlas shakes his head, an attempt to rid himself of the voices futile.

"It's Leda, Red. She said some of the members are experiencing sickness. But it's no sickness she's seen before," Keniph answers, fear lacing his voice. "She said they're starting to forget. Forget where we are, why they're here. Lesions are growing on their skin... They might not make it."

Atlas bites his lip, hoping any semblance of pain may wake him up from this nightmare. The margin of victory for their mission slims with every incapacitated member, whether injured, killed, or sick. Atlas realizes his team were no soldiers, the balance he struck between combative and intelligent a strategic move. But no soldier nor scientist could have prepared for what they were to face. Only the most skilled adventurer with knowledge of the druids may have been able to foresee all that had transpired in the realm. But with no team, the numbers game grows trickier. A balance.

Atlas's mind starts running through the math before he even thinks to question Keniph further. How many could they lose and still win? Was it more so a matter of who would be lost? Are there those that would be preferred sacrifices? Preferred losses? Was every loss equal? The wind cackles at his cold calculations. The air breathes down his neck, sending every hair on end. A reminder. *They were no more than sacrifices all along...* But no, no amount of power will teleport them out of this mess. No power he's accustomed to, but there's still the staff...

"You're positive Leda's not misdiagnosing their apprehension as illness?" Atlas asks, his tone of unconvincing hope. Keniph stares blankly at him, the question purely rhetorical to his ears. Atlas returns the stare, begging for optimism, or rather pleading for the cruel words to leave the lips of his commander so he would not be forced to voice his thoughts. *Hide the cruelty. Hide the malintent.* "Keniph, from the journal, do you remember if the ailment is contagious?"

"I'm not sure if it stated," Keniph responds. He scratches at his head as memory fails him, a strike of his own culpability in this predicament. Guilt festers in his throat as he chokes back a wince. Water builds in Keniph's eyes. "In honesty, I think leaving them behind may be the only option. They're not much use fighting in their condition. They'll quickly be turned into titan food."

"Then it seems we have no choice," Atlas says, his expression transforming as if a switch flips. Atlas's eyes lack the emotion they carried not seconds before, Keniph choking back an accusation he'd surely regret. Atlas continues. "You give the orders to the team. We're moving out. Those infected are to head back immediately. Understood?"

"But, Red..."

"That's an order, Jet. It was your idea, not mine. And I agree with your assessment. So, give the order. Understood?" Atlas's tone reveals his authority, wielding it as an effective weapon not uncommon for one so often in such a position.

Keniph's jaw slowly drops, not knowing how to respond. He realizes he must follow the command, yet he knows their team lacks the numbers to deal with the titans as they are. Losing even more members would prove suicidal.

The pair march to the structure Leda suggested as a quarantine spot from the rest of the group. Solemn eyes and struggling breaths meet them upon entrance. An expression of hopelessness, despair, and failure on every face. Puddles of bile and vomit sit in holes carved from the soil with the sicks' own fingernails, the debris caking underneath and marking their face and skin with every itching blemish they can't help but irritate further.

"I suggest you stay back, Atlas," Leda voices in a stern tone.

She leans over a team member's body, sanitizing then pushing gauze onto oozing, diseased tissue to prevent the bacteria ridden puss from infecting the others, not yet aware of the plan for the infected to return. Another member lay grumbling in agony, biting his hand to prevent himself from screaming for the sake of the secrecy of the team's location. Blood flows from his hands as well as from the open sores on his arms and chest, which are bare in preparation to be bandaged. Black spots circle the sores, blotting out any hope for survival from the disease. Atlas cannot find it within himself to lay eyes upon this particular member.

Atlas takes a count. Four. Four members down. Seventeen members left. Not optimal. Atlas turns to his left and notices movement in the shadows as they begin gathering for another meal. He cannot ignore their presence, nor can he ignore the whispers of Death in the wind, carrying its morbid message for the infected. He gazes at Leda, noting the glittering of her eyes in a futile attempt to help the members.

"Leda, we're moving out," Atlas states. Her eyes widen and she looks up at him. Her strong, maternal nature crumbles under the weight of the cruel reality. She licks her lips and her chest heaves, words unable to find her.

Atlas understood well that no one had the wartime experience going into this mission, except perhaps Keniph. His team was not prepared for such traumas and yet here they are, face to face with what may be only the beginning of their worst nightmares. Clouding their futures with fear and anxiety, paranoia following them wherever they go. Granted, Atlas had not expected most of them to make it this far, for, despite his faith in their abilities, they were not as strong as they needed to be. The time frame did not allow for any further training.

"Leda, we must go," urges Atlas. The authority he asserted when speaking with Keniph disappears from his voice. He cannot order or command Leda to follow his wishes, simply hope she'll agree.

"But... we can't..." she glimpses at the bodies, who don't respond to their conversation, as if they're not there.

"Leda," Atlas nods his head in the direction of the stirring shadows. She stands and steps away from the member's body. Her eyes express her devastation.

"What will they do?" Leda asks.

"If they survive, find their way out. I can ask no more of them in this battle."

Leda closes her eyes and bows her head. All four members lay motionless, even the man who was in agony prior appears to have found rest. The shadows rise from the ground and begin to sculpt themselves into individual beings. Atlas grabs Leda's hand and pulls her away from the graveyard of the diseased, now a meal for the creatures of the realm.

"I've failed," Leda mumbles as they round the corner and regroup. As a nurse and as a shaman, her job, her duty, lies in healing others. Not achieving that promise to all ends means a failure on her part. Though, perhaps it's the cruelty of this dimension, causing grief out of spite or amusement.

Members of the team glance at the three as they join the circle they had formed. Atlas clears his throat, ensuring all eyes find them. Keniph gazes at Atlas before quickly returning his attention to his flask, gulping down the water as if the chance to hydrate would never come again. Atlas glares, understanding Keniph now too fragile to give the command.

"We move out," Atlas says, a strong voice devoid of tremors or sadness, empty of all emotion, filling their ears. Furrowed brows and jaws agape form the only responses. Stillness settles over his team. Is it doubt? Fear? Or has their loyalty begun to degrade? Atlas clenches his jaw, his aura wrapping about him in a tight cyclone, forceful and in control. "Gather your things. We are nearing the end of our mission. You all will be compensated for your part and any lost shall rest assured that their family will be well taken care of." Tears escape some of them at this statement. "We move forward for something greater than ourselves. We move forward to preserve justice and fairness and to do what is right. And we are doing what is right. Come. To victory."

"Aye!" several shouts ring out, arms springing to the air, some pointing to the heavens as if their gods exist in this realm alike.

"Aye," Keniph murmurs, a delay in his reaction.

As Atlas moves toward the front of the team, the others prepare themselves, life force ready to be wielded at a moment's notice. Naht appears at Atlas's side and bows his head, while wearing no expression. They march at the front of the group, hesitant followers lagging a few meters behind, but following nonetheless. Keniph speaks with Leda at the back of the group, urging her to continue forward with them and to stop looking back.

"I'll pay you for the job of finishing them off when we get back," Atlas quietly remarks to Naht in a melancholic tone. The image of the sick man with sores and streams of blood, some of which formed from self-inflicted wounds, presents itself in full clarity in his mind. A shiver courses up his spine.

"Consider it a personal service unto this team. No contract, no payment," Naht replies. "Besides, one was in the state of being devoured by the shadow demons. The stench suggests he'd been dead for several minutes, but a low pulse suggests he hadn't fully been lost yet. But it was no use trying to heal them. Consider it a mercy."

"I have a feeling we're about to see much more than we bargained for."

The team exit the ruined marble town and begin their journey across the floodplains, as deprived of water and hydration as the soils they leave behind.

"Druidic historical texts state this was once a great river," Atlas says, stomping down the dried brush as they march. Tiny spiderlike creatures escape from their path. "The swirling blue banks dried up long ago, the town alongside it. Legend says the draught caused some in the city to flee to an area of greater economic advantage. These people were called apostates. Traitors to the faith. Most remained within the town, continuing to praise the gods whom they believed would save them. They hoped to right their wrong, believing they were being punished for some sin they committed. Unfortunately, despite their prayers and pleadings, their crops continued to wither, and the rain showers never came."

Atlas pauses, the distraction of the tepui entering his vision. He smirks.

"One day, following the death of several townspeople, their religious leader traveled to the altar atop the tepui. He never returned. However, soon after he was expected to arrive, illness plagued many of the townspeople, many of them crying out in agony about the voices and whispers calling to them. Those not infected never heard the voices they spoke of, though they grew irritated and paranoid about a resonant humming."

The breath of the wind hisses in his ear. Atlas licks his bottom lip.

Atlas and Naht tread carefully, Naht staring at the ground with a root of life force always traveling a meter ahead of them. The titans' origins are unknown, for they appeared after the town grew to be no more than ruins if the texts are to be deemed truthful. Atlas hopes if they conceal their presences well enough, the titans will remain undisturbed. However, Naht is not as optimistic.

As the tailing member, Keniph, enters onto the floodplains, the ground tremors as it had earlier. Keniph senses a difference, minute but recognizable. It's as if they are nearer to the epicenter, for the quaking feels shallow. Keniph's heart accelerates. Imminent danger lies ahead. No more fear for other teams, but those who claimed the land long before they arrived.

Naht holds out his arm, stopping Atlas and the train of people behind them. He carefully listens. The earth beneath them grumbles. He suddenly feels a presence behind the team and chuckles.

"The enemy's ahead as well as behind," Naht states.

Atlas turns back to the ruined city. The other team members follow suit, twisting their necks to observe what Atlas wishes to see, not noticing the grin to spread across his face. With a twitch of frustration and curiosity, Atlas parts the team and marches to meet their adversary.

"Well, well, I'm surprised to see you here," Atlas says. His lie would seem genuine but for everyone knowing it to be untrue. His grin does not fade, nor do his eyes give away any hostility or sense of fear. He expresses the face of one welcoming old friends, though they do not mirror his response.

"No need to lie to us," Merwyn responds, revealing an angered glimmer through slitted eyes. Not many could evoke such a hostile response from the Professional, but this was one man who had pushed the boundary one too many times.

Cefni stands next to Merwyn, right arm heavily bandaged with blood seeping through the cloth. He glares at Atlas and feels a rage burn within him, though, the pain derived from his cursed arm leaves his face in a constant state of anguish. Cefni tries to mask his pain but realizes his attempt is unsuccessful. Atlas's eyes glide from Merwyn to Cefni and slowly down to Cefni's wounded arm. Atlas chuckles.

"It seems there was surprise in neither of us. Who told you? Ms. Vayl? Seems there are traitors everywhere..." Atlas stops directly in front of the two Council members. His teammates remain motionless behind him, Naht feeling temptation leak into his thoughts as he looks at the ground, wondering if he should take that step.

"Ms. Vayl did not provide us intelligence, though you seem not too keen in holding her name in reverence, calling her a traitor before allowing us time to answer. No, we have another on our team who told us," Merwyn matter-of-factly answers. Naht, hearing their statement, feels his stomach shift. The two hold their discussion as if no one else is around, as if no danger exists. Cefni begins to feel uneasy with their nonchalance.

"Who, if I may ask?" Atlas inquires. His grin remains intact and his eyes glow with curiosity. Intuitively, Atlas understands he has an escape if the conversation strays from his control. Naht is well aware of the trigger, though, Atlas hopes they are in sync when the time arrives.

"We prefer not to talk about those not present," Merwyn briskly replies, feeling pleasure in defying Atlas. No more than a year ago, Atlas was his superior. Every project, research study, every report, he had to gain approval from Atlas, for budget and permissions, and any information gathered or learned would have to be revealed to Atlas Lurio. He let every member know who held control, who had the authority over all of which occurred within the Association. However, Atlas no longer serves under the Magistrate Association. Merwyn is free to reject Atlas any request. Cefni smirks at Merwyn's response, noting the irritation in Atlas's aura. Merwyn continues. "However, I believe we can entertain one another's interests. If you have the time?"

"Now you're talking my language."

"We'll start. You're aware five distinct teams entered through the gateway?"

"Yes. One team was dead before we left Qoterra."

"How many of these teams were once your allies?"

"Three of the four. Your team the obvious exception. My question." Atlas nods toward Cefni, his grin has faded. "How did that happen?"

"Unlike you, we've been fighting our battles," Cefni answers. He and Atlas never had an understanding relationship. The length of their understanding is that they would stay out of the other's business. "My turn, you've not yet fought, I can tell by your teammates' auras. However, if I recall correctly, you're down a few members-"

"Though not against another team, we've also fought some battles. Humans are the least to be feared in this dimension." Atlas and Cefni lock eyes. His eyes shift, wondering if they are attempting to catch him off guard by diverting his attention elsewhere. But, as he looks around and probes the environment, Atlas feels no presences not in his view. "Where are your other members?"

Merwyn and Cefni glance at one another. Cefni lowers his head to the ground as Merwyn exhales. "I suppose we've arrived at a question unknown to us both. During the last battle, we lost all traces of them." Cefni trembles, water forming in the corner of his eyes, the pain from his arm preventing him from calming himself. The sky reflects his own dismal attitude, clouded and ashy. Atlas discerns his reaction to be genuine, but a series of questions flood his mind. Naht finds difficulty in swallowing at Cefni's revelation. He stares at the ground, his mind forcing his body not to take the step.

"We don't wish to fight you, Atlas," Merwyn continues. "Too many have died for the sake of the staff."

"Oh, believe me. I understand," Atlas charmingly responds. His eyes swell with a feigned sympathy for all those lost, while internally enjoying his own pristine physical condition. Merwyn appears shocked at his reaction, but Cefni, untrusting of Atlas, sees through his stunt. Cefni begins to wonder what Atlas is strategizing or has already strategized. Atlas continues. "I betrayed that team because I did not seek the staff. Our goals did not align, not that I ever expected them to. I had my reasons for joining them, and it was always known by myself and my team we would leave them. Sometimes, in order to crush your enemies, you have to earn their trust. Learn what hurts them most. The staff was never my prize."

"You desired the staff to spite them," Cefni states in a cold tone. Atlas grins. "In fact, you're still willing to risk the lives of those loyal to you just to prove your strength and intelligence to those who didn't stick by your side, even if they're already dead. It's just a game to you. One you're too sore to lose. I'll never understand your definition of justice."

"I don't ask you to. But I will ask you to turn back. After all, beyond this point, nightmares enter reality." His grin widens. The ground beneath them rumbles once more. "Wouldn't want either of you getting hurt."

"You-" Cefni draws his revolver, though it quivers in his hand as he attempts to extend his plagued right arm. Merwyn closes his eyes, believing it unnecessary to involve himself in their conflict, rather focusing his energy on the individuals among his team, many of whose auras feel recognizable from his familiar earlier. Their auras spike at the threat, ready to attack. Naht glances at the crazed Cefni, before returning his attention to the ground, carefully listening to what sleeps beneath. Atlas makes no move, seemingly unafraid of the threat to his life.

"Shoot me," Atlas mockingly orders. Cefni breathes heavily. "What will that achieve, Cefni Medina? I'm not your enemy here. The staff should be entrusted to one who carries the will of humanity on his shoulders. Will you accept that fate? Or who would you choose? Vayl? Giacobbe? Ulton?"

"Give me one more reason, I swear I'll do it!" Cefni shouts. The earth quakes. Naht twitches his leg.

And then he feels it. Though well concealed, his senses are adept to minimal shifts in the environment. A strange comfort returns to Naht. His eyes slowly close and a smile spreads, an emotion he often hides yet unable to at the relief it brings him. Naht always tried to act the uncaring, stoic older brother, but he could not deny to himself that he would go to any lengths to save his siblings, despite his father's programming to rid his children of any possible weaknesses.

It hadn't worked on Nix, perhaps the effect was wearing off on Naht as well.

Naht's life force probes those around, realizing no one else noticed the others' presences taking shape at the edge of the flood plains. They're too enthralled with the spectacle created by Atlas and Cefni. Though Atlas may not realize, this is the cue. The moment to unleash the beasts.

Chapter Nineteen

N aht steps his foot beyond the threshold.

The ground ferociously trembles under them, indistinct noises, like horrid grunts and moans amplified to thrice the volume the average human may make, fill the air. All look around in fear, peering at the soil mounds all about the floodplains and understanding the geographic origins of such forms to have an explanation they had not anticipated. Not one needs told the causation of the quake. Lurking beneath the surface, awakening from their slumber within the crust, the titans rise to meet them.

Panic fills every eye as the earth crumbles around them. Dusty, dried soil forms a cloudy haze as the beings stretch their long-rested bodies. Lumbering arms and legs spring into the air, gargantuan hands reaching to the heavens. The packets of soil erupt to reveal barbaric forms as they unearth the last parts of themselves. The titans wear crude garments, tanned leather pieces slightly decomposed from their time under the soil. As they sit up, they use their monstrous hands to dig at their sides, unearthing rusted weaponry.

Atlas races toward Naht and the two run to the tepui. Every other person seems frozen in place. Cefni and Merwyn look at one another, unaware of their next move. Suddenly, they feel a gust rush past them as three figures run after Atlas. The shock grows within Cefni and Merwyn, though a temporary relief follows soon after.

Atlas's team enter battle mode, understanding their need to distract the beings so Atlas may reach the steps. The fight begins and the world continues to shake with every move the titans make.

Cefni and Merwyn nod to one another, arriving at yet another silent agreement. They join alongside Keniph and help to take down the titans, their resolve written on their faces. The fate of their team rests with the three. And the Council members know they will not disappoint.

As they run through the floodplains, Koepp trips as the ground rumbles. Botalia and Nix help him stand. They continue pursuing their target. No fear derives from the titans rising before and behind them. No focus is spent on the beings. Their vision tunnels toward their sole goal: stopping any from acquiring the staff. As they sat in the house after their battle with Bysciw, the three of them made a pact. And none of them have the slightest inclination of betraying the others. They duck and swerve to avoid the swings and footsteps of the titans, dodging them but refusing to use their energy in an attack. Botalia, Koepp, and Nix know their teammates will act as their support.

Cefni and Merwyn actively play their roles, gliding from side to side, knocking back, severing limbs, and defending their team from the titans. All others would be in awe of their ability if not worrying about their own lives. Cefni points his revolver at the rusted weapon of one, a shocking bullet hitting a copper sword and sending the electric current through its wielder. The electricity finds the titan's muscles and causes a spasm of uncontrolled movement. It knocks another with its sword, and both fall to the ground, dazed. Merwyn sculpts birds of prey to circle the titans' heads, pecking at their eyes and ears as an annoyance but also to prevent them from attacking any on the ground. The distraction would prove more useful if they didn't have to worry about the possibility of being crushed by stumbling feet.

Atlas's team also assists with distracting the titans, believing the three from the other team having no chance at beating their leader. The most impressive fighter on Atlas's team being Ilric, who manages to conjure life force missiles, aiming with pinpoint accuracy to ensure the defeat of solely the titans, sending them in directions where no person stands nor fights. The missiles release compact explosions where human nerves are typically located, hoping the anatomy of a titan, though much grander in scale, to be similar to a human. Many titans fall before him, creating a rush of satisfaction and confidence within him. Ilric glances toward Praecantatis Tepui and feels an urge arise, an impulsive desire. He maliciously grins and takes off toward the steps.

Keniph notices Ilric's shift in aura and yells after him, but to no avail. Keniph continues his fight, questioning his reasons for accompanying Atlas. Doubt and regret surface. He no longer fights for Atlas, but to preserve his teams', and his own, life.

He sees a figure run onto the floodplains, a new face entering the battle. The person is instantly recognizable to him. Keniph feels a pit enter his stomach, unaware of his best course of action. Though mentally his goal has changed, his aversion and trained hatred over the course of the past several months of this man, became embedded in his mind. A target by nature, not by choice. Keniph steps from the titan he and a few others were fighting, believing they contain the necessary strength to defeat it while he shifts his attention elsewhere for the time being.

"I won't let you pass this point, Tanten Flynn," Keniph remarks as he places himself in front of Tanten's path. Tanten slows his run until he halts in front of Keniph. Tanten examines the area around, noting many of the titans are falling but more continue to rise in the distance. That one step truly proved to be a chain reaction.

"You say that as if you are in control of my options," Tanten states, irritation evident in his voice. Tanten's jaw moves in a manner reflective of his tone, how one does when not sure what to say. He never expected to face defiance from such a lowly creature, a follower of Atlas no less. "I suggest you move. I don't wish to use my power on the likes of you."

"I cannot let you reach the tepui, on my own conscience," Keniph replies.

Tanten rolls his eyes. He sighs. Tanten unsheathes his dagger and examines it as he begins walking toward Keniph. Keniph attempts to take a defensive stance but finds himself frozen by some physical, invisible force.

Tanten grabs Keniph's collar in his left hand and positions the blade in his face with his right. Though Keniph stands taller than Tanten, he's not intimidated. He's simply frustrated at being delayed.

"Why don't you just return home to your two-timing wife and keep feeling like you're worth a damn? And meanwhile, act as if you don't know the truth," Tanten jabs. He lowers his voice to a whisper, "But I'll know. It'll do you well to remember who's in control." Tanten releases Keniph and sheathes his dagger. Dusting his hands, he walks around the obstacle that was once Keniph, though it's no longer any more than a shell.

Keniph clenches his fists as his anger swells within him, but he cannot find the power to confront Tanten again. Defeated, Keniph returns to fight alongside his teammates, though his motivation and resolve appear lacking.

Botalia and the boys run as fast as they can, conserving no energy for the inevitable fight once they reach their target. For they know if they cannot reach the staff in time, it will not matter the amount of energy they have left. However, their pace slows as they exhaust their stamina, Koepp's reaching its limits. The titans move in for the attack but are always stopped by the efforts of Cefni and Merwyn. Their life force projections and spells whir past the three, causing the titans to fall to the ground.

Botalia focuses ahead and a shock of realization jolts through her as her acute vision recognizes the man with jet black hair running alongside Atlas. A tumultuous windstorm of an aura surrounds him, whether fear or exhaustion filled the void the gusts typically whistled through, Botalia could not be certain. She glances at Nix, who has not yet noticed.

Botalia feels a strange twist in her gut, not able to discern her own emotions or internal conflict. What should she feel? Anger? Betrayal? Well, perhaps not betrayal because their meeting was the direct effect of him trying to assassinate her. However, with Nix having grown so close to herself and Koepp, she couldn't help but feel a bond had formed between herself and the Kufuta siblings. Their time on the island was short, but the experience was a sufficient amount of time to consider them like family given her zero contact with any human for the last ten years. Understanding that to be no more than a sentiment she felt for her circumstances, the twisting persisted as a new thought struck.

She had stolen Nix away, taken him to her isolated island, far from his family and never once considered contacting them. He was only a child, eleven years of age and she allowed him to make that choice. She thought she was saving him. Just as she had hoped someone would save her fourteen-year-old self. If anything, the Kufutas should hate her. They should want her dead for abducting their son, risking a reputation for the family business who failed to control even their own children.

She cannot decide on an emotion or how future events will play out given the circumstances she now faces. Should Naht Kufuta meet her with violence and wrath, Botalia could not hesitate. She could not hold back or risk losing Koepp or Nix. And despite her pounding heart pleading with her to do whatever it takes, Nix's reaction may be the deciding factor of the outcome.

"Botalia! Use your life force to stop them!" Cefni shouts from behind, breaking her from her thoughts.

Botalia bites her bottom lip, frustration coursing through as she allowed her mind to be her weakness once more. She claps her hands together and forcibly slams them to the soil, stumbling a bit in her tracks as she regains her posture to keep running after them. The life force dissipates instantaneously. Botalia trips over her feet, no longer focusing on her steps but the confusion circling that which transpired. Her knees and palms hit the soil, sending up a small cloud of dust. She tries once more.

Unmoving from her position, her life force flows from her hands and through her fingertips but stops as she tries to move it across the floor of the floodplains. An unexplained force prevents her life force from travel. In her confusion, Botalia and the others see a young male pass them. Botalia rises and stares blankly ahead. She extends both arms in front of her, left palm on the back of her right hand, and shoots a projectile at an incredible speed.

Ilric's face reads panic as the projectile flies past him. He quickly manifests a small pistol for safety and continues to run.

The projectile reaches the position of Atlas and Naht. It floats between the two for a few seconds. Both of their heads turn toward the orb, unaware of what to do. Before they can put much thought into it, the orb explodes in a flash of light. Atlas and Naht fall to the ground, their bodies temporarily stunned. Ilric slows his pace and gazes ahead as the two fall. Botalia, Koepp, and Nix overtake him, racing as fast as they can for the steps.

Atlas and Naht struggle to stand up, their center of gravity not yet in check. They shake their heads, attempting to readjust and find equilibrium. They look back and see four people approach at an alarming rate, decreasing the lead they once had. Atlas instantly recognizes Botalia and grins.

Ilric follows close behind the three. He raises his pistol and aims for Botalia's back. An electric shot hits his hand and his conjured gun dissolves. Turning to see his attacker, Cefni stares back at him, a satisfied smile on his face. Ilric grimaces and clings to his right hand, the pain excruciating.

Botalia gratefully raises her hand as she runs, a gesture of thanks to Cefni. The features on their targets' faces grow clearer. Botalia waits, the moment coming. When it hits, the air changes consistency, as if the little vapor available magnetizes one to another. The result of life force slipping from control. Nix's breathing becomes erratic and his aura appears like a twister. Koepp senses the shift and, face full of concern, turns to Nix. When his head faces front, he learns of the reason. His eyes widen.

As the three approach Atlas and Naht, they find the only one smiling to be Atlas. Botalia furrows her brow and clenches her jaw, the pounding of her heart filling her ears as the beast desires its chance to rip apart the prey. But that would be what Atlas desires, witnessing the beast coming out to play. His smile is nothing other than a trick of temptation. A distraction to their true goals. Botalia hates his mind games.

They stop running, almost as if against their will, and halt in front of the pair. Botalia's aura flares as her eyes move from Atlas to Naht. Nix stands paralyzed, staring at his older brother who avoids eye contact with him. The mass of titans swarm toward the battle near the ruined city, leaving them without worry of interference, with the exception of small tremors that manage to reach them. Ilric joins Atlas at his side.

"I'm so glad you could join us Ms. Ulton, Little Flynn, and," Atlas glances at Nix, who pays no attention to him in return, and chuckles. "Young Kufuta. You appear surprised? Though, I assume you all are. Granted, I'm surprised at the lack of hostility with Ms. Botalia and Little Flynn. After all, the Kufutas attempted to assassinate you both."

"I appreciated the company, no matter their ill will towards me. While I didn't appreciate the intent, I realize it was a job and no more than that at the time. Seems somebody wanted me dead," Botalia mockingly states. She and Atlas examine one another closely. His aura takes the shape of a violent, yet completely controlled, cyclone. It does not express his emotions but is a tool for intimidation, revealing his power.

"Why did you come here with him?" Nix asks with an irritated edge lacing his voice when regarding to Atlas. Rage circulates through him and his body trembles, though the exhaustion could be adding to it. He bites down on his lip.

"I should be asking you the same. Father would have never approved for you to be here."

"I don't need his permission anymore."

Naht raises an eyebrow, sealing his lips to prevent any further words from escaping. Nix's words sting in an odd way, as if they hold more power and weight than his brother realized. As if beliefs he never once questioned were now clouded by doubt.

Atlas opens his mouth as if to speak, but quickly snaps it shut, his eyes shift to the horizon behind the team. Naht and the others sense the presence as well, though those with their backs to it refuse to take their eyes from those in front of them. Botalia glances at Cefni whose eyes connect with her own for a split second. Botalia focuses her hearing.

"You stop him, Merwyn and I will stop these guys," Cefni whispers, his sentence indistinct to the others. Botalia nods.

Tanten Flynn does not pause as he races past them with only one thought on his mind. Ilric shoots at him, but Tanten artfully dodges the shots. The stairs at the base of the tepui are in sight, and he focuses wholeheartedly on reaching the top before the others. Botalia taps Koepp's and Nix's shoulder and they run off after Tanten. Atlas and his allies turn to follow, but Cefni and Merwyn successfully trap two of the three, Naht being the exception. Naht makes no hesitation and runs toward the staircase.

Atlas and Ilric turn to the Council members, an evident hostility in their eyes.

"It's just you and me, Atlas. You have no idea how long I've waited for this," Cefni states. Atlas smiles. Cefni's hands twitch and his life force prepares itself. His eyes appear similar to a predator watching its prey, patiently waiting for the moment to strike.

Ilric glares at Merwyn as a potent fear courses through his veins. He materializes a shotgun and aims it at his opponent. Merwyn raises a shield to block and grins after the life force dissipates. Not maliciously or out of jest, but of the pride he feels in seeing one so gifted in conjuration. Sympathy creases Merwyn's eyes as the sensation drifts to sadness at such a talent wasted with warfare, not to mention the unfortunate circumstance at being pitted against one of the greatest life force users in the known world.

Ilric shoots more shots at the figure of Merwyn, but the figure disintegrates and Merwyn's voice can be heard behind him.

"You have an impeccable talent. If I thought you'd agree, I'd ask you to become my disciple." Merwyn sighs. "Unfortunately, you've a long way to go."

Ilric turns to shoot once more but is pulled to the ground by Merwyn's conjured life force roots. The shotgun transforms into a knife and Ilric cuts through the vines. The blade he has constructed sends the life force racing back to the sculptor, the other roots dissolving after the first slice. Ilric panics as the need to be on a constant defensive is not the position of the victor.

Alongside them, Cefni and Atlas fly back and forth, defying gravity. A fight like none ever seen. A fight between two of the most gifted life force users in generations. Cefni continuously pulls the elements from the heavens above. Atlas, a severe glow emitting from his eyes, manipulates the space and fields about them. Anyone looking in on the fight would not be able to understand the complexity concerning the attacks being utilized.

Outside, time flows normally, but within their battlefield, it looks as if time has accelerated to higher velocities. For Cefni and Atlas, time slows. Each attack and each defensive block succeed in their purpose. Flashes of light and reflected units of life force create a show. They fight not for the staff or for their teams, but for the sake of their own pride. For the sake of righting the wrongs done unto them so long ago by the other.

Whether it be failed proposals or defeat by attacks on personal interest, Cefni and Atlas harbor a hatred toward one another that may only be diminished through the use of physical confrontation. They've both buried their history with one another long ago for the sake of the betterment of the Magistrate Association, Dominia, and the world as a whole. But within this new realm, the weight of responsibility and reputation no longer hold them back. They disinter their pasts and use it to fuel their battle.

Chapter Twenty

Tanten leads the pack, reaching the cobblestone steps before the others. Botalia and Koepp start the climb, but Nix freezes at the base and spreads his arms before his brother. Koepp slows as he notices Nix take a defensive stance behind. The glimmer in Naht's eyes as he slows to a stop causes a chill to race up Koepp's spine. Nix, Koepp's best friend, proves their bond to run deeper than blood. Tears fill Koepp's eyes as the concepts of sacrifice and inevitable death swirl there.

"We'll be together again at the end of it all," Botalia says between heaving exhales to ensure Koepp, the heat of whose aura prickles at her own. She attempts to keep her own eyes from watering, the flames of his aura packed with the emotion of his thoughts. "I promise."

Koepp nods and the two race up the stairs after Tanten.

At the bottom of the steps, Nix stands in front of his brother, wearing an expression that threatens to attack if Naht tries to pass him. Once a void of emotion, rage and wrath wrapped in despair find him. But masking it all is resolve to do what it takes at all costs. Nix does not plan on betraying Koepp or Botalia, not even for the sake of his brother.

"I can't let you go any further," Nix commands, his voice trembling. Naht squints and tilts his head, a quizzical look on his face. Nix extends his arms to his side, in a childish fashion, as if creating a roadblock with no more than his body.

"Did they threaten you? Or harm you, perhaps?" Naht asks. He carefully examines Nix but sees no sign of manipulation. Naht cannot comprehend the strange evolution apparently taking place within Nix. He appears stronger, yet more fragile, and purposeful in comparison to when they acted together as assassins.

"They saved me," Nix replies. He glares at Naht who ceases to understand the scenario. Nix's aura flares. "If you want to pass, you'll have to fight me."

"Assassins are not to fight amongst themselves. You know that."

"I'm not an assassin. I quit."

"So you were not abducted? You ran away. Father will be quite displeased with your decision. He was already concerned with your disappearance."

"He doesn't care about me, just the business."

A silence enters their conversation, for Naht knows he cannot disagree with Nix's last point. Naht looks to the ground. There is no point in arguing with a stubborn eleven-year-old, for their arguments go without reason and are often fueled by many irrational emotions. Though, Nix's insight is impressive at such a young age.

Naht sits on the ground, legs crossed, leaning back on his arms. Nix furrows his brow, confusion settling in, but refuses to lower his own guard, understanding the underhanded tactics his brother may be employing.

"Let's watch this fight play out, shall we?" Naht asks. He pats the soil at his side, signaling for his young brother to sit there. Nix steadies his breathing and notices the genuine disinterest in Naht's eyes, granted his eyes always held an emptiness. After a few seconds, Nix sits on the cobblestone step and gazes up toward Botalia and Koepp, praying they will succeed.

Botalia, Koepp, and Tanten ascend as quickly as they can, attempting to ignore their screaming muscles as they climb. They know if they so much as slow, they may never get back up to speed.

They may completely crash. Their hearts beat in their ears, powerful thumps threatening to shift their balance. A loud humming accompanied by indistinct whispers fills the air around them, as if one recites a chant, a spell. Koepp begins to feel dizzy, a sharp pain beneath his ribs as he breathes.

The stairs endlessly ascend, mirroring the feeling in Botalia's dreams. The images. They flash through her head, the altar, the staff, the staircase, the blurred figure... Botalia clenches a fist to her chest as it pulsates. The creature yearns to help, knowing its ability to aid in accomplishing her goal. Botalia feels indebted to the creature for saving her life on several occasions, but Botalia wants to accomplish this by herself. For her pride, her honor, for Koepp and Nix, Cefni and Merwyn, Tenebrant...

Botalia raises her right arm and emits her life force. It hits the step in front of Tanten, his reactions delayed due to running. Ultimately, it slows him down, the small pieces of stone broken from the step falling in his path. This provides the time needed for Botalia to catch up with Tanten. She reaches out her arm and grabs onto his leg. Tanten trips and pulls Botalia down with him, crashing onto the cobblestone steps. Tanten Flynn kicks at her, not doing so with much accuracy but furiously and with great force. She blocks his attacks with her life force, the entirety of her physical strength drained.

Botalia holds him down and rises, attempting to pass him. Tanten raises his hand and projects a life force missile at her. Her life force protects her from most of the damage, but the force of the impact pushes her forward, finding herself once again lying atop the steps. Her head lies close to the edge, able to see just how far she'd fall.

Koepp stands back, understanding given his position any attack will cause him to slide down the stairs. He watches the two fight one another like rabid animals, clawing, kicking, and punching one another as they try to gain the advantage. As he looks down the stairs, Koepp notices how far they've climbed, but looking up he realizes just how far they have to go. The clouds cover the steps ahead of them, and above that there is no telling how much farther they'll need to travel to reach the altar and, more importantly, the staff.

Tanten leaps to his feet and races up the stairs, Botalia following closely behind. She feels the bruises forming under her skin from the impacts with the stairs and his physical attacks. The pain makes the run incredibly unbearable.

"Almost there," Botalia constantly reminds herself. While she knows there is not much truth in such optimism, the hope fuels her to keep going, as does staring at Tanten's back. Again, she extends her arm and projects another bolt of life force. Tanten tries to reflect the beam back at Botalia and partially succeeds in his execution. They both stumble but remain standing.

As the three decrease their distance from the staff, their heads ring and ache with the abundance of noises and voices, both their own and some of unknown origin. Botalia's energy drains, the flicker of the creature's protective aura forming and retreating as the cage she crafted loses power. Botalia's arm trembles as she extends it in front of her. A chain of life force exits the palm of her hand and wraps itself about Tanten's ankle. Botalia pulls back, forcing Tanten to the ground. He digs his fingers into the stairs, ensuring he does not fall too far, for fear of giving up more ground.

Botalia stumbles past him, careful to avoid his flailing arms and legs in an attempt to grab her. Her breathing grows shallow as she continues to climb. Tanten appears as exhausted and weak as she does all while cursing under his breath. Passing into the layer of clouds, Botalia feels her entire body tremble. Tanten climbs not far behind her, but neither have the energy required to combat one another.

Her vision begins to fail her. Her chest pulses. She blinks several times attempting to remove the black spots from her vision. Her eyelids slide down. Her eyes water. Her heart pounds, echoing in her ears. The beat courses through her entire body. Her lungs scream out. Her mind gone, teleported away, no longer wishing to participate in this mission. Devoid of thought, all rationale, all emotion. All that drives her is an instinct. She'll continue to do what she set out to do at the bottom of the tepui. Though she does not know why. Why is she here? What is she fighting for? The questions float for no more than a nanosecond before drowning in the abyss.

Koepp gazes at the two, overwhelmed with emotion. His own physical fatigue disappeared as he watched those before him waste away to no more than mindless zombies. He overexerted his body to the point where he no longer feels pain, the only downfall is not being able to stop. Koepp knows the moment he stops, he will collapse and find himself unable to move, much like when Botalia awakened from her state of unconsciousness. He follows the pair. He wipes his arms across his face as the stream of tears begins to flow. Every once in a while, Koepp violently shakes his head, trying to stop the whispers and humming.

As soon as the three pass the threshold, they know. Their vision entirely fades to black. The stairs disappear underneath them. The sensation of falling overcomes them for a second before feeling solid stone form under their feet. Botalia and Tanten believed they had met Death, the shadows consuming their physical forms. But when they open their eyes, they see the Heaven that awaited them.

A beautiful marble altar, inlaid with gold and sapphire sits atop the tepui. Four spires rise from the corners, runic signatures etched into them. At the center of the altar, displayed in bountiful glory, hypnotizing any who look upon it, stands the legendary staff, gnarled at the top, carefully and masterfully carved of yew.

Tanten stares at the staff, a feeling of obsession and completion, the chance to obtain infinite power. He finds difficulty in swallowing as a chorus of muses seem to sing their angelic hymns about him.

The staff calls to him... It desires him to claim it... Tanten smiles, a sensation of pure joy fills him. A radiant beam of light issues down from the heavens to illuminate the staff. All for Tanten Flynn.

Botalia's eyes grow wide as the image of the staff sets in. She feels her entire body tremble. Botalia returns to her senses, her mind yelling at her to run, escape its presence before it's too late, before she falls under the staff's influence. A tremendous fear restricts her movement. The images, the noises, flood her thoughts, creating within her more fear and anxiety.

As she notices Tanten at her side, standing tall, enthralled by the radiance of the staff, she remembers she is not in her dreams, this is real... or as real as one's mind can make an event seem. Tanten starts to step toward the staff, his dreams within reach.

Botalia lunges forward and tackles Tanten to the stone foundation. A ravenous red glimmers in his eyes as he turns to look at Botalia, the last, annoying, insufferable, lowly ant in his way. He had fought too hard, lost too much, to be thwarted by an indignant lab rat who had forgotten her place. The only option is extermination.

He pushes the weak Botalia back and positions his knee in her abdomen. She gasps for air, trying to push him off but lacks the strength. With one hand, he holds down her wrist and unsheathes his dagger. Holding it steady, Tanten attempts to stab Botalia, a killing blow. She grabs his wrist with her free hand, slowing its movement toward her body, though, she cannot prevent its forward motion. She finds herself without the energy or strength to boost a rush of adrenaline. The creature calls to her, but she refuses. This is her mission.

The blade approaches her face.

"Stop it!" Koepp cries out and jumps on Tanten's back, arms wrapped around his neck.

Tanten throws him off, a loud sound of anguish and pain as Koepp crashes to the ground. A tear trickles down Botalia's cheek, escaping from beyond her control. Botalia trembles as she watches Koepp's rugged figure struggle to rise. Her vision blurs as she believes both of their deaths may be near. She failed him.

Her hand races up again to stop the attack on her person. She digs her nails into Tanten's forearm. His face never changes expression, a hypnotized rage burns within him, as if he is being manipulated by some unknown force to eliminate Botalia. His blood covers her hand, which start to slip up his arm, losing traction due to the slippery, red liquid. She inches her hand up his arm, past his wrist, and tightly grips his hand.

The blade grazes her neck, opening an exit for her blood. She clenches her teeth to prevent a cry of pain.

This is suffering. I thought I've felt it all. But this. Face to face with true horror, desperation, hopelessness...

A suffering not experienced through others, by others, but by herself. A suffering not felt since...

She fails to find breath, tensing every muscle in her body to stop the blade from penetrating her neck. Her left hand slips down the dagger, the blade slicing through her skin, her blood pouring forth. She tries to create a barrier between the blade and her neck, her hand the only available shield. Her eyes squeeze tightly shut, her legs flail in an effort to escape. She does the only thing she can. She prays. She prays for an end. The exact prayer from ten years before. Asking, begging for death. As if Botalia could shoulder the world's suffering, but cripples under the weight of her own.

A blurred figure rises behind Tanten. Koepp. Koepp peers at the staff, not with the look of desire or fear but rage. He cannot gaze upon Botalia or Tanten, his emotions outside of his control. His eyes fix on the staff, and he stomps toward it.

Slowly stepping onto the altar, a pressure pushes down on his body, as if the gravitational pull increases with every movement forward. Koepp pours every ounce of energy within him into completing the task. His entire body trembles, his torso stiffens as the resistive force attempts to stop him. As if the staff is a being of its own and understands his intentions. He clenches his jaw and stubbornly raises his arms, overcoming much difficulty in doing so. The tears drip onto the marble of the altar, Koepp leaving his mark. He refuses to be a burden.

With a last surge of energy and before Tanten can stop him, Koepp grabs hold of the staff, tightly gripping it in both hands. Strong winds begin to circle Praecantatis Tepui. The sky grows darker, a sole ray of light spotting the staff. Tanten jumps from Botalia, infuriated by Koepp's tenacity, as if believing he has a right to touch the Staff of the Gods.

Tanten screams some indistinct insult, but it cannot be heard over the howl of the wind. Koepp squeezes his eyes and releases a cry of his own. His entire body appears consumed by the aura of the staff. Strong surges of pure, concentrated life force course through him, feeling as though the strands are ripping apart every muscle, striking every nerve, paralyzing him. Koepp cannot move. He cannot see. For a moment, he cannot breathe. His mouth is open and a loud screech leaves, but it is not his own. He is powerless. Koepp cannot conjure the simplest of winces. Koepp cannot do anything.

The winds grow more violent per second. A dense fog closes in from a distance. Botalia pays no attention to the environment, but rather stares at Koepp, desperately wishing to pull him from the torrential aura of the staff, to remove him from his suffering.

"A Staff of the Gods is not meant for mortal man," Botalia thinks. "He's not strong enough for this, his body, his mind, his heart... they're dissolving, decomposing before my eyes. I have failed for I cannot save him."

Koepp pictures many memories from the course of his life. The power of the staff forcing the bad to rise to the surface. But Koepp's own will, his resolve and promise to those he deeply cares about, intersperse images to keep him sane. To give him a mental and emotional strength he'd thought he'd lost.

Koepp sees the blur of the man sneaking into the room where he constructed the fireplace, closing the door behind him and with a thin smile and hungering eyes. He sees himself now, as if observing the scene from the outside, his ephemeral form screaming to run, to attack, to do something, anything but sit there dazed. But he knows what happens next. As the hand grips about his shoulder, the memory flicks to Botalia placing a hand in that ill-fated spot. She congratulates him on his new high score for their math testing. He plops a jellybean into his mouth and displays a wide grin. With great force, the memory is ripped from him, and he feels the lash hit his back. *I told you two meters exactly! Not two and three centimeter! You'll learn not to do that again.* Another lash at his bare skin. Gritted teeth hold back a cry of pain. The tears sliding down his cheek were not simple despair but anger. Rage aimed at himself for his powerlessness. For being a failure and disappointment who would never rise. His guardians screamed at the blood-stained clothes when he arrived, how selfish he was to not take care of that which they granted. He punched at his wall when secluded in his bedroom, the stone splitting his skin at the knuckle. And then another punch and he was playfully sparing with Nix. His friend taught him some of the fighting forms he learned during his assassin training. Nix told him he'd feel like a superhero when he succeeded in landing a punch in battle. Koepp never told his friend he had no desire to be a superhero or fight people, he just liked spending time with him.

His memories. They were his, they were all he had. The only thing he had that no one else did. Some he wished to forget. Others he treasured. Botalia helped erase some painful attachments, but even viewing the bad memories from a distance caused a pain in his chest and made it difficult to breathe. As if holding his breath, wondering how things could have been different. But if they had been different, would he ever have met Botalia and Nix? Would he trade those bad times if it meant losing them forever...

But he would lose them forever. Because while he would hopefully remain in their memories for a short time, they'd grow to forget him and move on. He was willing to sacrifice himself here and for what? He didn't want to be the superhero. He never asked for this. He just didn't want to leave their side. He didn't want them to go and forget about him. He wanted his presence to remind them of who he was. But maybe his presence was a burden for them. Maybe his death will also prove burdensome. There was no light at the end of the tunnel. He would always be a problem for those he met. Maybe he could use the staff to go back. To make himself invisible from the start. That way no one would know him. No one would care. He would fade away and it would be no different than a meteorite entering the atmosphere and burning to a crisp. He would be no more than a flicker in their thoughts, just another pedestrian in the street, an ant on the ground.

Koepp yells at the top of his lungs, breaking through every sound barrier attempting to cloud his mind. A bolt of lightning crashes from the sky and hits the altar in a blinding flash. A thundering sound protrudes from the point of contact, the altar cracked in half. The staff erupts in a burst of flames, but Koepp refuses to let go.

Though screaming in pain, Koepp waits until the staff is weak enough, its aura detaching itself from his own, slowly dying out, and, holding the staff high above his head, Koepp smashes it into the marble altar. In a gust of wind, which pushes Koepp and Tanten to the ground, Botalia never having risen from the previous incident, the staff explodes in an array of colors and sounds. The whispers transform into screams. The humming into howling. The three feel strange sensations course through their bodies and their eyes drowsily close.

What seems like no more than a few moments later, her eyes open. Botalia picks the upper half of her body off the stone slab and sees a broken altar, the staff nowhere in sight. The skies are clear, and the sun shines cheerfully on the top of Praecantatis Tepui. Botalia scans the surface when tears instantly fill her eyes. She crawls to his mangled body as fast as she can. Tears fall like rain from her cheek and onto his own. Her mouth opens, but she remains speechless. He appears to her no more than a blurry figure.

She moves her bloody left hand to his chest and can feel his heartbeat. But, in this she finds no relief. To her side, Botalia notices Tanten's unconscious body, not yet having awoke from the explosion. Botalia cradles Koepp in her arms and rocks back and forth. She prays the others will come. Hoping the others will find them atop the tepui and take them home. Home. A word she never liked using to describe the house on that island. And yet, here, at this moment, she wanted to be there, more than anywhere else. Botalia gazes at Koepp's face. On it, there are no signs of distress or pain... or suffering. Only peace. She glimpses at his maimed arms before rapidly looking back at his face, not wanting to see the injuries, the corruption, only the innocence of a young boy who felt he was worth nothing. But he was worth so much to her.

Botalia keeps her hand on his chest and closes her eyes. She wishes only to feel his heart, to ensure it keeps going. His heartbeat is calm. As it should be. No more nightmares. Only sweet dreams. As Botalia rocks back and forth with Koepp in her arms, she begins to sing:

Close your eyes little warrior
Return to your dreams
Walk upon the red clouds
And sleep

Lu Li La Le
Feel the pain disappear
No need to fight on, fight on
The darkness draws near
Lu Li Lu La
Approach with gentle heart
Sense the monster's release
And sleep, and sleep
Sense the monster's release
And sleep
Lu Li Ly La Li Ly Le

Before she finishes the last line, Botalia falls into a deep sleep. Shadows dance through her eyelids as the sun finds her, heating the immense chill that threatened to consume her. In that space, silence is deafening, the void a powerful presence. The creature cannot escape the feeling, collapsing within the barrier where bars once prevented exit. But the cell dissolved with Botalia, no remaining energy for even the beast to grab hold of. This was not death... it couldn't be. After all, she still needed to make her wish.

Chapter Twenty-One

When Botalia wakes, the weight of Koepp in her numbing arms sends relief through her. A slight pulse can still be felt, her fingertips gripping tight to him as a tremble returns to her. Her gaze scans the top of the tepui. The marble altar crumbles, bits of debris hitting the stony, flat surface of the plateau with the sudden gusts to swirl through. Tanten has since departed, no sign he had ever been there left behind. Blood that once pooled crimson now dries to a deep auburn in the heat of the sun. Botalia wishes to continue taking it all in, but her head droops as gravity fights to beat the little energy she has left. She allows her head to lay limp, not risking losing the energy needed to not let Koepp slip from her grip.

"Koepp! Botalia!" an overly distressed voice calls out. An indistinct mumble can be heard after in a different voice.

Botalia does not have the energy to yell in return. Her jaw drops but no desire to make any sound or movement arrives. She does not want to disturb Koepp, whose heart plays a steady, tranquil melody, hauntingly slow and quiet.

"Koepp! Botalia!"

Though he continues to shout, Botalia cannot find it within herself to give him the affirmation he seeks. Nix wishes to know whether they are alive before he witnesses the scene. Any hope that he won't arrive to no more than bloodied corpses after such a long climb. Every shout loses the trill of hope once carried to him by biting nerves, the pit in his stomach releasing a corrosive despair ready to consume him should his nightmares be reality.

Their footsteps draw closer, patting against the stone steps with agility and without fear of heights. She cannot determine how many people will meet them, how many made it out alive and in such form to be able to climb the stone stairway, but the number does not matter. The fact that anyone would climb to the top of the tepui to find herself and Koepp gifts her with a sense of happiness and relief. Neither her nor Koepp had been truly abandoned. Not this time. The simple knowledge of this would force a smile to spring upon his face were he conscious. The thought tears at her and a wince escapes as the only sound she can muster.

Botalia blankly stares out at the horizon. The soft blues of the sky, the sun brightly shining onto the white marble ruins of the city. She turns her head to face the other direction. Majestic mountains rise from the land and stretch toward the heavens. The lack of all life, whether plants or animals, creates a dismal, estranged environment, like the lands of a foreign planet. Botalia feels the light breeze caress her face. She slowly closes her eyes, transcending the world around her. Traveling like a current through the lifeless soil, the nutrients long squandered. She senses the cumulus clouds forming in the distance. Perhaps rain.

"Koepp! Botalia!"

Botalia opens her eyes and watches as their heads enter her view. She thought she would feel relief in seeing their faces, but she feels nothing. As if all emotion drained from her, Botalia cannot feel anything as she examines them, believing herself to be in a dream. It doesn't feel real. An illusion.

The figures rush toward her, screaming out, crying. Botalia feels their hands against her skin, yet she does not move. Her face is expressionless, her eyes empty. The figures attempt to lift Koepp, but her grip on him tightens. They step back.

"Everything is going to be alright. We're here to help you," Merwyn calmly states. He places his hand on her shoulder but receives no response, not the slightest change of expression to accept the help.

Cefni stares at the same empty shell, an image which haunted his memories for years now transfiguring into a woman ten years older but still so alone. *Don't do anything rash...* The words echo about his mind, the scene before him no different than those he'd seen dozens of times as an investigator and yet he could not disconnect himself from the moment. *Why was it always so bloody?*

Nix stands behind the Professionals, jittering eyes unsure of where to focus. His hands clench and release as his breathing grows erratic. Naht takes a place beside his brother, a strange sensation settling in his stomach as he peers at Botalia and Koepp, the image unlike any he's seen, despite the family business.

Blood, a not uncommon sight for the assassin, came in many states. Dried into a deep auburn and painted about the body and clothes in ways that would suggest a torturous, mutilation technique not used by their business, was not a state he wished to ever see again. The blood's canvas, Koepp's body, which now existed without two limbs where his hands should be, draped across Botalia's lap, held as if the only possession saved from a devastating house fire. And every tensed muscle in her body suggested that despite her exhaustion, she would not fail to sacrifice herself time and again to save what little ember of life burned within him. Naht clamped his jaw shut as he realized it slid open, expressing more emotion than he would ever wish for any to catch sight of.

"Botalia," Merwyn begins, noting the shock on all other faces and hoping to be the solid pillar for the team. "Can you stand?"

Botalia nods. The response causes Merwyn to grin. Progress.

"Botalia," Merwyn starts in a hushed tone. He whispers into her ear, hoping the others will be unable to hear his question. "Is he alive?"

Botalia feels Koepp's heartbeat under her hand, announcing its presence. She nods. Merwyn gives a sigh of relief. He wipes his hand across his brow and removes any semblance of tears from his eyes. He turns to Cefni, and they offer a blink and head nod as some form of telepathic communication.

"Botalia, are you ready to return home?"

Her eyes water and her entire body trembles as the thought of life after this was even possible. The idea of home was not some sublime impossibility. It still existed there. And she still existed here, despite a skipping heart and flickering aura. Botalia closes her eyes, the pressure of her eyelids forcing the tears to stream down her face, and nods.

"So are we," Merwyn replies, a wide, reassuring smile on his face. He rises from his kneeling position and peers at the meeting of cumulus clouds in the distance. Having taken his eyes from the awful sight and allowing a different thought to enter, Merwyn wonders if he can look down upon them once more. A grim expression settles and he holds his breath, the sunlight reflecting from Botalia's tears enough to force some of his own. "Do you need assistance?" Merwyn extends his hand.

Botalia shakes her head. She attempts to stand with Koepp in her arms but finds her body won't listen. Her legs refuse to move. Her chest pounds. Botalia sits for a moment. She thinks. Her conclusion makes itself evident and she closes her eyes.

Her subconscious body travels through dark hallways, one so similar to that she knows from others' memories and slideshows. Yet she only traveled her own on few occasions before. Often she avoided this place, only in her weakest moments could she no longer keep this hallway trapped behind a wall of her life force. In those moments, the scarred memories would seep into her dreams, forming nightmares, always taking her back to that one night, where she lost her wits, and she lost herself.

A bright light shines from under a door in the hallway ahead. She stops in front of it. What she knew to normally be shielded by life force, that part which she concentrates in her chest, no longer bore a shield. She could easily touch the handle and swing the door open.

Botalia's footsteps echo as she enters the space. She grows alert, knowing that eyes watch her from the shadows. She searches for it and promptly finds it hiding in the corner.

The koroko. The part of her hybrid self she locks away, that part she separated from herself with The Hymn of the Beast those ten years ago. A part she was ashamed of, a part she resented, but more so a part of her she was afraid of.

Botalia bows her head and rapidly extends her arms in front of her, open palms to the ceiling. Her mouth opens but no words find their way out. She attempts to calm her breathing so as to not alert the creature, but fails.

After several seconds, the creature inches forward. It questions whether the sign of relinquishing control of the physical body is genuine. The last time it took over at the request of Botalia, its life turned into a nightmare as did Botalia's. However, it slowly begins to understand her downfall, as if the world is crumbling around her.

It reaches out, hovering an elongated finger over her hand, hesitating before taking hold, believing she may change her mind. When Botalia does not flinch, the koroko presses into her palms with its own. Their positions swap. The koroko winces at it feels the pain and exhaustion wrapped about the Botalia existing in the real world. It feels the anguish from emotion at that which transpired. It feels the weight of Koepp in her arms. The subconscious Botalia curls into a fetal position on the floor and shoos the koroko from the space, wishing for a moment of solitude.

The koroko stretches out its neck and legs and walks through the door down the hallway of memories, approaching the light at the end of the hallway, the moment of waking from this inner place and exiting into the real world. It's as if waking from a dream, opening the eyes to see the world around, knowing that where it once was doesn't truly exist. And yet it rarely sees this light on its own, through its own perspective, watching through Botalia's sights like the dream. Now, it was awake.

Merwyn carefully watches as Botalia's facial expression subtly changes. Botalia opens her eyes and looks about. Muscles scream but the being in control of Botalia pushes past the pain. The koroko, its movements awkward in Botalia's physical body, bends its knees and lifts Koepp with it as it stands. It remains silent and avoids making eye contact. Merwyn reveals a reluctant grin and looks to Cefni, who bows his head and turns toward the stairs. Nix follows without hesitation.

Naht gazes upon Botalia, noting the strange shape her aura now takes. Though Botalia's aura had always been unique, the shaped mimicked her own. The shape swirling about her now is not the outline of a human, but of a creature. This was it. This was the reason she could not be manipulated by another, because she was already sharing a mind with this beast.

"It's here to help," Merwyn says, noting the doubt lining Naht's expression.

"It? As in that thing now has control of her?"

"Botalia simply needs to rest."

Merwyn descends the steps, the koroko with Koepp in its arms following behind.

Naht stands alone on the top of the tepui and looks down at the sights. Atlas had not lied to him. A monster does live within Botalia and at the moment it was walking Koepp down the stairs in a maternal fashion. The idea of a gentle being slaughtering a gang returns him to thoughts of what animals do when threatened or protecting their young. He lets out a short, breathy laugh and shakes his head. Atlas may be obsessive and delusional, but at least he knows his enemies... better than they may know themselves.

The group walk in silence, passing through the floodplains. Downed titans and a couple of Atlas's team members, rest on the dried soils, those who survived having fled with the crack of thunder to shake the land. Titans can still be seen fleeing in the distance, moving on with their lives as they no longer are chained to these lands as the protectors of the staff. Phantom sand birds appear no more than vultures circling overhead, marble weavers, the arthropods who chased them previously, curling into their nests in the ground as they prepare to rest.

Merwyn leads the way into the ruined city, the broken marble structures a haunting sight, but less so with the absence of voices riding the winds. The shadows act as they should, none out of place or moving. As the wind blows the dust and debris about, the old cobblestone street slowly reveals itself.

Cefni tails the team. He gazes upon the structures and through the labyrinthine passageways in town. All fear of what lurks behind every corner, beyond the walls which have stood the test of time, has subsided. Though no more than a few hours have passed, he feels as if he's known this town his whole life. A familiarity and understanding one attains through hardships. Like a person you've known for a short time but share the experience of something joyful or tragic. A shaky bond constructed from the fragile threads of core memories being formed. One that cannot be simply broken... or forgotten. The kind of bond even should you wish to forget, your dreams offer the constant reminder. The image, the scene, vivid and tangible.

A droplet of water strikes Nix's forehead. He flinches, with head whirling in all directions, awaiting the attack. Cefni places a hand on his shoulder and points to the sky. Grey-blue clouds race over the town, the winds accelerating to bring them there. The sparse isolated drops grow into a gentle trickle. They close their eyes and allow the rain to hit their faces. The clouds weep alongside them, as a tear streams down Nix's face, disguised by the raindrops. The dirt and debris wash from their hair, skin, and clothes. The ground pools with the offering, the soil deprived of the moisture for so long slowly regaining its thirst for the sweet taste once more. The grime detaches from the marble ruins and they shine of alabaster white as they may have once done when the town was alive.

When they near the building where they first arrived, Botalia slows. She gazes at the exact location where the gateway should be should no walls exist between them. Hesitation grows in her will to follow Merwyn. When at the door, the being in control of Botalia's body halts.

"There it is. Our way home and luckily still opened," Cefni says with low tone, as if speaking too loudly may scare it. "Come on, Botalia. We're almost there. We're almost home."

The being in control of her body makes no movement.

"It's the aura of the gateway. Many Scholars have found that creatures have an increased sensitivity to fields that humans cannot sense. Hence why no creatures on Qoterra near the portal. The cryptochromes within such creatures allow them to sense magnetic fields, which can have adverse effects on creatures after extended periods of time if the field strength exceeds an uncalculated amount," Merwyn explains. Naht and Cefni share a similar blank expression, not wanting Merwyn's opinion of their intelligence to diminish. Merwyn, realizing he's lecturing a marble wall, turns his attention to the being that is Botalia.

"Botalia," Merwyn calls out, as if not talking to the being, but past it. "Naht, if you could please," Merwyn approaches Botalia, her facial expression spelling her caution as he nears. He holds his palms out, warranting peace and no ill will. Naht steadily walks toward Botalia, inquisitively eyeing her. Merwyn reaches for Koepp's figure, but the creature tightens its grip.

"We won't hurt him. We wish to help," Merwyn calmly pleads. The creature's eyes soften and it loosens its grip. "Naht, if you will. You're more capable than Cefni and myself at the moment." Naht hesitates as he reaches for Koepp's figure, and carefully lifts Koepp to hang over his shoulders. Naht bites his tongue, the odd sensation as Koepp's limp and broken arms lay against his back, sending a chill through his spine. Merwyn nods at Naht. "Thank you."

Naht steps back, takes a place near Cefni, and looks to his brother. Nix stares at the ripples caused by the rain in a nearby puddle, doing his best to dissociate himself entirely from their current conversation. Naht wonders why the urge to assure his brother of Koepp's heartbeat echoes in his mind. The assassin gazes into the distance, wondering how this realm succeeded in manipulating him.

"Botalia," Merwyn whispers, hovering a hand over her shoulder without making contact should he scare the creature in control. "We need you out here to pass through the gateway. Botalia? Can you hear me? It's time to leave. Please. You have all the time to relax when we return to our world. Botalia?"

The creature opens its mouth as if to speak but, rather than forming words, it closes its eyes.

"Tired already?" Botalia remarks as the koroko trudges into the room on all four limbs. She sits up, no longer willing to distract herself in the starless ceiling above. "I can't blame you. I've never quite prepared you for the world out there."

The creature holds out its hands to Botalia, which she accepts with a moment's hesitation. When they swap control once more, the koroko slinks to hide in the shadowy corner, preparing for another long rest. Botalia peers after it, worry lines deeply setting on her forehead.

"Thank you," she whispers, walking from the room and not shutting the door behind her as she leaves. Her life force circles about, waiting for the command that never comes before dissipating into the air, or more literally joining with the source of life force within her.

Botalia focuses her mind on every muscle in her body, concentrating on leaving this subconscious plane and returning to reality. She does not know where she will be when she wakes, for she never once peaked through the eyes of the creature since her relinquishment atop the tepui. Botalia feels the weightlessness of an atomic shift and the heaviness of a planet with ten times the gravitational pull all at once. Her body takes form about her, taking on the exhaustion and soreness of muscles and bruises, the itch of bug bites from Qoterra, the drain from tears, and the rain gently falling onto her body. The fresh air clears her head and Botalia opens her eyes.

Merwyn stands in front of her. Relief sweeps over as she scans every face before her, her team, almost whole and almost wholly well. Except...

"Koepp..." she makes the move to race but notices her legs refuse to listen. "Is he breathing?" she mumbles, her heart falls into her stomach. Naht stares in disbelief at the sudden change of the creature into Botalia before him and nods. Botalia exhales in relief. "Where's everyone else? They didn't... They're not..."

"No, no. Botalia, please calm down," Merwyn begs. He places a gentle hand on her shoulder. "We assume they've returned to the other realm, our realm, like we should be doing. Cefni, if you will. Lead the way."

Cefni holds out a hand for Nix, who shrugs at the gesture but obediently follows. They both enter through the gateway, the portal swaying and contorting at their entrance, moving them through time and space, dropping them into the caldera on Qoterra. After several seconds, Naht follows.

Botalia catches her breath and slows her heart rate.

"Let us get out of the rain," Merwyn suggests, offering his hand to Botalia. She glances at it and refuses, guilt swelling in her eyes as she knows unlike the staff of the gods, some curses may never be broken. Merwyn frowns at the muddy ground and enters the marble building. He motions for Botalia to continue through the portal before him. She bows her head gratefully, the warm, magnetic pull of the veil offering a call of home and normalcy.

She steps through the gateway and the instant release of the weight lifts from her shoulders. The sore, tense, exhausted muscles, nerves, every fiber of her being relaxes in a rush of tranquility only gifted by the songs of the insects, the chirp of the birds, the rustle of a gentle breeze through hydrated canopies. The island's scent, pregnant in the air, salty and flowery fresh. The taste of sweet honey on fried bread and ripe fruit with juices bursting into her mouth as she bites in. Every sensation of home meets her. Every memory of what home means returns. Koepp and Nix smile and fill the space she longed to be once more. The flash of a nightmare expunged by yet another wonderful dream. When the ground forms beneath her, Botalia doesn't want to open her eyes, she doesn't want to leave the dream.

With the ashy and iron smell drifting in the air to meet her, Botalia realizes the mission is not yet done. A chill courses up her spine, every hair standing on end, as the pain in her chest pulses once more. The strain of high emotions, devastation and loss, stress and anxiety born and driven by the masses. The gravity of this infinite potential well assures she may never forget the burden she is forced to bear. As the illness formed and bred on the battlefield may infect the minds, the mission all have faced and their obstacles in the ruined realm will never fade from their memories. They are all scarred. None will return to their homes the same. Even if their homes have not changed, the individual self has. And Botalia, the one cursed to uphold the weight of worldly despair, will have to

accept the fact, even if her own vision has transformed along with
their own.

A few seconds pass, and Botalia refuses to open her eyes. Her
body stiffens, refusing to listen even if she should so desire it. Strong
arms wrap around her with certainty, embracing the fragile form she
has become. Memories flood of when her father would embrace her
when winning an award or reaching a conclusion in what he deemed
a successful experiment, twirling her about with his exuberant joy
and bellowing laugh that could fill entire dining halls. The reassuring
feeling that she wasn't simply another experiment. The feeling that
she was loved.

Botalia opens her eyes and pulls away, finding Cefni before her.
A tear streams down his cheek, many others not yet flowing from
his eyes, but present and ready to push down the dam should any
more form. Botalia averts her eyes, not wishing to bawl as a child
and burden him with more fatherly concern than he should waste
on her. Botalia peers down at his arm, noting the bloody cloth. Her
hand hovers over the wound, his own pushing it away in an effort
to conceal whatever she may learn from the corrupted flesh. Cefni
shakes his head and nods towards the others. Botalia accepts the
distraction, though his desire to hide what happened reveals more
than what her life force may have divulged.

Because they returned in the dead of night, Cefni deploys small
light force orbs to illuminate the area. Botalia notices Koepp's body
leaning against the wall of the crater, in the location where they
first descended into the caldera. He still appears to be breathing.
Slightly turning her head, Botalia sees Naht and Nix standing beside
one another, Nix with his back to Koepp, Botalia notices, but no
more harmed than when she last saw him before ascending the
cobblestone stairs.

Botalia runs to Nix, a limping, dizzy sprint, lowers herself, and
tightly embraces him. His face reveals an immense surprise as wide

eyes hide the bags of exhaustion beneath them. Nix is unaware of how to react to such an action. Botalia uses one hand to pull him toward her while the other cradles the back of his head.

"I'm so glad you're alright. How are you feeling? Are you hurt? Have you eaten? Are you hydrated? You're soaking wet. Are you cold? Do you need me to help you dry off?" Botalia rapidly fires the questions without giving Nix the opportunity to respond. She backs away and examines his entire person before pulling him back in. "I'm so happy to see you're alright."

He stares blankly forward, the look of shock never wavering. A strange warm sensation courses through him, but he does not know what it is. It's a feeling he's never experienced. But he cannot doubt he felt happiness in that moment.

Botalia rises and connects eyes with Naht, noting the streaks of blood on his hands and shoulder where Koepp was lying for the journey. His eyes flicker something deeper than the dark void once filling the empty vessel, a glitter of tangible emotion, strung back but within reach of comprehension. Admitting vulnerability, Naht merely looks away and sighs.

"Botalia," Merwyn calls, taking form atop the altar.

Botalia smiles seeing his safe return and rushes to offer a hand to aid his descent. As he steps down from the marble, the gateway contorts and stretches before collapsing into itself and vanishing. A loud snap thunders in the air and sends a quake through the earth with the altar as the origin. A crack protrudes from the marble altar as it disintegrates before them, a sure sign of the staff's demise.

"It appears our quest has come to a close," Merwyn delightfully states.

"Would you call it a success?" Cefni questions, a furrowed brow as he determines the state of the entire team, corpses still littering the ground about the caldera.

"I would say so."

Silence fills the air, its weight heavy and solemn, pensive and transient. The voices in their minds, the images of scenes that would surely haunt their nightmares and corrupt their daydreams, float in and out like the devastation of the first high tide after a tsunami. The greatest battle is won, their lives intact, yet the lingering effects may prove worse in the long run. Naht wishes to be the shell once more, devoid of these thoughts. Botalia also considers regressing to that state as she once had. But to deny the truth would be to ignore a much larger problem, one brought to light by the mission and was perhaps much more prolific than first assumed.

"I understand the want and need to relax, but we're not home yet. We need to decide, as a team, if we rest here or begin heading back," Merwyn states.

Botalia bites her lip as she realizes the true decision rests in her ability. She feels her body screaming out, her muscles torn, her bones bruised, her entire person aching and throbbing. Her mental capacity has since rejuvenated, her emotions slowly returning to her control, but her physical capability may not be fully healed for weeks. Botalia glances at Koepp, knowing the sooner he reaches civilization the better. Taking a deep breath, Botalia reinforces her body with the life force she's recovered and smiles.

"I don't believe we'll be able to fully rest until far away from this place," Botalia says. "Perhaps the cabin?"

"Any objections?" Merwyn asks.

"Then, I guess we're movin' out," Cefni states. He goes to grab the bag of things he'd abandoned before entering the gateway and pauses. "Botalia, can you come here for a second?" Botalia walks toward him and follows the direction of his pointing finger. Above his bag, on the wall of the caldera, is the image of a crescent moon. Botalia smiles. She looks up to the sky.

"You know, I don't think I've ever been more grateful being given the opportunity to gaze at the stars. Looking at the stars above

Qoterra feels so... different," Botalia muses. "It's such a beautiful night."

With that, Merwyn summons his golem to carry Koepp, and the group return to the cabin. Their journey was silent for the most part, and any time they did speak, no one mentioned anything that had happened within the alternate dimension. No one spoke of hardships or sufferings, of pain or aches. They spoke of the joy of returning home. However, Naht and Nix never spoke. They trudged along, side by side, Naht's hand firmly grasping Nix's shoulder, Nix shivering every time someone spoke of "home."

Koepp remained in a deep rest. Barely moving, calmly breathing. The group trusts his care to the golem carrying him, for their hearts are already heavy on their trek, despite their feigned optimism. Not that they wish to ignore Koepp, but they feel no need to worry for the time being. What's done is done. They cannot help him any further. They can only wait, and there is no need to wait in misery.

The crew arrive at the airship in the early afternoon, reaching Mercuria, the city of the Magistrate Association late that evening. Word quickly spreads to the officials and many service vehicles race to the port. The media quickly catches word of some major event, though not quite understanding the circumstances. In honesty, many of the official magistrates sent to receive the heroes don't know why. They simply see a group of injured, tired, and exhausted individuals, two of which are Council members. Conspiracies rise, but most are so ridiculous few believe them.

Naht disappears upon their return, reluctantly leaving Nix behind. Nix joins Botalia's side and the two travel with Koepp as he is transported to the hospital. The Council members leave them to it, understanding the crowd that may follow if they choose to go as well. Vayl requests for the pair to return to the Association building, but both deny her, claiming they will talk to her as a team.

Days pass and the excitement dies down. No one learns of their deeds. No one cares. For on the mainland, Dominia, they are recovering from a war of their own. The schism has faded, many fatalities on both sides. A treaty was promptly created between the warring sides when they discovered early in the predicted civil war that they were pitted against one another with false pretenses and exaggerated language as to the other's beliefs and desires. The one who managed to start the conflict, stir the embers, fuel the fire, was never determined. The Magistrate Association hold the warring factions accountable for their actions and are in the process of trials for the licensed magistrates among their ranks, as well as questioning all others. Vayl sets the task to Rhys Champney and Atheas Maynard. Many prominent names are interjected in their interrogations, many naming Atlas Lurio. Though many fail in this claim when Atlas cannot be tracked down, none being able to support the claim that the ex-vice president took part in the battles. All attempts at an investigation of the claim are instantly dropped.

Chapter Twenty-Two

A week after their return, a council meeting is called into session. Cefni and Merwyn stand near the front doors of the Magistrate Association, waiting for the guests who will be joining them. Their team.

The car pulls up, tinted windows hiding the faces of those within, but this does not prevent wide smiles growing on the Council members' faces. Cefni Medina and Merwyn Giacobbe rush out of the building and towards the vehicle as it slows to a stop. Merwyn opens the door and Cefni leans inside.

He grabs hold of the young boy and lifts him from the vehicle, swinging him in a circle of joy before allowing his feet to find their balance on the ground. Unkempt black hair covering his eyes, Koepp struggles to find his footing, the world's rotation seemingly affecting him more increasingly every day.

"You look great as ever. I'm glad to see you again," Cefni excitedly states, masking any semblance of guilt which echoes in his thoughts. His beaming smile is met with little more than a shrug from Koepp, eyes unmoving from the pavement.

Botalia and Nix climb out of the vehicle.

"Be careful, Cefni. He's still getting used to it," Botalia says, the light tone of her voice not able to hide the hurt in her expression. Cefni and her eyes connect, the windows into their souls as pained and glossy as always.

"It is a great honor to be graced with your presence once again, Ms. Botalia, Mr. Nix, Mr. Koepp," Merwyn says, understanding not to expect much of a response. "Thank you for keeping us updated." He pats Botalia's shoulder.

"Of course," Botalia responds. She glances at Nix and, noting his expression, shakes him by the shoulder. "Shall we go inside?"

"Certainly," Merwyn says.

Merwyn places a hand on Koepp's shoulder, the boy flinching at the unexpected touch. The Professional leads them into the building. Many eyes find them upon their entrance, eyes lingering longer on Koepp than the rest. Metal arms hang at his sides, the prosthetics to replace that which was destroyed atop Praecantatis Tepui. His nerves and muscles had fried, the aura of the staff terrified of the raw magic of a child with the desire to destroy it. But Koepp succeeded in his wish, sacrificing his hands and forearms in the process.

Upon return to Dominia, the surgeons at the hospital amputated the torn parts of his limbs, his right arm at the shoulder and his left at the elbow. They attached the sleek, metal, fully-functioning prosthetics, paid for in full by the Magistrate Association. Botalia and Nix waited until the anesthesiologist's life force wore off to visit Koepp in his room. His eyes refused to meet the metal, a blatant refusal to move his prosthetic arms and hands forced Botalia to spoon feed him. In fact, he didn't move them until he was released from the hospital, told he could return to the island. He didn't hesitate to rip the identification bracelet and hospital robe away, no words to leave only the determined expression to return. But the island was still far away as they were forced to the Magistrate Association one final time.

Nerves threaten to flood Botalia as they trek that same route to the conference room. The images of her exile flash through her mind, and she forces them out and replaces them with happy thoughts. The happiest she can find. She never dreamed the thought of being alive would bring her happiness, but in this moment, it helps. Or at least she appears happy externally. Internally, Botalia feels as exhausted as ever, feigning happiness so as to prevent Koepp and Nix from diving into depression, as if it would help. She knows what a great trauma at a young age can lead to. She never wanted them to fall onto the path of self-destruction she took.

They walk down the hallway and Botalia sees Westin Sapotski standing outside of the door. Botalia and Westin share a smile as he opens the door for the team. Botalia takes a deep breath before plunging into the room of staring eyes, penetrating glares, and curious expressions.

Five empty chairs sit adjacent to one another on the opposite side of the table from the door. As they head to their seats, Merwyn and Cefni are greeted by numerous welcomes from their fellow Council members. Botalia notices the absences of Rhys and Atheas, presumably busy with the paperwork and cleanup concerning the schism.

"Welcome, heroes. Please, sit," Vayl starts with a smile. The five sit in their chairs. "So? Do tell us of your adventures. Now that you all seemed to have properly rested, not to mention regenerated. How are those prosthetics, Mr. Flynn?"

"Fine," Koepp reservedly responds.

"How lovely." Vayl smiles.

As Botalia prods about the room with thin stems of life force, her senses heightened and truly paranoid, she feels a suppressed hostility in a few of the Council members' auras. Perhaps her mind is playing tricks, slowly readjusting to the environment. But even Vayl seems to exude hostility in the thin wisps of misty aura to leave her fingertips.

The air about the Vice President is off, as if attempting to gain their trust, or mimicking Atlas's tactics to earn undying loyalty and respect by recognizing their sacrifices. But the hostility remains, surpassing the guise she attempts to wear. Obviously not as practiced as Atlas Lurio in the art.

"Ms. Ulton?" Vayl asks. Botalia quickly looks up to lock eyes with Azriel Vayl, hoping not to appear suspicious in doing so. "I believe you'll be pleased to know your plants were well taken care of as you requested. Our very own biological Scholar, Mrs. Entzia Weaver," as Vayl says this she makes a motion toward Entzia, "and her team provided the best care they could."

"And I would love to discuss much with you, Ms. Ulton," interjects Entzia, a large, genuine smile spread across her face. Botalia returns the smile, hoping her feigned expression measures up to the others in the room. Though Botalia feels she already knows most of the questions, she cannot decide how many of them she will answer truthfully.

A silence fills the space. After several moments, Vayl presses on.

"So... How was the journey? I imagine Qoterra was quite peaceful in comparison to whatever you experienced thereafter."

"Our journey proved difficult and many of us had to make sacrifices, Koepp Flynn perhaps more than the rest of us combined. And I do not believe our adventures should be discussed as fairytales or campfire stories. The events are fresh in my mind as I'm sure in my teammates'. And, while it's fresh, allow me to provide some intrigue," Merwyn offers in a monotone voice.

"Yes, please." Merwyn's offer seems to spark genuine interest in Vayl and the other Council members.

"As you knew before sending us, there were teams after the staff. Five, to be precise."

"How fascinati-" Vayl begins before being cut off by Merwyn.

"Allow me to finish." Merwyn interrupts Vayl with a voice of authority. She appears rather irritated by his tone, understanding her position to be above his own, but also confused, for Merwyn has always only been respectful. "We came into contact with quite a few of the teams. Many lost their lives due to human conflict, the beings in the alternate realm simply tidying the mess."

"Alter-" Guto, the druidic Professional, begins to question, surprisingly his first interruption of the meeting.

"Guto, please," Vayl orders. Her voice trembles and she shifts in her seat, hanging on to every word to leave Merwyn's mouth. "Go on."

"I'll continue. Anyone here may answer," Merwyn says as his eyes move around the table, connecting with every eye along the way. "Would it surprise you to know we met Atlas Lurio?"

"Quite," Vayl instantly responds, her eyes wide, whether it be of shock or fear.

"Hardly," replies Gwyn Sanoba, a stern expression on her face. She peers at Botalia, who in turn connects eyes with Gwyn. She understands something, a hidden layer of the conversation that Merwyn and Cefni also understand. Botalia feels the questions flood her. What is she missing?

Turin Vitas glances at Vayl and rolls his eyes, believing Vayl's responses lack confidence. As he looks at Merwyn and Cefni, he notices a stone-cold resolve on their faces. They know.

The other Council members turn to one another and express their shock or complete lack thereof. Many of them are familiar with Atlas and his numerous operations, few of which were known. As the volume among them rises, the five team members remaining silent, Vayl finds her patience wearing thin.

She is aware she must be the next to speak, regaining control of the conversation. Allowing Merwyn to dictate its direction may prove suicidal, too much information may leak. Vayl worries, wondering how much they know, for they obviously know something.

"Quiet, everyone," Vayl raises her voice in an attempt to silence the others. The voices fade after a few seconds expire and she continues. "I believe we're getting off topic. We sent our team of heroes out to reobtain the altar piece. So. Where is it?"

Everyone turns to the team. Botalia notices Koepp and Nix stare at the table. Glancing at Merwyn and Cefni, she sees the same blank, yet powerful, expressions. She chooses to copy their looks, but slowly it transforms into analyzing the table.

"We did not acquire the altar piece," Merwyn answers. A hushed murmur is heard.

"Then, the staff perhaps?" Vayl cautiously treads forward, hoping and praying for the answer she wishes to hear. Though, given their expressions, the probability seems very minimal... practically nonexistent.

"No." A simple response from Merwyn seems to cause an eruption within the Vice President.

"Who, then?" Vayl asks, appearing flustered. Some other Council members, Orphacia Glatz specifically, expressing their disbelief.

"No one."

"Impossible." Vayl's denial apparent.

"It's the altar piece or the staff. One or the other. Someone has to have one or the other." Orphacia interjects, unable to hold her silence any longer.

"No. No one does," Merwyn replies. A look of confusion covers many of the faces. Botalia notices Gwyn Sanoba and Ibovel Sobiski share a grin before hiding their feelings under stern expressions once more. Botalia feels herself begin to smile, but quickly prevents it. Vayl's heart accelerates and, though paying attention to her breathing, she fails to control it.

"What? What do you mean?" Vayl asks.

"We ensured the destruction of both." Koepp's arms twitch slightly, as slightly as metal prosthetics can. Orphacia cries out as if she's having a panic attack. The other Council members, the exception being Gwyn, Ibovel, and Turin, express their shock. Their suppressed whispers rapidly evolve into screams. Turin places his hands on his head and remains silent, glaring at Vayl. Vayl penetratingly stares at Merwyn, a look of utter consternation.

"De-destroyed?" The word demands another cry from Orphacia. "How do you mean destroyed? A legendary, all powerful, staff of the gods, destroyed?"

"Yes. Luckily our heroes came in the form of two young boys and a powerful young woman." Merwyn winks at Botalia, who's unaware of how to respond. She returns to analyzing the table and feels the burning wrath protruding from Vayl's and Turin's eyes as they stare at her. "I do not know if Cefni or I would have been so brave." Cefni nods.

"That staff could have led to hundreds if not thousands of discoveries, not to mention assist in creating a better world... a better future," Vayl calmly responds, attempting to contain her frustration and rage. Orphacia vigorously nods, ensuring all notice her agreement with Vayl's comment. Vayl suppresses her triggered emotions and plays to the majority's expression, dumbfounded. "And you chose to destroy it? As a team did you decide this? Who? Who thought this to be the best course of action?"

"Ms. Vayl," Merwyn begins, not expressing any reaction to her own, not allowing her the satisfaction of tearing them down. This is why Merwyn does the talking, for Cefni sometimes too easily grows irritated with the one he is in conflict with. "We traveled peacefully through Qoterra, and despite the numerous creatures whose homes we invaded, never once did they attack us.

"When we entered the gateway and arrived in the alternate dimension, not once did the foreign creatures target us without ourselves first provoking them. No. The true monsters were the ones after the staff, after the power. People. Like you and me. Reasoning, rationalizing creatures capable of thoughts and emotions that interdependently rely on others of our species. While we fought our battles against humans in a faraway land, you all fought your battle with humans here at home. They kill without care sometimes, if it means it is beneficial to themselves. Sometimes they do so out of selfish desires, not for the good of the species. Not for preservation or loyalty to a group but to oneself. The true monsters of the world are found within humanity.

"The staff would only prove to serve that fiendish desire and willpower, corrupting even those who deem they wish to help with its power. Its power is nothing to admire but fear.

"Only these three beside me, these who willing sacrificed their lives, not for honor but because they valued someone else's life more than their own in an instinctual moment. Instincts tell creatures like us to preserve our own self, no matter the circumstance because life, life is ultimately more important than power or happiness. But these three never fell to the staff's spell. They feared its power as they rightly should, seeing the bad not in the staff but in humanity.

"They've seen and experienced the bad in humanity and know full well that life can be cruel and consist of pure, concentrated suffering. Suffering dealt by monsters, not the world, seldom the environment, but humans. I believe Cefni and I have learned much from the four of them."

The use of the number "four" causes much confusion, however, no one speaks up. No one wishes to. Merwyn's monologue casts a spell of silence on them all, Vayl feeling not only unable to find words, but petrified.

"Ms. Vayl?" Merwyn folds his hands and places them on the table in front of him. His expression appears stern and hostile. Botalia doesn't believe she's ever seen him glare in such a manner. Cefni also glares, but perhaps to a greater degree, for the glow in his eyes shine like a wildfire.

"Yes, Mr. Giacobbe?" Vayl briskly asks, her voice quavering.

"You haven't asked about Tenebrant Mortu." The room freezes over. No one moves. Vayl's heart threatens to explode, her mind igniting and detonating in a series of explosions. Her rage is tangible. Merwyn continues. "Therefore, we have nothing left to say to you."

Merwyn and Cefni rise, motioning for Botalia, Koepp, and Nix to do the same. Vayl's eyes move from one to the next. Her mouth hangs open, but no words can find their escape. No one dares speak as they watch the five exit the room. Merwyn leads the way and Cefni tails, just as always. As Botalia exits, she notices the grins worn by Gwyn and Ibovel.

Cefni closes the door behind them, hoping the message is clear.

Merwyn turns and grins at the group, the atmosphere much lighter in the hallway. Botalia feels tears forming in her eyes.

"Well, I believe that is enough excitement for one day," Merwyn laughs. "You three should return to the island before they try to arrange another meeting."

"We'll not be in a good place after that stunt we just pulled," says Cefni with a wide smile. "It would be unfair to involve you three. These issues go way beyond that mission they sent us on."

"Let us see you off, then," Merwyn states. He grabs a light hold of Koepp's and Nix's shoulders and begins to tell them an exciting story, a smile covering both of their faces.

Cefni and Botalia turn down the hallway and sigh.

"Is it ever going to get easier?" Cefni asks, the scar as fresh for him as it is for her. However, she no longer thinks of her exile the same way she used to.

"Yeah," Botalia reassuringly says, and grabs hold of his hand.

A series of painful jolts course through Botalia, her eyes squeeze shut. She feels herself falling, blows hitting her from all sides, yet she cannot defend herself, let alone fight back. She struggles to find the ground beneath her feet, all the while being pelted and assaulted. Botalia feels her subconscious form hit the ground. A bright light flashes. A slideshow of visuals and audio move at high velocities in front of her. She feels constricted by the sheer amount circling her, and yet, she feels nothing but emptiness. Her skin slowly peels away to reveal a hollow interior. Nothing. Her invisible insides tighten and create immense pain, her chest pulsing, preparing for an escape. Her subconscious self begins to close her eyes but images, images of someone so familiar yet indistinct and distant, flash in front of her, a heavy surge accompanying each of them. Botalia reaches for the sky and focuses on her true body. Gradually, she's come through to reality.

Botalia finds herself on the ground, Cefni and the others beside her. Though they all appear confused, Cefni appears more so than the rest. He clutches a hand to his chest and stares intently at Botalia, wondering about the sudden lightness within him. Botalia finds her strength and stands.

"Shall we get going?" This time Nix and Koepp lead the way. They walk silently, but their strides show how joyous they are to be next to one another again.

"Botalia, what happened?" Cefni asks, his face serious once more.

She laughs. "Being a monster comes at a price. It's my mountain, but luckily I can see the stars from up here."

The five travel to the docks. All is quiet and still as fishermen and bargemen had already set out for the day, deck-loaders smoking from cigars and pipes lean against the wooden posts, staring at the small waves rippling in the horizon. A fish breaks the surface, jumping to catch an insect skating overhead.

"Let me go ask about renting a boat," Cefni states before Botalia stops him.

"No need. I can get the three of us back," Botalia responds. Cefni and Merwyn gaze at her in amazement.

"You never cease to amaze me, Ms. Ulton," Merwyn compliments. "Thank you, all three of you, for your hard work and bravery."

"Thank you, Mr. Giacobbe, for what you did back there," Botalia replies while wearing a somber smile. Merwyn leans in.

"Botalia, I don't think I need to tell you this, but please, don't follow Tenebrant's example. He has committed quite a few atrocious deeds," Merwyn whispers to her.

"I know. I simply wish to help an old friend." They share a grin and Botalia extends her hand. The pain and slideshow hit her and when she recovers she notices she's still standing. "It's been an honor," Botalia states, to Merwyn and Cefni alike.

"The honor is ours, truly," Merwyn says, hand to his heart.

Botalia smiles at Koepp and Nix who return it. She holds out her hands to her sides, Koepp and Nix understanding the routine.

"Be sure to come visit."

"Just because you're an exile doesn't mean you have to be alone," Cefni responds. He and Merwyn wave as the three disappear right before their eyes. They sigh and walk back toward the Association building, prepared to face the fire, but with a new set of armor.

Botalia, Koepp, and Nix arrive at the island. The smells, the sounds, and the sensations at being home fill Botalia with relief and happiness. She notices the trampled paths taken by the Scholars who resided here during their mission, Botalia hoping they cleaned up after themselves. Koepp and Nix sit next to one another on the porch and smile as they take in the surroundings. Botalia takes a deep breath in and spins in a circle.

"I'll be back by nightfall," she promises the boys. And with that she leaps into the trees, swinging through the canopies above. She visits every creature and plant, ensuring their health and showering them with her affection. She runs her hands through their hair and fur, across the leaves and petals, listening and breathing in the life around her. They return their affection, displaying their loyalty to her. Even the herba aduolant plants remember the trio.

Botalia travels the island and finds herself at the back of villa near the greenhouse. As she wanders inside, she notices a difference in the environment. Botalia squints as she carefully examines every plant, creating a current between herself and them. Her life force flows into them, one at a time, and determines their needs. Many are malnourished and distressed, residual hints of chemicals sprinkled on their leaves, leading Botalia to believe they performed tests on her plants. She counts the plants... and then she counts again. One is missing. One of the species "potentia herba." She bites her lip and shakes her head in an attempt to subdue her anger and frustration. Botalia decides to deal with the issue of theft at a later time.

She walks up the path to the veranda at the back of the house. As she climbs the stairs and gazes at the villa, memories resurface and position themselves in her mind. A smile grows on her face. She sits and faces the greenhouse and forest behind it. Slowly, her eyes lift from the ground, her neck craning back as her eyes move to the sky.

The sun sinks into evening, the call of the birds and insects echo in the distance. She hears the indistinct voices of Koepp and Nix from the front porch. A sigh of relief naturally leaves Botalia. She claps her hands together and takes a deep breath in. She separates her hands and places them on the veranda underneath her. Her life force travels from the palm of her hands and into the villa, heading toward the kitchen to prepare a meal, though, she's no idea what the grocery situation looks like.

After their meal of roasted potatoes and spiced rice, the three relax in the sitting room with full stomachs, the first opportunity of pure peace in weeks. They sit in silence, not wanting to disturb the tranquility of the moment. The soft, melodious sounds of the island find their way to their ears. After several minutes of relaxation, Koepp's gastrointestinal tract decides to break the quiet. Koepp and Nix bite their lips, attempting to hold back their laughter, but subdued snickers escape. A large grin covers Botalia's face, and despite trying her hardest, she is the first to lose. Her body hunches as she laughs, throwing her head to her knees. The boys follow her lead and their laughter bursts forth. After a while, the three forget why they originally started laughing, but that doesn't stop them from continuing.

Botalia leans back and smiles at the boys, her heart full of joy, as if the jolts of pain and suffering were simply a tool to remind her she's awake. Koepp turns his head to face Botalia, a wide smile still across his face. He carefully places his metal arms on his legs, so they do not scrape against one another, and locks eyes with Botalia, Nix doing the same.

"Botalia?" Koepp calmly questions, not knowing if his voice will catch her off guard.

"Yes?" Botalia leans forward to show her interest.

"Can you teach me and Nix how to use life force like you?" She notices a glimmer of embarrassment, and yet excitement, in his eyes.

"Are you sure you wouldn't prefer to learn about the history of Aldo Casquo and his scientific achievements in studying peregrin herons and their migratory patterns and mating rituals?" Botalia sarcastically asks.

Koepp giggles and Nix dramatically rolls his eyes. They shake their heads in a unanimous "No."

"Please?" Koepp begs.

"Why would a teacher deny her apprentices the opportunity to reach their full potential?"

Koepp releases an excited squeal, Nix, a loud sigh, though a smile fights to break through his stone face. Botalia observes the boys, but her smile quickly turns to a frown, images of her past resonating. The stings in her chest attempt to remind her of reality and yet she refuses to abandon the dreams she strives for, not for her alone but for the three of them. A family... or some semblance of one. No longer alone, the feeling of isolation gone... temporarily? No.

Botalia shakes her head and stares at the ground. The trophies and certificates in the room seem to grow eyes as they inspect her. Their eyes act as judgmental as society's, casting her out as if one action of an emotional incoherent teen defines her as a person... monster... thing.

She's not the only one to face such scrutiny. Many people fall victim to collective societal persecution. She can't help but think of the team, the dysfunctional team, composed of society's outcasts. No one would have minded if they never returned... though no one cared that they returned. And yet, they accomplished what so few could. And their reward? Life? As if they could return to "normal" lives after what they witnessed. Even on the island, Botalia's senses cease to relax, a constant state of paranoia, the slightest sound setting off her acoustic reflex. Koepp is slowly growing accustomed to his new arms, but no sensation will ever cross his fingertips again. Nix may never be accepted as a Kufuta, disowned for abandoning the family business and partaking in a mission outside of his assigned duties. No longer is he permitted to step near Kufuta Manor, trespassing punishable by death. On top of this news, reports of a killer in Dominia surface, no bodies left at the scene, the killer leaving the sole trace of a crescent moon drawn in the victim's blood.

As the sun sets, Koepp and Nix decide to head to their rooms to study the new material Botalia gave them earlier that day. Botalia's eyes follow them out of the room and up the stairs. As she lays back, she folds one arm behind her head and the other arms extends in front of her. She focuses her eyes but sees nothing. Her eyes slowly close. A voice, one she barely recognizes anymore, sings to her from the depths of her past, a quiet, calming hum, the words hardly audible. But Botalia's subconscious fills in the words not heard in the memorized lullaby.

Sense the monster's release and sleep, and sleep.
Sense the monster's release.

And sleep.

Author's Notes:

Hello, everyone! You've made it to the end of Book 2, but the story continues on. Thanks again for supporting me and the work I pour myself into. Check out my other speculative fiction under the name M. A. Morales. If you're into contemporary romance, you can check out my other works under the name of Elle Oaks.

Please check out our socials and our website. Please also rate if you read all the way through. For an independent author, reviews are a great way to show support. But again, just reading is very appreciated!